THE
TAMARACK
TREE

BY HOWARD BRESLIN

Whittlesey House

McGraw-Hill Book Company, Inc.

NEW YORK: LONDON

THE TAMARACK TREE

PUBLISHED BY WHITTLESEY HOUSE

A DIVISION OF THE MCGRAW-HILL BOOK COMPANY, INC.

PRINTED IN THE UNITED STATES OF AMERICA

For PAT

Stratton, of course, is real. The mountain still rears its ridge against the sky, though the crossroad now has only a church and a house. One can stand today in the clearing where the meeting took place, but the forest has shrunk it, and the marker that proclaims its history in metal words and Vermont rock is a few rods from the proper spot. The political events described in this book actually happened. The characters, however, except for those seeking or holding public office, are entirely fictitious.

PROLOGUE
May, 1840

Tʜᴇ ᴍᴏᴜɴᴛᴀɪɴ was not a peak like its neighbors but a ridge. It's long spine was clear against the sky, looking from below like a giant sleeping cat, its haunches high, back sloping down to rise again slightly at the neck. Like a cat, too, it was furred—covered with the thick, dark foliage of an uncut evergreen forest. There was power in the mountain's attitude. It had been there a long time. It had been there before the Indians, who had called it Manicknung. The white men had come with their axes and hewed out their places on the mountain's side, and they had clung there now for more than half a century. Being white men they named the mountain for one of their own—Stratton.

On the western slope of the mountain, six miles below the ridge of Stratton's summit, was a scar that covered 300 acres. No man lived in this clearing; no man cared who had ripped this vast space out of virgin wilderness. Ripped it had been—chopped, cut down, leveled in a wide arc that spread its half-moon shape across Stratton's side.

In the spring of 1840 the clearing was already old. The grass showed this, high as a man's knee, uncut and weedy, damp now from recent thaws. A few aging stumps showed it, too. In the very heart of the clearing, alone and towering, stood a single tree. A tamarack.

The tamarack tree was tall, magnificent. Each needle of its vivid green foliage was as clear in the sunshine as the lines of an etching. Trunk thick, full grown, its branches bright with seasonal freshness, the tamarack was in its prime. It stood, straight and proud as if challenging the clearing and the axes and the men.

What chance had saved it when its fellows crashed, what axe had passed it by when the field was cleared, would be at best a guess. This was fact: alone in the midst of that great clearing, untouched, the tamarack tree stood in the morning sunshine of the first warm day of the spring that came to Stratton Mountain, in the township of Stratton, in the state of Vermont, in the election year of 1840.

A partridge whirred up suddenly from the edge of the clearing, and a gun slammed. The report echoed higher up the mountainside. Untouched and flying fast, the bird crossed the clearing in a climbing, straight line, skimmed over the narrow mud road that bordered the lower end of the field, twisted into a quick, banking dive, and disappeared.

Four boys and a dog ran out of the woods. The dog bounded after the partridge, leaping through the grass. At the tamarack tree the dog gave up, barked twice, turned and trotted back toward the boys.

The smallest one's voice was shrill and mocking. "Missed! You missed, Put. Never touched it! Old Put missed!" He was dancing with excitement, shaking all his fingers.

Putnam Chester said, "Hush up, Davey." He looked down at the muzzle loader he held, turning the gun in his hands. Scowling, Put shook his head. The scowl darkened his blue eyes without affecting the rest of his round face. "Fire and brimstone!" he said, swearing. "She kicked, Asa. She kicked high."

"Warned you," said Asa Brayton. He was the tallest, a thin, stringy lad of sixteen, all arms and legs. Now his long face seemed to lengthen visibly, and his lips narrowed. "Warned you, Put."

"He did!" David shrieked. "He did! And you missed! Never touched one feather!"

Saying nothing, the fourth boy reached out, clamped a hand on David's collar, and yanked. The shrieker toppled over backwards. His assailant put a knee on David's chest and a palm over his mouth. Kneeling there, leaning on the muffling hand, he spoke pleasantly. "It was a hard shot, Put."

Asa stretched out a long arm for the gun. He said, "Lost the load." The words were almost toneless, but Asa's eyes were bitter.

"I'm sorry, Asa." Put gave up the gun.

4

"Sorry don't mend nothing. Load's lost. Lost." Asa was as stiff as the weapon he held. He glared at Put.

The squirming David tugged loose from his gag. He was raging, near tears. "You!" he shouted. "You Seth Purdy! Let me up! You hear? Let me up!"

"You ain't hurt," Seth said, smiling. "So you needn't bawl like a calf. Keep quiet or I'll scalp you." He rose, turned to the others. "What's done's done, Asa."

"E-yah." The Vermont affirmative twanged as Put agreed. "Shucks, Asa. The way you're carrying on, you'd think I meant to miss him."

"Missed him, didn't you?" Asa asked. "Missed him."

Even little David, intent on rubbing his bruises, heard the harshness in Asa's voice and looked up, mouth open. All three stared at the tall boy. He was the oldest, but there had never been a question that Put Chester was the leader. Now, suddenly, in uncomfortable silence, there was something in Asa, in their group, that was adult and alien and unpleasant.

Uncertain, not knowing what was eating Asa but sure that something was, Put swallowed hard. "E-yah," he said, stalling. "I missed. E-yah."

Seth Purdy moved around and stood beside Put. He was serious now. "Anybody can miss, Asa. No cause to get riled."

"It ain't that," said Asa. "It ain't his missing. It's just . . ." He stopped talking and blinked. The tension went out of him, his fingers loosened around the gun barrel, and he flushed. Looking away, he muttered, "It ain't nothing."

Put's tone was a soothing answer to Asa's. "Sure, Asa. Sure." He glanced around, looking for a topic of conversation. "Where's that fool dog of mine? Cap! Cap!" Put whistled.

The dog had wandered off, sniffing, and he came bounding back. He was a brown, long-eared mongrel, with black and white markings plastered indiscriminately all over him. Cap put his front paws up on Put's stomach and had his head rubbed.

"Find us something else, Cap," said Put.

Asa said, "No more loads."

"What'll we do now, Put?" David asked.

Put Chester pulled off his knitted cap and mopped his face with it. In the sunshine there were glints of gold in his brown hair.

"Warm," he said. "First real warm day we've had." He grinned, keeping them waiting, knowing his plan would startle them. "Let's climb up the mountain to Jones Pond and go swimming."

"Be mighty cold," the practical Seth said.

Put laughed. "Cold? E-yah. Might be. Too cold for sugar cakes and high-living Democrats."

"Cold for anybody," Seth said. His father was a Democrat, and he picked up the challenge of argument. "Freeze the hide off your old Tippecanoe."

"General Harrison," said Put, "ain't fat and soft like foxy Van Buren. My father . . ." Put paused. His father was minister of the town, and clerical opinion carried weight. "My father says Martin Van Buren is doomed to defeat."

Seth Purdy scowled. He resented Put's bringing in parental authority. The dicta of the Reverend Chester overpowered those of Seth's father, a stage driver. "Whig talk, Put. Nothing to do with swimming anyway."

"Old Van wouldn't get his feet wet. Lives too high! Made the White House into a palace, didn't he? Eats off gold plate!"

"Wears a corset!" David Tarbox said.

Asa Brayton, arms crossed, leaned on his gun and listened.

The small boy's plunge into the discussion annoyed Put. He frowned at David and clapped Seth on the shoulder to indicate the political argument was over. "What say, Seth? Swim?"

"E-yah."

"Asa?"

The tall boy threw back his head and gazed up past the tamarack tree at the sun. He squinted and shook his head. "Can't," said Asa. "Getting on to noon. Got to get back."

Little David spluttered his excuses. "I dassent, Put. Ma would whale me. Anyway, I got to get back too. Got to help around the inn. I'll go along with Asa."

They separated without formality. Put whistled for his dog, and Cap, bounding, raced ahead. The two left in the clearing waited till the sounds of the others had died away. Then Asa Brayton swung the butt of his gun over his shoulder.

"Coming, Davey?"

"E-yah."

They walked across the clearing and leaped down the bank onto the road. It was the stage road across the mountain, wide

6

enough for one vehicle. The two deep grooves of the wheel ruts were slick with mud, brown and gleaming in the sunshine. Even the higher, middle ground between the ruts was spongy beneath their boots, but it held fewer puddles than the wheel tracks, and the boys marched down it in single file.

They went east toward Stratton church, Asa walking with the long-legged, loose-kneed stride of a farmer, David skipping along behind. They didn't talk. Asa plodded steadily, brooding, chin on chest, his lips narrow. David needed all his breath to keep close behind his taller companion.

Not far from where the big clearing ended they passed a farm that lay south of the road. Here the fields were wide and level, and stone walls held back the forest. Both boys knew that this was the Chittenden place. Sheep grazed on the slope behind the dusky red barn, and David counted the sheds that linked the barn to the big yellow house. In the barnyard a woman turned and raised an arm in greeting. David waved back. Asa trudged on without taking his gaze from the road.

Once past Chittenden's trees hemmed in both banks of the turnpike, cutting off the sunlight. The road wound and curved. For most of two miles Asa and David walked through shade.

They emerged from it as they approached the crossroad settlement and began to pass between clusters of houses. A little farther on was the blacksmith shop, and the clank of hammer on iron was clear and vibrating in the morning air. David glanced into the shadows behind the smith's open door but all he could see was the orange-red splotch of the fire in the forge.

The two boys kept on to the crossroad. It was not truly a cross since only one road branched from the turnpike, running northeast. Here, at the joining of two roads, was the mountain's spring of solace and sustenance for body, soul, and mind. There were three buildings—the inn, the church, and the parsonage.

From the stage turnpike the branch road ran out perpendicularly, forming two right angles. In the western angle stood the inn, a square yellow building, two-storied, showing the same face to both roads. The other angle held Stratton church, long and white, its gable front toward the more important highway, its squat, flat-topped steeple a little higher toward heaven than the chimney of its secular neighbor.

Across the stage road from the inn was the L-shaped parsonage

7

where the Reverend Chester and family lived. Its gable, too, fronted the turnpike, and the two high windows in the peak gave the impression that it stared disapprovingly at the inn opposite.

Asa Brayton turned into the branch road and, without changing his pace, nodded a curt farewell to the smaller boy. David returned the nod and trotted up the path beside the inn. He hurried, planning to get a winter apple from the barrel in the kitchen. He was eleven years old and nearly always hungry.

The inn's big kitchen was empty when he entered, and he went straight to the apples. There were not many left. David had to lean deep into the barrel, teetering as he reached, his feet off the floor, the rim of the cask across his middle.

His mother caught him there as she came out of the pantry. Lydia Tarbox chuckled at the sight of her son's wriggling, round bottom and spanked it as she passed.

"Hey," yelled David. Scrambling back, he nearly upset the barrel. He rubbed himself and scowled at his mother with indignation. "I didn't do nothing. You said I could always take an apple."

Lydia laughed. "There's ways of taking, Davey, and ways of taking. General Ethan Allen took Ticonderoga, but he was too sharp a man to leave his rear guard sticking out. Just inviting attack, he would have said." She laughed again, a plump, pretty-faced woman, her hair as crisp as her apron. For one who had borne four children and lost two, her laughter bubbled as easily as a girl's.

She stood a moment, with an armful of pewter mugs, her sleeves rolled up above dimpled elbows. The fire in the great cavern of the inn's fireplace twinkled reflections on the mugs, and Lydia twinkled at her youngest. She glanced at the iron pot hanging from a crane over the fire and said, more seriously, "Don't spoil your appetite, Davey. It'll be dinnertime in an hour or so."

With a swish of skirts Mrs. Tarbox turned through the door and went into the inn's public room. It was big, cool now, and dark. Even the sunshine that beamed through the windows didn't penetrate it far. The wide planks of the flooring were scrubbed so clean that a guest could see the marks the adze had left when they were shaped. There were tables in the room and chairs, all well made and polished. The fireplace backed on the kitchen's and, while not so large as the other, was not small; its brickwork,

8

wet and shiny, had an odor of sour milk. Sitting back on his heels before the hearth, the innkeeper, milk pan beside him, was studying the results of his polishing.

"Finished in here, Dan?"

"No." Dan Tarbox didn't turn. "Fire's got to be laid." He snorted, glaring into the empty fireplace. "This time I ain't a-going to light it till somebody comes!"

"Folks'll come."

"Maybe."

"They'll come. You won't need the fire till nightfall in this weather. But folks get dry when it's warm." Mrs. Tarbox's laugh tinkled. "Especially menfolk."

"Maybe."

"It's Saturday, Dan. Don't we always do better on Saturday?"

"E-yah."

"Winter's really over. Up till now I wasn't sure, but today I feel it. The worst is over, Dan. The stage'll run regular, and things'll pick up."

Her husband rose and turned. He was a broad man, with a broad face and bald head. Everything about Dan Tarbox was broad. His nose spread wide; his hands were huge.

"You sound certain sure, Mrs. Tarbox."

"I am. Wait and see."

Lydia finished arranging the twelve pewter mugs on the little bar in the room's corner. She stood off to admire the effect, and Dan moved closer for the same reason. The tankards were the inn's pride, and both husband and wife felt the satisfaction of ownership.

Half hoping to hear her refute him, Dan said, "You're just wishing. If wishes were horses you'd have more than Justin Morgan himself."

"You mark my words. Folks'll come now."

"Coming ain't spending, Lyd. They can't spend if they don't have the money. And that dumb Dutchman has fixed things so that nobody has any!"

"Dan! Mr. Van Buren is our President!"

"Not mine, he ain't! Not by a damn sight!"

"Dan!"

He saw her quick glance toward the kitchen doorway and low-

9

ered his voice. "He ain't your President either. Nor nobody's in this family. Him with his Panic and his hard-money talk. What kind of President takes the food out of the mouths of people like us? Anybody—even me—could do better down there in Washington than that pig-headed, la-dee-da, York State Dutch, horse's ass!"

Pursing her lips, Mrs. Tarbox nodded thoughtfully. "That's right," she said. "He is York State, ain't he? It never pays to trust that crowd." The old quarrel between the New York colony and the Hampshire grants still rankled in Vermont memories. Bloodshed, Ethan Allen, and statehood had silenced New York's claims, but the innkeeper's wife voiced the general opinion of the neighboring state's intentions.

"Nothing good for Vermont," said Dan Tarbox, "ever come out of Albany! Van was governor down there once, and he's still thick with that whole Regency crowd. We'd be living in York State if Albany'd had its way!"

"I know. General Allen fought them till the day he died."

"E-yah. They won't try that again! Not that this panic of Van's ain't almost as bad!"

"I thought you blamed that on Andy Jackson."

"Jackson and Van Buren! Jackson molded the balls, and Van fired them! Let me explain once more. It's as plain as the nose on your face. This inn—our living—depends on folks spending money, don't it?"

"E-yah."

"Who's got the most money?"

"Around here?"

"Anywhere!" The innkeeper shouted with exasperation. "The places with the most money is banks, ain't they?"

"E-yah."

"E-yah. And folks get their money for spending from those banks. But Van Buren wants to put them out of business. But if there's no banks, folks can't get money, can they? And if they can't get it, they can't spend it. And if they don't spend it, we suffer, don't we?"

Mrs. Tarbox, bewildered, nodded.

"And that's why Van Buren's a menace to the country! Him and his whole Democrat gang!" With which piece of logic, Dan Tarbox drew a twist of tobacco from his pocket, bit off a chew,

10

and glared at his wife. He was about to say more when he heard the rattle of wagon wheels and stiffened.

With a lightness surprising in one so broad, he whirled and leaped to the windows. He gazed out through the checkered panes at the side road.

Mrs. Tarbox stayed where she was but prompted him. "Passing?"

"E-yah." Dan didn't turn back. He was so close to the window that his breath, as he spoke, frosted one small pane. "Joel Patch and son Nathan. The light rig. The one with the yellow wheels. Nathan's driving." Dan clucked in admiration. "Them's a right pretty team of Morgans."

"Team, Dan? You said the light wagon."

"E-yah. One horse in the shafts, and t'other following along behind. Must be taking it to the blacksmith's." The innkeeper hunched, peering carefully. "E-yah. That's it. That trailing mare moves like she throwed a shoe." He straightened and nodded. "E-yah. Turning up the mountain."

His wife was already at the windows that faced the other road. Watching the wagon pass and the two men on its seat, Mrs. Tarbox wrinkled her nose, sniffing. She didn't care much for Joel Patch even if he did own a sawmill. The man was a mite too sharp for her taste. Nothing you could put your finger on, but—well—sharp. Talked like nobody knew as much as he did, too, and put on airs. Sensing her husband behind her, Lydia said, "Dressed up, ain't he?"

The innkeeper chuckled. "E-yah."

"Wonder whose wood lot he's got his eye on now?"

"Now, Lyd, there's no call for that kind of talk. Joel Patch's all right. No harm in a man liking to wear a beaver hat."

"Maybe. Depends on what's under the hat." Mrs. Tarbox flattened her cheek against the middle pane of the lower sash and followed the wagon's progress. "E-yah. Like you said. Going to stop at the blacksmith's."

Dan Tarbox began to untie his apron. "Mightn't hurt to stroll down that way. Just thinking of business. Sitting around that forge can be mighty sweaty on a warm day. And talking politics and such is dry work. There's just a chance somebody might suggest wetting his whistle."

"Joel Patch won't."

11

"Maybe not. But somebody might. E-yah. Never can tell." With an elaborate wink that screwed up one whole side of his face, Dan Tarbox left the room.

In the past more talk, small and great, was forged under blacksmiths' roofs than iron. The constant fire was one reason for this. It gave warmth in winter and was always friendly. Perhaps that was why the gods were so furious with Prometheus: they knew that men gazing into flames would draw from those dancing tongues some heat that would loosen their own. Fire ranks with alcohol as a mental lubricant, and if the thoughts that both produce are seldom earth-shaking, at least they add to the sum of man's laughter and draw him closer to his neighbor. And fire is the better of the two. Nobody ever worked up a crying jag, that catharsis of frustration and revolter of companions, by sitting in front of a hearth or forge.

There was something about the smell of a smithy, too, that induced conversation. Wood smoke whipped at the nostrils; charcoal gave off gas. There was always a hint of dampness from the vat where the white iron was plunged. Most important of all, the odor of horses clung to the corners of a blacksmith's shed. Usually a horse or two was present in the flesh, replenishing the odor. Why a mixture of lather, sweat, ammonia, and manure, wet leather, damp hair, and burning hoofs should have stirred anyone to discourse has never been decided. Still, men talked in that atmosphere.

Part of it was the pure joy of sitting idle and watching someone else work. The smith was busy. Hammer clanged on anvil. The bellows wheezed. There was clatter and bustle. To watch all this, while he waited, lounging at ease, gave a man a sense of well-being. For the time of his stay at the blacksmith's each customer was a wealthy loafer, and others worked for him. Naturally, few could keep silent.

They talked. All but the blacksmith. He gained a reputation for profound wisdom by being too busy to say much. But, for conversation, someone must be the listener, and the smith was perfect for the role. There were even rhythmic pauses in his hammering that seemed meant to be filled by the farmers' pungent sentences. No wonder the blacksmith was a personage. A

12

poet, not without honor, sensed part of this feeling and immortalized muscles and a chestnut tree. He should have listened to the loungers as well.

Abner Reed, the only blacksmith on Stratton Mountain, had no idea that there was poetry in his work, for it was still a year before the poet's poem would appear. As soon as the Patch wagon came in sight, though, he knew he was in for another session of talk. Abner sighed. The long, quiet morning that he had spent alone, reinforcing a whiffletree, was over.

From within his doorway Abner watched the wagon approach. The two men side by side on the high seat seemed cast from the same mold. No onlooker could mistake that these two were father and son. By some trick of eugenics, it was the older who was the copy of the younger; the father appeared patterned after the son. A hand skilled at woodworking might have taken a block that was young Nathan and trimmed it down to produce Joel. An adze, hewing to the line as a log is planked, might have brought from the younger man's figure the smaller-scaled father, keeping the outline yet chipping away the excess, leaving planes and angles as such a blade does.

Joel Patch was an angular man. There was, however, nothing wooden about him as he squirmed on the wagon seat and shouted for the blacksmith. "Abner! Abner Reed!"

The smith came forward out of the shadows. "Morning, Joel."

"Sadie's throwed a shoe." Patch jerked his thumb at the mare tied to the tail of the wagon. "Want it fixed right away. Show him, Nathan."

"No need," said Abner. "Left hind, ain't it?"

Patch nodded. It was more like a snap of his head. All the man's movements were quick and jerky. He said, "Can you fix it?"

"Always managed to."

"I mean now! Right away! Time's money, Abner! I ain't got all day!"

The blacksmith sighed again. He was used to Patch's habit of announcing his arrival with peremptory demands. Abner never bothered to argue against the bugle of his customer's voice. "We'll see," he answered. "Lead her in, Nathan."

Nathan unhitched the sturdy little Morgan mare and led her into the shed. Abner crouched, swept the hoof into his lap with

13

one deft movement, examined it. "E-yah. That'll need a new shoe."

"Knew that when we brought her!" Patch said. "If you ask me, there ought to be a rebate. Shoe couldn't have been put on right if she throwed it so soon!"

Abner looked at Patch. "E-yah," he agreed.

"Ought to be a rebate."

"Get it where you got her shod," said the smith. "That ain't my work and you know it."

"It ain't?"

"It ain't." Abner's tone was resigned but definite.

Patch showed his teeth. "Do tell. My mistake, Abner. Mite hard to know them matched Morgans of mine apart. Maybe it was t'other one."

"No." The smith's gaze was steady. "Last time they was re-shod your hired man did for the pair of them."

"E-yah." Patch's nod saluted defeat. "Guess that's right. Well, get busy at it, will you?"

Behind his father's back, Nathan grinned. The old man was a smart trader, but he'd run into a stone wall that time. Nathan was pleased, too, at the smith's lack of animosity. Sometimes, he reflected, Pa's trickery made you feel hot and ashamed, but Abner just took it as a matter of course. He wished he were more like the blacksmith and, suddenly, fiercely, wished his father were also.

Working his bellows to bring the fire to the glow he wanted, the blacksmith noticed the listeners gather. Dan Tarbox sauntered in and seated himself on a keg of nails.

"Morning, Joel . . . Abner . . . Nathan."

"Morning, Dan."

Peleg Nason hobbled through the doorway, the tip of his cane thudding on the ground. The old man was close to ninety, bent and rheumatic. He didn't walk but staggered, pitching forward in short spurts as if about to fall on his face at any moment. Peleg rattled his cane against the bench, slid down onto it, and gasped, catching his breath.

Abner Reed grunted. He liked old Peleg, but Peleg was a veteran; he'd never forgotten it, and he did his best to see that no one else could.

"Morning, Peleg."

14

"Fine day, ain't it?"

"E-yah."

Glancing up from his forge the smith saw that Will Carpenter, who farmed without working, was leaning against his usual place on the wall, chewing. Sitting cross-legged in the dirt, his mouth slack and loose, was the Pierce boy, who didn't have all his wits. Abner pushed the bellows' handle angrily. It's like they pop up out of the ground, he thought, one minute nobody's here and the next the whole crowd is.

There was no hurry about starting the talk. Every eye followed the blacksmith as he selected a shoe, clamped it in the tongs, thrust it into the coals. Joel Patch, conscious that it was his mare being shod, walked up and down as if supervising the smith. It was Peleg, with the impatience of age, who broke the silence.

"How be things up to the sawmill, Joel?"

"Slack, Peleg. Same's everywhere."

"Ain't cutting?"

"Oh, we're cutting. But hardly enough to keep the saw busy. Cutting ain't selling!"

"E-yah. Guess that's so."

"Ain't cutting prices, are you, Joel?"

"My price is fair, Will Carpenter! You won't get better at Pike's or White's!"

"Didn't say I could. Just wondered."

"Three sawmills seems a lot for one mountain."

"There'd be business for three, only folks ain't building. Nobody's buying. No cash."

"Same all over. The inn feels it too."

"Blame that on the Panic, Dan. That's what did it. The Panic!"

"That was three years ago, wa'n't it? Thought it'd be over by now."

"It ain't over up here, Peleg! Nowhere's near! It took a long while to climb up to this mountain, and it's going to take longer getting off."

"E-yah. You got it right, Joel."

"E-yah."

"Must be them bad roads." Peleg cackled at his own wit. "You ought to do something about them roads, Joel!"

Joel Patch spread his legs wide and shook a finger to catch

15

his audience's complete attention. When he had it, he spoke slowly, with force. "What we ought to do something about is those that's responsible for causing Panics and hard times. Those in public places, high places, who have betrayed their trust! They've been lining their pockets by taking out of ours. And so long as we let them go on doing it there ain't never going to be a chance to make a dollar in this miserable, unhappy country! I guess you know I refer to the tyrannical, corrupt administration led by that arch-hypocrite Martin Van Buren!"

"E-yah."

"Ought to hang that Dutchman!"

"Hanging's too good for him."

"York State bastid." Dan Tarbox's tobacco juice splashed.

"Mark my words," Joel Patch said. "Mark my words. The fat little leech is sucking the blood out of the whole United States. First he helped that damn fool Jackson wreck the cornerstone of our financial system, the Bank of the United States!" Patch repeated the impressive title. "The Bank of the United States."

"That's right."

"E-yah."

"Him and Jackson."

"But that wasn't enough! Not for Van! He got that senile idiot, King Andy, to make him President, and then the fur really flew. It ain't enough smashing the big bank, he has to go after the little ones! The White House ain't fancy enough for Van! He's drinking out of gold goblets, but he wants more. Sent out a call for specie. Hard money! And that brought the whole kit and caboodle down around our heads! The Panic! Didn't hurt him any! Didn't even bother him! Still didn't figure he had enough for his drinking and eating and parties, so he decided to set up an independent treasury to make his own money! Guess you know who that money's for!"

"The Democrats."

"E-yah. The Loco-focos."

"Why do they call them that, Mr. Patch?"

"Call them what?"

"Loco-focos."

"Oh." Patch glared at the questioner who had derailed his train of thought. Young Pierce, gaping, waited for his answer,

16

his mind too dull to sense the speaker's anger. Others volunteered information.

"After the matches, boy."

"E-yah. Democrats want to play with matches."

"Want to burn everything down."

"Burn the Constitution."

"E-yah."

Forced into reply by this barrage, Patch shouted, regaining control of the conversation, "That ain't the right of it at all. I know all about that. Fellow down to New York told me. It happened down there. The Democrats was holding a meeting in their hall. Planning some new devilment. And somebody put out the lights on them!"

The audience exploded into laughter.

"I want to know!"

"Put out the lights, did they?"

"That's the way to fix them!"

"Where was Moses when the lights went out?"

"Didn't work," Patch said. "Smart trick, but those Democrats got Satan's own wiliness. Every feller at that meeting ripped out a packet of them new-fangled matches and lit up. They've been Loco-focos ever since!"

"You don't say!"

"Mighty quick thinking."

"E-yah," agreed Patch. "They're foxy, all right. The Loco-focos can figure out more ways of grafting and cheating than a man'd think possible. You got to get up real early to get around that kind. Passel of blackguards!"

"Thieves, and whores," Peleg said, waving his cane. "Thieves and whores! Every one of them!"

"E-yah."

"Plenty of that down there in Washington!"

"Ain't noticed any scarcity in these parts."

"Been looking, Dan?"

"Not specially. I leave that to the younger men."

"Bet old Van doesn't."

"That's why he's Van, the used-up man!"

This time Patch joined the laughter. He realized the difficulty of switching the gathering from man's favorite subject and surrendered. Shaking his head, he said, "The carryings-on in Washington are a national scandal."

"Maybe it's the weather."

"Maybe. Hot down there, ain't it?"

"All the time."

"Having it hot helps."

"You sound like your blood's getting thin."

"Science says females react to heat."

"Shucks. I got a heifer says the same thing."

"Send her down to Washington. Take care of her there!"

"Guess they ain't passing any laws against that."

"Too busy working at it."

"That Peggy Eaton now."

"E-yah. She was a looker."

"High-stepping filly."

"That's old stuff. She ain't no chicken any more."

"Maybe Will likes them prime."

"Don't have to, Joel. Not in Washington."

"Plenty more where she come from."

"More'n one color too."

"I don't hold with that!"

"Can't tell the difference in the dark."

"But nigger women!"

"Don't ask me. Ask Colonel Johnson."

"E-yah. Ask the Vice-President."

"He's got the right title. Vice fits him!"

"How many is it he's had? Three or four?"

"Whole herd of them."

"Every shade."

"And that's the kind of man who is President of the Senate."

"Old Tecumseh Johnson."

"Sure got far by just killing that Indian."

"If he did kill Tecumseh."

"Harrison was the commander."

"E-yah. But Johnson got the credit."

"Guess it was the only good thing he ever did!"

"He didn't figure it a good deed. Just habit."

"Habit?"

"E-yah. Johnson's from Kentucky. All they do in that state is

kill Indians. There was Tecumseh, and there was Johnson. Bang!
Dead Indian. Force of habit."

Patch showed his teeth as the laughter rocked around him. He
teetered, toe and heel, well satisfied with the effect of his remark.
He noticed that Peleg Nason wasn't laughing. The old veteran
hammered his cane against the bench.

"Now, hold on," Peleg said. "Hold on just a minute. If the man
did do a killing, that might account for things."

"Account for what things, Peleg?"

The old voice was thin and quavery. "Might account for his
actions. The black women. All those things. I ain't excusing him,
mind. Ain't excusing him one bit. But when you've done a killing,
things is never the same as they was." Peleg Nason bubbled in a
deep breath, crossed both hands on the crook of his cane, and
went on before anyone could stop him.

"You all know that I went out against Burgoyne. I was just a
young fellow then, living down Marlboro way, but I went. All us
young fellows went, and most anybody that could shoulder a
gun was welcome. The Revolution wasn't going so good, and
there was the Redcoats coming down out of Canada and getting
ready to let loose all them red savages on us. 'Course we went. No
two ways about it. The bunch I was with, we didn't half know
where we was going. We just walked west over the mountains.
Up one side and down the other. More damn mountains. And
after a while we joined up with some other fellows heading west.
And then some more. And the whole lot of us sort of linked onto
the tail end of General Stark's army. General John Stark, of New
Hampshire. He knew where he was going all right. I was just
getting my feet rested from all that walking, when off we go
again. Still pushing west. And the first thing I know we've pushed
smack into the middle of Bennington Battle.

"I guess maybe you've all heard of that battle. I know that
everybody I've heard tell about it tells it different. I even read
about it in a book the parson has up to his place. It was the biggest doing in the war line we ever had in this state. Maybe Saratoga, over in York State, where Burgoyne give up, was bigger, but
there mightn't have been no Saratoga if we hadn't been to Bennington. That's history. But what I can't understand is why nobody
ever tells about it the same way. That book now. Maybe Ben-

nington Battle was like it tells in that book, but if it was, then where the hell was I that day?

"A battle's a kind of confusing thing. You and the fellows with you are walking along in one direction, and all of a sudden you hear the guns start popping way ahead of you. More guns than I ever heard all at once in my life. And everybody stops dead still and listens. Then they all start pushing and bumping into everybody else, and some fellow on a horse, he's yelling to beat the band, and nobody can make out a word of it. But the whole mob runs off the road in another direction, and me with them. That was even more confusing 'cause we didn't seem to be going toward that gunfire at all. No, sir. We crossed a stone wall and a field, and then we were in among some trees. The shooting wasn't any nearer, but everybody sat down and waited. I got tired of looking at nothing but leaves and pushed forward to where I could see something.

"Mostly it was smoke, and folks running back and forth. More smoke than folks. Out in the open was this bunch we was fighting, and the best part of them weren't Redcoats at all. They was wearing a blue uniform not red. But they weren't our side, because our side was shooting at them. There was this whole rank of these blue fellows, big men, standing packed as tight as the trees on this mountain. And they're fighting by count. One, two, three, shoot—all the guns going off at once, and the smoke hiding them. Volley they call it. Me, I couldn't figure out what they thought they was doing, but I had sense enough to want to move up closer and take a shot at them. You couldn't have missed, they was that tight packed. The boys that were shooting at them were knocking them down fast. I was just about to get going when something gleamed, and I saw that they had a little brass cannon. And that cannon gave a puff of smoke right at me, and I got going all right. So did everybody else. Off we all went, rampsing away for dear life in still another direction. And that was all I ever did see of the battle proper.

"You see, I tripped over a root and twisted my ankle sore. Left ankle it was. I got up and hobbled as best I could, but I couldn't get along very fast. And I got left behind. My ankle was hurting like fury, and I was hot and tired, so when it got a little quiet I sat down.

"I don't remember how long I sat in that one spot, but the day was getting along when the boy come. First thing, I heard somebody running through the woods, so I took up my musket and looked at the priming and cocked the hammer. It was loaded, all right. I hadn't fired it once. Then I sat there, with the gun across my knees, and listened to the noise coming closer and waited.

"The boy come out of the brush real close. He wasn't no farther from me than Abner's anvil is now. He was a little blond fellow, and he'd lost his hat, and there was dust all over his uniform. But his coat was red, red as a heat sunset. I saw it and didn't wait. I threw the musket up and fired.

"He was close, like I said. You could hear the ball hit. He went down like he'd been poleaxed.

"I grabbed the musket by its barrel and hobbled over to him. I was young, remember, and it was the first Redcoat I'd seen in my life, and I guess I figured I'd just about won the war and the Revolution.

"But he wasn't dead. That was the hell of it. He wasn't dead, and he had a face like a baby's. You could see the down on it like peach fuzz; he was that young. And he kept looking up at me sort of surprised like any boy his age caught stealing jam. But not mad at me any. Just surprised. He tried to talk. His lips moved but nothing came out. And after a little while he died.

"It wasn't like killing in battle. Not that way. Just the boy and me. It was more like murder. I thought so then, and I think so now. I went off a ways and was sick. I hadn't et much all that day, but I was sick anyhow."

Peleg Nason stopped talking. He sat with his eyes squeezed tight, breathing hard. After a while he said, "I fought in other battles later. But they wasn't like Bennington. That's what I meant about the Johnson man. If his killing Tecumseh was personal-like, it makes a difference. Things ain't the same after you've done a killing."

The blacksmith tossed his hammer aside with a clatter. "Here's your mare, Joel," he said. "All shod."

Nathan Patch had slipped out of the blacksmith's shed when his father started talking. After all, it wasn't as if he hadn't heard it all before and often. He knew his parent's opinions and agreed

21

with them and thought of himself as a Whig too, even if he hadn't voted yet. But a man could stand just so much politics, and Nathan had other business on his mind. He grinned up at the sun and ambled back along the mud of the road toward the parsonage. It was seldom that Nathan got to the settlement during working hours, and he meant to make the most of it. Suddenly conscious of the Chesters' curtained windows, he stiffened his shoulders and walked briskly. From behind those curtains Lovina Chester might be regarding him.

Skirting the gabled front of the house, Nathan went around to the L. The kitchen door was open, and before he reached it, the warm, pleasant scent of bread filled his nostrils. Nathan stood for a moment enjoying the aroma, then took off his square cap and smoothed his hair. Frowning, he ran his index finger along the bristles on his chin and wished he had shaved. Nathan shrugged, rapped a knuckle on the door's panel, and stuck his head inside.

It was baking day in the Chester kitchen, and the long room that occupied the L was hot. A fire roared in the fireplace at the room's outside end, and the air was thick and heavy. Spice and dough and pastry mingled, fighting vainly against the deeper odor of the oven. Five female Chesters, busy at their tasks, gave the kitchen a thronged appearance.

Their bustle took the starch out of Nathan. His knock had gone unheeded. He cleared his throat and said, too loudly, "Morning, everybody."

Sally Chester, peeling apples on the settle, looked up and nudged her sister, Martha. The two chorused their greeting as one, "Morning, Nathan."

Little Josepha, licking a spoon at the table, swung around. She jammed the spoon completely into her mouth, and gazed at the visitor with the fixed, frightening solemnity of an eight year old.

Nathan winced and looked away. His glance met Lovina's and he gulped. A slow flush started in his neck and climbed up his face, like a tub filling. He was stricken with the knowledge that his coming was a mistake. For Lovina Chester was glaring.

Sleeves rolled up, arms deep in the bread trough, Lovina was hot and furious. She was conscious that her dress clung damply to her back, that she was splattered with flour, that dough was caked on one cheek, and that her hair was tumbled in her eyes. I never looked worse, she thought bitterly, never in my whole life. She blew the hair up from her forehead and glared, hoping to blast Nathan Patch with one look that would drive him back out the door he had entered.

Mrs. Chester saved him. She left the big oven set in the brick of the fireplace and came forward. "Good morning, Nathan. Come in, come in. Don't stand on the doorsill. How nice you dropped by."

The girls on the settle tittered, but their mother's quick look silenced them.

"Mattie. Sally. Those apples won't peel themselves. Go on with your work. Nathan needn't bother you."

Sally tossed her head, muttering, "He isn't bothering *me!*"

"That will do," said Mrs. Chester, not daring to steal a peek at Lovina but aware of her eldest daughter's rigid back. The minister's wife was not stupid, and she felt a twinge of sympathy for Lovina. Men, she thought, never fail to make a mess of things. Of all moments to drop in unexpected! Still, there was no need to insult the poor youth. Remembering that Nathan was Joel Patch's only son and that the sawmill owner was the wealthiest man on the mountain, Lovina's mother smiled graciously. "Draw up a chair, Nathan. And sit down out of the way. We've only this second batch and then we're finished."

"Thank you, ma'am." Nathan was grateful.

Lovina went on with her kneading, twisting the doughy mass skillfully under her palms but with such energy that the bread trough shivered. She felt a trickle of sweat run coldly down between her breasts, and every bad word she'd ever heard jolted into her mind. She tightened her lips against them, digging her fingers into the dough.

"And how is the Deacon?"

"Who? Oh, Pa. Fine, ma'am. Just fine."

"And your sister?"

"She's fine too. Thank you, ma'am."

The conversation died of its own weight. The lad's a lump, thought Mrs. Chester. She was a tall woman, ample, with a strong, almost masculine face and more ability than patience. She had work to do, and she was not in the habit of taking nonsense from

23

any of her children. She turned to Lovina, facing the issue squarely.

"Lovina. Nathan's here."

"Yes, Mother." Lovina implied she wished him elsewhere.

"You may leave that."

"It isn't finished."

"I'll make it into loaves. I said to leave it."

The clash of wills was almost audible.

Nathan sensed a crisis and stumbled to his feet. "I can't stay," he said. "Just dropped by to pass the time. We're having the mare shod down to the smithy and . . . "

Mrs. Chester interrupted. "Nonsense. You're always welcome. I'm sure there's no need to rush off. Lovina." The last word was no louder than the rest but it flicked like a whip end.

"Please," Nathan said, with sudden craft. "Could I have a cup of your cold well water? I'm a mite dry." He wanted to escape from the kitchen. Nathan realized that Mrs. Chester had already magnified his original blunder and, with an instinct that showed his Patch blood, he carried the war to the enemy. "If you don't mind, Mrs. Chester?"

"Not at all. Lovina will show you."

Lovina led the way into the sunlit back yard, taking the dipper from its nail as she passed out the door. She remembered that she was wearing several less petticoats than usual. It was more comfortable for working in a hot kitchen, but she hadn't expected company. Very conscious of the male behind her, the girl attempted to walk without swinging her hips. She bit her lip and tried not to hurry.

The Chester tomcat, Toby, was sunning his tiger stripes on the lip of the well. Lovina scratched his ears as she watched Nathan draw up the bucket. Toby seemed to realize that the scratcher wasn't concentrating, and he grew restive; he walked from under the hand with offended dignity, leaped down, and stalked away.

Nathan splashed water into the dipper and stepped back. "You first," he said.

The water was cold in Lovina's mouth, and her teeth clicked on the dipper's tin as she gulped hungrily. When she lowered the vessel the anger was gone from her face. She sighed, patted the hem of her apron against her lips, and held out the dipper, smiling.

24

Nathan took it and drank. Gazing at the round disk of the dipper's bottom, he was thinking of his next move. That first perfect sentence refused to form in his mind. He had no more ideas than the clear water lapping beneath his nose.

"You'll founder yourself," Lovina said.

It took him by surprise. He lowered the dipper hastily. "E-yah. Tastes so good though."

"Dry work. Visiting."

He knew then that she wasn't going to let him off. The certainty lessened his worry, and he found words. "Lovina, I'm sorry. I thought you might be glad to see me."

"You heard Mother. You're always welcome."

"I didn't come to see your mother."

"No. It was the mare needing shoes, wasn't it?"

"That ain't fair, Lovina."

"If you think that, you're free to go."

"No." Nathan shook his head; his tone was stubborn. "Not till I get something straightened out. You're put out 'cause I caught you when you weren't all prettied up. I saw that right away."

"Why should I care what you think?"

"Far as that goes you've got no reason to care. Maybe this is a work dress, and you've been working, but you never looked prettier."

"Pretty!" Lovina sniffed, but she was pleased. She turned and looked down into the well.

"E-yah. Pretty's what I said. A man'd have to be blind not to see it. I ain't blind, Lovina. You know that fine feathers don't make fine birds. And no matter what apparel you might wear, you would always have my admiration and respect."

The formal tone brought Lovina's head around. This was courting talk, and she looked at him. Her own reply was equally studied. "Thank you, Nathan. It seems I owe you an apology for my rudeness."

"No apology is called for, Lovina. I have never wanted anything except that you might entertain friendly feelings for myself. Feelings that, I assure you, would then be mutual."

Poor Nathan, thought Lovina, suddenly sorry for him. In spite of her mother's encouragement, or perhaps because of it, the girl had never regarded him as a serious suitor.

Nathan soared to greater heights. "In such a case, valuing your

25

friendship as I do, I would regard myself as the most fortunate of men."

Lovina knew that he didn't mean friendship and giggled inwardly. But these formal, courting speeches led to an inevitable answer, and she decided to end them. She was pleased and flattered, and when she spoke there was no pretense. She said, with simple sincerity, "I'm sorry, Nathan."

Her tone toppled Nathan from the clouds. He understood. His eyes narrowed; his voice sharpened. He was suddenly even more like his father. He said, "Somebody else, Lovina?"

"I'm afraid I can't answer that, Nathan."

"Charles Chittenden?"

"Nathan, please. You have no right to question me."

"Ain't settled, is it? You wouldn't have listened to me if it was settled for keeps."

"Nathan Patch!" Lovina stamped her foot. He knew as well as she did that there was nothing settled between herself and Charles, but she was in no mood to be reminded of it. "You stop that talk this instant!"

Nathan blinked at her. "I can wait," he said doggedly. "Pays to wait sometimes. Never can tell what might transpire."

Spots flared on Lovina's cheeks, and fury deepened the blue of her eyes. She blazed out at him. "That will do! You'd better leave!"

"No hurry," said Nathan and set his teeth.

From beyond the roofs of the parsonage a voice like a trumpet blasted.

"Nathan! Nathan Patch!"

Nathan jumped. "Oh, thunder," he quaked. "That's Pa. I got to go, Lovina." He started at a run, hurling his farewell over his shoulder. "Bye, Lovina. I'll drop by again soon."

"You hear me, Nathan!"

"Coming, Pa. Coming!"

Lovina watched him lope out of sight around a corner of the house. "Scared to death of his Pa," she said. The scornful remark disposed of Nathan, and she began to think about Charles. All through the long winter Charles Chittenden had managed to find time to call. Barring the two blizzards, he'd come down from the farm nearly every week, besides Sunday meeting.

It had always been Charles for Lovina since she was seven. Eleven

26

years, she counted. But this winter, at eighteen, she had thought there was something different in their relationship. At Christmas they'd exchanged gifts. She'd knitted the mittens for him herself; she'd read every word of the book he'd given. Poetry, too—"Thanatopsis" and other poems, by William Cullen Bryant. And, if it wasn't precisely the poetry she expected, at least it had Father's approval, in spite of Mr. Bryant's being a Democrat, and showed that Charles respected her mind.

Not that Charles was any dry stick. They'd skated on Holman's Pond as long as the ice had lasted. They'd been sledding, too—five times, wasn't it? Lovina flushed a bit, remembering the Sunday they'd sneaked away with the toboggan. She, a minister's daughter, had enjoyed the sinful sport every bit as much as Charles. The flush warmed as she recalled how Charles had pressed her tight to the sled; she hoped he didn't recall exactly where his hands had pressed, at least not so vividly as she did.

They had laughed a lot during the winter, and she'd felt very sure. Now, prodded by Nathan's discourse, she racked her memory vainly for any ardent declarations from Charles. There'd been that one quick kiss at the Nasons' husking bee last fall, but that was in jest because Charles stripped the red ear. Her mother had made a to-do over nothing about that. No, there was certainly nothing really settled between herself and Charles.

Today made two weeks since she'd even seen him, not counting last Sunday when it had rained and the Chittendens had gone off before she'd finished putting the hymnals away. Lovina plucked a blade of grass and chewed it thoughtfully. It was Saturday, and maybe Charles would come that evening. She'd been counting on it. That was why she'd talked her mother into letting her take her first spring bath this afternoon, even though it might come on cold again. Maybe Charles would notice if she took a chill and died.

With sudden panic, she remembered Mrs. Chester's anger about Nathan in the kitchen. If her mother forbade her the bath as punishment she'd die. Especially with Charles coming. Lovina turned toward the kitchen. Smiling, she determined to placate her mother no matter what the cost.

Bouncing into each pit and over every rock, its four wheels deep in the muddy ruts of the road, the four-horse team dragging it by

27

sheer strength, the stage toiled slowly up the east side of Stratton Mountain. The stage was a high Concord coach, painted dark green with gold trim, and somewhat shabby. But all the metalwork on stage and harness was polished and gleaming.

There were no passengers. High on the box the driver, legs crossed, lolled at ease. Lot Purdy was as fine a stage driver as his son, Seth, believed him to be. He had a broad, strong-chinned face, weatherbeaten almost to the color and texture of the reins he held. Neither tall nor heavy, he looked muscular and competent. The black fur cap had its ear laps neatly tied over its crown; his trousers were tucked tautly and smoothly into his boots. Lot's one luxury of dress was on his hands; he wore smooth, expensive-looking buckskin gloves.

He had made them himself and considered them the badge of his profession. For in Lot's mind stage driving was a profession, and one that took skill and training to learn. He liked his work. He had the salaried craftsman's easy contempt for farming as a livelihood. It was drudgery, back-breaking labor, dull. There was nothing dull about driving stage. Each trip was different. The weather, the horses, the passengers changed constantly. Lot Purdy found them all interesting.

Sleeping at home only one night in three didn't bother Lot. He preferred the freedom, although he was aware that it set him apart from his neighbors on Stratton. Atop his stage Lot Purdy was as authoritative as a ship's captain; in the crossroad settlement he was as the sailor among landsmen. He brought the news from the world off the mountain. With the glib familiarity of his kind, he knew everybody and had few friends. Tate Jones, the mountain's trapper, was the driver's closest companion. They made a good pair. Tate Jones, the hermit hunter, was suspected of being an atheist; Lot Purdy was known to be a Democrat.

The horses, sides heaving, topped a steep rise and shuffled to a halt. They were on a level stretch, a regular resting place, and, from one of the high banks that hemmed in the road, water trickled down a wooden trough and was caught in a hollow log. The lead horses plunged their noses into the water noisily; the rear team whinnied, eager for their turn.

Stamping his brake set, the driver jumped down and pushed the horses away from the water before they drank too much. He watered the wheel pair from a bucket. Then, with a glance at the sun, he climbed back on the box and took his lunch and a bundle of mail from the cavity under the seat.

Lot unwrapped both. He munched bread and cheese while he weeded the letters from the mail and fanned out the residue of newspapers, periodicals, pamphlets, and broadsides. He grinned at the pile. Only when the stage was without passengers could he scan the publications before they reached the subscribers. Not that he carried many passengers. It was over three weeks since he'd brought that young fellow up from Arlington, the one who had got out and looked over the big clearing as if he was buying it. He wasn't, though; he'd spent the night at Dan Tarbox's inn and went on down this side to West Wardsboro.

The driver read the names and titles.

The *Vermont Phoenix:* last week's copy from Brattleboro. Nearly everybody on the mountain took that paper.

The *Boston Advertiser:* that was for Joel Patch.

The *Boston Atlas:* one for the parson, another for Patch.

North American: a magazine. The parson.

New-England Magazine: the parson again.

Log Cabin: a whole mound of this newspaper, all consigned to the inn for resale.

Lot Purdy swore. All Whig publications. Not a decent Democrat paper in the lot. And that mess of *Log Cabins!* That young Horace Greeley must have a mint the way he scattered his newspaper around.

Shaking loose the most recent of Mr. Greeley's papers, the driver read a few lines:

> What paupers are th' ambitious rich!—
> How wealthy the contented poor!

"Sweet Jerusalem!" said Lot Purdy and spat.

He unfolded another paper to a cartoon and winced. The woodcut depicted the Whig candidate for President, General Harrison, battering, in prize-ring style, a fat pugilist labeled Martin Van Buren.

"Cow dung," Lot Purdy said.

He shuffled through the rest, noting one ever-recurrent printed phrase. "Tippecanoe and Tyler too! Tippecanoe and Tyler too!

29

Tippecanoe and Tyler too!" Lot rattled the words like a parrot, derisive and scornful.

They're making an awful lot of that log-cabin, hard-cider business, the driver thought. Whatever Democrat opened his mouth about that ought to be jailed. The Whigs sure cracked it up something wonderful, making out that Harrison was just common folks. Lot Purdy doubted that any general lived in a log cabin.

From his pocket he took a broadside, the strongest Democrat ammunition he'd found so far, and read it aloud, rolling the title on his tongue. *The Producer's Election Hymn, or an Address to Poor Men.*

Poor men, thought Lot. That should hold the Whigs at the inn. He skipped quickly through the stanzas.

> Arise! Arise! Sustain your rights,
> Ye sons of labor rise!

> ✦ ✦ ✦

> *The Paper Plague* afflicts us all,
> Its pains are past enduring;
> Still we have hope in Jackson's robe,
> Whilst it wraps around VAN BUREN.

> ✦ ✦ ✦

> Then to the polls like victors go!
> Rushing like a river's flow,
> Urged by wastes of melting snow:
> Mark a Whig, and lo, a foe!
> That would enslave you, work your woe!
> Therefore support Van Buren!

Suddenly there was a rustle of leaves, and a catamount leaped into the road.

The panther landed squarely in front of the lead horses, froze in surprise, and snarled. Then it flashed through the air, a tawny streak, its long tail held straight, cleared the opposite bank, and crashed from view in the underbrush.

The horses reared, screaming in panic. The stage teetered, wheels locked. Cursing, Lot Purdy kicked the brake loose. Before he could sweep up the reins, the horses were racing.

Lot let them run. He stared back, his mouth open. "God Almighty," he said. "That cat must have been seven feet long!" He braced his legs against the wild careening of the stage, tucked away the broadside, and pulled up his tangled reins.

"God Almighty," he said again. Then, grinning, he settled back and began to slow the team.

Dinner at the Chittendens' was always a noisy affair. Eratus Chittenden was a large man, six feet five in his socks, and he had a voice that fitted his size. It boomed down the long table, drowning but not stilling the chattering five young Chittendens. Not that the noise bothered Eratus. He liked it. Dinner was his favorite meal, with the noon sunlight brightening the kitchen, and the whole family present.

He checked the attendance now and frowned when he noticed the absence of Peter, his eldest son, and Peter's wife Jennie. Eratus refrained from commenting on this when he remembered the reason why Peter had driven Jennie down the mountain. He hoped the doctor found it to be true; he wanted to be a grandfather.

Eratus always served standing, looming over the table as if his giant frame needed all the space it could get. From this position he could survey the entire kitchen, the fire roaring on the hearth, the copperware gleaming ruddily on its row of hooks, the height of the logs in the wood box. From it, too, he could direct the movements of his children. Best crop he'd raised, Eratus felt, and grinned down the table's length at his wife, Mary.

Mary Blood Chittenden smiled. She was a slender woman, small, with a generous mouth and wide-set, bright eyes. One cheek had a deep dimple, and both glowed with the color of health.

Her husband nodded, "Talk, talk, talk." The big voice boomed. "They're your brood all right, Mary!"

Mary winked at him. "I've never denied it."

Eratus guffawed and covered himself by a rapid-fire issuing of orders. "Charles. Pour the milk."

"Yes, Pa."

"Amos. That's not enough bread. Cut more."

"Yes, Pa."

"Henry."

"Pa?"

"That woodbin's your chore. Don't look too full from here."

31

"I filled it this morning, Pa. Ask Ma."

"That's right, Eratus."

"Fill it again after dinner. It don't look full to me."

"Yes, Pa."

"Nancy. That spoon's not to play with, miss."

"Yes, Pa."

"Miley! Sit still, child!"

"Yes, sir."

Having squashed the diners into some semblance of decorum, Eratus bent over the huge pie, each mound of the upper crust barely tinted with brown, and wrinkled his nose in a sniff. "What's this, Mary?" he asked. "What's this?"

"Rabbit potpie."

"Rabbit potpie!" Eratus lifted his carving knife, brandished it, and plunged it into the crust. Steam hissed from the pie. "If it eats as good as it smells, it'll eat all-fired good!"

"Eratus." Mary rapped with her fork to arrest his attention.

Knife point poised, Eratus stared at her. "E-yah?"

"We haven't given thanks."

"Oh." Eratus pouted and laid down the knife. Then he squinted to disguise the look of glee that came over his face. "And to whom do we give this thanks, pray? I swapped some powder to Tate Jones for three of these rabbits. And Henry snared the other one. Easy enough to thank Henry, but how do I find Tate?" He beamed, relishing his children's laughter, hardly able to contain his own.

Mary Chittenden said, "It is only fitting in these hard times to give thanks that we're a little more fortunate than others."

"Your mother's right," said Eratus, accepting the rebuke but placing the onus where he wanted it. He gazed down the laden table, noting the heavy crockery, the piles of bread, the blue-gray Bennington milk jug. A dish, heaped high and smoking, caught his attention. He pointed at it.

"Milkweed greens," said Mary. "The last of the jars I put up last summer."

"E-yah. Your mother's right. We wintered better than most. Let us give thanks."

Every head at the table bowed. Eratus, hands clasped behind him, scowled at the potpie and cleared his throat, thinking. A twist of smile twitched the corner of his wife's mouth. Sometimes Mary believed that she insisted on grace at meals just to hear what her husband would say this time. She could judge the state of his appetite by the length of the blessing.

"God!" Eratus thundered suddenly, as if afraid the Deity might be busy elsewhere. "We give thanks for this here bounty which Thou has provided in spite of too much frost and Martin Van Buren!"

Eratus brought both arms from behind his back, scooped up knife and spoon, and began dishing out the potpie. His command to his second son was exactly the same tone he had used to his Maker. "Charles! Pass the plates."

The endless, tossing chain of food finally stopped. Everyone waited while Eratus forked a bite of the pie into his mouth, munched, and gave a hearty grunt of approval. As one, the younger Chittendens shoveled into their dinners. They ate with intense concentration; there was no sound now but the scraping of forks, the tap of spoons, the slight thud as a heavy mug was set down. Even the necessary replenishings of bread or milk were indicated by nods and gestures; every mouth was too busy with business more important than speech.

Charles Chittenden finished first. He scraped his plate clean with a morsel of bread, popped it in his mouth, and sat back. Almost twenty-one, Charles lacked but an inch and a half of his father's height. He had the same shoulders, but his frame was rangier, not yet filled in completely. His coloring was his mother's; he had her brown hair and hazel eyes. He stared into space, thinking. He wondered about the best method of approaching his father. Charles wanted very much to borrow a horse and wagon after supper. If he could, he would take Lovina Chester for a ride. If it was a fine night, if it didn't come on too cold . . . He sighed. There were so many ifs. And the biggest was whether or not Eratus would let him have a horse.

Blaze or Whitefoot? Charles weighed the points of each. Both horses had worked hard with the first turning of earth that morning and would work hard all afternoon. Eratus wasn't likely to deprive a horse of a well-earned rest. Charles knew his father's devotion to all the livestock on the farm, cattle, sheep, and pigs, as well as horses. In fact Eratus Chittenden's passion for animals was one reason they were hard put to it to make ends meet. They were overstocked, even if Pa wouldn't believe it, but Charles let that problem wait and concentrated on his own.

Tilting back on the legs of his chair, he decided to ask for Whitefoot. The big gray was stronger than Blaze. Besides, he looked better in the shafts and liked to run and would take to the exercise as a sport and not a task. Yes, Whitefoot and the light-weight Sunday-go-to-meeting wagon. If only his father would see it that way. Charles sighed again.

"What's the matter with you?"

The slam of the paternal voice brought Charles back and his chair down with a crash. He looked around wildly. The whole family had finished, and every face was turned toward him. Even his mother, head cocked, was looking amused.

"Nothing," Charles said. "Nothing. I was just thinking."

"Thinking?" Eratus snorted. "You were bellowing like something set heavy on your stomach."

As if the remark were a signal, the family started in on Charles. Automatically, as usual, the raillery came in the order of ages.

Amos, dark-haired and black-eyed like Eratus, said, "Spring fever, Pa. He's got it bad."

"Or vapors."

"Only girls have vapors, Nancy."

"E-yah. It's the weather."

"Makes the sap run."

"Fetch the sulphur and molasses, Ma."

Charles had led this same wolf pack too often to be routed by its howling. He grinned at them. "I said I was thinking," he said, and his glance flicked at his father. "Somebody has to do the thinking in this family."

"That so?" Eratus rose to the bait. "Well. Since you've appointed yourself the family brain, suppose you let the rest of us in on these great thoughts. Eh?"

Too easy, thought Charles. He took his time, waiting till the others were expectant, guessing from his mother's smile that she knew his plan. He risked one more verbal feint at his father's guard. "It was mostly about the blessing, sir."

"The blessing?"

"E-yah. Sounded a mite odd to me, Pa."

"Odd! My blessing?" Eratus shook the windows.

34

Grinning, Charles sank his barb. "Yes, sir. A man who voted for one Democrat shouldn't blame things on another."

"You whippersnapper!" Eratus hammered his fist on the table. "Now, just a minute! I voted for Andy Jackson 'cause he had it coming! This country owed him something! He'd been out there fighting for it and licking the British and doing his best! Van Buren's another kettle of fish entirely."

"Everybody says he's Jackson's man."

"Everybody says! I don't say it! I never said it! He's no Indian fighter, like Old Hickory. He's no more like Jackson than you're like George Washington."

The family listened with wide-eyed delight.

"Van's a Democrat. So was Jackson."

"Being in the same sty don't make pigs the same pigs! You might as well call me a Democrat just because I voted that way a couple times." His son's quizzical nod brought a new burst of pounding on the table. "I'm as good a Whig as anybody else! Jackson earned the Presidency! The people wanted him! And he'd been euchred out of it by that horse trade between J. Q. Adams and Henry Clay! That's why I voted for him!"

"I don't see what difference . . ."

"Of course you don't see! You've been talking mighty big for your boots considering you've never voted for a President in your life! You don't see! You've been listening to all that buncombe they spout down to the crossroad. Well, let me tell you something. General Jackson got to be President 'cause lots of folks rose up on their hind legs and yelled. Including me. But Van Buren got there by sneaking around behind doors and pulling strings and buttering folks up—including Andy, I'll admit—and building up a corrupt party. Now, if you don't see any difference in them two things, you'll swallow anything!"

Charles nodded as if impressed. He said, "I guess you've got the right of it, Pa."

Capitulation always caught Eratus by surprise. He looked a little disappointed, then said, "I'm pleased you admit it when you've been mistaken, son." A titter from the table swung the father's head around. "What are you sitting here waiting for? There's work to be done! Scat! The whole lot of you!"

Charles waited till the kitchen was nearly emptied. Only his mother and Nancy remained, stacking dishes. He drew his father aside, lowering his voice. "Pa. Could I ask a favor?"

"What favor?"

"I'd like to borrow a horse. Tonight. After supper."

"Horse? What horse?"

"Whitefoot," Charles said, wincing at the carrying power of his father's question. "And the Sunday wagon. I want to go down to the village."

"Got feet, ain't you?"

"E-yah, but . . ."

"Horses work, same as we do. Need their rest."

"Eratus." Mary had come close without their noticing. She smiled from son to husband. "Let him have Whitefoot. He wants to pay a call on Lovina Chester."

"That right, Charles?"

"Well—yes, Pa."

"Speak up. Speak up. Nothing to be ashamed of! Lovina's a fine-looking girl. Never hold a candle to your mother at her age, but fine-looking. Built right. Long in the flanks."

Speechless, Charles looked at his mother.

Mary said, "You've got what you wanted. Go along now."

"Thank you, Ma. Thank you, Pa."

Eratus watched his son bolt through the kitchen door. He grinned at his wife. "Land, Mary. They're growing up. Peter married and expecting, Charles out sparking the minister's daughter."

"Don't you notice anything, Eratus? This isn't new."

"It isn't, eh? Why didn't you tell me?"

Mary shrugged. "Figured it was his own business."

"E-yah." Eratus stared at the door. "Guess it is. But I hope he ain't in any hurry. He's young yet."

"That didn't hold you back much."

With a quick hug, Eratus clutched his wife to him and swung her off her feet. "The woman, she tempted me!"

"Eratus! Stop!"

"True, ain't it?"

"Nothing of the sort! Let me down!"

"Pay toll."

Nancy Chittenden ducked back into the pantry out of sight. Honestly, she said to the shelves. At their age. But she felt pleased.

36

The slap of the strap sounded flat across the sun-drenched barn-yard. Zilpha Brayton, staring at the woodshed door, licked her lips and counted. Thirty-one. The boy had never held out so long before. Zilpha shrugged, a movement of scorn. Asa was a young fool. To her practical mind it made better sense to give in quicker. Lem would just keep beating his son, rage increasing with each stroke, until Asa broke into the usual, wild, pleading screams. Asa was Lem's son all right. God knows he was more like Lem every day—the same mean, stubborn streak, the same whining when he was licked.

Thirty-two. She felt a grudging twinge of admiration for Asa. There must be a grain or two of herself in the lad. He couldn't make me squeal, she thought. Not Lem. Even when I was caught and made him marry me, it was him that did the squealing.

Again the strap slapped, and this time a loud, bubbling shriek followed so fast that the two sounds blended.

"Don't, Pa! Don't! Oh, stop!"

One of the ox team munching at the barnyard trough raised its white head and gazed placidly at the woodshed. Zilpha Brayton's face showed the same bovine lack of expression.

"Please, Pa! Oh, don't! Don't!"

Unconsciously, Zilpha brushed her fingers together as if dusting her hands. She stopped bothering to count the number of Asa's lashes. She leaned up against the back doorway, one arm raised and resting on the jamb. The posture tightened the lift of her bust and stressed the curve of a hip. She was a buxom woman, and her fine figure, with its small waist and straight back, had the smooth lines of sculpture. There was little beauty in her face, but it held a hint of sultriness; it was in the lower lip of the wide mouth, in the milky paleness of the skin, in the green eyes. Her hair was the color of oiled red leather.

If she heard Asa's broken pleadings or the crash as Lem hurled the strap against the shed wall, she gave no sign. She watched her husband push the boy out into the barnyard. Asa, naked to the waist, was sobbing rackingly into the wad of his shirt.

Lem Brayton said, "Stop that sniveling, now! You ain't hurt! Stop it, I said, 'less you want more!"

Staggering under another push, Asa muffled his sobs, pressing the coarse homespun stuff of his shirt against his mouth.

37

"Yoke up them oxen!" ordered Lem. "Hear? And get them out to where I left the stoneboat! And next time I send you after game with three loads maybe you'll remember not to waste one. Powder and shot ain't free! Hear?"

Asa's head bobbed in a nod.

"Three loads means three pieces of meat! If you can't shoot straight, I'll lace you till you learn! Now, get a move on."

"God bless our home," Zilpha said. She turned and went into the kitchen.

She heard her husband stamp in after her. "I'll learn him!" Lem said. "Goddam him! I ain't made of money, you know!"

Zilpha's laugh was mirthless. "E-yah. I know."

"Well, times is hard, Zilpha."

The whine in the voice brought the wife's head around. She looked at her husband. Lem was a spare man, no taller than herself, with a perpetual stoop and thick, overlong arms. He was dark, and a black stubble that matched the fur on his forearms covered his unshaven chin. Strangely enough, the hair on his head had receded back from a long widow's peak that accentuated his narrow face. With his jutting nose, Lem, front face, resembled an axe with its edge foremost.

"Times, my foot. When wasn't times hard for you, Lem?"

"Aw, Zilpha."

"For God's sake, stop whining!"

"Well, it ain't my fault. It's this Goddam land! I'm working my fingers to the bone for you, ain't I?"

"E-yah." Zilpha saw the white, pinched lines that stretched from Lem's nostrils to the corners of his mouth begin to relax. She knew those lines. They had raised from her husband's face like welts when he'd examined Asa's gamebag and shot pouch. All through the silent noon meal the lines had whitened as Lem let his fury mount inside him, keeping Asa on tenterhooks, enjoying his son's expectant terror. Now the tenseness loosened in the man's face as his eyes brightened. Oh, God, thought Zilpha. He's like that again.

"Zilpha."

"What?" She knew what. There was some link between Lem's beating Asa and wanting her. There was something queer about the whipping stirring him up this way.

"Zilpha."

38

"Now don't start acting the fool!"

"Aw, come on."

"No."

"Come on."

"You've got work to do."

"Mending a stone fence! Them rocks won't walk away. They'll wait."

"So will you."

"Aw, Zilpha."

"Have you gone daft? It's broad daylight."

"That never bothered you before."

"This time's different."

"How is it different?"

"Just different, that's all. Now, leave me alone!"

Lem reached out, hand curved, toward her breast. She brought her wrist against his hard, flinging his arm away.

"Stop your pawing! I said no!"

"But, Zilpha . . ."

"I just don't feel like it! After all these years you ought to know there's times when I don't! So stop sniffing around like a mink!"

Zilpha's glare was too much for her husband. Lem backed away, more whiny than ever. "All right," he said. "All right. You don't have to get in a tizzy. I thought you'd like it."

"When I want it, you'll know it! But it ain't now!"

"I'm just a hired man around here! A nigger slave gets more consideration than I do! A black, stinking nigger slave! I got feelings, ain't I?"

"You're abused, you are!" Zilpha shouted after him. She heard Lem's heels scrape across the shed floor. Him and his feelings! Only one feeling was bothering him, and she wasn't having any of that. Lem never could face her down; he didn't have the gumption. Epithets occurred to her and, being alone, she indulged in them. The foul-mouthed, horny, spineless little weasel!

Zilpha stared down at the iron skillet she was holding. With sudden convulsive fury, she hurled it into a corner. The heavy pan smashed against wall and floor.

"God!" Zilpha said. "When you got hitched, you got good and hitched!"

She stood brooding for a moment, then, shrugging, picked up the skillet and snatched a kettle from the fireplace crane. She attacked the dirty dishes as if each plate were a personal enemy. The hot water brought beads of sweat out on her forehead, and at intervals she mopped at them with one wrist. She dried and stacked her work with the same concentrated speed. When she finished she was hot and wet, but she felt better. She tossed the gray, scummy dishwater into the barnyard, and her anger splashed out with it.

After drinking a dipperful from the crock in the water room, Zilpha went and sat on her front step. The afternoon sun threw the shadow of roof and chimney across the tiny patch of overgrown yard that sloped down to the road. Zilpha sniffed the spring breeze with relish. She spread her legs wide and pulled dress and petticoats up over her knees; her legs were bare, thrust into shapeless boots.

The stone wall that hedged the grass from the mud of the road set her thinking. Asa and Lem were busy mending the pasture fence, which was also of stone. As a girl back in Massachusetts, Zilpha had helped build stone fences, and she was proud of a skill uncommon in a woman. The wall she was looking at was an example of her handiwork. She had built it with Lem's help when they first settled on the mountain. Zilpha remembered how she'd worked, selecting the stones carefully, fitting shape into shape, weight on weight, quick and sure with the knowledge that they would lock tight.

Stone fences. There were enough of them around. Lines and lines, wriggling across hills and flats, cutting the land up into squares. Back in Massachusetts some of the walls were so old nobody knew who'd put them there. If they were made right they never wore out, never caved in. You could see them in places where no folks had lived for years. Even if you walked in thick woods there might be a stone fence barring the way. Sometimes it seemed as if the stones had been piled up for the want of something better to do. Maybe to get rid of them. There were so many fences it was a wonder there was a single stone left.

Not that there was any scarcity of stones on Stratton. There seemed to be almost as many rocks as there were trees. Any ground a plow went into spewed up hundreds. And after those were cleared out there were always more. The whole of Vermont was one big lie. Green hills and mountains and valleys as pretty as anybody could ask. And just about skin deep underneath it was nothing but a chunk of granite that had litters every season.

The rattle of wagon wheels ended Zilpha's reflections. She listened. Somebody was coming up the road, heading for Stratton church. It wasn't likely that old Patch would pass back and forth twice in one day. And that trapper fellow, Tate Jones, he'd cut across, he wouldn't bother with the road. It must be one of the Carpenters or Isaac Mead.

Zilpha pulled down her skirts and poked at her hair. Any passer-by was welcome. It would be mighty fine to talk to somebody different. She was still on the sunny side of thirty-five and a body got lonely on a farm.

She recognized Isaac Mead's white horse the instant it bobbed into sight. You couldn't mistake that near wall eye. Zilpha Brayton smiled and settled back on the step. Isaac was a fine-looking man, a bachelor. He had a farm way out near the Bondville road, and he dressed like it made money.

The horse lurched closer, and the man in the wagon raised his whip. "Howdy, Miz Brayton," he called.

Sitting primly, feet together, hands folded in her lap, Zilpha Brayton bowed. "Afternoon, Isaac. Aiming to go somewhere?"

"Whoa, Nick. Whoa." Accepting the question as an invitation, Isaac reined in his horse. The wagon bumped to a stop. Atop its high seat the driver was on a level with the woman on the doorstep. "Just to the inn," said Isaac. "Got to meet the stage."

"Do tell. Expecting company?"

"No. Can't say I am. Just a couple or three parcels. Tobacco and suchlike."

"Fine weather, ain't it?"

"E-yah. Guess maybe spring got here after all."

"Been quite a spell coming, I'd say."

"Moderate, Miz Brayton. Just moderate. I've known a lot worse winters than this one. The thermometer up to the farm only froze solid a couple of times."

Zilpha laughed. She liked the way his teeth showed when he grinned. Isaac wore his hair long; it was about the color of a maple table. Looks as soft as silk, she thought.

"E-yah," Isaac said. "Ain't been real cold if your thermometer's still working."

"Only thermometer around this house," said Zilpha, "is a body's

41

pelt. And that got cold enough, let me tell you." She wondered if the remark was too forward, but his chuckle reassured her.

"Didn't get anything frostbitten, I hope."

Enjoying the banter, Zilpha crossed her legs. She smiled as she noted Isaac's glance drop to where the cloth of her skirts was taut along her thigh. Let him look, she decided. He ain't such a bad sight himself, decked out to the nines. There's no homespun in that coat and those breeches. Maybe he didn't wear a plug hat, but at least it was felt and not a fur cap or knitted. She spoke slowly, considering.

"Frostbit? No. Not that I've noticed."

"Nor me." Isaac leaned forward, put his fist up under his chin, and stared. Deliberately, he let his gaze travel from shoe tip to red hair and back. "Nope. Can't say there's anything seems to be missing."

Zilpha felt her color rise. She recognized the flutter in the pit of her stomach as an almost forgotten excitement. Her breath came a little faster. She bent her head and made her tone demure. "Far as you can see?"

"Far as I can see."

"Nose is still there? And both ears?"

"E-yah. Everything seems in its proper place."

"'Course what I was really worried about don't show." Zilpha waited through his shout of laughter, then rebuked it lightly. "Meaning my marrow, Isaac. Like folks say, I got chilled to the marrow."

"Heard the expression."

"Thought it likely." Zilpha raised her eyelids and looked him full in the face. She said, "But it's spring now, Isaac. And it's thawing. Slow but sure, it's thawing."

"E-yah." Isaac said the word thickly. "E-yah. Guess that happens, Zilpha." His lips twitched as he swallowed. Their glances were locked and steady, across the slope of grass.

"Natural course of events, ain't it?"

"Guess it is, Zilpha."

"Nothing to be alarmed about, you don't suppose?"

"Alarmed?"

"Sometimes them spring thaws do a lot of damage. They get a little out of hand. They can be—dangerous."

Isaac Mead sat back and waited before he spoke. He said, assured and calm, "I don't scare easy, Zilpha."

The woman laughed at him. "Maybe you don't, at that," she answered with admiration.

With a start Isaac jerked his gaze away from Zilpha. She followed his look. Lem Brayton was standing by the corner of the house.

Zilpha fought against a flash of panic. How long had Lem been there? What had he heard? She tried to keep her voice cool. "Hello, Lem. I didn't hear you come back."

Lem didn't look at her. He said, "Afternoon, Isaac."

"Howdy, Lem."

"Would you be wanting something?"

"No," said Isaac, unruffled. "Can't say as I do. Bound to meet the stage. Just passing."

"We've been having a real sociable chat, Lem."

"E-yah?" Lem glared at his wife, his eyes hard with suspicion. "Concerning what, for instance?"

"Folks," said Zilpha. Anger had replaced her panic, and with it came contemptuous belief that she could handle Lem no matter what. The sneak, she thought. Cat-footing up behind us that way. It would serve him right if I really put horns on his head, instead of just play-talking around with Isaac.

"E-yah," said Isaac. "And politics, Lem." The lie was plausible; it was the common subject of the day.

Lem's face showed his disbelief. He didn't speak. An awkward silence made the passing seconds seem interminable. Isaac's embarrassment became hostile. Thrusting his head forward, the man on the wagon tried to stare Lem down. Zilpha, already linked in secret alliance against her husband, watched, pleasantly excited by the contest. When Lem's eyes shifted, the wife laughed.

"Isaac was just getting along. Wasn't you, Isaac?"

"E-yah." Isaac grinned and nodded. "Guess that's right. Well. Afternoon." He clucked to his horse, shook the reins. "Hup, Nick." The horse leaned into his collar and started with a jerk.

The Braytons watched him go without comment. Lem merely nodded; Zilpha raised a hand as farewell.

Until the wagon rounded a curve that hid the house, Isaac Mead held himself so stiffly that his neck and back muscles were rigid. He listened intently for any speech behind him, but there was none

43

while he remained in earshot. Once he was well around the turn of the road, Isaac let out a great gust of breath and relaxed.

You got out of that one, Isaac Mead, he said to himself, by the skin of your teeth. He had no large respect for Lem Brayton, but custom required one for the rights of a husband. Not even Lem would take kindly to familiar talk between his wife and another man. That Zilpha. Remembering, he chuckled. Her and her marrow. Well, if Lem wasn't man enough to take the chill out of it, there were others who'd find it a pleasure. She was a fine-looking female, put together neat and compact like a Morgan horse. He bet she'd be a real cosy armful on a winter's night. With them breasts and that red hair. Mentally, he began to undress Zilpha, humming tunelessly through open lips.

The sight of the stage drawn up before the inn brought Isaac out of his imagination with a start. He'd missed the arrival and, if he didn't hurry, he might miss whatever news Lot Purdy, the driver, had brought from off the mountain.

Heedless of the fact they were climbing a grade, Isaac Mead lashed his horse. "Hup, Nick," he shouted. "Ha!" The clatter of the turning wheels redoubled as the horse broke into a trot.

A mound of white petticoats was piled high on the seat of the wooden settle drawn up before the long fireplace in the Chester kitchen. The settle's high back screened the hearth from the rest of the room, and blankets hung from cords that stretched from the tops of both wings to the brick mantel. In the alcove thus formed Lovina Chester was busy with the first bath of the spring season.

Facing the fire, her knees as high as her chin, Lovina sat steaming in a round wooden tub. On the floor were strewn all the necessary pieces of equipment—towels, scrub brush, her dropped wrapper, pail and dipper, a jar of homemade soap. Two huge iron kettles were alongside the tub; another hissed over the flames. The air in the improvised cubicle was warm and damp, and, in spite of her cramped position, Lovina was wearing as her only adornment a contented smile.

At the moment she wasn't using much energy. She sat, revelling in the feel of the hot water against her skin, not at all upset that its surface rose no higher than her calves and her navel. The fire was warm; her shins and knees baked in its heat; warmth wrapped her whole body. She uttered little murmurs of pleasure that were much like purring, and her hands idly lapped water higher on herself. One cupped handful rose to her breast, trickled down. She touched herself tentatively, putting a palm under each breast, raising them.

Gazing into the flames, not seeing them, Lovina was dreaming. She felt drained, relaxed, as if she had no muscles. She was naked and clean and happy.

Everything had worked out well so far. Her mother hadn't been at all difficult about the bath, and her sisters had taken her going first as a matter of course. Rightly, of course, since she was the eldest. Now, if Charles came, and he just simply had to, she would be all ready.

Thinking of being ready for Charles made her blush. He's certainly not going to see this much of me, she reflected, and giggled. A noise on the road outside, followed by shouting, startled her, and she listened. The stage arriving, she decided. You could always tell the stage. Mr. Purdy galloped his horses to finish with a flourish.

Lovina settled back and tried to remember where her thoughts had been. Charles. With a guilty glance at the blankets, she wondered if he'd like her if he saw her this way. Maybe her shape was why he hadn't declared himself. Pouting, she leaned forward and scrutinized her body. Her legs did look on the long, skinny side. But still, she curved nicely at the hips, and her bosom was good, too. Her skin was smooth and white. She ran a hand along one flank and nodded.

She dreamed about marrying Charles. It was an unmaidenly dream, she knew, but exciting. Father would marry them, of course, and the whole township would be there. Mattie and Sally would be bridesmaids, and Mother would let her wear the family wedding dress that was up in the attic. She and Charles would go away somewhere afterwards.

Afterwards didn't worry Lovina in the least. She was a farm girl, and she had raised a younger brother. She knew how men were built and was quite sure she knew exactly what happened. You shouldn't have such thoughts, she told herself, and then yielded to them guiltily. Maybe it wasn't right for a minister's daughter to know all that, but she couldn't help it if her father farmed, too. Anyway, that part of it must be very exciting. It was even exciting to think about. Although of course it wasn't proper to do yet.

45

"Lovina!"

At the sound of her mother's voice Lovina jumped. Even as she answered, one arm shot swiftly out, and she scooped a handful of the strong soap from its jar. "Yes, Mother?"

"Land, child! Don't take all day in there!"

"I'm nearly finished, Mother."

When Mrs. Chester poked aside a blanket and peered at her daughter, Lovina was busily rinsing lather from her thighs. The mother sniffed. "You might think of your sisters. They're entitled to baths, too, you know."

"I'm sorry, Mother." Lovina stood up, back to her mother, and stooped for the dipper.

"As it is," complained Mrs. Chester, "it's nearly time to start getting supper. I'll have to wash Josepha and make Sally and Mattie wait till after."

Filling the dipper, Lovina smiled. Baths would effectively get her sisters out of her path when Charles came. She heard her mother walk away and glanced to see that the blanket was back in place.

Lovina tilted the dipper. Cold water splashed on her chest, ran down. She sucked in her breath with ecstasy. "Oh, wonderful!"

The liquor served in the inns of a country is never a constant; its strength varies in direct proportion with that of the political opinions of its imbibers. The men gathered in the common room of the Tarbox inn had a taste for potent drink and violent argument. Now, supplied with both, the entire company listened as Lot Purdy, the stage driver, read aloud a poem from a printed sheet. The innkeeper frowned, listening. The blacksmith's face was expressionless. Isaac Mead, who had just been served, was shaking his head.

Two other men present, Will Carpenter and Clem Galusha, the Patch hired man, looked at each other and shrugged. The stage's arrival was the event of the day, and they all had to depend on its driver for their off-mountain news. Sometimes, like now, Lot Purdy's being a Democrat made it kind of hard.

Therefore support Van Buren!

Lot finished with a shout. He picked up his tankard of cider, drained it, and wiped his lips with the back of his hand. Squaring himself, he said belligerently, "What do you think of that?"

The answer was obvious. The others let the host speak. "Don't think much of it," said Dan Tarbox.

"Don't deny there's truth in it, do you?"

"E-yah. Afraid I do, Lot." The innkeeper poked a finger at the broadside. "In the first place it ain't named right. *Address to Poor Men!* Where does old Van Buren get the right to talk to poor men? He ain't poor!"

"E-yah."

"You got the right of it, Dan."

"That Dutchman's got a fistful."

The chorus had no effect on Lot Purdy. He hooked his thumbs in the armhole of his vest and waited. When it was quiet, the stage driver spoke. "I don't ever recall coming across a poor banker. And they ain't no friends of Van's. Whigs, every man jack of them!"

"What's that prove?" Isaac Mead asked.

"It proves that the rich are against Van Buren. And the poor are for him!"

Three men snorted in unison. Dan Tarbox and Isaac Mead both talked at once.

"Proves nothing of the sort!"

"That's just Loco-foco gab!"

The innkeeper captured Lot's attention by taking his mug and refilling it. As the cider gurgled from the tap, Dan said, "We ain't rich, are we? And we ain't for him!"

"By thunder, I ain't!"

"Nor me!"

"Hope to spit!"

"You Democrats are always putting on a poor mouth!"

"Will's right. Being poor ain't no exclusive Loco-foco privilege!"

"Comes to that, who made folks poor?"

"Who? Van, that's who!"

"Ain't you ever heard of the Panic, Lot?"

"E-yah," said Lot, refusing to be badgered. "I heard of it, Clem. You hear a lot of things driving a stage. But I never heard that Van Buren went around putting padlocks on bank doors! If you want to talk Panic, them doors was barred from the inside! By the men that owned them!"

"After old Van robbed the horse!"

47

"He made them shut up shop!"

Ignoring the side remarks, the stage driver fastened on one victim, hoping to confine the argument to a two-man debate. He saluted the Patch hired man with lifted tankard. "You, Clem. You ought to recognize Martin Van Buren—and the Democratic party—as friends of labor! Being a laborer yourself!"

Clem Galusha turned beet red. "Who's a laborer?" he cried angrily. "I'm as good as anybody else!"

"E-yah."

"No call for that kind of talk, Lot."

"No insult intended. I call myself a laborer, too. Drive stage for the company, don't I? Get paid for it, don't I? Same as Clem works down to Joel Patch's sawmill. Anybody that works for somebody else for pay is a laborer, a worker. And they ought to be for them that's for them! President Van Buren is a friend to labor. And I can prove it!"

This statement silenced the opposition. They exchanged glances uneasily, wondering just what new information Lot Purdy had picked up on his stage route. His assurance was upsetting; a man couldn't get an answer ready to something he hadn't heard about before.

Isaac Mead rubbed his chin. "Let's hear your proof," he said.

"All right," Lot replied. "On the thirty-first of March, this year, the President signed an order that said nobody that worked for the Federal government on any public works had to work more than ten hours a day! And they'd still get the same wages they got before!"

The speaker leaned back against the bar and gulped a long swallow of cider. He gazed around the room in triumph.

The listeners digested the news thoughtfully. Again it was Isaac Mead who broke the silence.

"I don't believe it."

"It's true, Isaac," said the innkeeper. "There's something about it in one of them new papers Lot brung in today."

"What's he mean by public works?"

"Navy yards and such."

"Ain't no Navy yards up here, is there?"

"Fool idea, anyway! Stands to reason you got to work till you're done!"

"How come Congress let him pass that?"

48

Dan Tarbox said, "Old Van never asked Congress. Did it by executive order. Just signed a paper."

"Just like him!"

"Crafty Dutch trick."

"Knew it wasn't legal."

"It is too legal!" Lot Purdy tried to shout them down. "The President can sign an order like that any time he wants! It's the same as a law!"

"Thought Congress made the laws."

"Nope. Van makes his own."

"Just signs a paper."

"Thinks he's a king."

"Better than that. Thinks he's Joshua and can make the sun stand still."

"Now, whoa. Whoa." Lot clenched his fists, shook them. "You fellers are letting yourselves run off with the bit in your teeth. I never said anything about cutting down the hours in a day."

"We heard what you said, Lot."

"A farm would sure get away from you if you only put in ten hours a day."

"Cows wouldn't take to it, either."

"Maybe that'd suit Van. Wreck the farms along with everything else."

"Hope he don't get any more sharp ideas before election!"

"E-yah. Tippecanoe wouldn't hold with that nonsense."

"He's a farmer."

" 'Bout time we put a farmer in the White House."

"Tippecanoe and Tyler too!"

"Tyler!" Lot Purdy bellowed the name. "Tyler ain't no farmer! He's a Virginia aristocrat!"

Isaac Mead said, "Simmer down, Lot. Nobody's talking about making Tyler President. Running for Vice-President, ain't he? Works out fine that way, don't it?"

"How do you mean, Isaac?"

"Common sense, Clem. That's all. We elect Harrison, a farmer like us, to be President. And we put Tyler, a smart lawyer, educated, in as head of the Senate. Where he can do some good shutting up them talkative Democrats."

Everyone laughed but the stage driver. He glowered at them. His reply was muttered. "Two Virginians! Harrison was born there, too!"

"Now, Lot," said the innkeeper. "You can't blame a man for where he was born. Not all of us was born here in Vermont."

"I told you," Isaac Mead put in again. "Tyler don't count. He ain't going to hurt anybody just being Vice-President."

"Isaac's right."

"E-yah. Tyler's sort of like the lazy horse in a matched team. He keeps in step, and he looks right pretty in there, but he ain't doing much pulling."

"At least the Whigs got a team."

"Van ain't got no running mate!"

"Old Johnson was a little too gamy even for Van!"

"How about that, Lot?"

The stage driver knew better than to try to defend the incumbent Vice-President. Cannily, he decided to change the subject. He rapped the base of his tankard on the bar and said with apparent abruptness, "Dan. Hear if anybody lost any stock lately?"

"Stock?" Dan Tarbox sounded puzzled. "No, can't say I have."

"Why, Lot?"

"Just wondered," Lot said. He made the words weighty and mysterious.

"Who'd be losing stock?"

"What're you talking about, Lot?"

Lot Purdy smiled. He said, "I'm talking about a catamount."

"Catamount?"

"A panther?"

"You mean there's one around?"

"E-yah." The stage driver nodded. "Coming up I near ran over the biggest damn catamount I ever saw in my life."

"On Stratton?"

"Holy Moses!"

This was news about their own mountain, and they gathered around, avidly eager to hear. The election belonged to the future; the mountain lion had been seen that day. Settling his elbows on the bar, Lot Purdy let them coax before he told his story. The innkeeper, busily refilling pewter mugs, beamed at the stage driver. Recognizing the catamount as an asset to brisk business, Dan Tarbox thought that Lot Purdy wasn't really a bad fellow at all. For a Democrat.

On the mantel in the parsonage parlor the Terry clock ticked loudly: click, clack, click, clack. The brass sun of the pendulum flashed back and forth through the elliptical window in the painting below the clock's face. Click, clack, click, clack. The pendulum swung from painted house to painted willow tree. Then, with a whirring in its insides, the clock struck seven.

The Reverend Jedidah Chester continued to gaze over the tops of his spectacles at his only son. Tall, thin to the point of gauntness, Reverend Chester locked his long, narrow fingers together in an attitude of prayer. The flame of the candle on the desk was triply reflected: twice in the glass of the minister's spectacles, once on the high, curved dome of his bald head.

Reverend Chester sighed. He said in a gentle, tired voice, "I am waiting for your explanation, Putnam."

The boy stood, head bent, with his hands clasped behind him and his feet wide apart. He spoke without looking up. "There isn't any, Father."

"You did go swimming?"

"Yes, Father."

"After your mother had expressly forbidden it?"

"Yes, Father."

"I'm afraid you force me to only two conclusions. Either you forgot your mother's admonition and went, or else you indulged in willful disregard of her wishes and went. I have no desire to insist that you eliminate one of those conclusions."

Put Chester didn't answer. Here it comes, he thought, and wondered what it would be this time.

With a sigh Reverend Chester reached for a book. "In either case you neglected your duty to more than earthly authority. You recall the story of Abraham? Genesis 22?"

"Yes, Father."

"That is pleasing. A trifle belated since it has to do with obedience and concerns a father and son, but pleasing. You will recall it even better after you have copied it out for me."

"All of it?"

"All of it. And in a round, legible hand, please. No blots." The minister held out the Bible open to the place. "You will find quills, ink, and foolscap on the arm of the writing chair. And, since I am working at my desk, you may have the wrist candle." Reverend

51

Chester waited while Put lit the candle, fastened it to his left wrist, sat down, and dipped his pen. Then the parson picked up his own quill and read what he had written.

It was his sermon for the morrow's service, and he was worried about it. The text was from Paul to the Romans, the first chapter, the fourteenth verse: "I am debtor both to the Greeks, and to the Barbarians; both to the wise, and to the unwise." The sermon was the minister's attempt to pour oil on the rising bitterness of the year's political struggle. Reverend Chester sighed. He was sure it would please no one. The Whig majority of his congregation would think it too easy; the few Democrats would believe it a defense of Whig policy.

The parson scratched out a scholarly reference to Athenian democracy, quoted from Plato. He drew lines through Greek words and English translation, alike. God help me, he thought, with an inward groan, I am a milksop preacher. They don't want to hear logic and languages; they would be much happier with a constant diet of hell-fire and the wages of sin. He began to write, forming each letter with care and precision.

For a time the only sounds in the room were the fire, the clock, and the two pens. Reverend Chester was the first to speak.

"Putnam?"

"Yes, Father?"

"Was the water cold?"

Put grinned at the inkwell. The day's sin had received its merited punishment; it had been judged and dismissed. He said, "Very cold. Seth Purdy turned blue."

Wheels rattled on the road outside, and a man's voice called a horse to a halt. As if on signal the parlor door opened and Mrs. Chester, followed by Lovina, swept into the room.

"Father," Mrs. Chester said. "That wagon is stopping here."

"Perhaps someone needs me, my dear."

"No. It isn't that."

Lovina said, "I think it's Charles Chittenden." She ignored her brother's knowing grin.

"And we shall want this room, Father. The other girls are bathing in the kitchen. Lovina can't very well receive callers there."

Reverend Chester sighed and looked at his sermon. "No. I suppose not. Well, go let him in, Putnam. Our literary labors must wait upon etiquette." He turned his chair from the desk, folded his hands together, and waited.

Mrs. Chester plumped down in the rocker by the fireplace. Lovina, very crisp in a dress of yellow poplin, seated herself between her mother and father. All three faced the doorway as Put ushered in Charles Chittenden.

He wore his best black suit, white linen, and a maroon cravat at his throat. Charles stopped at the threshold and bowed formally, hat pressed to his chest.

"Evening, sir."

"Good evening, Charles."

"Mrs. Chester."

"Good evening, Charles."

"Lovina."

"Charles."

Each salutation was accompanied by its own bow or nod. Everyone seemed relieved when the formalities were over. Charles took a step into the room and halted, looking down from his height at the assembled Chesters. Thank God, he said silently, that this time the other girls aren't here, too.

"Your family is well?" asked the minister.

"All, sir. Thank you."

"Let us hope they remain so. If the spring weather continues we should have much less sickness."

"E-yah." Charles hesitated, then made his request. "I was thinking, sir, since it's such a fine night—a mite chill, perhaps, but the mildest we've had—that, well, if you had no objections, sir, and it met with Lovina's wishes, we might take a short ride in my wagon."

"Indeed?" Reverend Chester glanced at the manuscript of his sermon and smiled. "I can think of no objections."

His wife could and did. "Father! The night air!"

Lovina had sense enough not to venture an opinion. She merely looked at her father and hoped. Charles followed her example.

The parson said, "My dear, that notion is as obsolete as witchcraft, though it seems to die harder. In my calling I have been out at all hours of the night on duty bent. I can't say it has affected my health one way or the other. However, I leave the decision to Lovina."

"I would be pleased to accept," said Lovina, not looking at her mother. She rose, smiling. "I will fetch my cloak and bonnet." She hurried out of the room, skirts murmuring.

Mrs. Chester set her lips. She liked Charles personally but not as a suitor for Lovina. He was only a second son, and once the Chittenden farm was divided among all those children each portion would be small. She said, "You will not be gone long, I hope."

"No, ma'am." Charles sensed the hostility and wondered if it was just Mrs. Chester's usual attempt to be bossy. He remembered the saying, "Like mare, like foal," and hoped it wasn't true in Lovina's case.

Once the girl returned Charles bowed out as quickly as possible. He handed Lovina up into the wagon, climbed alongside, and tucked a blanket around them both. The night was cold, and such actions were customary etiquette.

They were well away from the settlement, Whitefoot trotting steadily, before either spoke.

"Where are we going?" asked Lovina.

"I thought maybe the big clearing."

They looked at each other and laughed. The road was dark where the trees bordered it, but the stars were bright and countless. There was no sound but the wheels and harness chains and the even clop-clop of the horse. An edge of moon was behind them, peering over the shoulder of the mountain.

"You're quite a stranger, Charles."

"E-yah." Expecting rebuke, he was relieved to find her tone casual. Charles was suddenly gayer. One thing about Lovina, he exulted, you didn't have to explain things. He wasn't good at explanations.

Lovina dug her nails into her palms. Was that all he was going to say after two weeks? She began to feel the night's chill and the warmth of the thigh that was against her own.

"Lovina."

"Yes?"

"We've been a mite busy out to the farm. The red cow calved."

"Bull or heifer?"

"Heifer." Charles warmed to her interest. His circle of feminine companions wasn't large, but he had a vague idea that most girls didn't care to talk farming. It was another point that made Lovina different. "Fine calf, too."

"Good," said Lovina. She had accepted the mention of the farm as an apology and was willing to discuss it until they reached the clearing. There'd be time for other talk later. "Your Pa should be pleased."

"E-yah." Charles frowned at the horse's bobbing tail. For a moment he was tempted to tell Lovina the news about Peter and Jennie. He didn't. There was a world of difference between calving and his sister-in-law's pregnancy, and the latter wasn't a suitable topic for him to go into with Lovina. Anyway, it wasn't his business to spread the news.

They clattered past the Chittenden farm, dark except for a light in an upstairs window.

"Somebody's still up, Charles."

"E-yah. That's Pa-and-Ma's room. Guess they're talking." Charles carefully kept the worry from his voice. He imagined his parents joyfully discussing the prospective addition to the family. He scowled, thinking of his father. A man that made farming such a happy, hilarious venture ought to be more successful. They had enough to eat and were better off than some, but there was never any cash, any surplus. Too many mouths to feed. Charles had a deep, protective love for the blustering Eratus and a well-hidden concern for his brothers and sisters that would have surprised them all.

A hole in one of the wheel ruts bounced Lovina against him. Charles held her steady, putting his arm around her. He said, "That was a real thank-you-ma'am."

"Wasn't it," said Lovina, leaning on him happily. Bless it, she said to herself. Her cheeks were warm in spite of the breeze.

Charles didn't remove his arm until it was time to wheel White-foot into the clearing. They bumped up the bank and across the starlit, uneven patch of ground. West and northwest, they could make out the massed bulk of the Taconics, shouldering each other against the lighter, flecked sky. Above them their own mountain rose, black and brooding, to its summit.

The horse stopped not far from the long shadow cast by the tamarack tree. They sat there, gazing at the night, and the noises awoke around them. Trees rustled; a stream gurgled; frogs chirruped throatily. Somewhere in the distance a dog bayed, and, from even farther away, the faint, long-drawn wail of a catamount rose and faded.

Lovina shivered. She did it deliberately, hoping that Charles would put his arm back around her, and he did. Maybe tonight, she thought. Maybe tonight, just us, out here, he'll say something about an understanding.

"Cold?" asked Charles.

"No. Not really."

"That cat's miles away." Her softness in the circle of his arm made him very masculine. He smiled fondly at the shadow under her bonnet. She needn't worry; he'd take çare of her. "We're safe enough here, Lovina."

"I know." The girl stared at the tamarack tree, uncertain what to say next. She was eager and restless, and it was somehow hard to talk. "Why do you suppose they left that tree there?"

"The tamarack? I don't know."

"Strange, isn't it? Just that one tree."

"E-yah. I guess so."

"Like—like it was watching us."

Suddenly, so fast that neither knew how it happened, they clung together. Lovina's face lifted; they kissed. It was a long kiss and left them both breathless.

"Lovina," said Charles, in a strained whisper. Surprise, delight, and doubt scrambled his thinking. He hadn't planned this; it was stronger than he'd expected.

Lovina, pulses pounding, snuggled closer. Everything was all right now. She let her breath out in a long, relaxing sigh.

They sat there, in each other's arms, not speaking. The night seemed to cut them off from all problems, and the warmth of their bodies was a bond all their own. They were both excited, and liking it.

After a while they kissed again, more slowly. Lovina murmured and held his face in her hands. This is wonderful, she thought. He does love me. He does.

Charles tightened his arms. He tried to speak but had nothing to say.

The girl rubbed her forehead against his smooth cheek. She realized that her bonnet had fallen back and didn't care. It was all wonderful; it was just the way she had dreamed it would happen.

Again they rested, breathing in unison. Charles started to say something, but Lovina's fingers pressed his lips. She didn't want speech just yet. She was content, secure. The rest would come naturally—the proposal, the acceptance, the wedding. But it was all too lovely to hurry.

Charles, holding her, felt proud. He was sure of Lovina's love, so sure that his mind was only on kissing. He waited with tender patience, confident that this was best. It seemed a long time before he slowly slid one hand up under Lovina's breast. She gasped and stirred.

"You're awful pretty, Lovina. Vina."

"Charles." The word was whispered. His touch frightened her, even as she liked it. Maybe they shouldn't do this. But it was Charles, and they were going to be married. Married, she thought blissfully, in our own place, and raise children.

When they kissed this time their excitement mounted. Lovina was almost dizzy with it. She rested, panting, against Charles while he fondled her. Now, she rejoiced, throbbing. Now, surely, he would ask her. She was still scared, mostly for herself, at his fingers on her breast, and she put a hand over his, holding it close but quiet.

"Vina."

"Um?"

"Oh, Vina!"

Out of her dream and her fright, love, and guilt, Lovina thought suddenly of her father. She wondered if he'd approve of all this kissing. But it was really all right. He'd marry them himself. She said, in a half voice that was almost drowsy, "Father will be very surprised."

"Who?"

"Father."

The word was like cold water on her escort's spine. Charles gulped. Thoughts came surging into his mind. Lovina's father was a minister. If they told him, it meant marriage. He wasn't ready for marriage. In panic, flustered by the love-making he did exactly the wrong thing. He held the girl away from him. "Vina. Your father? Why *him?*"

Lovina was startled. She said, "But, Charles . . ."

"This is just between us, Vina."

57

"Of course, but . . ."

"We—we can't get married, Vina."

"Charles!" Lovina stiffened; her voice was almost harsh. "You don't want to!"

"It isn't that. We can't yet."

"Well, not tonight! No!"

"You don't understand." Desperately Charles tried to keep the discussion from becoming an argument. He explained, doggedly, badly. "I don't know when we can, Vina. I have no right to ask you."

"No right?" Close to tears with reaction, Lovina tossed her head to keep them back. "A minute ago . . ." She couldn't put in words what they'd been doing a minute ago.

"I know. Maybe we shouldn't have. It's my fault."

She was suddenly very ashamed. She wanted to slap him. She drew away. "You don't love me!"

"I do. It's just—well, getting married . . ."

"Your brother Peter did!"

"That's just it. There's no room at home!"

"We could live somewhere else!"

"Leave the farm?"

"Is the farm more important?"

"Vina! They need me! This year, anyway!"

Lovina fumbled for her bonnet, straightened it, retied the ribbons at her throat. He had smashed her dream; she was angry, hurt, unhappy. She said, "I'm sure I don't. Not this or any year!"

"Vina!"

"I don't care to discuss it further, Charles!"

Charles chopped the air with his fist. He was angry, too. She wouldn't listen. He thought his reasons good, hers, unreasonable. He made another mistake. He said, "All right, then!"

For a long time they sat, not speaking, not looking at each other. Lovina's voice, low and miserable, broke the silence.

"I'm cold, Charles. Take me home, please."

In Boston the mist was thick in the streets, and the man at the window stared out at its pale smoke. There was a coal fire in the grate, and the room was well lit with candles. The round table

58

was covered with maps and papers, glasses and a decanter, cigar ashes and butts. Both the men at the table were smoking.

They watched the back of the man at the window. It was a wide back, and the shoulders filled the gray swallow-tailed coat. The coat looked well tailored and expensive. Hands in pockets, the man stood squarely, blocking the high, narrow window, gazing through the curtains. His head, from behind, was large, almost massive. It might have belonged to a Roman emperor.

The thinner of the two at the table took his cheroot from his mouth and shuffled some papers. He cleared his throat, shrugged at his companion, and spoke. "Then, Senator, they'd like to hear you in Vermont."

"Vermont!" said the Senator, not turning from the window. He had a deep, resonant voice that caught the ear. His words came with ease of long practice, but there was bitterness in his tone. "Vermont! In the Convention, seven votes for Winfield Scott. They were certainly set on a general!"

With a patient sigh the thin man said, "Sign of the times, Senator. The military is still popular. Don't you agree, Judge?"

"Completely, Rufe." The Judge, a round little man, held his glass of port up to a candle and squinted at it. "Jackson taught us that."

"Not that Scott had a chance, Senator. Harrison was the choice from the beginning."

The Judge said, "Only took five ballots to nominate, Daniel. Even Vermont shifted to Harrison on the fifth."

"The party's choice, Senator."

A snort was the only reply from the Senator. The Judge sniffed his port and continued, "If you wanted to stop that movement, Daniel, you should have been there and not in England."

Senator Daniel Webster of Massachusetts swung around. His eyes, angry now, were deep-set, beneath too-prominent brows. From front face he looked even more like a Roman, but a tribune, not an emperor. His lips had a thin tightness that might have been copied from a bust of Cato, the censor. He said, "Can you stop a flood, Judge? I knew it was cut and dried. I'll support the Whig candidate, of course. But I didn't count on gadding all over the country making speeches for him!"

"We want to win, Daniel."

"Mr. Clay is doing it, Senator."

"Clay!" Senator Webster's grin was sudden and surprising. "God, I'll bet it chokes him!"

"Daniel, Daniel." The Judge's reproof was light. "Remember that you and Henry Clay still jointly rule the Whig party. 'United we stand.'"

"General Harrison won't forget, Senator."

"All right, Rufe." Webster's gesture was impatient. "All right. I said I'd speak, didn't I?"

"Vermont, too?"

"Vermont, too! Though I don't know why! They wouldn't go for Van Buren if he was the Angel Gabriel. Not when he's from York State!"

"Are they still fighting that one?" asked the Judge.

Daniel Webster took a cheroot from the table and bit off its end. He nodded, leaning forward to light the tobacco in a candle's flame. "They've never forgiven New York for claiming them, Judge. But let's get on with it. When do they want me, Rufe?"

"July, Senator. Early in July. We've only scheduled the one speech."

"Where?"

"Well, that brings up another question, doesn't it, Judge?"

"Go on. Tell him."

"Vermont's eager to hear you, Senator. They want you all over the state. Manchester, Bennington, Brattleboro, Bellows Falls. Everywhere!"

"You said one speech!"

"Sure, Senator. Sure."

"Just the one, Daniel."

Rufe drew a map toward him. "Question was where to put it, Senator. But we worked out a fair system. We drew lines from the big towns, diagonally. And where they crossed was the spot we picked." Rufe's fingernail stabbed the map.

"Almost where they crossed," corrected the Judge.

"Well, close enough, anyway. It's on top of a mountain, Senator. We're planning to hold a big Convention way up there on the mountain. Nominate a congressman."

"Another circus!" Daniel Webster swore. "This isn't a campaign! It's just a mumbo-jumbo, hocus-pocus freak show!"

"It's working, Daniel."

"Sure it is. Folks like it, Senator. And anyway, the Democrats started it. Jackson appealed to the rabble."

"Jackson never stooped to half the things we're doing! 'Tippecanoe and Tyler too!' Good God! What a way to ask for votes! We might as well have run Chang and Eng, the Siamese twins!"

The Judge said, "We're not arguing a case before the Supreme Court, Daniel. We're trying to win an election. For the good of the country. Any method that will gain votes is worth trying. The banks will foot the bill. Nicholas Biddle will spend any amount to lick Van Buren!"

"I know." Webster sat down. He made a mental note to remind his bankers that they were late with his retainer again. "Let's hear the details, Rufe."

"We'll turn out the whole state for you, Senator. There's a big clearing up on this mountain, sort of a natural amphitheatre. I sent one of our Bennington boys up there to look it over a few weeks back. It's perfect. We'll camp the whole shooting match in that clearing. They'll come from miles. Thousands, maybe. On top of a mountain!"

"Which mountain is it?" asked Webster. "I was born in New Hampshire. I know that country pretty well."

"Stratton, Senator. There's a little town named Stratton, and that's the name of the mountain, too."

"Stratton." Daniel Webster inhaled deeply and blew a great puff of smoke toward the ceiling. "No. Never heard of it."

THE FIRST DAY
July 6, 1840

THE SKY OVER Stratton Mountain changed color at the approach of day. It was as if the inky blackness of night were rapidly being diluted, first to dark blue, then to gray. The gray spread, erasing clusters of stars as it moved westward. Along the ridge of the mountain's summit the shadows sank, and the forest emerged. A pale shaft of gold was suddenly visible in the eastern sky, and the mist began to roll itself back and up. It rose from the valleys and fields; it twisted more sluggishly from the brooks and streams. Above the millpond behind Joel Patch's sawmill it clung as if the water steamed. The black bear, squatting beside the pond, had beads of it in his fur.

Leaning forward, the bear suddenly scooped one paw into the water. He missed the fish, snorted, and shook his wet foreleg. Then he stiffened, raised his head, and peered through the mist toward the dim bulk of the sawmill. Across the pond a voice spoke; a chain clanked; wood scraped. There was a sound of water, first splashing, then tumbling. With a protesting creak, the big mill wheel began to turn.

The bear rose and, without haste, waddled off into the woods. Paddles dripping, the wheel revolved on its axle, picking up speed. Water swirled, and spray tossed out into the mist. The noises were not loud enough to drown the voices inside the mill.

"Come on. Come on," Joel Patch said. "Time's money."

"E-yah." Clem Galusha made the two syllables toneless. The hired man smiled wanly at his employer and looked at the saw. In the morning half-light inside the mill, the metal blade seemed cold and dull. It was a big saw, a yard in diameter, and its teeth were wickedly hooked. There was no gleam from the semicircle that showed; it was pale and unshining, like a much-used silver coin. Clem blinked and shivered. He didn't like the saw. He was afraid of it, and his fear was greater in these early hours before the cutting started. Clem thought of the saw as waiting, menacing, deadly.

Joel Patch said, "Well, get started!"

"Belts all right, Tim?" asked Clem, stalling.

Tim Frost, Clem's helper, yawned and glanced at a belt taut between wheels. He was sitting on a log ready in the carriage. Both blade and carriage were in a direct line with the water wheel that gave them power.

"E-yah," said Tim, sleepily.

The mill owner stamped a foot. "Of course they're all right!" Patch was proud of his circular saw. It was the most modern piece of equipment on the mountain; the other mills were still using jerky gash saws. "That saw cost a mint of money, Clem Galusha. And it was rigged by experts. There ain't many like it around, and you know it!"

"Pays to make sure sometimes."

"Stop dawdling!" Patch said. "You're wasting water! I don't know what's come over you, Clem! This order for the Whig Convention is the first decent job we've had in months. And you've done nothing but crab, crab, crab!"

"We turned it out, didn't we?" Clem kept the argument going, watching the day lighten in the open side of the shed. "They got their wood!"

"We ain't finished! The meeting's tomorrow and there ain't half enough in that pile of shingles!"

"Why shingles?" asked Tim Frost. "The cabin's finished. Roofed and everything! What in thunder do they want with so many shingles?"

Patch grinned. "That was my idea, Tim. You just wait and see." He teetered, heel and toe, nodding with satisfaction. "E-yah. Maybe I did have to share the logs for the cabin with the other mills— though you'd think anybody'd know I'm the best Whig in the bunch—but them shingles, now, are totally mine." He stopped, glared, and shouted, "Clem!"

"All right," said Clem. "All right." He shuffled forward, grasped the hand lever, and pulled. There was a metallic click, and the saw spun, humming.

Tim Frost released a brake, and the carriage edged forward. As it jerked its way toward the spinning blade Patch's eyes matched every movement.

The saw bit into the log with a high-pitched whine. Sawdust spurted up. Clem Galusha, wincing, set his teeth. The screaming noise seemed to go through him, deep inside, along every vein. It wasn't warm in the shed, but he began to sweat.

"Shave it close!" Patch yelled.

Inch by inch the saw cut along the length of the log. The trimmed board dropped at last, bouncing on the floor. Clem glanced up at the tally board that hung over his head. The flat wood was honeycombed with holes. He moved a wooden peg over one space and shut off the saw.

The sawmill owner crouched and inspected the plank. "Too thick, Clem!"

Clem was breathing hard; he wiped his face. "I told you," he said. "You can't make proper shingles this way!"

"I know what I'm doing!"

"You can't slice a log like a ham!"

"Too thick, I said. I ain't wasting no wood!"

"All right," said Clem. He helped Tim run back the carriage and marked the log. "We'll try her again."

Again the log jounced forward until the teeth met it. The whine filled the shed, so that it could be heard over all the noises of belts and wheels and water. Clem watched the glittering arc of the saw with a look that was glazed and unblinking. When the plank dropped, thudding, his ears ached with the sudden change. Under his breath he cursed Patch and the log, the mill, and the saw.

Patch clapped his hands. "That's it! That's just right! E-yah. Keep the boards that thin and cut them into eight-inch lengths!"

"Shingles that thin," said Tim Frost, puzzled, "won't keep rain out long!"

"You leave that to me, Tim," said Patch. "Who said they was shingles, anyway?"

Clem said, "You did. Shakes. Shingles. You been calling them that right along."

"Have I, now?" Patch chuckled. "Well, I had to call them something, didn't I? You wait and see what them shakes get used for. It's new ideas makes new business. There's a whole passel of people coming to that Convention tomorrow, and I want just as many—er—shingles as there is folks. Good Whig wood for good Whig voters."

"You got four, five hundred now."

"Four or five hundred!" Patch sniffed at the figures. "That's a drop in the bucket. They're aiming to have a lot more folks than that. Bet that crowd will run to thousands, not hundreds!"

"You really think that, Joel?"

"E-yah. Got reason to believe it." Laying one finger alongside his nose, Patch winked. "Them fellows staying down to the inn. They're pretty big Whigs." He cackled, surprised at his pun. "Bigwigs in more ways than one! E-yah!"

Tim Frost laughed dutifully. Clem Galusha folded his arms and waited.

"They know a thing or two, them fellows," Patch continued. "And they're counting on a mighty big shindig. Making arrangements for as many as five, six thousand people."

"Six thousand?"

"Up here on Stratton?"

"E-yah. This ain't going to be no piddling town meeting! We're having the best speaker in the country. Remember the Bunker Hill speech? And the debate with that Southern fellow, Hayne? Dan tied him in knots slicker than slippery elm! E-yah. When it comes to orating there's nobody like Dan Webster."

"Ever get to hear him, Joel?"

Patch frowned at Clem and evaded the question. "We'll all get that pleasure tomorrow."

"If it don't rain."

The frown deepened; Patch glared. He said, "It ain't going to! And that's enough chatter. Tomorrow's your holiday, not today. Get at that cutting!"

After he had watched several more boards sliced from the log, Patch left the mill. Remembering Clem's remark, the sawmill owner cast a sharp, calculating look at the morning. The sun was fairly up now, and the sky, clear blue, was dotted with clouds as white and puffy as popcorn. As he walked through the still, wet grass toward his house, Patch noted that spider webs hung in the blades, glistening when they caught the sunshine like so many jeweled handkerchiefs. He jerked a nod of approval at these signs of fair weather. The mist was rising, and it looked like a spell of clear days. Still, Patch reminded himself, it wouldn't hurt to look up the date in his almanac. It might pay, he decided, remembering his lumber pile, to be ready to erect shelter if necessary.

Patch made a quick inspection of the housekeeping. He expected important guests on the morrow, and he wanted everything perfect. All three of the women in his household were hard at work. His daughter, Sarah, was cleaning windows. Lizzie, Clem's wife, was sweeping furiously. In the kitchen Rhoda Hapgood was on her knees, scrubbing the wide planks of the floor.

He had started to pass through when he noticed that the girl had stopped work. Patch stared, surprised and disapproving.

Rhoda looked up from her pail. She was a thin, small girl, with a pug nose that gave a pinched appearance to her narrow face. She brushed a strand of hair away from eyes that were the same faded blue as her dress. She smiled uncertainly but did not speak.

"Well, Rhoda?" asked Patch, impatiently.

The girl bent her head. When she spoke it was into the scrub pail and almost indistinctly. "I—I was wondering, Mr. Patch."

"E-yah?" Patch waited, tapped his foot. "Speak up, Rhoda. We've no time for stalling! There's work to be done."

"Well. Could I—can I go? To the meeting? Tomorrow?" With one frightened glance at Patch, Rhoda dipped her brush and scrubbed hastily.

Looking down at her, Patch jingled a few coins in his pocket. He considered Rhoda, a homeless orphan, as an investment. In exchange for an amount of work incredible for her size, Patch had for a number of years given Rhoda her board and keep. Not many men, he reflected, would have taken such a waif into their homes. He was not sure he approved of her request.

"It's a political meeting, Rhoda. You can't vote."

The rasping scrub brush paused, went on.

"We're having visitors, you know. Mr. and Mrs. Dunklee. He's an important man. A banker." Patch pinched the tip of his nose, thinking. It might look better in front of Humphrey Dunklee if he let the girl go. Showed that the success of the Whig Convention was more important to him even than household duties. Patch nodded. "It might be managed, Rhoda. We'll see."

69

Rhoda gasped her thanks to his retreating back. Patch stamped out of the house. "Nathan!" he shouted. "Nathan!" He was only halfway across the barnyard when his son hurried out of the barn. Patch stopped and waited. His voice threw questions across the lessening distance as Nathan approached.

"Chaise washed?"

"Yes, Pa."

"Harness polished?"

"Yes, Pa."

"Team curried?"

"One of them, Pa."

"All right." Patch looked up at the taller Nathan. "I want everything in apple-pie order tomorrow. Humphrey Dunklee runs a bank down to Bennington."

Nathan nodded.

"Pays to make an impression with a banker. Keep that in mind. And be real polite to his wife. I'm going to have a talk with her about your sister Sarah."

"About Sarah?"

"E-yah. Time we thought about a match for Sarah. She ain't getting younger. Twenty-one next birthday. That's mighty close to an old maid. The Dunklees might know of somebody suitable. Ain't nobody around here. And I ain't aiming to have Sarah on my hands for the rest of her days!"

"Pa," said Nathan and gulped. "I been meaning to mention a similar subject."

"The Chester gal? Guessed that."

"Nothing's settled, Pa. But lately I'd say my stock had gone up a bit."

"Ain't surprised. You're a good match, Nathan." Patch regarded his son as he might weigh the points of a horse. "And it ain't a bad connection—the church. Not that she'll bring much else, unless the parson's got something put away I don't know about! And that ain't likely. But Lovina's all right; she's been raised right—she'll work."

"E-yah," agreed Nathan.

"Now, you get busy. Hitch up the bay and haul a load of them shingles down to the clearing. Tell the fellow in charge I sent them. And don't dawdle down there. There ain't nothing worth

70

while going to happen in that clearing till tomorrow. Today's for work!"

"Pa. About them shingles . . ."

"Don't ask questions! Do as you're told!"

"Yes, Pa."

Patch turned and walked away. He felt very pleased. The shingles had them all puzzled. Just showed that a man could make money lots of ways other folks never thought of, long as he kept his wits sharp. He blessed the Whig party and Dan Webster for holding the Convention on Stratton.

Helping folks make a dollar, Patch thought, wouldn't do Tippecanoe a mite of harm. Exactly what the country needed. Yes, in more ways than one, that Convention was going to be a blessing.

Standing on Seth Purdy's shoulders, Put Chester reached for the lowest branch of the tamarack tree. The bark of the bough just scraped the tips of his fingers. Put stretched, swaying, but he still couldn't get a grip. He jumped, caught hold. There was a yell from below as he chinned himself up on the branch. He squirmed into the tree and looked down.

Seth Purdy sat on the ground, rubbing one shoulder. "Dang you, Put!" he said.

"Couldn't reach, Seth."

"Well, you might have said something. Instead of kicking like a mule."

Put laughed. From his perch in the tree he could see the whole clearing. There was plenty of activity; the woods above echoed with the flat sound of hammering. For the hundredth time, Put admired the length of the new log cabin. It was the biggest building he'd ever seen—bigger than his father's church. Workmen were carrying planks into it. He knew they were for flooring and partitions. Closer, almost in the shadow of the tamarack, other men were driving nails into a board platform, its wood white and new against the green of the clearing. One of the hammerers grinned up at Put and waved.

"Need any help?" called Put.

The workman shook his head, slammed a nail home.

Seth called from below. "Now that you're up there, you see anything new?"

71

Put shook his head. It had been his plan to climb the tree to get a fresh view of a now too-familiar sight. Ever since the first workmen had appeared in the clearing and the first logs had been hauled there, both boys had spent every available minute at the place. They had watched Tippecanoe's log cabin go up rapidly, notched trunks locking the walls together; even Seth, a Democrat's son, had pulled on a rope and cheered when the roof was raised. They had carried water to the workmen; they had examined and tested every tool.

Now Put dangled his bare feet and looked around once more. The wheel tracks of the workmen's wagons were fresh scratches on the ground, crossing and crisscrossing, mud ruts gouged through the grass. But they were few compared to the breadth of the clearing; most of the wide expanse was still untouched. The field was blooming under the early July sun. Its green was frothed with white sprays of field daisies and wild blackberry. There were carelessly scattered dots of yellow buttercups and the orange-flame blooms of hawkweed. Put was not impressed by the colors; he only marveled again at the size of the clearing. He thought it would take an awful big crowd of people to fill it.

"Seth."

"E-yah?"

"You figure many'll come today?"

"Maybe." Seth shrugged. "Some, anyway. Them as can't wait for the doings to start."

"And want to get the best spot." Put nodded wisely.

"You got that right now," Seth said, grinning. "You could spit on Webster's head from there."

"I ain't no Loco-foco Democrat!"

Seth blinked at the angry tone. "I didn't say you was, Put."

"Spitting on a great man like that would be a low, dirty, Democrat trick!"

"You needn't take on so, Mr. Chester." Seth spoke slowly; his cheeks were flushed. "Democrats got manners same as anybody. There ain't no call to say they spit at folks."

"They ain't holding this Convention! The Whigs are! And I wouldn't want no Democrats to go spoiling it just because it's for Tippecanoe and Tyler too!"

Something caught Put's glance, and he leaned forward, pointing. "There's something new, Seth. They got stuff piled behind the cabin." He swung off the branch in the whirl known as "skin the cat," hung, and dropped. "It's all covered up. With canvas or something. And there's a fellow with a gun sitting on it."

"With a gun?"

"E-yah. Come on. Let's go see." Put started off at a brisk walk.

For a moment, Seth didn't follow. Then curiosity got the better of anger. But, even as he took the first step, his attitude changed. Pile of stuff, he said to himself. Some more Whig tomfoolishness.

They skirted the rear of the cabin. There was a canvas-covered mound a short distance farther, and there was a man sitting on it. He was talking to another on a roan horse.

Put identified the latter. "That's the man in charge. The one they call the Captain. He's staying down to the inn."

"I know!" said Seth irritably.

The Captain turned his mount and started away. The roan horse broke into a gallop, clods flying up under his churning hoofs, and raced across the clearing.

Put whistled in admiration. "Rides good."

"E-yah." Seth wasn't conceding a Whig anything.

They watched the rider out of sight, then walked closer and stared up at the man atop the mound. He was a tall, lanky man in a long coat and a broad-brimmed hat. A rifle lay across his lap, and he was chewing tobacco. He calmly gazed down at the boys.

"Morning," said Put.

The man nodded and spat.

They hadn't met him before. Seth looked at Put. Nodding, the latter casually kicked a bare foot at the edge of the canvas. Both boys glanced at the man. He watched them, chewing.

Put placed his hands on his hips and faced the man squarely. "What's under the cover?"

"Kegs."

"Kegs?" Put bent, lifted the canvas, and peered beneath. Seth watched the man. The tempo of the chewing jaws didn't change; the eyes under the broad brim followed Put's movements. "What kind of kegs, mister?"

"Cider."

"Oh." Put grinned. "Cider, Seth. For tomorrow. Log cabin and

73

cider. Like they said old Tippecanoe drank. The cider, I mean. He lives in a log cabin!"

"I know!" Seth's irritation was sharper.

"It's hard cider, ain't it, mister?"

"E-yah."

"E-yah. And you're guarding it with a rifle so's the Democrats can't steal it!"

Seth Purdy's lips tightened. Stealing now, he thought. Put seemed to figure he could pin anything on the Democrats. They was just as honest as the Whigs any day. More so, from what Seth's Pa said.

"How many barrels is there, mister?" Put asked.

The man in the broad-brimmed hat sighed. He shifted the rifle and his cut of tobacco. He spoke one word.

"Scat!"

It wasn't loud or violent. But both boys knew he meant it. Put tried to stare the man down and failed. He nudged Seth. They walked away slowly, with as much dignity as they could muster. Neither looked back; they ignored the fact of their retreat.

They reached the upper edge of the clearing before Put spoke. He laughed and said, "Fire and brimstone! That fellow thought he was old Nick himself!"

"Maybe he is," Seth said.

"Huh?"

"Whig, ain't he?"

Put's mouth opened; he stared at Seth. Then he chuckled. "That proves he couldn't be! It's old Van who's one of the devil's followers! A fiend in human form!"

The words were spoken in jesting imitation of a preacher's sermon, but Seth had passed the stage where any barb thrown at the Democrats could be amusing. He jerked his thumb in the direction of the cider cache and said, "He still scared you."

"Scared who?"

"You."

Each speech dropped a few years from their ages. The boys faced each other belligerently. Put saw no reason for Seth's attitude. The accusation of cowardice made him determined to refute it. "He ain't scaring Whigs," said Put. "Just Democrats."

The accumulation of the morning's slurs made Seth stubborn, and he enjoyed the feeling. "Scared you!" he repeated.

"Did not!"

"Did!"

"No!"

"E-yah!"

Put, glaring, thrust his chin forward. "I was not scared!"

Seth uttered a disbelieving laugh.

The sharp crow lashed Put's anger; his face went white. He took a single, catlike step toward Seth. He said, "Seth Purdy, are you calling me a liar?"

The question was too great a temptation for Seth. He remembered Put's boasts about Tippecanoe, his numerous insults at Democrats, his irritating possessiveness of the morrow's convention. The answer came quickly.

"All Whigs are liars!"

Put hit him. The blow was sudden and savage. It caught Seth on the cheekbone, drove him back staggering.

White rage blurred Seth's eyes with tears. He charged, swinging. The wild punch missed, and Put hit him twice, right and left. Put's fists rammed in. Blood gushed from Seth's nose. He choked out a single sob and came on.

Ready, both hands cocked, Put tasted triumph. Got him, he thought. I can lick him sure. Then, even as he dodged Seth's rush, Put was suddenly shocked.

Pain and rage contorted Seth's face; it was wet with blood and tears. Put felt sick. This was Seth. His friend. One certain thought leaped into Put's mind. If he licked Seth now they would never be friends again. Put knew it. He swallowed hard and dropped his hands.

Jarringly, Seth's fist smashed against Put's ear. There was a ringing in Put's head. The blow shook his teeth and his resolve. But he clung to the idea of friendship. I hit him three times, Put remembered. He's got two more coming. Seth's next swing seemed to take forever to land. Put shut his eyes and took it.

He let the wildly flailing Seth hit him again, flush on the mouth. Then with a bound he flung both arms around Seth, hugging him tight. They wrestled.

"Quits!" he yelled. "Quits, Seth! And even!"

Seth tried to shake loose; Put clung.

"Quits and even!"

They were both panting. Seth stopped struggling. He was still trembling; he said, choked and strained, "Quits, Put?"

"E-yah! And even." Put let go and stepped back. He tried to smile; his hand jerked out. "Even, Seth. I hit you three times. You hit me three times."

Seth snuffled his bloody nose and took the offered hand. "All right, Put. Even." They stood there, shaking hands, breathing hard, for a full minute. As one they flopped on the ground and grinned at each other.

Put dabbed at a cut lip, looked at his fingers. "You hit!" he said, accusingly.

Trying to stop his nosebleed with his knuckles, Seth giggled. "Ain't so bad yourself." He twisted his head to keep from dripping on his shirt.

"We'd better get washed up," suggested Put.

Together they went toward the gurgle of a stream. In the cool shadows of the trees Put was gay, lighthearted, happy that it had ended all right. With tender affection he helped bathe Seth's face. They lay back and looked up through the foliage.

"Seth."

"E-yah?"

"That fellow with the gun."

"Oh, him."

"Maybe he did scare me a little."

"Hell! Who cares? Scared me, too!"

The cuss word showed strong emotion. Put appreciated it. He dabbled one foot in the noisy little brook.

"Put."

"E-yah?"

"I guess some Whigs ain't liars."

"Some Democrats ain't, either."

Put sat up and scratched his head. "I'm for Tippecanoe. You ain't. All right. No sense fighting about it. You shoot better than me. I can run the fastest. All right. Like you said. Hell. Who cares."

"E-yah!" Seth gave a hearty approval to this long speech.

"Listen!" Put stiffened.

They both heard it. Faint and distant there were strains of music. The boys stared at each other.

"What is it?" asked Seth.

"I don't know."

Through the trees came the thin melody. Bugles blared; fifes shrilled; there was the steady double beat of drums.

Seth said, "Music." It was a judgment.

"E-yah." Put's eyes brightened; he grabbed Seth's shoulder. "Seth. Seth, I bet I know. It's a band!"

"A band?"

Neither had ever heard one, and they looked at each other with mounting excitement.

"A band!" Put shouted. "Coming to the Convention!"

"Let's go see!"

Whooping with joy, Put leaped the stream. Seth followed, clearing the water easily. They began to run toward the music.

The undersigned respectfully invite the young men of the 1st Congressional district of Vermont, & all others opposed to the oppressive measures, the extravagant expenditures & corrupting influences of the present, profligate NATIONAL ADMINISTRATION & in favor of *Harrison* and *Reform;* to meet in convention at the Log Cabin to be erected in Stratton, for the occasion, on the Green Mountains, a little east of the height of land near the Turnpike Road leading from Arlington to Wardsboro, *Tuesday the 7th of July next,* at 12 o'clock M., for the purpose of discussing the political affairs of this country: to nominate a suitable candidate to represent this District in Congress: to respond to the nomination of State officers and Presidential electors which may have been made by the State Convention, at Burlington. And to transact such other biz. as the exigences of our political affairs may seem to require for the advancement of the cause of the people & the overthrow of their oppressors.

The biz. of the convention, it will be perceived, is of no small importance, & we doubt not there will be a strong rally, from all parts of the district, of the Young—Middle Aged—& Old Men. A day or two spent in discussing the affairs of an oppressed Country, in the pure air of the Green Mts., beyond the reach of the miasmatic taint of Loco Foco corruption cannot but invigorate the devoted patriotism, which has ever characterised the honest Yeomanry of "ALWAYS FAITHFUL" Vermont.

It is expected several gentlemen from neighboring states will be present and address the convention.

The invitation, cut from the pages of the *Vermont Phoenix,* issue of July 3, 1840, hung from the fireplace mantel in the common room of the Tarbox inn. Several gentlemen from neighboring states, none of whom were expected to address the Convention, glanced at it as they lunched. They were alike, these gentlemen, both in dress and in a certain facial shrewdness. All wore long black coats and tight trousers; all had plug hats. Only in shapes and waistcoats did they show their different points of origin. The Man from Boston was fat; his waistcoat was green. The Man from New Hampshire, lean, wore a double-breasted gray vest. The small, bald Man from New York showed purple beneath his coat. The one they called Captain was completely in black, but there were tiny gold threads and silk lapels on his waistcoat. Whatever the color, it covered a politician.

The Man from New York pointed his knife at the dangling clipping. "Ain't no mention of Webster," he said.

"He'll be here," said the Captain.

"He'd better be."

"God, yes!"

Wrinkling his green waistcoat, the Man from Boston leaned forward and tapped the table. "Gentlemen, please. You can count on Senator Webster. He contracted to be here tomorrow, and he will keep that contract."

"He better had," repeated the New Yorker. "I know these Vermonters. They've been promised Dan Webster and they won't take any short change. They'll raise merry Ned if he doesn't get here."

"You needn't worry. Boston delivers the goods."

The Man from New Hampshire guffawed. "So I notice. Got a Democrat governor down there now, ain't you?"

"That's right. We bust a gut putting a Whig in Albany. Right in Van Buren's own state! And you beaneaters manage to lose Massachusetts."

"Gentlemen!" The Captain's voice was firm. "Our immediate concerns are this state and this year's election. We Vermonters want that Convention tomorrow to be something the voters will remember. I've had a hand in the arrangements. We can count on Webster. And after you leave this mountain I think you'll all be able to say to your folks back home, 'Vermont is in the Whig column!' "

"I still think somebody should have rolled a ball."

78

The Captain shook his head. "There are some things that just won't go in this state. And pushing a ball from place to place is one of them. Seems silly."

"It's popular in the West. And some of our New York clubs think well of it. There's a song goes with it, you know.

> "As rolls the ball,
> Van's reign does fall,
> And he may look
> To Kinderhook."

"No," said the Captain.

"Kinderhook," the New Yorker explained. "That's where Van Buren lives."

"We know."

"That sort of tomfoolery would never go in Boston."

"He's right. Let the West keep it. And York State, too. New England is doing all right sticking to the Log Cabin and Cider campaign."

"Precisely, Captain."

"You'll see tomorrow."

"What if it rains?"

"It won't. But it wouldn't stop the Green Mountain boys. A little rain may cut the crowd down. But they'll come. They've been looking forward to it. Dan Webster and hard cider. A good time. They'll come."

"Who's going to get that nomination for Congress?"

"Hiland Hall, sure as shooting."

"You agree, Captain?"

"E-yah."

"All your arrangements are made, eh, Captain?"

"Think so. The cabin's all ready. The platform's up. I've got a man watching the cider. Plenty of badges and gimcrack log cabins."

"By the way, Captain"—the Man from Boston lowered his voice—"has there been much talk along that line?"

"Along what line?"

"Tippecanoe's log cabin. We hear quite a bit of it down to Boston."

"Quite a bit of what?"

"Speak up, man."

"Well"—the Bostonian coughed—"it seems that General Harrison's dwelling isn't exactly a cabin. Quite palatial, in fact."

"Is that right, Captain?"

"Doesn't he live in a log cabin?"

The Captain shrugged. "How the hell should I know!"

Dan Tarbox bustled into the room. He hurried to an open window, looked out. He crossed to the other wall and looked out there. The political gentlemen watched him.

"What's the matter, innkeeper?"

"A band!" said Dan. "A band's coming somewhere! You can just hear it!"

"Thunderation!" The Captain groaned. "The early birds! How am I going to keep them happy till tomorrow? Damn and blast! There goes my meal! I'd better get out to that clearing!"

The band that was heard by the gentlemen in the Tarbox inn was not the same one whose music had attracted Put Chester and Seth Purdy. There were two bands trudging up the side of the mountain. Both were small, and both had deliberately started a day early to be the first band on the spot. Each planned on having the field to itself, in the choicest site, before competition arrived. One was coming up from the west, from Arlington; one was climbing the eastern slope from Wardsboro. Neither was aware of the other.

As it passed through the crossroad settlement, the band from the east made a brave show but a big mistake. Encouraged by the cheers of the onlookers who ran out from inn, houses, smithy, and parsonage, it began to play. The leader, a lanky fifer with a big nose, strutted proudly out in front. Behind him came the bugles and the drums and, in their midst, a flapping white banner with the green-lettered slogan, *Tippecanoe and Tyler too.* Jolting along in the rear of the marchers were the wagons and carts of their loyal neighbors. These waved at the spectators, bravely sang with their band. The parade wound past the settlement's last house and followed the road in its twistings through the trees.

Trunks and leaves were not such stimulating onlookers. The sun was hot, and the road continued uphill. One by one the musicians found that lungs needed wind more than instruments. As the music faltered and weakened, so did the following singers. Even the lanky leader, nose shining with perspiration, finally lowered his fife and succumbed to the effort of marching. For the last of the several miles to the clearing only the drums beat out any semblance of a tune.

Then, when the thinning ranks of the trees showed the destination to be close, the drums abruptly stopped. The marchers stopped too, stood still, listening. The leader, mouth open, gestured wildly with his fife. Even the folks on the following vehicles stared at each other in surprise and consternation. Ahead was music. Band music. And song.

> Let Van from his coolers of silver drink wine
> And lounge on his cushioned settee.
> Our man on his buckeye bench can recline,
> Content with hard cider is he,
> The iron-armed soldier, the true-hearted soldier,
> The gallant old soldier of Tippecanoe.

With a squeal like a note from his fife the lanky leader ran forward. The rest of the band followed. They hurried around a curve out of the trees and halted, staring. The clearing with its new log cabin was stretched out before them. No one as much as glanced at it. For, drawn up in the road, serenading the townspeople who had followed it up the other side of the mountain, was the band from the west.

The eastern musicians groaned. The big-nosed fifer swore. Men voiced their disappointment.

"They beat!"

"Licked, by Joshua!"

"Diddled!"

"And we started 'fore dawn to be first!"

"Now, hold on!" The lanky leader screamed. "We ain't licked yet, you spineless buzzards! We ain't licked yet!"

"We ain't, eh?"

"Like hell we ain't."

"Your eyesight's failing, Luthur."

"Deef too. Listen to them."

Swinging his fife like a club the leader threatened the nearest heads. He shouted at them. "I hear them all right! That's just it,

81

you crawling half-wits! Maybe we're licked marching, but we ain't licked playing!"

The band looked at its leader and listened to its rival. Eyes began to shine. A drummer hitched his drum higher; a bugler wiped off his mouthpiece.

"Maybe there's something in that, Luthur."

"'Course there is!" Luthur's lanky form scurried about as he gave orders. "Form ranks there! Get in line! We'll show them fellows they ain't the only rocks on this here road! We ain't never been licked playing by no band from the west side of the state and we ain't going to start now!"

"What tune, Luthur?"

"'Little Pig's Tail, Luthur?"

"E-yah! 'Little Pig's Tail!'" Luthur raised his voice. "And you folks back there on the wagons! You know the campaign words for it. Sing fit to bust your buttons!" He took his place in front, raised his long arms, and held the fife above his head. "Step sharp now, boys. Left foot first. Soon as they stop."

They waited like soldiers set for a charge. As soon as the band from the west finished playing, Luthur's hands jerked the fife down to his lips. Music and marching started together.

> What has caused this great commotion,
>   Motion, motion,
> Our country rolling through?
> It is the ball a-rolling on, on.
> For Tippecanoe and Tyler too,
> Tippecanoe and Tyler too,
> And with them we'll beat little
>   Van, Van, Van!
> Van is a used-up man.
> And with them we'll beat little
>   Van, Van, Van!

The drums slammed out the repeated syllable of the President's nickname. In line, banner high, every instrument at its loudest, the band from the east swept up the road. At their head the lanky Luthur marched erect, lifting his knees with each step. Behind the band came the wagons, horses prancing, people roaring the words of the song.

It was a fine display, and it won deserved applause. The folk

82

already in the clearing, the workmen, and visitors from the west cheered and clapped. Even the musicians who had arrived first tucked their instruments under their arms and beat their palms together.

Luthur wheeled his band in front of the other. Halting, they finished the tune with a flourish. One sweep of Luthur's arm stopped the music. In the sudden silence, his voice carried to the ends of the clearing.

"Thought maybe the folks up here might like to hear a band."

Like a thunderclap, laughter burst from the crowd. It was the sort of impertinence they appreciated, and the enemy musicians guffawed as loud as any. The members of Luthur's band beamed at their leader, broke ranks to pound him on the back. Both bands intermingled, exchanging remarks.

"Showed you fellows a thing or two, didn't we?"

"Not to notice."

"E-yah."

"We got here first."

"Just fool luck if you ask me."

"Sour grapes."

"Right shiny bugle you got there, mister."

"Dressing up a fife don't make it sound sweeter."

"Me? I like my drumskin a mite loose."

In the friendliest fashion the visitors from both sides of the mountain pitched camp in the clearing. On his roan horse, the man they called Captain pointed out the sites. There was some grumbling about the distance from the big log cabin. Tents went up; wagons and carts were arranged in lines; horses were unhitched and tethered. A few men went off to cut spruce boughs and ground pine for bedding; several women unpacked cooking utensils. Seth Purdy directed some boys to a stream where they could draw water. Put Chester helped a lady pile stones for a campfire. Mostly, men and women both, the visitors wandered about the clearing. A steady stream of paraders strolled around the big cabin and drifted in, examining the insides.

"Big, ain't it?"

"It'll do."

"Built real solid."

"My! I wish my house was this size!"

"It'd cost."

"Right fine timbers."

" 'Course it ain't what I'd call chinked proper!"

"Never winter."

"Well, it ain't permanent, you know."

"That's right."

"Note the flooring, Fanny? Real planks."

"Partitions, too."

"Land sakes! They even got rooms inside!"

"That's pine, ain't it?"

"Them boards? Pine, all right."

"Pine."

"Big, ain't it?"

Whatever the comment, the visitors were impressed. The size of the log cabin was measured and memorized. It was the first solid sign of the Convention, and it made the trip up the mountain worthwhile. They had come various distances, in some cases farther than they'd ever been from home, and over difficult roads. They had left farms and work, stock and businesses, and their expectations were high. The cabin assured them that the meeting would come up to those expectations. They were proud, too, that they were the first to arrive. Those who came later would have to concede that earliness showed devotion to the Whig cause. General Harrison ought to appreciate such stout support. Tippecanoe and Tyler too.

Everyone had his own camping arrangements. There was little notice of discomfort. They were all country folk, used to hardship and rough living. Some families spurned tents or shelters and planned to sleep in their wagons—or under them. Camping out, in the fine July weather, was no great privation. It was a shared adventure, a welcome change in routine, and something to be remembered. For a couple of nights they would cook and eat and sleep surrounded by friends and strangers; the greater the crowd, the better. It did a man good—and a woman, too—to meet a whole herd of friendly folk at once. On some of their farms months passed without the sight of a neighbor.

Once again the clearing rang with the sound of axes as men cut firewood. One mother, wishing to wander through the cabin, hitched her small daughter to the tamarack tree. No one else paid it the slightest attention. The tree's aloof position, if noticed, was not mentioned. They had all seen plenty of trees.

They had not seen anything like the two riders that came trotting along the turnpike from East Arlington. The campers in the clearing stopped work and stared. Wives called their husbands to look. Children pointed. Talk dropped to surprised whispers.

"Fire and brimstone!" said Put Chester to Seth Purdy. "Will you look at them?"

Staring, Seth said, "E-yah."

On a big black gelding with a coat like satin, the first rider was startlingly resplendent. He was tall, slender, and he rode well, sitting the saddle as if he belonged there. He was young, and the varied colors of his clothes became him. The thigh-length coat was deep sky blue with silver buttons. His trousers, fawn-colored and tight, ended in calf-high, polished boots of black leather. He wore a tall beaver hat that was almost white.

The second rider caused even more comment. He rode a chestnut horse, several hands smaller than the leader's, and he, too, rode well but with a lazy slouchiness. He was clad in purple livery. His low-crowned, shining coachman's hat was black. An audible gasp drifted through the crowd when the watchers saw that the man's face and hands were of the same shade.

"A black man!" said Put, who had never seen one before.

Seth stuttered in excitement. "E-yah. A nigger."

This was an event, and both boys ran to the roadbank to get a better look. The young man in the lead reined his gelding to a halt in front of them. Patting a gloved hand on the horse's neck, he smiled down at them. He had an easy, pleasant smile that brightened his brown eyes. He was a very handsome young man.

"Is this the place where the Whigs are meeting?" he asked.

"E-yah," Put answered. He was surprised at the rider's speech. The man's voice was soft and low, slurring the words, barely pronouncing some parts of the alphabet. It was Put's first encounter with any dialect but his own; he didn't recognize the accent as Southern, but he found it strange.

The black man reined in behind the other. "This here place, Mr. Tom?" The voice was strikingly like the first in spite of its disgust.

"It appears so, Hoc." The tall young man grinned, gazing at the encampment. "The young gentleman seems sure."

Put said, "Convention's going to be right here in this clearing. Tomorrow."

"Mr. Tom! We can't camp in no open! We'll catch our deaths!"

The other laughed. "I'm afraid you're right, Hoc. Accommodations do look a trifle airy. But perhaps you could direct us to something more sheltered, boy."

"Well," said Put, not sure he understood. "There's the inn."

"An inn? Eureka! You hear, Hoc?"

"Yes, sir. I hear, but I don't see."

"It's straight on down the road. Couple or three miles."

"Couple or three." The young man chuckled. "The usual understatement, no doubt. Well, we'll find it. And thank you, young sir. Come on, Hoc." He wheeled his horse, heeled him into a trot. The black man sighed and followed.

Put watched them out of sight. He said slowly, "You know what, Seth?"

"What?"

"That black one. He's a slave."

"You think?"

"E-yah. The other fellow owns him same as he owns the horse." Put nodded his head. "A slave. I never seen one before."

"Me neither." Seth barked a laugh. "But then, I never seen anybody done up like that first fellow, either. Where do you suppose they come from?"

Thomas Jefferson Dunbar, trotting his gelding toward Stratton church, had come from far-off Virginia. He had just finished his first year in the College of New Jersey at Princeton and had decided to spend his vacation visiting in the North. The decision was approved and encouraged by Tom's parents, both of whom were somewhat worried by their son's too evident interest in a neighbor's daughter. The elder Dunbars were no prudes, but there was something in the air of any room in which Tom met this particular young lady that reminded them of the uneasy pause between flashes in a lightning storm. Mrs. Dunbar blamed the girl for a forward hussy; Mr. Dunbar, more justly, wondered what his young devil of a son had been doing. Since Pulchramonte, the Dunbar plantation, bordered the neighbor's acres, and since

86

it was known that the daughter's hand was promised to a third county family, a scandal would have strained relations. Tom's request for money to spend on his tour was speedily and generously answered.

With Hoc, who had been his body slave since childhood, Tom spent several weeks at the fashionable Saratoga spa. He liked the girls and hated the water. Both proved to contain unpleasant surprises. The young Virginian was startled to find that the mother of one fair escort took his bantering attentions as serious. Tom Dunbar was anxiously planning to move on when he heard of the Whig Convention on a mountain over in Vermont.

The Dunbars were Whigs and ardent ones. They believed that fitness for office was determined by bloodlines and breeder's book. Tom's grandfather, the one who fought at Saratoga as an officer of Morgan's rough riflemen, had been convinced that he and his like were the only logical ruling class. The dogma was handed down in the family with the silverware. Grandfather had voted for Jefferson because he was a gentleman; he approved of erratic John Randolph of Roanoke for the same reason. His son, Tom's father, considered Andrew Jackson an upstart and Van Buren worse. On the porticoed porch that faced tidewater, all the Dunbars clucked over Calhoun of South Carolina as a gentleman gone wrong. The man was too fiery, a troublemaker. . . . Now that John Tyler, a family connection in the ninth degree of kinship, was being linked with Tippecanoe, Tom Dunbar considered the election of a Whig President a personal cause. It was high time the White House was returned to those it really belonged to—the Virginia gentlemen.

Naturally, he rode east to hear Daniel Webster speak. And where Tom went, Hoc went too. Only a few months older than his master, Hoc was the lone survivor of triplets born to a slave girl at Pulchramonte. Mr. Dunbar had named all three infants after Latin pronouns, *hic, haec, hoc*. Young Hoc accepted slavery as the natural order. He had grown up with Tom, played with him, served him. They were fond of each other. Hoc admired his master's horsemanship and his way with the ladies. It was indicative of their relationship that it never occurred to either that they were riding through a free state.

As they passed Chittenden's on their way to the inn a man was sharpening a scythe in the barnyard. Whetstone rang suddenly on blade as Charles Chittenden stopped and stared. Tom Dunbar raised his hat, but only the curve of steel, catching the sunlight, seemed to show any response. The two riders clattered on.

Their arrival at the crossroad caused more stir than had that of the band. The innkeeper took one look at the horses and rushed out. Little David gaped so at the black man that Mrs. Tarbox finally pushed him away from the window. Men peered from the shadows of the smithy; the idlers gathered.

Tom Dunbar dismounted, stretched, and tossed his reins to Hoc. "You're the innkeeper, sir?" he asked.

"E-yah. Name's Tarbox. Dan Tarbox."

"A pleasure, Mr. Tarbox." Tom bowed, lifting his beaver. "Thomas Jefferson Dunbar. I'd like rooms, please."

"Rooms?" The plural upset Dan. He bit his lips. "Well, we're a mite crowded. There's a passel of folks coming for the Convention."

"I know. I'm one." Tom grinned. The soft voice was insistent. "Rooms, please. For myself and my man."

"Him?" Dan jerked a thumb at Hoc. "He can make out in the stable, can't he?"

"Hoc?" It was Tom's turn to sound surprised.

"The stable's fine, Mr. Tom," said Hoc quickly. "That way I can take good care of the horses!"

"As you wish, Hoc. That leaves only myself, friend host. Surely you can find something for a loyal Whig who comes all the way from Virginia. 'I am sick to my heart, and I fain would lie down,' as the song has it. Actually, I'd like to wash and have something to eat."

"This way, Mr. Dunbar."

"I'll want the saddlebags, Hoc. But see to the animals first." Tom watched the slave lead away the horses. He followed the innkeeper, turned on the inn doorstep, and surveyed the settlement. "This would be Stratton, Mr. Tarbox?"

"E-yah. Same as the mountain. Stratton."

"Interesting," Tom Dunbar said. "Very interesting."

"Girls! Come away from the window!"

Mrs. Chester's voice was sharp, insistent. She clapped her hands and singled out her daughters by name. "Lovina! Mattie! Sally! Come away this instant! What would your father say to such behavior!"

The girls scattered from the window like frightened hens. Like hens, too, they all cried out in protest.

"Did you see him, Mother?"

"That horse! And those clothes!"

"So handsome!"

"Handsome is as handsome does," said Mrs. Chester, frowning. "I thought you all had better sense. Rushing to the window, giggling like little ninnies. Suppose the young man had seen you! A fine sight, I must say. What opinion would he have formed of your immodest attire?"

Sally blushed; Martha tittered nervously. Both girls were in petticoats and underwaists, with shawls around their shoulders. The kitchen was littered with dresses—strips and pieces of cloth of many colors and textures. There were homespun and cotton, poplin and dimity, even silk. On the long trestle table was a large sewing basket and the scattered impedimenta of dressmaking.

"He didn't see us," said Lovina. Being fully clothed, she could come to the rescue of her sisters.

"No fault of yours!" Mrs. Chester bit off the argument as neatly as her teeth snapped a thread. She measured the width of the hem she was basting and nodded. "This one will be fine when it's finished. But there's still plenty of work if you expect to have new dresses for tomorrow."

The implied threat sent the two younger girls scurrying back to their sewing. Sally, threading a needle, asked, "Where do you think he comes from, Lovina?"

"The South, I judge."

"You mean because of the black man?"

"That will do," Mrs. Chester said. "If you intend to discuss every stranger that arrives you'll find time for little else. Besides, your father abominates slavery." The parson's wife looked around the busy room and sighed. Those that have slaves, she thought, have servants. It would be nice to have all the help you needed. "You may resume the reading, Lovina."

"Yes, Mother." Lovina picked up her book and searched for her place. She was much more interested in the young man on the black gelding than in the Lady's Pocket Library. Slavery or no slavery, Lovina said silently, he is good-looking. His finery would certainly put Charles Chittenden's in the shade. She wanted fiercely to see Charles overshadowed by the stranger.

"Can't you find the place, Lovina?"

" 'Rudiments of Taste!' " Mrs. Chester's tone was impatient. " 'By the Countess of Carlisle!' "

"I know, Mother. Oh, here it is. Letter V."

"Well, go on. Go on. And all of you pay attention. After such an exhibition I'm sure you can use some advice on good manners."

Clearing her throat, Lovina began. Her voice was slightly louder than normal, smooth but monotonous. She recited the sentences of the Countess with the same emotion that a schoolboy might show while repeating the multiplication table.

" 'By all means,' " Lovina read aloud. " 'By all means cultivate a taste for reading, but take care that your taste be a just one—that is, be more desirous of instruction than amusement or you will profit but little by literary pursuits. Those who read merely to please the imagination, may be sure of not reading to advantage, and do seldom acquire a relish for works of solid merit and utility. I have never known a young person who was fond of novels capable of relishing any thing superior to them. For my own part, I had rather see a girl wholly ignorant of the alphabet, than attached to that species of writing; for I am convinced that infinitely more have erred in the conduct of life from that cause, than from any other.' "

Lovina's voice droned on. Under it, in soft accompaniment, were the noises of dressmaking. Scissors snipped; cloth rustled. Each of the sewers had occasion to fumble in the sewing basket. Once Mattie dropped a darning egg and was reproved by her mother's glare. But none of the listeners spoke until Mrs. Chester held up a dress and shook it.

"We'd better fit this before I go any farther!"

It was to be Sally's dress, and she jumped up, tossed her shawl aside, and stood in the middle of the floor. Lovina rose to help. They had just drawn the folds over Sally's head when the door rattled under a knock.

Mrs. Chester said, "Oh, my goodness!"

Sally uttered a muffled squeal.

"Stand still," said Lovina, tugging at the cloth. But the dress was stuck, wrapped around Sally's head like some huge, ungainly turban.

"Who is it?" called Mrs. Chester.

"Me," said a voice beyond the door. "Mrs. Purdy."

Mrs. Chester gestured helplessly. "You girls better retire. Lovina, would you . . ."

"Yes, Mother. Don't worry. I'll fit it. Mattie, bring the basket."
Guiding the blinded Sally, Lovina led the way from the room.
Mattie gathered up an armful of equipment and hurried after them.

Mrs. Chester raised the wooden plug that held down the door
latch and let in Mrs. Purdy. The stage driver's wife was a small, thin-
faced woman whose movements were quick but graceful. She was
carrying a high, cloth-covered package, and there was something
furtive about the way she came into the room. When the door closed
behind her, Mrs. Purdy blew out her breath in relief and grinned.
The thin face was suddenly pretty as the grin brightened it.

"Land!" said Mrs. Purdy. "I hope nobody saw me."

"Saw you?"

"E-yah." Mrs. Purdy set down her package and whisked off the
cloth. Five pies, neatly stacked, were revealed. Offering the top one
for inspection, Mrs. Purdy continued, "Somebody'd be sure to tell
Lot. And then he'd know for certain where all our mincemeat went."
She grinned again.

Mrs. Chester smiled. Both women wore the look of conspiracy and
triumph common to their sex when a male has been outsmarted.
Mrs. Chester said, "Your husband's bound to guess."

"Guessing ain't knowing. Lot's fair that way. But he'd take on
something wonderful if he figured our house was helping put a
morsel of food in a Whig mouth."

"It's awful kind of you."

"Fiddledeedee!" Mrs. Purdy chuckled. "We're members of the
church, ain't we? Even if we are Democrats! I'd never feel right if
the Methodists had a bigger showing of pastry at tomorrow's supper.
I don't care if the visitors are Whigs. We wouldn't want them thinking the Congregational church was niggardly."

"I'm not worried." Mrs. Chester sounded satisfied. "We have the
best cooks."

"E-yah." Mrs. Purdy agreed. "But the Methodists've baked an
Election cake!"

"You don't mean it?"

"Fact. Heard it from Miss Nason herself. They used her oven!"

"But how could they? An Election cake takes thirty quarts of flour!"

"And twelve pounds of raisins, Mrs. Chester. Not to mention the
brandy. But they did it. Everybody contributed. And that sort of
puts us on our mettle, don't it?"

Mrs. Chester nodded. "Indeed it does. We'd never hear the end of it if those Methodist ladies got ahead of us."

"We'd better get these tucked away in your pie cupboard. Before someone comes along."

Mrs. Chester went over to a corner of the kitchen and raised a hinged board. The plank suspended under the floor was long, but there were already so many pies on it that the two ladies had trouble finding room for Mrs. Purdy's five. Mrs. Chester counted the collection before she closed the pie cupboard.

"Almost fifty," she said. "You think that matches an Election cake?"

"Well, it's a mite close for comfort."

"We should get a few more. But they won't be as good as what we've got now."

Mrs. Purdy said, "That don't matter. Bulk's what counts. Those men will get so het up over their politics, they won't know if they're eating sawdust!"

"Men!" said Mrs. Chester.

"E-yah."

"If they're going to vote for somebody why don't they just do it and not stir up all this fuss about it!"

"I know." Mrs. Purdy shrugged. "But some women are just as bad. Look at that Fanny Wright."

"Oh, her."

"She must be crazy. Making speeches and all. Haven't we women got enough trouble without getting mixed up in men's politics? Who's going to keep them out of trouble if we don't?"

"You can't keep them out of trouble," said Mrs. Chester. "Not men. They go looking for it. They'll even drop work to talk politics. Suppose we ran our kitchens that way?" The parson's wife sighed. "Even the Reverend Chester is a problem sometimes."

"This time," confided Mrs. Purdy, "I'm real worried about Lot. I don't rightly know what we'll do if he leaves off stage driving."

"Leave stage driving? Lot Purdy?"

"He threatens to, Mrs. Chester. It ain't just the Convention and having mostly Whigs as passengers. But now it seems the stage company wants him to drive a log cabin up here tomorrow."

"A log cabin? On wheels?"

"E-yah. They've got one down to Wardsboro or around there. And they want Lot to drive it. Six horses. And they figure there's nobody else can handle them. Lot, he says he just won't do it, being a Democrat. Says it's more than flesh and blood can stand!"

Mrs. Chester clucked sympathetically.

"It ain't like he was here where I could help, either." Mrs. Purdy shook her head. "I ain't never heard Lot talk so hard before. And down there off the mountain there's no telling what he'll say to folks. He's liable to get everybody's back up." Mrs. Purdy shrugged helplessly. "Men!" she said.

"E-yah," said Mrs. Chester.

Lovina stuck her head in the door in time to catch the last two words. "Mother," she said, "the dress is fine except it has to be taken in. Do you want to do it or shall I?"

Mrs. Chester said, "You go ahead, dear. I'm talking to Mrs. Purdy."

"All right." Lovina went back to her sisters. She was smiling when she joined them. From what I heard, thought Lovina, everybody in this house is discussing the same subject. Men. When the two younger girls saw that Lovina was alone, they resumed the conversation where she'd left it.

"Southern men," said Mattie, "aren't as nice as Northern men." She was sitting on the floor hugging her knees.

Sally, standing on a chair, sniffed. "How do you know? You've never met any."

"I know, that's all. Are they, Lovina?"

Lovina moved around Sally adjusting the dress. "Men," she said darkly, "are all alike."

Sally looked at Mattie. The latter made a face at Lovina's back. Sally said, "What do you mean, Lovina?"

"Never mind. Stop squirming."

"Come on, Vina," Mattie coaxed. "Tell us what you meant."

"No."

Over Lovina's head Sally winked at her younger sister. "Charles hasn't been around lately, has he?" She jumped and nearly toppled from the chair. "Vina! You stuck me!" Sally rubbed the wounded part.

"You will move," said Lovina, with a blank face.

"Vina." Mattie hitched herself closer. She glanced toward the kitchen and lowered her voice. "Vina. Did you . . . ? Have you ever . . . ? I mean . . ." She paused, rocked back and forth as if at

93

a loss for words. Finally she blurted it out in one quick sentence. "Did Charles ever kiss you?"

"'Course he did," said Sally scornfully. "At the husking bee. Shucks, Mattie. I've been kissed."

Mattie dismissed this impatiently. "I don't mean that way. Games and bees and things. I mean really. You know."

"Oh." Sally blinked. Then she stared, bending over to get a look at Lovina's lowered face. Sally's mouth opened. She said in delighted surprise, "Why, Lovina Chester. You're blushing!"

"I am not!"

"Tell us," said Mattie. "Tell us, Vina."

"We won't tattle, Vina."

"Not a word. Honest!"

"We just want to know what it was like?"

Lovina merely laughed. It was a cool laugh, and when she spoke her voice was calm. "You'll find that out soon enough. Maybe too soon, the way you're talking."

"Oh, Lovina."

"Was it Charles, Vina?"

"No," lied Lovina swiftly.

"Somebody else? Nathan Patch?"

Lovina laughed again, shaking her head. "You can stop asking. I'm not going to tell you anything."

Mattie giggled. "Then we'll have to find out for ourselves!"

"E-yah." Sally's giggle matched her sister's. "And for once there'll be a whole lot of boys around. Tomorrow."

"And we'll have new dresses."

"You two," said Lovina. She stepped back, surveyed her work. "You can take the dress off now, Sally. And I'll get Mattie's." She walked out of the room, then leaned against the wall. It had taken all her control to laugh and dismiss their questions lightly. The blush had almost given her away. She bit her lip, fighting back tears of reaction. She heard Mattie very clearly.

"Sally."

"E-yah?"

"You think Lovina did?"

"Mmm. Maybe."

"You think she—she kissed somebody we don't know?"

"Mattie!" Sally sounded shocked.

94

"Well, I just wondered!"

Lovina clenched her fists, shaking. Fury seethed inside her. Fury at Charles, at herself, at her sisters. She wanted to scream, to rant, to stamp her feet. That would show them. She knew she couldn't. She hadn't been near the clearing—not even to watch the building—since that spring night with Charles. Now she'd have to go. If Charles were there she'd be very polite and distant the way she'd been whenever they met these last weeks. She wanted to hurt him; she'd even encouraged the visits of Nathan Patch. But nothing seemed to do any good.

Lovina pressed her hands against her cheeks. I think I'll burst, she admitted, if something doesn't happen soon.

Zilpha Brayton stood at her front window and watched the wagon pass. It was the fifth vehicle to come up the road from Jamaica that day, and all had held strangers. Zilpha had never seen so much passing in a single day. She was excited, nervous with anticipation. This was going to be one time when she wouldn't complain that nothing happened on the mountain. There'd be more passing, many more; these were only the early comers. Tomorrow would bring the largest part of the crowd. She wondered if the other roads up the mountain were getting as much traffic as her own.

Zilpha felt grateful to General Harrison, with his outlandish nickname of Tippecanoe. She began to speculate on just what Daniel Webster would look like. She'd heard he was a man that any woman would set her cap for—not big, but right smart. Godlike Daniel. Zilpha sniffed. She guessed that Mr. Webster wasn't any more godlike than the rest of men. Married again, wasn't he? Not that Zilpha thought that proved anything. Men lasted longer than women, that was all. They wear us out, reflected Zilpha. Her eyes narrowed at the thought. If Lem had his way there'd be half a dozen brats running around, and she'd probably be under a tombstone up to the cemetery. Zilpha stretched, grinning. She knew she was stronger than her husband; if anyone wore out, it wouldn't be her. I'll bet, said Zilpha silently, that for all his fine talk and his big name, Daniel Webster ain't a mite better-looking than Isaac Mead.

She heard someone come into the room behind her and stiffened, sensing it was her husband. Conscious that she'd been thinking of Isaac, she mentally accused Lem of spying again.

Lem said, "Zilpha?"

"E-yah?" She didn't turn.

"You going to spend all day watching the passing?"

"If I like. For once there's something to see."

"This? This ain't nothing. Just you wait till tomorrow." There was glee in Lem's voice, and he laughed.

Zilpha turned around, surprised. He was so seldom in good humor these days, and laughter was a rarity. Zilpha stared, lips parted. Lem's tangled mat of stubble was gone; he was clean-shaven. The lean line of the man's jaw where the whiskers had been was the dusty gray of long-dead ashes. Lem was coatless, but Zilpha noted that he wore the trousers of his black go-to-meeting suit. She said, "What's got into you?"

Lem's chest puffed at her interest. "I'm taking Asa down to the settlement," he said. "Business."

"Business? Asa?"

"E-yah. This Convention's going to make a lot of difference to us, Zilpha. I've been telling you all along that what I needed was just a chance. A man ain't rightly to blame when times is hard, is he?"

"I've heard all that," Zilpha said, with an impatient wave of a hand. "Say your say."

"You know what's coming up this mountain? With every wagon. Cash, Zilpha. Hard money. Fistfuls of it. I'm aiming to see that some of it finds its way into my pocket. Asa now—he's strong and able-bodied. Dan Tarbox down to the inn, he's busier than all get out. He needs help, and Asa's going to be it."

Zilpha nodded slowly. "Pay?"

"Half dollar a day!" Lem cackled with triumph. "Dan didn't want to pay so much. Said he could get the Pierce boy for less. Go ahead, I said. You go right ahead. Them fine, rich, traveling folks will be mighty pleased. E-yah, I said. Mighty pleased being waited on by a half-wit. Dan, I told him, that will certainly add tone to your inn." Lem threw back his head and guffawed. "You should have seen his face, Zilpha."

"He took Asa!" Zilpha's laugh echoed her husband's.

"E-yah. He did. Tarbox squawked like a chicken with her head off, but I had him, and he knew it. There'll be extra too, maybe. Folks sometimes pay the boy something special for chores, you

96

know. Boot polishing, carrying slops, fetching hot water. Things like that. Asa can make maybe another few coppers that way."

"Guess them folks have more money than brains."

"Maybe. Leastways I'm going to show I've a mite of brains myself. Here, wait." Lem fished in his pocket and drew out a wad of ribbon. "Take a look at this."

Zilpha unfolded the ribbon. It was a strip of white satin, bordered with gold thread, and in its center, worked in the same color, was a rough picture of a man, a plough, and a log cabin. Zilpha read the motto.

Like Cincinnatus. He leaves the plough to save his country.

Lem said proudly, "I'm selling them."

"Selling them? But—what is it?"

"A badge! A Tippecanoe badge. That's supposed to be him on it there. And every good Whig that comes to the meeting will wear one to show he's on the right side. They'll just have to buy them."

"But where did you get them?"

"That's the best part. Fellow down to the inn's got a whole trunk full of those badges. They don't cost me a red cent. Each time I sell one, he gets one-half and I get the other!" He watched his wife finger the ribbon and added, magnanimously, "That there's a sample. You can keep it if you want."

Zilpha didn't think it was much of a present but nodded. "Think you'll sell many?"

"E-yah! They ought to go like anything!"

For once they hadn't paid any attention to the noise of a wagon on the road, but now a voice hailed them. Zilpha started, turned back to the window. She was relieved to see that it wasn't anyone she knew. It was a family in an open four-wheeled cart. Man, wife, and three children.

Lem opened the front door and called out. "You want something, mister?"

"How far to the camping grounds?"

"A piece. About a mile to the church. Then you bear right for a couple or three miles more."

The stranger was a young man, wiry and worried. The woman was young, too, and very pregnant. Not looking at her, the man said, "Likely there'll be a crowd, eh?"

97

"Likely."

"E-yah."

"Come far?"

"New Fane."

"Oh."

The young man looked everywhere except at Lem. The woman sat placidly patient. Fumbling with his reins, the man said, "Hard to find a place to stay, eh?"

"Depends."

"Eh?"

"Depends on what you want. There's the inn."

A headshake dismissed the inn.

"Most folks are camping out."

A slower, reluctant shake of the head.

"That's about all, mister."

"I sort of figured," the young man said, "that maybe we'd do better a distance from the meeting place." He cast a swift glance at Lem's barnyard. "Better to be under cover for the night, eh?"

"E-yah."

"Just anything. A shed. With a place for the horse. Only under cover, eh? I'd pay, of course!" The last sentence was clear and belligerent.

"Pay?" Lem licked his lips.

Zilpha nudged her husband. "The barn," she whispered.

Lem stared at his wife, then back at the wagon. Greed and suspicion struggled with each other in his face, clouding it as visibly as if someone walked in front of a light. When Zilpha nudged him again, Lem glared. His fingers opened and shut several times, but he didn't speak.

"You wouldn't know anything like that, eh?"

"No." The word seemed forced from Lem's lips.

The young man nodded, slapped his reins on the horse's back. The wagon lurched away. Only the children glanced back.

"Lem Brayton!" cried Zilpha. "Have you lost your senses? That man was ready to pay good money. He wouldn't hurt the barn any!"

"I didn't like his looks," Lem said, sullenly. He was already regretting his decision, and the regret made him defend it the more. "Something about him!"

"Why I never saw a nicer-looking young fellow!"

98

"E-yah. You noticed that, didn't you?"

Lem's tone stiffened Zilpha. Slowly anger mounted with her realization of her husband's reason for refusing shelter. For once she was speechless, inarticulate with fury. He would, she thought. He would think something like that. About a perfect stranger. The memory of Isaac Mead came into Zilpha's mind, and increased her anger at Lem. When she finally spoke, her voice was low, shaking with loathing.

"You!" Zilpha said.

"It ain't that," said Lem, lying and trying to mend things too late. "It ain't. It's just that the woman looked ready to calve any minute!"

His excuses only made Zilpha surer. In that moment she decided she would make Lem pay for his jealous distrust. She looked down and found that her hands were twisting the satin ribbon of the Whig badge. Contemptuously, she tossed it on the floor.

"Aw, Zilpha."

"You'd better go about your business."

"It was on account of the woman! You wouldn't want to have to be midwife, maybe miss Webster's speech!"

"Get out."

"Well." Lem took a step away, came back. He said, "The next party comes along—take them in. A—a nice married couple."

Zilpha's laugh was like a dropped knife.

Summer was the season for raising the crop; it would be harvested in the fall. The campaigners of both parties had it figured as simply as that. Throughout all twenty-six states of the Union, roads were dry, men could travel, and it was easy to assemble partisans. Heat and sunshine were assets, and the politicians watched the weather more anxiously than the farmers. During the hot July weeks those who controlled or sought to control votes were as busy as ants.

The sunshine brought the usual malarial shimmer from the swamps of the nation's capital, and the shrewd little person who was President of the United States mopped at his forehead and smiled. He had just signed the Subtreasury Bill and, practical politician though he was, he was impractical enough to think it would make a difference in the campaign. The news had not yet reached Tennessee where a battered old man baked his bones in the sun, wrote letters of praise for his latest patent medicine, and hated. His name was

Jackson, and he had no hate left for the Whig candidate. He was content to dismiss him as a mediocre general. Mediocre or not, General William Henry Harrison had thoroughly learned one Army dictum: to take orders and keep his mouth shut. He watched the sunlight dapple the Ohio, took orders, and kept his mouth shut.

The sun wasn't interested in any of these men, their opinions or beliefs, but went about its business of bringing summer to the land. Rays sank into the earth, warmed roots, helped growth. Plants sprang up in their proper seasons. Flowers, crops, berries, and rank weeds blossomed. On Stratton Mountain, where people were gathering to wait for Daniel Webster, the grass was high in the fields—high and sun-baked and ready for haying.

In the south mowing of the Chittenden farm the men of the family, good Whigs but farmers, were sharpening their scythes. Webster, Conventions, and Tippecanoe could wait; Eratus Chittenden intended to cut his hay.

The big meadow stirred with each passing breeze. The grass stood thick, stalk-clear, a sun-drenched expanse that mirrored the shadow of each passing cloud. The hubbub of the group in the clearing was out of sight and earshot. There was no sound in the meadow but the harsh friction of whetstones on steel.

Eratus Chittenden pocketed his stone, raised his scythe, and flexed his big arm muscles. He made one testing sweep; the curved blade swished through the air. Eratus grinned, set the butt of the polished ash handle on the ground, and looked at his sons.

"Come on!" The bellow frightened a bird nesting in the grass. "You're all slower than molasses! You could shave with that edge now, Charles!"

Charles licked his thumb, gingerly tried the cutting edge of the scythe, and nodded. He said, "Ready, Pa."

"Amos! Sharpen it, don't slap at it!"

"Yes, Pa. It's ready."

"Henry!"

Henry was nervous; he dropped his whetstone. This was the first time that he would take his place with his brothers, and father in the line of mowers. His jaws ached from his gritting determination that he would hold his own. Like the boy that held it, the scythe was new, untried. Eratus had presented it to him that morning, and Charles had sharpened it for him. The smooth, fresh hand pegs felt slippery under Henry's wet palms. He said, "I—I'm all ready, Pa."

"Good. Go first!"

"Me?" Henry's voice broke on the word. The squeak brought a blush to his face.

Eratus ignored the sound. "You!"

Amos turned away to hide a smile. Charles, face blank, gazed out across the field. Henry gulped and stepped forward.

"Right! Right!" Eratus waved the boy toward his position. "Then Amos. Then Charles. Then me. You set the pace, son. We'll take it from you. Remember it ain't no piddling handkerchief we're mowing. Take your time."

"E-yah." No subaltern ever accepted an order with more heartiness. Henry was almost fifteen, and today he was taking a man's spot, to do a man's work. He hurried to his place, took a practice swing curiously like his father's, watched the others spread out alongside.

Eratus glanced down the line. Charles grinned at him. Amos plucked a blade of grass, clamped it in his teeth. Eratus called, "Start!"

Henry raised his scythe, lowered it, raised it again, took a deep breath.

His father's big voice boomed across the meadow. "Today, Henry! Today!"

The boy's blade flashed in the sunlight, turned, swept down. He knew the stroke was ragged and bit his lip. He took a step; again the scythe passed through its arc. At the third stroke Henry thought he felt the smooth motion come into his arms, like a living thing that passed from the blade up the bent handle. The tenseness went out of him; he knew he could set the pace. His ears quivered, waiting for Eratus to speak behind him. There was no shout. Henry didn't dare turn. The grass swirled under his blade, fell away. He began to sweat and enjoy himself, swinging smoothly, letting the scythe do part of the work.

Amos allowed Henry to take four paces, then stepped out, watched his younger brother, and swung the scythe up. Both curves of shining steel swept down together.

"Pretty," murmured Charles, nodding to Eratus.

Eratus chuckled. He was watching Henry. "Boy's all right. E-yah. Smooth and easy like I told him."

101

Taking his beat from Amos, Charles flung one remark over his shoulder as he took his first cut. "Pace too fast for you, Pa?" He grinned at the sputter of rage behind him.

Three scythe blades, obliquely in line, rose and fell as one.

Squinting at his sons' three backs Eratus indulged in a moment of pride. Good boys, he thought, strong and know how to use their strength. He gave himself credit for teaching them that. Nothing pleased him so much as working with his sons, and in haying there was definite teamwork, drilled precision. Eratus came forward on the balls of his feet, brandishing his own scythe as if it were weightless. At the proper moment he moved with an ease surprising in so big a body. The sharp edge swished down, slipped through the grass as if it was water, and left it flat and tumbled in a wide swath.

The four Chittendens moved through the field like a four-bladed mowing machine. A single wake showed behind their line; each cut into the border left by the one ahead.

It was perfect unison mowing, and when Mary Chittenden rode the farm wagon to the edge of the field, the mowers were halfway across. She stood up and gazed at them. Except for size and the different colors of hats and shirts, the four figures looked as one. Steadily, smoothly, the oblique line flowed through the grass and made it fall. At the top of each upstroke the sunlight caught on bright steel, four sudden spots of reflection flashed together like diamonds and were gone an instant later as the scythes dropped.

Mary glanced at her husband. Lips parted, she watched Eratus mow, the big frame striding surely, the easy sweep of his arms. After all these years, she mocked herself, there is still a warm glow at the sight of his strength at work. She knew that a part of this was because Eratus was hers and that she, more than anyone else, saw beneath all the bluster and strength the underlying gentleness, humor, and kindness. The corners of Mary's eyes crinkled as she smiled at her husband's back. She breathed deeply, drinking in the sweet mixture of sunshine and fresh-cut grass.

Then she looked at Henry. The boy was youngest, smallest, and deepest into the field. Her menfolk made an occasion of the haying, and Mary realized that it was another strong thread by which her sons were woven into the family fabric. Henry's being one of the mowers was a step toward manhood, and Mary felt a lump rise in her throat. For a moment she gazed critically: the boy would hate to weaken or falter. She was a farmer's wife and she knew how a mower should work. Henry's path was close-cropped and even; the sweep of his scythe was smooth. Mary relaxed, smiling.

On the seat beside her Peter chuckled. He said, "Henry?"

Mary turned to her eldest son and nodded.

"He's all right. Look at him."

"E-yah. I was."

Peter frowned out across the field. He twisted the reins in his hands. "I wish Pa'd let me mow," he said. "Anybody can drive the team."

"It was time Henry took his place mowing."

"But he's younger. He drove last year."

"Last year. But your father wanted him to have his chance to-day. It means a lot to Henry," Mary said. "And this way Jennie gets more of a chance to see you." She glanced out into the meadow. The hayers had reached the upper end and were clustered in a group, talking. Mary waved and saw Eratus throw up an arm in reply. She could hear his hail, though the words were unintelligible.

"Black Dan Webster himself," Peter said, laughing softly, "is going to have to go some to beat Pa at hollering."

"When your Pa aims to say something, he says it." Mary's rebuke was gentle; she grinned. "And if Senator Webster don't speak up good and clear tomorrow, I'm afraid Pa will have something to say."

Peter frowned. "Ma. About that Convention. Jennie's a mite shy about going. Seeing all those folks passing up the road—bands and all—wagonloads—it sort of made her a mite queasy."

"They ain't coming to look at Jennie," Mary said. Then, because she was truly fond of her daughter-in-law, she softened the remark. "Not that I blame her much. I never did see such a crowd. But she needn't worry. We'll all take good care she don't get jostled or anything."

"It ain't that."

"I know." Mary laid two fingers on her son's hand. "I felt that way with my first, too. You, Peter. Like everybody was just bound to notice. But they don't. Leastways not till you're a lot farther along than Jennie is. Goodness, she don't hardly show at all."

"I'd hate her to miss it."

103

Mary said, "She ain't going to miss it. Nothing like it's ever happened on this mountain before, and us being the nearest farm to the clearing it's practically on our doorstep. Miss it, indeed! She'll never get another chance like this one."

"E-yah. That's what I told her."

"Going to that meeting will do Jennie good. Take her out of herself. Don't worry."

"Well," Peter, hesitating, looked away. "If you're sure it—it won't hurt the baby or anything. You know—mark him? Or anything?" He looked at his mother suddenly, bewildered and anxious.

"Fiddlesticks!" said Mary gently. "Old wives' tales. Take my word for it, Peter." She lifted her chin and laughed. It was a gay, light sound. "If that child of yours turns out a great talker it won't be on account of Mr. Webster. You can blame that on your father!"

Peter laughed with his mother. There was relief and gratitude in his glance. He said, suddenly older, "I didn't really take much stock in that, of course."

"Of course you didn't," said Mary, thinking how like Eratus all the children were. She recalled her husband's same worry before the son beside her was born. A bolting bull had frightened but not harmed her. Mary remembered how she had laughed Eratus into ease, while fear knotted within her that their child would bear some sign of the beast. She smiled. After you'd borne a couple or three you learned only to worry about the real things. She turned and gazed at the mowers.

They had spread out again and were working back toward the wagon. Now Charles was in the lead at the front of the line, and Henry was next to his father. Mary nodded. Trust Eratus, she thought, to put the boy where he would be easy to watch.

Bodies half-hidden by the waist-high grass, the four approached her. The quartet of scythes flashed up and down, up and down. From the wagon Mary couldn't see any effect of the cutting, but the line came steadily closer. Once she had seen a militia company at a muster advance through grass like that, bayonets gleaming, but the soldiers had held rifles stiffly across their bodies. The hayers were in constant motion.

"E-yah," said Peter, intent on his own thoughts. "That meeting sure has made a change around here."

"Change!" Mary said and shrugged. She gazed around the meadow. It was hemmed in by the forest on all four sides, and she

104

thought it looked much as it did in all the past haying seasons she had known. Henry was in line today instead of Peter, but that was the only major change. Her husband and sons were cutting hay to feed the stock. The sun was warm through the cloth of her dress, and the sky was clear, flecked with thick white clouds. To the east the moon, new and early risen, hung like a curl of ash from some forgotten fire. Mary smiled, secure and happy.

"E-yah," she agreed. "Perhaps." There would be a kind of change, she reflected—a nice one. Having visitors and Webster and a meeting bigger than any roof raising you could think of. But they'd all go off and things would settle back like they always did. Of course they were holding the Convention in the hope they could change some things, like who was going to be the next President. But Mary, without letting on to Eratus, had never noticed that it really made much difference who was. Only the changes inside the family were important—what wives her sons brought home, how the girls grew to be women. More money or less, good year or bad, Democrat President or Whig, there would be hay to cut in this field next summer, and Charles, for example, without losing a stroke, would flick the sweat from his face with that funny toss of his head as he did now.

As long as there's no sickness, Mary prayed, with sudden fright. It never paid to count your blessings into the future, and she forced her mind away from it. Then she chuckled as again Charles jerked his head, his hat bobbing. She wondered where he'd picked up that habit.

Charles, a bit drugged from sunshine and the monotony of his own motion, was not aware that he tossed his head. He knew he was hot; that was to be expected haying under the sun. Dimly he was conscious of the fact that his shirt clung between his shoulder blades and that he seemed to radiate heat. He watched the grass in front of him, and the blade of his scythe cut true and even. As far as he knew he ignored the perspiration pouring down his face. Happy in the certainty of his stroke, he didn't even concentrate on his task.

Back, shoulders, and arms moved as they should. Muscles performed easily each time they were required. His feet set themselves properly without seeming guidance. Charles rolled mechanically with each swing; the scythe swished through its arc again and

105

again, again and again. The grass toppled over by the square yard. It was perfect mowing, coordinated, smooth; like all endlessly repetitive exercise it had a certain soporific quality. Charles, in the large section of his brain not needed to control his body, was dreaming of Lovina Chester.

He was not stupid, and he knew that Lovina was angry with him. For the hundredth time he reviewed the evening they had driven out to the clearing, and each time Charles thought of several things he might have said. Now he rehearsed again the speeches that would make everything all right. First, with dignity, he would ask for the pleasure of escorting her to the Convention tomorrow. Charles frowned. Lovina might refuse. The few times they had met recently she'd been a different girl, treated him like a stranger. Sighing, he decided that women were unpredictable. All he asked was a chance to speak to her alone, and it was pleasanter to imagine that this was possible.

He listed the arguments that Lovina would be unable to resist. Item—he loved her. Item—he had no right to make such a declaration at this time. Item—his intentions, though of the most honorable, must not yet be mentioned. Item—his future prospects were negligible. Item—could he, dare he, ask her to wait for him until some indefinite, not-too-close date? Item—she, Lovina Chester, was the most wonderful of all the females he had ever heard about, read about, or seen.

Charles snorted. He doubted that he could say any of these things to Lovina's face without feeling like a fool. Even if he could they didn't sound so irresistible once he considered them. He was sure that Nathan Patch could think of much better things to say. Charles glared. Nathan Patch needn't wait to get married. Nathan Patch's father owned a sawmill. Nathan Patch!

With an angry hiss the scythe cut down some five hundred Nathan Patchs, all as alike as blades of grass, that stood in front of Charles.

"Charles!" Eratus roared.

Henry, panting, said, "Charles!"

"Charles!" repeated Amos.

In mid-stroke Charles stopped and turned. He stared, surprised. The other had fallen behind. He was a good nine paces ahead of Amos.

"What in blazes are you trying to do?" cried Eratus, shaking his scythe. "Kill yourself? Nobody could keep up that pace! What in thunder is the all-fired hurry?"

Charles looked past Amos's grinning face and saw that Henry was breathing hard. Contrite, he called, "Sorry, Pa." He straightened and waited.

"Sorry!" Eratus chopped the grass out of his path with quick, savage strokes. "If it's a race you want, I'll match you—stroke for stroke—my pace—for the whole rest of the field! We'll see who cries quits first!"

Recognizing that his father was really angry, Charles calmly wiped his blade and drew out his whetstone. He spoke to the cause of the anger. "It wasn't done on purpose, Henry. Must have lost my edge without noticing."

"I'm all right," Henry said, quickly.

Over the boy's head Eratus accepted the apology by stoning his own scythe. "Ought to watch that, Charles," he said. "Thought you had better sense. E-yah. A dull scythe doubles the work. How's yours, Henry?"

Henry held out the curved blade.

Eratus squinted at it and nodded. "Fine! Fine, son! Just right!" Ignoring the boy's flush of pleasure he fussed over the sharpening until Henry stopped puffing. He nodded toward the edge of the field. "Your mother's waiting for us with the water jug. Ready now, Charles?"

"E-yah!"

"Start!"

They resumed in the same formation. Three dozen strokes carried them to the border of the field, and they finished as smoothly as if there had been no interruption. Mary was pouring spring water from the stone jug before Eratus dropped his scythe.

The father drank first, the others waited. Eratus rinsed his mouth, spat, swallowed a mouthful, and handed the dipper to Charles. "And don't rush that," he said. "Or you'll come down with colic!"

Charles hid his grin behind the dipper.

"Spell anybody?" asked Peter.

Henry gripped his scythe tighter. Eratus snorted. "None of us need spelling. We ain't hardly begun to sweat!"

107

"Eratus." Mary drew her husband aside. "What happened out there? Why'd you all yell at Charles?"

"Didn't you see him? He kept getting faster and faster." Eratus's idea of lowering his voice was to pitch it so it could be heard only ten feet away. "Dreaming about his girl, I guess." A hoot of laughter from the brothers brought their father's head around. Charles, grinning sheepishly, had a scarlet face. Eratus said, "I'm talking to your mother!"

"Yes, dear," said Mary. "But they can probably hear you up at the meeting."

"Let them!" Eratus scowled down at his wife. "Get them used to tomorrow's whirligig. There's going to be some high and mighty spellbinding at that meeting. From Webster down! A lot of nonsense!"

"You're not going?"

"Going? Of course I'm going! You know blame well . . ." He spotted the twinkle in Mary's eye and stopped. He raised a huge hand, and she ducked in mock terror. Eratus said, "Getting right sassy, ain't you, ma'am? Remind me to take you down a peg. E-yah. Maybe this is the proper time."

"Eratus! The boys!"

The big man laughed and stretched. "I'll save the lesson till later. But only because I've got haying to do." He was turning away when his wife stopped him.

"We haven't settled yet about where folks'll sleep."

"Folks?"

"The Kidders! Our guests! Eratus, you invited William Kidder to stay with us when they came to the Convention! Don't tell me you've forgotten?"

"Course I haven't. Will Kidder's one of the Manchester delegation. Naturally he'll stay with us. We've been friends since we were no higher than toadstools. Plenty of room, Mary."

"He's bringing his family."

"E-yah. I never have seen the youngest girl!"

"Eratus! Will you listen a minute? We have to decide where they'll sleep!"

"In bed, Mary." Eratus was very solemn. "In bed. Will's civilized, and I expect he's brought his children up the same way."

Mary reached up and grabbed her husband's shoulders. She tried to shake him. Her arms vibrated, and she jumped completely off the ground. Eratus, grinning, stood as immovable as rock. Mary gave up, laughing. "Seriously, Eratus. There's six of them. Will and Hester, two boys, and two girls."

"E-yah." Eratus glanced at his sons, winked at his wife. "Will never could get ahead of me in nothing. Except maybe pitching horseshoes."

Mary said, "That will do. We can't move Peter and Jennie. But if we put the Kidder boys in with our boys that room'll be awfully crowded."

"Won't hurt any of them for a few nights."

"Maybe not. But if I move Nancy in with Miley and put the two Kidder girls in with them, that leaves only Nancy's room for Will and his wife."

"E-yah," agreed Eratus. "That figures out right, don't it?"

"Eratus Chittenden! They're our guests, and that's an awful small room!" Mary bent her head, glanced up at Eratus and away. "They really ought to have the best room. Coming all that way and everything."

"The best room? You mean ours?"

"You don't have to shout."

"Well, of all the hare-brained, blame-fool notions . . ."

"You don't have to swear, either."

"Who's swearing?" The blasting voice thundered. "We ain't giving up our room to nobody! Not if Dan Webster himself didn't have a spot to set his bottom on! Not if Tippecanoe was bedless! And Tyler, too! Not for the whole blasted Whig shebang! No!"

"But, Eratus . . ."

"Put them anywhere you like, Mary! Anywhere else, I mean. Move the youngsters around every which way if you want. But you and me are sleeping in our own bed, same as we always did! I ain't an unhospitable man, but I draw the line at some things!"

He strode back to his sons and yanked his scythe from the ground. Glowering, he continued, "I'm a Whig, and I'm all in favor of that Convention! In spite of the balderdash and high jinks it's in a good cause. Any cause that'll help lick that Dutch fathead in the White House is a good cause! I'm glad they're holding it here on Stratton—it's nice and handy! But I ain't aiming to lose one wink of sleep on account of that meeting! And it ain't going to put me out or upset my life . . ." He paused, hunted for a word, then snapped his fingers with a report like a pistol. "Not that much, Mary!"

"All right, Eratus," said Mary. "All right." If I didn't laugh so hard at his tantrums, she thought, maybe I'd get my way more often. She wondered if Eratus was aware of that.

With the hand that held the scythe's long, bent handle Eratus waved his sons toward the field. "Well!" he yelled. "You aiming to loaf here all day, talking? The grass is still standing, ain't it? It won't mow itself!"

> Twenty white horses,
> On a red hill.
> Now they run, now they run,
> Now they stand still.

The proprietor of the Wardsboro livery stable looked uneasily at the singer. "Now, Lot," he said. "Now, Lot." The stableman's voice held apprehension.

Lot Purdy took another swallow from a flask. His gloved palm almost covered the flat, green-glass bottle. The only visible effect of the liquor was that Lot squinted, and his tanned face was even darker than usual. He recorked the flask with careful, competent movements, tapping the cork into place with the heel of his hand. He said, "Only it ain't twenty white horses, Sem. It's six. Six white horses."

"E-yah. Fine-looking team, Lot."

"And it ain't a red hill, either," Lot continued, as if the other hadn't spoken. "It's a green mountain named Stratton. But the last line's true as gospel. 'Now they stand still.' Question is, will they stay that way?" Lot leaned against the jamb of the wide stable door and stared moodily at the ground.

"You ain't going to do it?" asked Sem.

"Not if I can help it!" Lot cursed, a long sentence of selected words, efficiently voiced. But his tone lacked conviction.

Sem said, "Now, Lot."

"I'm a stage driver, Sem. They got no right to put me up on the box of an outlandish contraption like that. A log cabin on wheels! God Almighty!" He bit the cork from the flask and took another swig. "Sem?"

110

"Don't mind if I do." Sem accepted the offered bottle, wiped its mouth, and drank. He coughed and looked around nervously.

"'Lot,' he says, 'you're the best driver we've got.'" Lot used a polite, unctuous tone when quoting his employer. "'We're counting on you to handle them six horses. Lot,' he says, 'I'd take it as a personal favor.'"

Sem grinned his appreciation of the imitation. "What'd you say?"

"That it wasn't my regular run." Lot snorted. "'It may be a trifle irregular,' he says. 'But there's nothing wrong with the money the Whigs have put up to charter the outfit. We're in business, Lot,' he says. And he sits there smirking at me, with those little pig eyes of his like two chips of marble. 'Of course,' he says, 'I wouldn't ask any man to go against his principles, but with us the company should come first.'"

Sem nodded and made a clicking noise with his tongue.

"E-yah," agreed Lot. "I know what it means, too. Drive it or quit. He didn't fool me a mite with his buttering. The blasted Whig son of a weasel!"

"Now, Lot," said Sem. "He's always treated us fair."

"You talk for yourself, Sem Briggs. Paying wages cause he has to ain't being so blame fair! You've seen some of the spavined nags he's tried to get another week's work out of! E-yah. He's put those cobs in a man's shafts and then raised a rumpus if the stage was a couple of hours late! Fair, my foot!"

"But there's a bonus for driving the cabin."

Lot stiffened. He moved toward Sem so menacingly that the other took a backward step. "E-yah! A bonus! He mentioned that! I'm supposed to forget everything I think and turn Whig for a price. And it ain't even thirty pieces of silver! It's a measly three dollars."

"Three dollars," Sem said, "ain't measly."

"I live up there, Sem! Everybody knows my political color! How am I going to look—a Democrat—driving that blasted log cabin? Like a turncoat, that's how I'm going to look!" Lot emptied his flask, raised his arm to hurl it against the wall, remembered the horses, and placed it on the ground. He said, "You know Tate Jones?"

"The trapper? Up on Stratton?"

"E-yah."

111

"Heard of him."

"Tate's my best friend. And he's got the right idea. He don't work for nobody! Just hunts and traps and fishes. Makes out real well, Tate does! Doing what he pleases and not having to answer to anybody." Lot sat down on a keg and put his head in his hands. "Tate's smart."

The stableman said, "Was that your last bottle?"

"Only thing," Lot said, going on, "he don't believe in nothing. He ain't a Democrat and he ain't a Whig. He don't even go to church. God Almighty! A man's got to believe in something. He ain't got a horse, either."

"Speaking of horses, Lot. You ain't seen that white team."

"I don't want to see them!"

"Pretty."

Lot raised his head. "You got them here, ain't you?"

"E-yah. Come on. It won't hurt nothing to take a look."

They walked along the line of stalls. There were a dozen horses in the stable. One white mare whinnied a welcome.

"Left lead," said Sem.

"E-yah." Lot stroked the mare's flank. He examined all six white horses carefully. He looked at Sem and swore. "The best animals I've seen in months, and he puts them dragging a cockeyed do-hinkus!"

"They ain't his, Lot. Borrowed. Belong to some rich feller."

"Another Whig. If they was my team you wouldn't catch nobody else driving them."

"Well," Sem shrugged and spat. "I'd say they was too much for the feller. Not everybody can handle six."

Lot's laugh was derisive. "Just like the Whigs. Want to run the country, and they can't even drive a six-horse team!" He shoved his face close to Sem's. "Takes a Democrat to handle six horses! They won't even get their log cabin up there without a Democrat driving!"

"That's right, Lot."

"E-yah."

Sem scuffed one foot in the dust. He watched the stage driver. Lot was staring straight ahead. Sem said, "You seen the cabin on wheels? It's out back."

"Let it rot there!"

"It's made real smart, Lot. Won't do no harm to look, will it?"
The stableman led the way.

Behind the stable was a four-wheel turnout with a small-scale
log cabin built upon it. It was complete, logs notched, roof shingled,
openings cut for windows and door. Someone had even tacked a
squirrel skin to one wall.

Lot Purdy stared at the stretched hide and swore. "Skinned!"
he said. "Skinned and pegged!"

"Lot. It ain't my business. But there's times when it's a mite
foolish to fight the bit. Maybe you ought to consider." Sem
shrugged. "Your making a fuss ain't going to keep folks from that
Convention. There must've been twenty wagons come through here
today."

"And for what?" Lot's query was almost a snarl. "What's fetching them? 'Twenty white horses on a red hill.' They all want to
see Webster's teeth galloping on his lying red tongue!"

Sem looked around like a man in a hostile alley. He said, "Nobody's asking you to vote Whig, Lot. Driving's your job."

"E-yah. And if I don't drive?" Lot scowled. With a sudden swing
he slammed his left fist against the wheeled cabin. "Blame fool
outfit! I'll drive you all right! But it ain't that I'm scairt of losing
money! It ain't that stage driving's not easy to get! It's just that
all this tomfool junketing ain't important! Ain't worth a tinker's
dam!"

"'Course it ain't, Lot."

"The hell it ain't," said Lot, with sudden, weary defeat. "The
hell it ain't, Sem."

All afternoon the wagons had been arriving in the clearing.
Some came behind one horse, some behind two; there were even a
couple of teams of slow-moving oxen. Every type of vehicle was
represented: chaise, dray, cart.

The arrival of these early comers was spasmodic. Sometimes a
single carriage would lurch into the clearing and disembark its
passengers almost unnoticed. Sometimes a whole group would
arrive together—neighbors who had journeyed as a unit for mutual
protection and who mingled with the throng more noisily. Another
band, with train of followers, climbed the road from Somerset.
This group of musicians didn't march. They rode a hay wagon

113

the entire distance and played lustily as they drew up in the clearing. By sunset one side of the clearing was bordered with an impromptu village larger than many in the state—a village that had three or four hundred inhabitants.

The setting sun, a red ball balancing on the rim of the Taconics, tinted the canvas of the many tents and turned them into pink pavilions. Its rays softened the etched foliage of the tamarack tree, subdued the bright green, sent the tree's long shadow across the upper part of the clearing. The tamarack, stretching high above men and beasts, was the last thing to be touched by the light.

Most of the men and as many women admired the sun's flame-red color. The admiration was not so much for its hue as for its promise of fair weather.

> The evening red, the morning gray,
> Sets the traveler on his way.

For a few hours the proverb was even more popular than the oft-shouted slogan, "Tippecanoe and Tyler too." Every person in the clearing felt that he or she had a stake in the success of the morrow's meeting. They were there, encamped. If it rained now there would be no staying home for them.

The crowd was never still. Each newcomer hastened to pay his respects to the log cabin. Several groups inquired about the covered mound of cider kegs and were rebuffed by the taciturn man with the rifle. Women swapped work and gossip. News was a coin of value and exchanged only for another of equal weight. They discussed politics and hard times and Daniel Webster, of course, but saved their choicest arguments for the next day. Mostly the talk was of crops and breeding, of marriages, cooking, childbirth, and deaths.

When orange splashes of flame began to leap up from several campfires, Put Chester and Seth Purdy remembered they had homes. The visitors bustled about preparing their evening meal; the tang of wood smoke mingled with the smell of cooking food. The two boys reluctantly left the clearing. They cut through the woods, not bothering with the road. That was why they didn't see the red wagon arrive.

It was a high wagon, roofed, and it swayed dangerously as the dun-colored horse pulled it up the bank into the clearing. The

114

wagon looked like a candy box on wheels. It was painted red, the same dusky shade as the country's barns, and trimmed in bright yellow. The trim framed each side of the body with scrollwork and curlicues as elaborate as those on a gilt picture frame. Inside the two fancy rectangles were words, printed in tall, bold letters.

MERRIFIELD'S
EPIZOOTICAL
ELIXIR

Below, much smaller but plainly readable, were two single lines of script.

Dr. Portus J. Merrifield, A.B., D.P., M.H., Founder.

There was a pair of figures on the wagon's seat: a man, driving, and a young girl. The man was portly; his torso made up in breadth for what it lacked in height. His face was broad, too, round and perpetually flushed. He wore square spectacles, halfway down a long nose, and his eyes twinkled and seemed to dart above and below their upper rims. His clothes were a trifle old, both in fashion and physical age. The black swallow-tailed coat was frayed in spots; the tall beaver hat had lost some of its nap. But the white stock at his throat was spotless, and the heavy links of the watch chain were bright across the maroon waistcoat. Oddly enough his feet, planted firmly against the dashboard, were tiny, and the small fingers that held the reins were as fat and dimpled as a baby's.

Standing up, the man reined in the horse. He removed his hat with a flourish and bowed. He said in a clear, soft voice, "Friends, Whigs, and countrymen! Good evening! A most salubrious day!"

The bystanders gaped. A woman tittered nervously; another said, "Well!" Several men read the writing on the wagon's sides aloud. One voice staggered questioningly over syllables.

"Eppy—zoo—tick—al?"

Smiling, the man on the wagon smoothed his hair. It was slate gray and reached to his shoulders. "Allow me," he said, with another bow. "Dr. Portus J. Merrifield. A man of science and a true Whig. At your service."

The girl beside him stirred. Her speech reached only his ears. "Now, Doc? The spiel?"

"No, Mercy." Doc Merrifield, blandly facing the crowd, let the words fall from a corner of his mouth. "The time ain't ripe. Never skim the milk till the pail is full." He raised his melodious voice. "If some kind soul would show us where we may encamp. Some spot that will not inconvenience others." Scanning the whole clearing over the heads of the onlookers, Doc selected his site. He picked it for much the same reason that a general chooses a battleground. It was not too close to any possible enemy; the forest protected it in the rear; in case of hasty retreat the way was straight and open to the turnpike.

Doc Merrifield clicked his tongue, and the dun horse started forward. The spectators parted. As the horse walked through the crowd its driver chattered, aiming his sentences at individuals.

"Stand away from the horse's head, son, please. Duke's a mite fractious. You, sir. You inquired about a word on my sign. Epizootical. Means affecting many animals. Exactly what my Elixir does. Good for sheep, horses, cows, and the human animal. Man or beast. But forgive me. I come here not to ply the marts of trade—if such a term can be used about a medicinal extract that benefits mankind—but to add my small support to the noble Whig cause. You, young man, should feel proud to cast your youthful vote for Tippecanoe and Tyler too. Is that charming lady your wife? No need to blush, my dear. My compliments. Ma'am, that's a fine, handsome baby you have there. Take good care of his health. An ounce of prevention, you know. Would anyone mind if we stopped here? Well, that's a splendid Morgan over there. Yours, sir? You're an excellent judge of horseflesh. Whoa, Duke! Whoa! I thank you one and all for directing me."

Since not a single direction had managed to penetrate the round man's patter, the red wagon halted where its driver wanted it. In a few moments Duke was unhitched and tethered. Doc Merrifield stretched a strip of canvas from the wagon's roof to a pole and under it set a battered iron box, its front side open, a grid for its top. Shavings and kindling were already laid on the floor of this rude stove.

The crowd marveled at the fat man's dexterity. Without seeming to move fast he set up camp with the easy speed of long practice. Whenever he turned to the girl in the wagon she was ready to hand him down another object.

Two light chairs were whisked into place under the canvas, one a rocker. A kettle and an iron spider went onto the grid. The dropped back of the wagon was propped up to make an efficient table; it even had a red cloth tacked to its inner side.

"If that don't beat all," said a bystander.

"E-yah."

"All the comforts, ain't you, Doctor?"

"That's the way to travel, Jeremiah."

"Regular home on wheels, ain't it?"

"That's smart, that is."

"E-yah," Doc Merrifield said. His use of the word was an excellent imitation, though it lacked the precise tone of the natives. "Practice. Just practice. I travel a lot. Being sort of a missionary. Carrying balm and easement far and wide."

"This here Elixir now. . . ."

"Just what is it, Doctor?"

"Thank you for your interest, ma'am," Doc said. "But this is no time for a long, scientific discourse. The Elixir is a discovery of my own after years of study. A panacea for humanity. But let us not sully this beauteous sunset with talk of sickness, disease, and the curing thereof. I'm afraid I keep you from your suppers. And my own must be prepared."

"You ain't selling this medicine?"

"Not here. Not now. Daniel Webster and the cause of our oppressed country drew me to this hallowed spot. 'Sic semper tyrannis!' Or, down with the Dutchman!"

The crowd dispersed slowly. A few watched while the doctor lighted his fire, and sliced strips off a side of bacon. When the last straggler strolled away, Doc Merrifield looked up at the girl on the wagon seat and grinned.

The girl stretched. Her laughter was a cool ripple, like water running over rocks. She said, "You old scoundrel!"

"You're referring to me, Mercy?"

"E-yah. You."

"E-yah. Me."

Both seemed to find the two-syllable affirmative amusing. They laughed together. Doc Merrifield helped the girl down from the wagon. Mercy was small and slight, with a pale face, jet-black hair, and big, startlingly blue eyes. Her dress was lavender with white

117

collar and cuffs. She wore her hair drawn back into a big knot. Dress and hair stressed her pallor. But there was nothing languid about the way she moved, and when she winked at the doctor her wan, serious expression suddenly changed to one of gamin glee. On the wagon seat she had looked twenty; grinning, she looked ten. Actually, Mercy was fourteen years old.

Doc Merrifield mopped his face and gazed at the sunset. The red disk had dipped behind the western range, and one of the peaks, a jagged silhouette, gave the appearance of a roughly cut slab in a pie. Doc said, "Weather should hold. With that crowd tomorrow we ought to sell every blasted bottle of Elixir we've got."

"How much a bottle this time, Doc?"

"Two bits."

"Doc!"

"Why not, Mercy?" Doc grinned. "That'll be a spending crowd. You saw those Reubens just now. They were nibbling like trout. And, you know, when they get just a mite more curious, I might sell them some Elixir."

"But, two bits . . ."

"Shucks, Mercy. The Whigs is out to bring good times back. Penny pinching is all Van Buren's fault. Hell, we got Dan Webster himself spellbinding for us. We can't lose if we play our cards right."

"If *we* play cards, Doc," Mercy said, "we're liable to lose. It's happened before." The smile she gave him was very wise and knowing.

Doc shrugged. "Don't worry, my dear. This time I will select my companions very judiciously. But we'd better eat. There'll be work to do later."

"All right." Mercy squatted before the fire. The reflected flames gave color to her face. Frying bacon, she spoke over her shoulder. "We go on with the rejuvenated invalid act, Doc?"

Doc Merrifield considered, rubbing his chin. He shook his head and said, "I don't think so, Mercy. You can rub that white stuff off your cheeks. These folks ain't got much interest in poorly young ladies with the vapors."

Busily cooking their supper, Mercy paused and laughed at him. "Who's a young lady?"

The fat man squeezed himself into the rocking chair and laid

118

his hat on the grass before he spoke. "You are," he said. "Or getting there." Doc's round face was grave. "I took up with a little girl. Never figured on her growing up on me. Time I started."

"Fiddlesticks!" Mercy said. She turned back to the stove.

Sitting there, watching the girl's movements in the fire's glow, Doc Merrifield remembered the eight years they'd been together. Now, in the blue-gray pause between sunset and darkness, it was easy to recall the snowy, bitter-cold night when he had first stumbled across Mercy. He, Portus Merrifield, ex-scholar, ex-Thespian, ex-gambler, ex-doctor's assistant, ex-musician in a bawdy house, had been drunk. He had been weaving his way through the crooked maze of New York's Five Points, cursing the snow and the biting wind.

As he staggered around a corner, he had almost tripped over Mercy. The child was blue with cold, a ragged waif, all eyes. She stood in the snow singing for pennies, singing in a high, quavering treble. Doc Merrifield frowned at the memory of the song's lyric; it had been hair-raising even in Five Points.

The song and the shivering child had shocked Portus Merrifield sober. With his last few dollars he had bribed the old crone who employed the girl, and he had left Five Points with Mercy in his arms. She was homeless and nameless, pitifully thin, and raging with fever. Fearful because of past beatings, she cried out at any sudden movement. The word she cried was "Mercy." That was what he called her.

Remembering, Doc Merrifield felt again the white, impotent rage against anyone who could so abuse a child. They had spent the rest of the winter in a waterfront garret, living on his winnings at cards. The following spring they had taken to the road, the fat man driving second wagon for a peddler. In midsummer, the peddler had lost his second wagon to its driver across a card table.

The Epizootical Elixir followed. It was an easy concoction to make; even Mercy found it simple. The main source of supply was any running stream; added to the water were a few harmless herbs, a pinch of drugs, syrup, and coloring. Bottles proved the greatest expense, but Portus Merrifield had a great talent for talking strangers into extending credit.

Following birds and sunshine, fairs and races, any event that attracted a crowd, the red wagon had journeyed the roads from Maine to the Carolinas. Beside it now, rocking in his chair, Doc Merrifield glanced at the list of self-bestowed degrees: Dr. Portus J. Merrifield, Bachelor of Arts, Doctor of Physic, Master of Herbiology. Impressive, he thought, and high-toned—something of an achievement for a boy who'd run off from a Latin grammar school because he wouldn't be birched.

Watching Mercy break eggs into a skillet, Doc Merrifield frowned. He blamed himself for Mercy's lack of education. The girl could sign her name and read the large print in a primer, but that was all. He had intended, time and again, to teach her more, but something had always interfered. There was a sheriff to dodge, or a near-by card game, or they must reach a distant gathering like this Whig convention. They were on the move so blasted much. In the wagon were books: Shakespeare, several of Scott's novels, Dryden's translation of Plutarch, *The Home Physician*, Thomson's *Quackery Exposed*. Mercy knew them as well as he did himself. But that was because she liked to have him read aloud. He enjoyed it, too; it kept his voice well tuned.

Doc Merrifield sighed. In a year or two Mercy would be a grown woman, a young lady. And she couldn't read or write or cipher, though she knew the value of every coin or shinplaster that passed through her hands. She's smart as a whip, Doc reflected, but the things she's learned ain't schoolroom learning. Mercy sang in a true, clear soprano, gayly or sadly depending on the taste of her audience. She could play almost any instrument one gave her. She was skilled in a hundred shady ways to beguile a crowd into buying Merrifield's Epizootical Elixir. A hell of a fine upbringing, Doc groaned silently, for a young lady.

"Supper, Doc," said Mercy and put the plates on the table.

They ate in silence. After Doc wiped his plate clean, he took out a battered cheroot. Mercy brought him a flaming splinter from the fire. When the tobacco was glowing properly Doc spoke.

"Mercy."

"Yes, Doc?"

"I've been thinking." Doc exhaled a cloud of smoke.

Mercy waited. She knew he was worried, and she guessed at the cause. She could nearly always tell when something bothered

120

Doc. He puts on a great show, Mercy thought, and folks get taken in by it, but he's never fooled me yet.

Around them was the clatter of the camp. Voices called; a woman nagged at her children in a grating whine. Noise was constant, never ceasing. The clearing was high enough so that there was still daylight; against the sunless twilight the campfires looked garish, too vivid. From where Mercy sat she could see a wisp of moon that seemed to be tangled in the top branches of the tamarack tree near the speaker's platform. In a sky whose blue was slowly fading the first star blinked tentatively.

"I've been thinking," repeated Doc. "Why should we suffer the slings and arrows of outrageous fortune, when we don't have to? Suppose, here, when the hurly-burly's done, victory sits upon our helm?"

"You mean if we make a killing?" Mercy bit her lip to keep from laughing. It was funny how Doc always fell back on Shakespeare when he had trouble explaining something.

"Precisely. If we make a killing—and we should, we should—let's cash in our chips and pull out of the game. I'm not getting younger, Mercy. I'd like to spend my declining years sitting still instead of flitting about like a gadfly."

This time Mercy let herself smile. She was older than her years, and she knew every variation of Doc's voice. She had heard that sad, pitiful note before. It was exactly the way he spoke when he was trying to trade a horse for a better one. She said, "You're tired of the road?"

"Aye." Doc put a hand to his head. "This bickering. This creeping at Duke's petty pace from day to day. Speaking speeches trippingly. A disguised cheater. A prating mountebank. And for what?" Carried away by his own eloquence Doc slapped the arm of his chair. "For what?"

"For Hecuba," said Mercy.

" 'What's Hecuba to him, or he to . . .' " Doc choked off the quotation and coughed. He gazed at Mercy sternly over his spectacles. Then slowly a grin spread over his face. The girl's laughter joined his guffaw. Still chuckling, Doc said, "I was going to say to sell bottles of slops to a pack of dim wits."

As if it wasn't meat and drink to him, Mercy thought. He loves being actor, doctor, and gambler all rolled into one. "Doc," she

121

said, "even if we sell every bottle we have we won't have any fortune."

"There's ways of adding to it. Money makes money."

"How?"

"Well—investments!"

"Investments? Such as—which is the best horse in a race?" Mercy sighed. She determined to be more careful in the future. Somehow Doc had got an inkling that she dreamed of staying in the same place for more than a week. Selling Elixir had been a great romp when she was younger; now she was aware that the men who watched her perform looked at her in a different way.

Doc put his hand over hers. "Mercy. This is no life for a young lady."

"You're aging me mighty fast, Doctor Merrifield. Almost as fast as you age that Elixir of yours. And you're counting your chickens a mite early, too. We ain't sold a single bottle yet."

"We will," Doc said. "We will."

From the corner of the wagon a voice said, "Evening, Doc."

It was darker now, and the speaker's face was shadowed. But there was recognition in the way Doc and Mercy exchanged glances. "That would be George Stiles," Doc said.

"Correct!" The man came forward. He was of medium height and wore the plain, neat clothes of a respectable farmer. Stiles had a face that sloped back from chin to forehead as if it had been squashed by a shovel. It gave him a vulpine look. "Evening, Miss Mercy."

"Hello, George." Mercy moved away, removing the dishes. She didn't like George Stiles.

"Ill met by moonlight," said Doc.

"What's that again, Doc?"

"What wind blew you in?"

"Same as fetched you," Stiles said. He rubbed his thumb against his forefinger. "I saw you drive up. Had some business so I couldn't get over to pay my respects. Too bad." Stiles sighed. "You had a nice-sized crowd around."

"Stay out of my crowds, George."

"Aw, Doc."

"No purse lifting around us!"

"We mean it." Mercy sounded cold. "You've caused enough trouble."

"But, Miss Mercy, I ain't even seen you and Doc since last summer."

Doc said, "We remember. Albany. And we can't show our faces there on account of you. They thought we were in cahoots. We had to run for it." Doc pointed his cheroot at the pickpocket. "Stay out of my crowds, George, or you'll wish you had."

"Whatever you say, Doc."

"And pass the word along," Doc said. "I doubt not that others of the fraternity are in attendance also. Crimpy, perhaps? Joe Matson? The Gypsy?"

"Joe ain't here. He got nabbed in Portsmouth."

"A pity." Doc Merrifield shrugged. "But I'm sure there are others who will take his place."

"There's a couple here I never seen on the road before."

"The buzzards gather. The vultures flock." Doc frowned; he spoke seriously. "Let them shun my wagon like the plague. It's a big clearing. There will be room for them to conduct their chicanery elsewhere. And you might mention that any precipitation will spoil business of us all."

"Precipitation, Doc?"

"Yes, George. Never stir up the bees till they've made all their honey. In short—wait till tomorrow when the real crowd comes. I suppose friend Crimpy is equipped with his usual walnut shells?"

"Correct."

"Crimpy is a fool," said Doc without venom. "That particular manipulation is getting hoary. These folks are coming from all over. Some of them are bound to've seen a shell game before. And Vermonters are hell-bent when they're riled. Still, that is Crimpy's affair. As long as he stays out of my sight."

"Luke Brooks is down to the inn, Doc. There'll be a game."

"So?" Doc avoided looking at Mercy; he tossed his cigar aside. "Luke's a gentleman. He deals an honest hand and wins on superior skill."

"I just thought you'd like to know." Stiles moved away. "Evening, Miss Mercy. Rich pickings, Doc!"

Doc Merrifield put the tips of his pudgy fingers together and frowned. "And we are confederate with this damned pack. Well, the brotherhood of the road should cheer for Tippecanoe. These log-cabin gatherings are proving a blessing to George and his like." He plucked out his watch and peered at it. "Seven-fifteen, and getting dark. I must away, my dear."

Mercy watched him rummage in the wagon and stow bottles in his coat. "Luke Brooks?" she asked.

"Well—where Luke is there will be games of chance." Doc Merrifield smiled ruefully at Mercy. "Oh, what a rogue and peasant slave I am, eh, Mercy? But I feel that fortune may smile on me tonight. Never fear. I won't lose all."

"You sound as if you were sure you'd have something to lose."

"I am." The Elixir's inventor tapped his bulging coat. There was a clink of glass. "I counted a dozen small babies as we drove in. Babies, removed from their surroundings, are apt to be fretful. There is in Merrifield's Epizootical Elixir a certain quality most soothing to the crying infant. Laudanum. It is, as you well know, about the only drug of note in the blasted stuff."

"Suppose these babies ain't crying?"

"My dear." Doc Merrifield bowed and clapped his hat on the back of his head. "Babies always cry. Especially at sight of me."

As the shadows moved up the slopes of Stratton Mountain and the early moon over its summit became brighter against the darkening sky, a restless anticipation spread like an epidemic. The birds felt it; the few who nestled in the tamarack tree left their branches because of the noise below; all within a mile of the clearing slept fitfully. Animals felt it also. Deer trembled in their thickets; rabbits hid; porcupines waddled about with quills half raised. Wildcat and catamount crept stealthily toward the encampment, drawn by its dozens of fires. A black bear kept his distance; deep in the woods that stretched to the summit he showed no fear but, at intervals, he pointed his muzzle toward the glow and noise and growled. Man, in numbers, was on the mountain, and he was planning something. The wildlife was wary.

Man, in numbers, had a sense of shared excitement. This was the eve of a great event, the night before the Convention. Restless anticipation was natural to the celebration of such an eve. The clearing rang with nervous laughter, hastily voiced plans, argued speculations on what the next day would bring. There was singing around several campfires; ballads vied with hymns. The lamest jest was greeted with lusty guffaws. Long stories, mostly of absent neighbors, were told to eager listeners. The whole space seethed with movement; figures passed constantly before the flames; no one sat still very long. Mothers watched their daughters. The girls scanned the youths for possible swains. Some men, sauntering carelessly, found their way behind a wagon where there was a jug.

It was almost dark when torches glowed through the windows of the big log cabin. The sight of the suddenly yellow rectangles in the dark walls caused a commotion throughout the crowd. People stood up, pointed. Some pushed, some scrambled on wagons to get a better view. Questions were scarcely uttered when there was a cluster of torches before the door of the cabin. A drum rolled, the beats tumbling on each other. A trumpet blared. Someone scraped a bow across the strings of a fiddle in quick staccato.

"Junket! Junket!"

The shout came from one of the men in front of the building. He faced another direction, cupped his hands, and bellowed through them.

"Junket! Junket!"

Four times, to the four main points of the compass, the call went thundering across the clearing. The crowd from the parked wagons poured toward the caller as if a dam had broken.

Boys hurdled the fires and ran. Maidens grabbed up ribbons, poked at their hair, and ran. Men loped; women scuttled. A farmer, who had doffed his boots for comfort, tugged at them frantically and hobbled. A woman with a baby in her arms hesitated as if she intended to toss it aside, thought better of the impulse, tucked the infant under an arm, and hurried toward the cabin. Cries of joy echoed above the racing throng.

"Junket!"

"Dance! Dance!"

"Contry dance!"

"Sister! Wait for me!"

"Get in the same square now, Daisy."

"Hurry up, Austin! Hurry up!"

"Junket!"

"My! I ain't danced in ages!"

"Be my partner, Lucy? Huh, Lucy?"

"E-yah!"

"Hustle along, Ma. We'll show these young folks!"

"Who ain't spry?"

"Dance!"

"Johnny! Come *on!*"

In the shadows behind the cabin the Captain watched the crowd cross the clearing like a charging army. He nodded and swung himself up on his roan. Looking down at the man who guarded the cider, the Captain said, "That ought to keep them happy. They'll probably dance till dawn."

The guard spat tobacco. "No cider till tomorrow?" he asked.

"Not a drop! That's for the Convention! Understand?"

"E-yah." There was a rasp and click as the hammer on the rifle was cocked.

"I'll be at the inn if you need me," said the Captain, and heeled his horse. He let the roan pick its way carefully around the edge of the clearing, but once the road was reached they went at a gallop. Thudding down the center of the muddy lane, they swept past the lights of the Chittenden farm and on toward the crossroad settlement. It was getting colder. The rider felt the chill of the night wind as he rode out of the trees. Countless stars were in the blackness overhead, and the first-quarter moon gleamed like a polished sickle. The Captain reined in before the Tarbox inn.

The same restlessness that had filled the clearing was apparent in the tavern's common room. There was some difference in degree; the visitors in the smoke-filled room were richer, better dressed, more worldly than the campers. It was the difference between homespun and broadcloth. Here there was more liquor drunk, more tobacco puffed and chewed, shrewder calculations made about the morrow. But, if the talk were lower pitched, the laughter not so loud, it was still plain that everyone begrudged the hours of the eve and waited only for the day.

Since he had turned innkeeper Dan Tarbox had never seen such trade. In the candlelight his bald head was shiny with sweat. His apron was askew. The left pocket, bulging with hard money, pulled the corner down; the right, lighter, held greenbacks. Dan was never still; he hurried from this table to that, served drinks, made change,

126

chatted with people, popped back of the bar and out again. His eyes were dazed, as if he couldn't believe in the rush of business. He had no idea how many suppers had been served, but he had been forced to send little David asking neighbors for more pie. Three meals a day took a lot of pie.

At the table against the wall the inn's regular customers, the men of Stratton, were grouped, watching the foreign element. They crowded together, seldom speaking, somewhat suspicious of the well-dressed invaders. It was a full quorum. The blacksmith faced the room; Isaac Mead was at his left; Will Carpenter was beside Isaac. Both the Patch hired men were at the table and so was Nathan, though he didn't intend to stay. Even old Peleg Nason, who never sat up late, was there sipping a toddy, which he raised with both trembling hands.

The politicians formed another clique. The varicolored waistcoats of the gentlemen from neighboring states rubbed against the same table edges now as at the midday meal. Cigar smoke clung thick above their tall hats, and even the Man from Boston drank with a speed and efficiency that was startling. The Captain, entering, took a chair they had kept for him.

Visitors were at other tables or ranked along the bar. A dozen were lodged at the inn; others had hired rooms in near-by homes. Quite a few had left wives and children at the clearing to seek entertainment here. Several young men, dandies and friends, were obviously intending to spend the night drinking. There were no women in the room.

One man sat alone, playing some form of solitaire. His black dress, pale face, and quiet manners gave him the air of a gentleman parson. A heavy gold ring on one of his long, narrow hands winked as he placed a card. He answered to the name of Brooks, and he could have instructed Hoyle on certain points of card playing.

Asa Brayton was helping serve. The tall boy's shirt was dark with perspiration. His lips were tight with the effort of trying not to drop whatever he carried.

Looking around, the innkeeper noticed that only one male guest was missing. That young Virginian was still upstairs in his room.

Although missing in person, Thomas Jefferson Dunbar was certainly present as a topic of conversation. His appearance, native state, horses, manners, and slave were all subjects for discussion.

Young Asa, carefully putting tankards before his fellow townsmen, answered a question.

"E-yah. Saw it myself. Saw it."

"I told you, Isaac."

"Asa's got no call to lie."

"Ain't lying," said the boy. "It was just like I told you, Mr. Carpenter. I took the hot water up. I ain't lying."

Isaac Mead said, "It ain't that I doubt you, Asa. I just ain't never heard the beat."

"Tell him the whole thing, Asa."

"E-yah. I fetched the hot water, and he told the black man to give me a copper." Asa didn't identify the he; it wasn't necessary.

"Did he?"

"E-yah. Got the copper in my pocket now."

"Land of Goshen!"

"Hush up, Nathan. Let the boy tell it."

"Thank ye, Mr. Reed. Then I was a mite curious, I guess. I sort of left the door open a crack and watched. E-yah. Maybe I shouldn't have. But I was a mite curious."

"Don't blame you, Asa. Don't blame you a bit."

"Go on. What happened?"

"Well, *he* sits down in a chair."

"The Southern fellow?"

"E-yah. Him. Dunbar."

"Who'd you expect, Nathan?"

"E-yah. Guess both of them's Southern."

"You got the right of it there, Abner."

"Consarn it! Let the boy tell it!"

"All right, Peleg. All right."

Asa glanced over his shoulder at the innkeeper and bent closer to his listeners. "Well, the black man. That Hock. He lathers the other feller all up and whips out a razor about a foot long."

"No?"

"E-yah. And he shaves him!"

"Asa saw him!"

"Well!"

A shout came from across the room. "Asa!"

"E-yah, Mr. Tarbox. Coming!" Hurrying off, Asa called back over his shoulder. "Gospel truth!"

128

"What'd Asa call him?" asked Nathan Patch.

"Who?"

"The nigger."

"Hock. That's his name."

"Hock? Like part of a horse?"

"Outlandish, ain't it?"

"That Dunbar's lucky it ain't Hack."

"If you ask me that Dunbar's another part of a horse."

"How's that, Clem?"

"Can't shave hisself!"

"Them Southern fellers never lift a finger. The blacks do all the work."

"Slaves."

"Mighty risky business, I'd say."

"Risky, Will?"

"E-yah. That shaving."

"Shucks, you've seen barbers down to the city."

" 'Course I have, Abner. It ain't that."

"What then? What?"

"That Hock's a nigger ain't he? A black slave? Well, you wouldn't catch me letting him near me with no razor!"

"Me, neither!"

"Especially a slave!"

"Slave or free!"

Peleg Nason thumped with his mug to get attention. "You fellers," he said. "You fellers ain't never been to the South. You ain't got the right of it at all. That Dunbar. He's a Virginian. Like Washington. Washington, he had slaves too. I was at Yorktown, you know. That's Virginia. Yorktown, Virginia."

"E-yah."

"We know, Peleg."

"E-yah. I was there right through the whole battle and whole surrender. Washington, he outsmarted them. They're smart, them Virginians. Look at the way they passed the Presidency around. Hand to hand, almost. And they ain't afraid of their slaves. The blacks like them! Yorktown was where the British give up, you know. I come home after that. Walked most of it. But I was telling you about the surrender."

"Wait a minute, Peleg. Dan!"

"Dan!"

"Dan, we're empty over here!"

Dan called back. "Just a minute, Clem!" He put a tankard in front of the Captain and wiped the table. "Everything all right up to the clearing, Captain?"

"E-yah. Folks are dancing."

"Dancing." The innkeeper nodded and moved away to spread this news.

The Captain took a long swallow of his drink. "I put my horse in the stable. Any of you get a close look at that black gelding?"

"E-yah."

"That is a horse," said the Man from New Hampshire.

"Thoroughbred," agreed the Bostonian.

The Captain said, "A damn fine animal! *He* must be made of money." Again there was no further identification of the pronoun. The Captain could be speaking only of Thomas Jefferson Dunbar.

"Slaveholder!"

"I was speaking of horses," said the Captain. He stared coldly at the Man from New York. "That sort of talk is out of place."

"Especially this year."

"Harrison's a Virginian like this lad."

"Tyler, too."

"I don't hold with slavery!" The New Yorker sounded stubborn.

"I hold with minding my own business."

"The Captain's right."

"Young Dunbar is a Whig after all."

"The party comes first."

"Mr. Clay has some slaves, I believe."

The barrage was too much for the Man for New York. He drained his glass and said, "It's just my personal opinion. Nothing to do with politics."

"Absolutely nothing."

"The Southern vote's very important."

"I know that!" Irritated, the New Yorker chose attack as the best defense. "I suppose Boston ain't the abolition center of the country!"

"Nonsense." The Bostonian was unperturbed. "A few riffraff. Loco-foco Democrats mostly. Never amount to a row of beans."

"Troublemakers."

"Precisely."

"After all, the plantation owners of the South are our natural allies. Men of education, breeding."

"Whigs too, ain't they?"

"Some."

"Enough to win, Captain?"

"I hope so."

"Mr. Clay thinks so. And this Virginian coming here is an encouraging sign. Now, if Calhoun should join us . . ."

"Calhoun!"

"Hell! You never know where he stands!"

"He just hated Jackson, that's all."

"Perhaps. Perhaps not."

"If they count on Calhoun in Boston no wonder us Whigs got licked down there!"

"Calhoun is for Calhoun!"

"And Carolina."

"Gentlemen," said the Captain, shrugging. "Neither Calhoun, Carolina, nor Virginia is our concern at the moment. First things first. Tomorrow we hope to obtain Vermont for Tippecanoe and Tyler too."

"Let's drink to that!"

"Mr. Tarbox! Another round! My score!"

Dan was pouring drinks. He pushed them across the bar, snatched up a coin, ducked from behind the counter, calling, "Asa! The Captain's table!" The innkeeper shouldered his way to the kitchen and burst through the door. "Lydia!" Dan's voice was an angry shout. "We need more clean mugs!"

Mrs. Tarbox, elbow deep in a tub of water, jumped. "Dan! You don't have to yell! I'm doing them as fast as I can! I only have two hands!"

Little David and his older sister, Marcia, were both busily wiping. Marcia said, "Here's a finished stack, Pa."

"Give me those!" Dan snatched up the tray. "And hurry up with the rest!" He slammed the door behind him.

Marcia Tarbox looked at her mother. Plump, almost pretty, Marcia wore her hair in two brown pigtails. Her figure, at fifteen, was mature, fully curved. "Land," she said. "I've never seen Pa take on so!"

"I know." Mrs. Tarbox sighed and mopped her forehead. "He's tired. He's been on the go since early morning."

"So have you."

"It ain't the same. Your Pa's so—so excitable."

David, polishing a cup, waited. He was in the middle of telling something and, with the dogged patience of his age, intended to return to his story at the first opportunity.

His mother splashed water viciously. She said, "I—I wish this Convention thing was over and done."

"Ma!"

The shock in her daughter's voice brought loud defiance from Mrs. Tarbox. "Well, I do, Marcia! Nothing's worth going on this way! I ain't had a civil word from your Pa all day! Not even so much as a thank-you for running my heels off!"

"But, Ma. With Mr. Webster coming and all . . ."

"Webster! Don't talk to me about him! That's another thing! All your Pa worries about is will Dan Webster stop here! And where in time he's going to put him!"

Marcia said, very casually, "Mr. Dunbar's got the best room."

"E-yah." Mrs. Tarbox gave a short laugh. "Webster may be quite a speechmaker, but that young Southerner has a way with him too!"

"E-yah," agreed Marcia. She felt her cheeks getting warm and bent to take a kettle from the fireplace. The posture reminded her of a similar position assumed while laying the fire in Mr. Dunbar's room. She straightened hastily, face flaming.

"Money," said Mrs. Tarbox, not noticing the girl's confusion. "Money talks, you know. Right out in church sometimes."

"I'll make lots," said David, plunging into the midstream of conversation. "I already asked him, and he said he would."

"What, Davey?"

"I told you, Ma."

"I guess I wasn't listening."

David was annoyed but patient. "The black man. Hoc."

With a child's unconscious mimicry David pronounced the name correctly. "I'm going to make Put Chester and everybody pay to talk to him."

132

"Davey!"

"Pay!"

"E-yah. Hoc says he wouldn't do it for anybody else. But he likes me. And he says only pickaninnies can come."

"Only what?"

"Pickaninnies." David used his new word loftily and explained. "That's what black folks call little boys and girls."

"David Tarbox! I don't want you learning any outlandish heathen talk!"

"Hoc ain't heathen, Ma! He's Episcopalian!"

"Well." A trifle set back by this information, Mrs. Tarbox relapsed into muttering. "That ain't so much better."

"What's Episcopalian, Ma?"

"Church of England," stated Mrs. Tarbox with an air of taking care of the whole matter. "It's a lot more common in the South than in these parts. When General Ethan Allan made us independent of England he went the whole hog!"

Marcia said, "Then Mr. Dunbar must be that, too."

"Likely."

"He is. Hoc said."

Maybe that accounts for it, thought Marcia. She put a hand behind her and touched the place Tom Dunbar had pinched. Maybe they ain't so strict in that religion. Blushing, she reviewed the whole incident. He'd laughed when she jumped. That nice soft laugh. And the easy way he talked. Marcia was sure he'd meant no harm. It was just his way. Even when he'd tickled her ribs and stolen that kiss he hadn't scared her any. She smiled dreamily.

"Marcia! You'll rub the lustre off that pitcher!"

"Oh. Yes, Ma." Startled, she almost dropped the pitcher. She felt very guilty that she'd enjoyed the tussle with Mr. Dunbar. She knew Ma would whale her if she ever found out. Not that there was anything wrong, really. But Marcia decided she'd stay out of Mr. Dunbar's room. She was hot with shame. Squealing like that. What was it the slurred speech had called her? Oh, yes.

"Ma."

"E-yah, Marcia?"

"Are we Puritans?"

133

"Whatever put that in your head. You know very well that we're Congregationalists!"

"E-yah!" David said with scorn.

Marcia concentrated on her wiping, puzzled. Somehow, in view of what had happened, it didn't make good sense for Mr. Dunbar to call her a Puritan. There was something wrong somewhere.

Hoc came down the back stairs and into the kitchen. He was carrying a tray of piled-up dishes. He said, "Evening, Master Davey."

"Hello, Hoc."

The three members of the Tarbox family watched the slave set down the tray. "Mr. Tom said I was to make myself useful." White teeth gleamed as Hoc grinned. "Mr. Tom said you all looked busier'n a pack of foxhounds." Already wearing an apron over his livery, Hoc deftly plucked the dishrag from Mrs. Tarbox's fingers. He was washing tableware before the good lady knew what had happened.

Not sure she approved, Mrs. Tarbox said, "You're very kind, I'm sure." Her tone was stiff.

Hoc flashed her another grin and kept on working.

"Is—did Mr. Dunbar come down?" asked Marcia.

"Uhuh." Hoc nodded his head toward the noise beyond the wall. "He's in there with the other gentlemen. I expect they'll be playing cards before long."

Hoc knew his master. Tom Dunbar's entrance into the common room had caused a momentary silence. The assemblage was conscious of the fact that the tall young man had been the cause of much debate and speculation. In the sudden lull, the voice of the Patch hired man, Clem Galusha, was clear. Clem was a little drunk and not at all shy.

"That the feller? Regular prize pumpkin, ain't he?"

Dan Tarbox glared in Clem's direction and hurried toward his guest. Everyone in the room started to talk at once.

Grinning, Tom waved the innkeeper back. He was not even slightly disturbed by the remark. Tom Dunbar expected to cause comment when he entered a room. He stood gazing around, confident of his looks and dress. He had changed his boots for pumps, and his linen and cravat were fresh. The neckpiece was royal purple.

Tom's roving glance paused on the quiet man playing solitaire. Of all the men in the inn, the Southerner was probably most familiar with the professional gamester. He recognized the type and walked directly to the table.

Luke Brooks rose. Both men raised their hats and bowed. The preliminaries were swift but punctiliously polite.

"My compliments, sir."

"Mine."

"If I'm not intruding?"

"Not at all."

"Perhaps I err, but you have the appearance of one who finds a gentlemanly game of cards a worthy evening's amusement."

"Often, Mr. Dunbar."

"The advantage is yours, sir."

"Brooks, sir. Luke Brooks."

"A pleasure, Mr. Brooks."

"I trust so, Mr. Dunbar. Would you do me the honor?" A quick, smooth movement spread the cards in a wide fan across the table top. "High choice, Mr. Dunbar."

Formalities properly finished, the gentleman grinned at the gambler. The latter smiled back. Both knew exactly where the gulf between them ended. Across a card table they were skilled opponents and, though one played for excitement and the other for bread, both intended to win.

Sitting down, Luke Brooks raised his voice slightly. "Perhaps some of the other gentlemen would care to indulge?"

Some of the others did. The Captain sat in and the Man from New York. Clem Galusha lurched over and took a chair. A young delegate from Rockingham sat down, too.

The card table became the quietest corner of the room. There was only the murmur of men requesting cards, the riffle and slither of the deal, the clink of coins, and the crackle of greenbacks. There were no chips; each player had money piled before him. All except Clem Galusha smoked; a gray haze hung over the tables. The innkeeper kept the tankards filled. The Captain lost and drank. Clem won several deals and drank. Tom Dunbar sipped his drink with the same easy assurance he wore when playing cards. The crowding spectators failed to notice that Luke Brooks seldom more than wet his lips.

Fortune seemed to wander haphazardly around the table, stopping first at this place, then at that. The young delegate, losing, quit and was replaced by a salesman of Tippecanoe badges. Clem and Luke Brooks were the most frequent winners: the one with amazed, drunken luck; the other, shrewdly valuing each card.

Tom Dunbar became bored and bet recklessly. He raised the stakes, wagering a sum that brought an awed murmur from the crowd. The Captain swore and tossed down his cards. Only Luke Brooks, smiling, thrust an equal sum into the center of the table. Remarks came from the watchers.

"Will you look at that pile of eagles?"

"Mite reckless, ain't they?"

"The Panic must be over."

"E-yah."

"Good money, too."

Doc Merrifield shouldered through to the table. The fat man took in the situation and grinned at Luke Brooks. "My," he said. "What fools these mortals be! Evening, Luke."

"Evening, Doc."

Tom Dunbar said, "Your play, I believe."

Luke Brooks showed his cards. They won.

"Touché!" Tom Dunbar laughed. "My compliments."

When Clem Galusha saw the gambler scoop in a sum greater than a hired man's yearly salary, he pushed back from the table without a word and staggered away. Doc Merrifield chuckled and spread himself over the vacated chair. "May I, gentlemen? Thank you."

"Been expecting you, Doc."

"I was delayed, Luke." Doc began to pile coins on the table. "By scenes of revelry. They're having a dance up to the clearing, and . . ."

"A dance?" Tom's interruption was quick with interest. "A dance, sir?"

"E-yah. Trumpets and hautboys! When the fiddlers play, the ladies are gay!"

Tom pushed back his chair. "In that case," he said, "I'm afraid I'll have to leave you. Perhaps I may have better luck at other types of hazard." He bowed to each player and left.

136

The gambler watched the tall white hat bob through the crowded room as Tom departed. He looked at Doc Merrifield and sighed.

Doc grinned. "Parting is sweet sorrow, Luke. But he left some ducats behind."

Fingering his depleted money, the Captain said bitterly, "Stop dawdling! Deal!"

"Cut, Doc?"

The fat man split the deck. "This, my friends, is probably the most unkindest cut of all." The pudgy hands swept up the first card; the eyes behind the ill-balanced spectacles took one look. "Alas," Doc moaned. "Et tu, Brute?"

The New Yorker glared. "What? What's that?"

Dealing, the gambler's fingers were a pale blur of movement. "Don't mind Doc," he said. "The louder he cries, the better he holds."

Galloping his black gelding up the road to the clearing, Tom Dunbar passed Charles Chittenden. The latter's wagon was headed in the same direction, and on a night-dark curve the horseman swerved to avoid a collision. He thundered past. Charles, startled, shouted; Tom whooped in reply. The gelding raced on; its rider was happy and excited. After the stale smoke of the tavern the cold air felt bracing. Tom faced the prospect of the new gathering with zest. Card games, he thought, were all pretty much alike, win or lose, but anything might happen at a dance. Although he expected it to be very rustic, the dance held definite attractions for Tom. In Virginia there had been much talk of the blue-law North, the puritanical narrowness of New England. At Saratoga he had found the Boston ladies stiff models of correctness, great talkers on—of all things—intellectual subjects. He had higher hopes for the inhabitants of this Vermont mountain. Puritans? Tom grinned into the blackness. A gust of wind tugged at his hat and he settled it at a jaunty angle. As a matter of scientific research he determined to find out for himself whether or no these New England misses were as straitlaced as he'd been told. Tom Dunbar laughed. Already he'd learned that these Puritans danced.

That little girl at the inn, recalled Tom. She hadn't reacted so

137

differently from other serving maids he'd met. A trifle more skittish, perhaps, and quicker to blush. Tom judged that she hadn't really been offended in spite of her squeals. But a tavern wench was one thing; a lady, another. A man of the world could be successful with both but was forced to make distinctions between them. Even as he rode, the gelding racing beneath him, Tom Dunbar managed to swagger.

He heard the music and the din of the dancing before he reached the clearing. There was more din than music; the pound and stamp of many feet slammed out in cadence. But through the noise the tune came clearly, lively, true. Urging his horse forward, Tom began to beat time with his fingers.

Against the massed darkness of the forest the many campfires looked like glowing gems stretched along the chain of some giant necklace. Light streamed from the windows of the long log cabin and seemed a visible conductor of the warm, melodious, rhythmic sounds from within. It was evident that even so large a floor had not been able to contain the crowd. Groups were clustered outside each window staring in at the dancers. Torches brightened the space in front of the door, and Tom reined in the gelding beneath their spluttering flames.

As he hitched his horse the music ended. There was a burst of clapping and shouts of approval. Tom pressed through the crowd around the entrance. When he had a clear view of the dance space, he gazed with grinning delight.

The main room of the cabin was a large rectangle, and all four walls were banked with rows of people. In the wide space within this human hedge the dancers were crowded, still grouped in the positions where the music had left them. Only by sexes were the dancers equally divided. They were all ages, all weights, and all sizes.

Their costumes, too, were varied in wear, material, and fashion. Black appeared to be most common—the good black dress, the Sunday suiting. Still, the throng was splashed with many moving colors as if the torchlight were being filtered through a prism. The young women and girls wore yellow and brown, green, red, purple, blue. If Tom Dunbar saw more of homespun than he did of satin or silk, it was less noticeable than that the fashions were somewhat older than those of Saratoga, New York, or Richmond.

138

There were other differences from the fashionable balls and cotillions with which he was familiar. Here there was no concerted pause for refreshments or flirtation. Even as Tom watched one of the squares dissolved, dancers panting, to the sidelines, and another stepped forward to take its place. One aged farmer refused to halt a moment; he practiced his Pigeon's Wing even without music. Women, laughing, tried to repin the hair shaken loose.

Tom Dunbar examined the maidens who, flushed of face and happy, waited for the musicians to start up again. He examined and approved. Jove, he said silently, some of them are really pretty. He found it a pleasant surprise.

In a corner the musicians stopped passing a jug and picked up their instruments. The band was small: three fiddlers, a flute, and a bugle. One fiddler, the prompter, stood. He was the same lanky Luthur who had led one of the bands up the mountain that morning, and he called the figures through his big nose.

Luthur flourished his bow. "Choose your partners!"

The music burst forth in the lively strains of "Hull's Victory." Tom Dunbar saw the dancers form lines facing each other. Each set held six or eight couples. At the first words of the prompter's call, the dancers were moving. Tom's foot began to tap on the floor. He turned to a near-by lounger.

"I beg your pardon, sir."

"E-yah?"

"Is it permissible for anyone to join in?"

"Huh?"

The other's amazement was so obvious that Tom explained. "I mean do I have to be introduced to a lady before I ask her to dance?"

The lounger stared. With an initial grunt, he said, "Guess you don't go to dances much, do you?"

Tom chuckled. He was becoming used to the native habit of answering a question by asking another. He judged that formal introductions were unnecessary, and the man confirmed this.

"Ask 'em," he said. "If they don't aim to be your partner, they'll let you know."

"Thank you," said Tom, bowing. He was aware that every feminine eye in the room, even those of the women already among the dancers, had registered his presence. The gaze of the older ladies was direct and suspicious; the young ones glanced covertly. With the serene choosiness of any male in his brightest plumage, he scanned the crowd for a partner.

He took his time, boldly gazing at each set of dancers, into every rank of spectators. Tom's standards of age and beauty considerably narrowed the field. Since he found many of the figures in the dance strange, he decided he had better choose somebody graceful. Several girls met his qualifications. One, in yellow poplin, happened to be near him. Tom concentrated on her.

Even while winding through the fast, complicated maneuvers, her hand hotly grasped by Nathan Patch, the girl in yellow was aware of Tom's scrutiny. Lovina Chester was glad that the heat of exercise would cover any blushing confusion. Nathan danced with grim, unsmiling efficiency; the young Southerner looked as if he would enjoy himself.

"Swing your partners!"

Every male swung his escort off the floor and whirled her. There was a great rustle of skirts and petticoats. The dance floor seemed suddenly covered with dozens of unfurling fans.

Tom Dunbar watched white petticoats foaming under a billow of yellow poplin and was confirmed in his choice. That was a trim ankle, he judged. He hoped the girl's partner wasn't her husband.

When the music stopped Lovina dragged Nathan from the floor. She swept aside his protests. "Nathan! You have to dance with Sally! You promised!"

Nathan glowered. He felt an angry conviction that he'd been swindled and, what was worse, outsmarted. He'd brought news of the dance to the parsonage with crafty intent. Lovina liked to dance; he'd escort her. Instead, he'd found himself saddled with all three sisters. He said, almost pouting, "There's plenty of other partners!"

"Nathan! You fetched us!"

"E-yah." The acknowledgment was bitter.

Sally ignored his reluctance. She hadn't danced yet, and she wanted to. With much the same swiftness that one post rider uses to accept a burden from another, she took Nathan's hand from Lovina and pulled him back toward the dance floor. Then his surprised grunt caught her attention. She turned for a backward

140

glance. The handsome Southern boy was bowing before Lovina. Sally giggled. Trust Vina, she thought.

Lovina dipped a curtsy to the bow. She wished Charles Chittenden were there to see. She was pleased and flattered that the stranger had singled her out. She found the soft, slurred speech pleasant, if a mite hard to follow.

"Thomas Jefferson Dunbar, Esq.," Tom said. "At your service, Miss. And would you do me the honor of a dance?"

"Thank you," said Lovina. "My name's Lovina Chester."

"Lovina." Tom's voice caressed each syllable. "That would be for loveliness. My compliments to your parents, Miss Lovina. They sure found the proper name."

Goodness, thought Lovina, what a way to talk. Down South they must crack everything up something wonderful. She said, "It's a family name, Mr. Dunbar."

Tom laughed. He found the frankness refreshing. There were no coy flutterings, no ejaculations disavowing his compliment. Grinning, he said, "So's mine, Miss Lovina. I think Grandfather had a tea at Monticello once."

Thinking furiously, Lovina remembered that Monticello was the name of President Jefferson's home. Her laugh held some relief. "Not the White House, Mr. Dunbar?"

"Grandfather believed it uncomfortable, Miss Lovina." Tom stiffened as the music started again. He said, with delighted surprise, "That's 'Sir Roger de Coverly!'"

"E-yah."

"A quadrille!"

"E-yah." Lovina was surprised at his surprise.

"Let's stir ourselves, Miss Lovina. I was raised on quadrilles. At this I can do my dancing master proud."

The dancers were quickly forming into squares for the quadrille. Tom and Lovina attached themselves to one. The girl recognized some of the other dancers as neighbors. Zilpha Brayton had her husband for her partner; Isaac Mead, in the same square, returned Lovina's nod. There was no time for introductions. The prompter called the measure, and they started.

With the first few steps Tom chuckled and pressed Lovina's hand. The girl laughed up at him. Each knew that he'd found a partner of skill and grace.

141

To their delight the musicians played a succession of quadrilles. The square remained the same. Lovina noticed that Mrs. Brayton danced well, while the exercise colored her pale cheeks. Isaac Mead, too, seemed to be enjoying himself. Lem Brayton marched through the figures glowering. Over Tom's shoulder, the girl caught a glimpse of Charles Chittenden, tall among the spectators near the door. Lovina didn't look again. She devoted herself to her partner, laughing gaily, the picture of merriment.

When the perspiring musicians finally stopped, there was a commotion at the cabin's doorway. Men jostled in the opening; from outside came voices raised in anger. Lovina, with Tom at her side, was in the crush that pressed forward to see.

In the wavering torchlight that brightened the night in front of the cabin, the crowd, with solid disapproval, was watching a noisy group. While their three companions hooted, two youths tried to drag a struggling girl toward the cabin. The girl was Doc Merrifield's Mercy. In contrast to the laughing pair that held her Mercy twisted and fought with silent, white-faced anger.

Lovina Chester stamped her foot. "Those Bondville roughs!"

"Who?" asked Tom Dunbar.

"Those boys. They're from north of here a piece. Live in the hills above a place called Bondville. They're always making trouble!"

Tom Dunbar nodded. "Backwoodsmen," he said. A note of amazement came into his voice. "They're drunk. Even that little tadpole!"

The quintet was a motley crew. Its members ranged in age from nineteen to twelve. The two that held Mercy were obviously the eldest. One wore a coonskin cap and fringed leggings; the other, bareheaded, was clothed in old-fashioned knee breeches. The three cavorting boys were equally antiquely dressed; the smallest had a battered three-cornered hat on the back of his head. All were flushed and loud with liquor.

With a sudden thrust Mercy tripped one of her captors, broke his grip. Instantly the girl slashed her free hand across the face of her other tormentor. The blow knocked the coonskin cap into the air and brought a yowl of pain. Loose, Mercy whirled to run. The struck boy moved fast. His arm shot out; fingers dug into the girl's long hair and yanked her back.

142

"Flay the jade!" cried he of the tricorne hat. "Flog the wench, Jabez!"

Jabez's arm was raised to strike when Charles Chittenden caught his wrist and sent him sprawling. A roar of approval burst from the crowd.

"Capital!" cried Tom Dunbar. Then Lovina gasped, and her grip tightened on his elbow.

With a catlike bound Jabez leaped to his feet. The long blade of a sheath knife was glittering in his hand.

Charles had caught Mercy as she tottered, and he swung her behind him. A low growl came from the spectators; several men stepped to places beside Charles.

"None of that, now."

"Put up the knife."

"Thrown fair, wan't you?"

"Deserved it, too."

"E-yah."

"And more."

Faced with this mass of disapproval, Jabez hesitated. His followers ranged themselves behind him, but five had no chance against such numbers. Jabez shrugged. He tossed his knife up, blade flashing, caught it deftly in his palm, and sheathed it. He said, "Marry! There ain't no cause to get galled. We wasn't harming the wench any!"

"God's blood!" The boy in knee breeches supported his leader. "She stirred more tempest than a pilloried whore!"

Their speech was even more ancient than their clothes. It held the frank idiom of an earlier day, and English almost Elizabethan was mixed with the local dialect. All the listeners recognized that these mountaineers were a race apart. Their manner of talking emphasized the barrier.

A man with an air of authority shook his finger at the boys. He said, "We don't want any of your tricks around here, Jabez Tute. I know you of old. Yes, and you, too, Noll Butler. And both you Dale boys. You'll behave yourselves in this clearing, or I'll see the sheriff hears about you."

"A fig for the sheriff!" said Jabez Tute. But he turned away. The little band drew out of the light and seemed to dissolve in the shadows.

Mercy smiled up at Charles Chittenden. She said, very simply, "Thank you."

"Are you all right?" asked Charles.

"Yes. I was standing under that tamarack tree, listening to the music. And they sort of took me by surprise." Mercy rubbed her wrists. "I don't know how I'd have managed if you hadn't been so handy."

The fiddles scraped from inside the cabin. A little annoyed at losing their audience, the musicians set out to win them back. Like some melodious charm the music scattered the crowd. It broke up; couples strolled into the cabin and back to the campfires. Tom Dunbar started to turn away, but Lovina's grasp kept him. He glanced at her, judged she was interested in the conversation between rescuer and rescued. His judgment was correct.

Charles looked up and saw Lovina. His eyes shifted as he took in the tall Southerner. His voice was suddenly loud and clear. "Perhaps you would care to dance if asked a little more politely?"

Neither Tom Dunbar nor Mercy understood the reason for the volume of the question. The Virginian thought it a natural invitation; the girl was pleased that Charles had accepted her as older than she was. In the dancing shadows of the torchlight no one noticed how Lovina's teeth clamped on her lower lip.

Mercy was tempted. She knew she could dance, and for a moment she wavered. She refused for two reasons. Doc might need her dancing before this crowd to help sell Elixir; closer inspection, especially from the women, might show her real age. She said, "Thank you very much. But no."

"At least," Charles said, "I will accompany you back to your wagon." He offered his arm; Mercy took it. "Those roughs may still be about."

As they moved away Lovina's laugh rang out. "Shall we dance, Mr. Dunbar?"

"At your pleasure, Miss Lovina."

The dance continued. Tom Dunbar danced with all three Chester girls and a couple of other pretty maidens. But Lovina had the greater part of his attention. Nathan Patch grew increasingly sullen. Charles Chittenden, returned from escorting Mercy, asked Lovina for a dance and was haughtily refused. He bowed stiffly and found partners elsewhere.

144

For the most part the crowd in the cabin remained the same. Only a few conservative souls went back to their wagons and to sleep. The musicians, untiring, sweated, played faster, and let themselves be stimulated by copious swigs from the jug. Stamping, skipping, weaving through the intricate convolutions of quadrille or contry, the dancers showed no signs of weariness. It was well past midnight when the festivities were interrupted. Again the interruption came from outside the cabin. It was the unmistakable sharp crack of a rifle.

The crowd rushed out. Those curious enough to investigate found the man who guarded the cider ramming a fresh wad and ball into the long barrel of his rifle. He was unperturbed and laconic.

"What happened?"

"Nothing much."

"Did you shoot?"

"E-yah."

"What was it? An animal?"

"Nope."

"What, then?"

"Thieves."

"You—you mean somebody was after the cider?"

"E-yah."

"Who was it? How many were there?"

"Dunno. Counted five."

"Five? Land's sakes!"

"If you ask me it was them Bondville boys again."

"Bet 'twas. Were they young, mister?"

"Dunno."

This new excitement was the cause for much talk. The raid was attributed, and rightly, to the five young mountaineers. None of them was around to affirm or deny the accusation. The guard resumed his perch, rifle ready. The crowd chattered and dispersed. Lovina Chester noticed, for the first time, that the moon had set.

"Sally!" she called. "Mattie! We've got to get home!"

"Aw, Lovina!"

"You heard what Mother said. We promised not to stay late. Where's Nathan?"

"Right here, Lovina."

"Miss Lovina," said Tom Dunbar, softly. "Would you do me the

145

honor? I'm going your way. I'd be right pleased to take you home."

Tom made the request sound daring, enticing. Lovina's sisters gasped; Nathan Patch stood speechless, mouth open. It was the sight of Charles that decided Lovina. He was standing in the light from one of the cabin windows and could hear every word. After all, Lovina thought, he took that little snip home. This would be paying him back in his own coin. She said, "Thank you, Mr. Dunbar. It's very kind. I'd be delighted."

"Lovina!" Nathan said, crushed.

"Take care of the girls, will you, Nathan?" Lovina's tone was regal. "Your arm, Mr. Dunbar."

Lovina was startled to find that the high, black gelding was Tom's only means of conveyance. She didn't get a chance to express her indignation before she was even more startled. Two strong hands caught her by the waist and lifted her to the saddle. Swaying, Lovina grabbed at the cantle to steady herself. Tom slipped one of her feet into the stirrup.

Sitting sideways, Lovina looked down at him. In the moonless dark Tom's face was a blur, but she knew he was grinning. She bit back the cutting remark she had ready. After all, she thought, it is an adventure.

Using a stump as a mounting block Tom vaulted up behind Lovina. The gelding pranced but not nervously. Tom turned the horse toward the road.

Lovina sat tensely. She looked straight ahead, rigidly aware that Tom's arms were around her waist. It was impossible to avoid contact with his body. They were very close. Every movement of the gelding threw them against each other. When Tom spoke his breath stirred the girl's hair.

"Down home, Miss Lovina, you'd be riding pillion. Behind me. Ebony's been ridden double often. But not having expected such fair company . . . This way's a heap safer and more comfortable."

The casual tone relaxed Lovina. Riding double was evidently a common occurrence where the Dunbars lived. She laughed, feeling a little foolish at her qualms. "Comfortable, Mr. Dunbar?"

For answer Tom tightened one arm around her and drew her back against his chest. "You are now," he said, close to her ear.

Lovina gasped but had to admit it was true. Pleasantly excited, she told herself that Tom was every inch a gentleman and that sharing his horse was certainly more interesting than going home in Nathan's dull company. Just as harmless, too, she thought, and hoped fervently that her mother didn't see her arrival at home.

As the gelding cantered down the road Lovina's enjoyment increased. They passed the lights of the Chittenden house and went on. The wind whipped at her hair; her cheeks glowed from its brushing. She was warm enough, and Tom held her securely. The darkness of the night, riding between the black walls of trees, gave the impression that they were alone in the world. The thought pleased Lovina, and she held it. A man, a girl, and a horse: the only living creatures moving under the stars, and nothing but shadowed depths around them.

It was an intimate feeling and drew her closer to the one who shared it. It's even romantic, Lovina said silently. Like something out of Scott.

Tom Dunbar, perfectly at ease, hummed a few bars of the dance music. He considered that the night had gone well, was still going well. He mentally bowed to himself. Miss Lovina was attractive and, Puritan or not, here she was riding along in his arms. He began to sing a fragment of a tune he'd picked up in Saratoga.

> Oh, a starry night for a ramble,
> Through the flowery dell;
> Stop 'neath bush or bramble,
> Kiss me; never tell.

His laugh ended the song. Tom said, "We're sure enough rambling, Miss Lovina."

"Ebony is," said Lovina primly.

"I don't rightly think Ebony's in danger of getting kissed."

"He'd never tell, Mr. Dunbar."

"That's right. Mighty fine chaperon, old Ebony."

The sight of the settlement took them both by surprise. Moving through the night they had lost track of time. Lovina stirred and sighed. Tom said, "Well. Home stretch." He reined the horse to a walk.

Light still blazed through the tavern's windows, streaming out across the road. Lovina flinched to see how bright it made the front of the parsonage.

147

Tom had his own reasons for desiring less illumination. "Miss Lovina," he said. "I wouldn't like to be the cause of any talk." His voice was gentle, tempting. "We're sure enough careful about that sort of thing down home. If there was just some way we could sashay past that inn."

"There is. Back of the blacksmith shop there's a lane—a cowpath. It comes out behind our barn." Lovina welcomed the altered course. She was more anxious to avoid her mother's scrutiny than the inn's customers.

The smithy was dark and silent. The plodding Ebony's hoofs seemed very loud. Lovina directed them in whispers.

Tom dropped his voice to match hers. "First one sees a nightcap wins."

Lovina tittered. "Shh!" she hissed.

Their careful passage and the whispering made them fellow conspirators. Lovina blew a breath of relief when they stopped in the shadow of her father's barn.

"Thank goodness that's over," she said.

"Journey's end," said Tom Dunbar. "In the usual manner." With a tightening of his arm too swift for struggle, he drew her close and kissed her. Then, with a laugh, he was gone from the horse.

Lovina stared down from the saddle. She was upset, a little startled, not too displeased. She could still feel the pressure of Tom's lips; her cheeks grew warm.

"Jump down, Miss Lovina."

The words were a dare, a promise. Lovina knew that she'd be kissed again; she wanted to be. She swallowed hard, trying to still the pulse beating in her throat. Why not, she thought. Why not? All the hunger of weeks rose inside her. Somehow kissing this young Southerner, a stranger, handsome, was easy and not connected with any scruples of her youth.

"Don't be afraid, Miss Lovina. I'll catch you."

Miss Lovina, the girl's mind repeated, and she fought an impulse to laugh at the title, at once formal and familiar. That too made it different, easier. Suddenly Lovina thought of Charles Chittenden. With a choked laugh she kicked free of the stirrup and slid down the side of the horse.

Tom caught her as she dropped. Skirts and petticoats hiked up

148

from the impetus of her descent. He held her tight and kissed her thoroughly.

"Oh, no," murmured Lovina against his mouth and kissed back fiercely. She seemed to have no strength in her legs and clung to Tom. "Oh, no," she said again. The gasping protest was directed not at Tom but at herself.

"Honey child." Tom's endearment was so thickly Southern it was almost unintelligible. He was having a wonderful time. Well, I declare, said part of his brain, it's just that these poor gals never had any advantages. He congratulated himself on his success and cupped one hand over Lovina's breast.

Lovina shivered. His touch didn't frighten her as Charles's had. They kissed for so long that she was almost giddy. She twisted her fingers in Tom's hair, pulled his head away.

"Please," she said, panting.

Laughing, Tom pecked little kisses on her eyes, her nose. "Don't fret, missy," he said. "Nobody's going to hurt you. Just close your eyes and leave the rest to me. Kissing goodnight's a fine old custom."

Dimly Lovina heard voices. She had lost count of the kisses, but she pushed Tom back and listened. She recognized her sisters by their laughter. She said, "My sisters! Nathan! They're home! I must go!"

Tom sighed. "That's how it always happens."

"I must." Backing away Lovina was aware that her petticoats were hitched up every which way. "Good—good night, Mr. Dunbar." The farewell sounded very inadequate.

"I thank you, Miss Lovina," said Tom, with a deep, courtly bow. "For a most enjoyable evening."

Tugging at her garments Lovina turned and ran. With each step shame mounted. She was too flustered to think clearly, but she was aghast at her sinfulness.

Thomas Jefferson Dunbar picked up his hat and wiped off the dew. Grinning, he stroked the gelding's nose. It had been a very enlightening night. Educational. Both for himself and for Miss Lovina. And tomorrow was another day.

"Ebony horse," said Tom Dunbar. "You want to know something?" The gelding nickered at his master's chuckle. "For July

149

they wear the damndest number of petticoats in these here parts."

Winding up the weights of the Terry clock on his parlor mantel, the Reverend Jedidah Chester noted the time. Actually, he thought, it's tomorrow already. The seventh. The day of Daniel Webster's speech. The parson sighed, put the clock's crank under the pendulum, and closed the glass door. He reflected that time was an arbitrary measure; for Stratton it was still the eve of the great occasion. There were still noise and lights in the tavern across the road. His three older daughters were not yet home from the dance at the clearing. He had not finished the entry he was writing in his daily journal.

Moving back to his desk the parson looked down at the thick volume. The journal lay open, showing half a page of fine, small script; it was flanked by two burning candles. A smile wrinkled Reverend Chester's thin face. The desk had a definite Papist air.

Picking up his quill the parson read what he had written. He made a faint hissing tune by holding the pen's feathered edge against his teeth and whistling through it.

As was his custom, he had started his entry with a quotation. Tonight's was from *Robinson Crusoe*, a book the parson had read and reread many times. On the white page each word was carefully lined, neat, and clear.

. . . that the middle station of life was calculated for all kinds of virtues and all kinds of enjoyments; that peace and plenty were the handmaidens of a middle fortune; that temperance, moderation, quietness, health, society, all agreeable diversions, and all desirable pleasures, were the blessings attending the middle station of life. . . .

The minister sighed. Certainly, he considered, his own manner of living, the busy combination of preacher-farmer-husband-father, was best described as "the middle station of life." But he was not so sure that it was attended by Defoe's list of blessings. The parson wondered whether his wife, if pressed, could not enumerate an equal list of inconveniences and discomforts. Mrs. Chester did not refer to it frequently, but her husband knew she had expected more from their marriage than a mountain church.

Settling himself, the parson reached to dip pen in ink when he heard the rattle of wagon wheels. Quill poised over brass inkwell.

Reverend Chester listened. A horse stopped; his daughter Sally laughed. The preacher laid his pen aside, linked his narrow fingers, and faced the doorway.

Called farewells and more laughter made the parson frown. He cast an apprehensive glance toward the back of the house. The girls would rue it if their chatter awakened their mother.

The parson knew that his candles must have been seen; he waited. The front door squeaked. There was a rustle in the hallway.

"Father?" It was Mattie's voice.

"Hush!" said Reverend Chester. "Don't wake the whole house, girls." He spoke quietly, but the admonition was effective. There was an instant silence. Then Sally and Mattie tiptoed carefully into the room.

"Mother's asleep?" asked Sally in a whisper.

"E-yah." The parson smiled. "I was told that she requested an early homecoming. I trust that your judgment of time would meet with her approval."

There was a quick patter of feet along the hall. Lovina swept through the door. "Still up, Father?"

Her father said, "Obviously, my dear." His smile took any sting from the words.

Mattie said, "Vina, how did you . . ."

Lovina's swift look silenced her sister. "Mattie, this is not the time for any discussion. We might wake Mother."

"The thought," said the parson, "had occurred to me. Perhaps you'd prefer to make your explanations to her?"

"It's early, Father."

"The hour is, Sally."

"It's my fault," Lovina said. "I forgot the time. But we came away before anyone else. The dance is still going full tilt."

Reverend Chester looked at his eldest daughter. The girl seemed agitated. Her face was flushed, rosy; her bosom showed her rapid breathing. Puzzled, the preacher said, "Your quick acceptance of blame is commendable, Lovina. But hardly cause for such trepidation. The matter is not of great moment."

Mattie nudged Sally. Not meeting her father's gaze Lovina managed a smile. "It may become so, Father. If . . ." She didn't have to finish the sentence; a gesture toward the rear of the house was enough.

151

Trying to look severe and failing, the parson nodded. "These matters can wait till morning. Take your candle and go up, my dears." He watched Lovina light a candle from one on his desk. The girl's hand shook so that the wax plunged into the flame. "Are you all right, Lovina?"

"Yes, Father." Lovina steadied. The candle flame split as she withdrew her light. "Just tired. I danced my feet off."

"We all did," said Sally.

Mattie sighed. "It was the biggest dance I ever saw!"

"Then you'd better get some rest. Tomorrow will be a big day, too. Good night, my dears." Each daughter dipped a curtsy; Lovina led the way out. From the hallway came two hurried whispers.

"Vina! Where'd you come . . ."

"Shh. Not now!"

Jedidah Chester rubbed his chin and turned back to his journal. Girls, he thought, and their innocent little secrets. His fingers toyed with the quill as he meditated. All through the long afternoon the parson had felt a growing uneasiness. He had welcomed the thought of the Convention, but its actuality was disturbing. For the first time he wondered if the influx of visitors was an entirely good thing. Lovina's nervousness, for example, was due to overexertion at the dance, but there would have been no dance if the Whigs had planned their Convention somewhere else.

Dipping his pen, the Reverend Chester began to write. Line after line spread down the paper like rows of knitting.

Today, the sixth of July, has seen no little change in the even tenor of that "middle station of life," mentioned above, which is the common lot of most of us folk here on Stratton Mountain. Truly, Mahomet has come to our mt.—many Mahomets—and it is my most fervent wish that any heathen, or over worldly qualities which these travellers may have brought will not be sowed, like the cockle of the parable, among the furrows of my neighbors, be they fellow church members, or no. Already several hundreds of wagons of all descriptions have passed this parsonage, and I doubt not that the other roads, leading from other directions, have held similar numbers. This is the more surprising when one considers that those already in our midst can be no more than an indication of those to follow on the morrow. "Εντευθεν εξελαυνει," so Xenophon was wont to begin each chapter, and if I may make the judgment, it is a phrase that will aptly fit most of the people in this district within the next twenty-four hours. "Thence, they marched!" And we, here on our mountain, are at the other end of that "thence"; we have supplied the arena. I count myself a true Whig, though I cannot join my fellow clergymen in castigating the entire party of Democracy as irreligious, radical, and atheistic; there must be men of good will even among the Democrats. Yet, while not approving of the present administration or Mr. Van Buren, I admit to a certain reluctance in accepting the thesis that revelry and huzzaing, festivals tinged with bacchanalian pigments, are the proper methods for choosing the Republic's Chief Executive. To refer to the above quotation of D. Defoe—this day has seen little of the blessings attending the "middle station of life." I have noted few signs of temperance, fewer of moderation, none of quietness. Diversions, and pleasures, are present a-plenty, but whether they will be found either agreeable or desirable is a matter for conjecture, and must be left for the day to come. I worry! *"Timeo Danaos et dona ferentes!"* My Whig friends are not Greeks, and to hear Mr. Webster speak is a gift indeed, but still—unjustly or not—I fear the outcome.

To digress—my fervent wish is that General Harrison will be elected, since I doubt if one calls the President "Tippecanoe," the sound of which is beginning to nauseate all my sensibilities!

Reverend Chester sat back and stretched. He was cold and stiff. From ankles to knees his legs seemed as brittle as icicles. The parson yawned, then blew out one candle. Before he rose, the quill scratched out one more sentence.

So endeth this day's record.

THE SECOND DAY
July 7, 1840

It WAS NOT the first streak of sunrise that ushered in Stratton Mountain's great day but the turning of wheels. On all the roads that wound from the valleys to the heights, from Arlington, Somerset, the Wardsboros, the Jamaicas, the wheels started to turn even before the sky changed from its sullen, predawn gray. Horses, carriages, and men were merely dark figures at that sunless hour, but they were moving. The countryside for miles in every direction lost its usual stillness. Axles creaked; whips cracked; the metal of wheel rims and horseshoes grated on rock, slogged through mud. When a voice spoke it had that curious, alien quality that human speech seems to contain during the minutes just before daybreak.

At each change of the roadbed the numbers of the travelers increased, moving in the same direction, like so many black columns of ants converging on a single hill. Wagons jolted from isolated barnyards into side roads, turned from side roads into highways, branched off the highways onto the narrow tracks that twisted up Stratton. It was a mass pilgrimage. Farms were locked and deserted. Whole villages were left empty except for a few, lonely, stubborn Democrats. Many of the anti-Whigs were unable to resist the current and joined the processions, protesting they went only to jeer, fearful that they might miss a great event. On horseback, on wheels, on foot, ten thousand people made their way through the chill dampness, and all eyes turned toward the brightening eastern sky. What weather the sun would bring was, for the moment, the most important question of the Convention. Even the most reliable local forecasters felt qualms. A man could never tell when the elements would decide to be unpredictable.

The sun came up suddenly. It pushed gray clouds from the mountaintops and burned them into wisps with a swiftness that seemed incredible. Along every road, in every cortège, men, women, and children gave a spontaneous shout of joy. Before the last of these had died out the whole bright disk was revealed, glorious and promising.

Climbing to the driver's seat of the log-cabin wagon, Lot Purdy saw the sun and swore. He stood, one raised boot thrust between wheel spokes, cursing steadily for over a minute. Lot hadn't expected bad weather, but he thought God had missed a wonderful chance to put the Whigs in their place. When breath and vocabulary were exhausted, Lot felt better. He swung himself up to the box, inhaled deeply, and grinned. It was the sort of grin displayed by men on the gallows.

Lovina Chester lay on her back in her bed at the parsonage and watched the ceiling seem to absorb the shadows. She had been staring at it for a long time. Her sisters still slept. On the other four-poster in the corner, she heard Mattie toss and little Josepha whimper; Sally's hair was tumbled on the pillow beside her. Lovina didn't glance at her bedfellow. She knew by the regularity of the breath against her cheek that Sally was sleeping as she always did. This morning Lovina didn't want to see Sally curled up, one hand under her head, her face childish and shining. So innocent, thought Lovina. They all sleep so innocently. She felt old and weary.

She enjoyed a sense of superiority over these sisters that shared her room. They were young, too young for wickedness. None of them would have wanted to kiss the young Southerner the way she had or taken pleasure in it or lain awake with the drab knowledge that it wasn't what she wanted after all. Outside the bedroom birds began to greet the sun. Lovina remembered this was a special day. She tried desperately to retain her melancholy, but thoughts of her new dress intruded. She wondered if Charles would like her in it. Then her eyes filled, and she began to cry, soundlessly, so as not to wake the others. Turning toward the window she saw it was going to be a lovely morning.

The sun's yellow matched the trim on Fred Streeter's militia cap. The reveille roll he was beating on his drum was no quicker than the excited pounding of his heart. In the roadside field where they had rested, the troopers and bandsmen of the Young Men's Whig As-

158

sociation of Brattleboro, mostly militia, stirred themselves to renew the march. Fred Streeter rattled the call on his drumhead, slam and flam. He was joyously impatient. He would be seventeen in a few weeks, and the previous night had been the first he'd ever spent away from Brattleboro. The drummer boy was anxious to get on to Stratton and the big doings. He added some extra flourishings to his drumming, and the drumsticks flashed in the early sunshine.

One of the first rays glinted on a window of the inn at Townshend where Daniel Webster slept. The Senator turned his face to the wall and burrowed deeper into his blankets. In sleep the great lung power that everyone waited to hear explode in eloquence produced only a catarrhal snore.

On every road the wheel ruts deepened under constant friction. Hoofs and feet churned the roadways into mud. Men hurried on, urging their beasts. As it came into view, each traveler looked toward the ridge that was Stratton Mountain.

In the clearing the tamarack tree filtered the sun through its upper branches. The encampment was quiet; more animals stirred than humans. Outside the long cabin a torch still spluttered, burnt low, its flame wan and garish in the daylight. From inside came the vibrant pulsations of many snores; the last of the dancers and the exhausted fiddlers had gone to sleep hardly an hour before. Horses whinnied for their feed. Two infants woke and cried for the same reason. Some of the campfires still smoldered, and a few early risers, mostly women, tried to poke or blow embers into flame. There was a rattle of pots and pans. A boy on his way to fetch water paused and stared at a pewter plate nailed to the tentpole of the Rockingham delegation. A banner hung limply under it, and the boy read the words, forming them silently with his lips.

Harrison men don't use gold plate.

The boy grinned in appreciation and went on toward the noise of a stream. He began to whistle; the tune was piercing.

> For Tippecanoe and Tyler too!
> For Tippecanoe and Tyler too!

The shrill notes penetrated Jabez Tute's consciousness. He stirred, rolled over, and fell off the edge of the speaker's platform. He hit with a jarring thud and, having forgotten where he went to sleep, woke in panic. Fringed leggings swished as the leader of the Bond-ville roughs twisted into a crouching defense. His knife slid into his hand. He grunted, relaxed, and sheathed the knife. Jabez saw a bottle in the grass, pounced on it. When he found the flask was empty he ripped out an ancient and unprintable oath. He hurled the bottle at the tamarack tree. It struck the trunk and shattered with a crash.

On the mound of cider kegs behind the cabin the guard sat up and reached for his rifle. Finding his trust unassailed, he kicked off his blanket, stretched, and scratched himself. The guard looked up into the sky and said, "E-yah. Today."

As the sunshine slipped down the tamarack the camp awoke. By the time the tree's full shadow was dark against the grass, the clearing was again seething with life. Food sizzled over fires; chil-dren yelled; men and women chattered. There was even more noise than before. They were mostly suspicious, taciturn folk, but the night in the open had dulled their fears, loosened their tongues. Now they shared a common experience, a neighborly bond. They felt no surprise at talking more than usual; this was not an ordinary day.

"Come on fair, didn't it?"

"E-yah. Thought 'twould."

"Whig fortune, I calls it. Whig fortune!"

"Florilla! You stop that singing!"

"Pass me a slab of that pie, will you?"

"Pork eats good, don't it, brother?"

"Ought to. Raised it."

"When do you figure he'll get here?"

"Dan Webster, you mean?"

"E-yah. He's the big attraction, ain't he?"

"He'll be along. It's a mite early, you know."

"Florilla! Come away from that horse!"

"Ought to be a fair-sized crowd."

"Twice as many as is here now."

"You figure, John? *Twice* as many?"

"How many you think? How many?"

"Might run as high—four, five thousand."

"Might, at that."

"Dan'l Webster. You can thank him."

"He ain't the only cow in the herd."

"No. This meeting's for Tippecanoe. Guess he gets some credit."

"Tippecanoe and Tyler too!"

"Florilla!"

Near the flamboyant wagon that belonged to Doc Merrifield, the group around one fire was strikingly quiet. A single voice droned out, telling a story. The speaker was a large woman, ample. Her entire figure seemed to be composed of different-shaped melons stuffed under a black dress. Even her bonnet couldn't conceal the roundness of her head.

"E-yah. This Tippecanoe Convention will have to stir itself to match the excitement we had down to Bennington some years back. Murder, it was. Two brothers got the blame for doing in their sister's husband. Couldn't find no body anywhere, but there wasn't no doubt about it. One brother confessed. Told just how his brother did the deed. E-yah. Folks was getting ready to hang them both when somebody found the murdered man over in York State. Wasn't dead at all. He'd just up and run off from his wife. Course they had to let the brothers go. Confession or no. E-yah. But them two brothers wasn't never so thick after that."

Doc Merrifield, sitting beside his wagon with his head in his hands, rolled his eyes in the direction of the droning narrator. "Oh, Lord!" he said. "Won't that woman ever shut her mouth?"

"You'll feel better when you eat," said Mercy. She sounded stern. The fat medicine man groaned.

"Eat," repeated Mercy. "Food. Eggs. Pork and beans. Meat and potatoes. Your usual breakfast."

"Hold!" Doc said and moaned. "Hold, enough!"

Mercy was relentless. She stood over him and shook her finger. The gesture made her seem younger instead of older, as if she were a child rebuking a doll. "Doc Merrifield. You wouldn't feel like that if you'd said 'Hold, enough!' last night. What you need is a nice big dose of Epizootical Elixir!"

Doc put his pudgy hands over his face. He peeped up at her through his fingers. His voice, though muffled, was pleading. "The quality of mercy shouldn't be strained, my dear. Desist. Mislike me not for my digestion." He pulled his hands apart to reveal a broad grin. "Anyway, Mercy, I won."

"Doc!"

161

Doc Merrifield chuckled. He drew some coins from a pocket and tossed them on his palm. "Behold. Three beautiful American eagles. Ducats, my daughter. Ducats." The money, much handled, looked like gold buttons.

Mercy's arm flashed out; she snatched one of the eagles. She bit it, rubbed it. A flick of a thumb sent it spinning upward. With a deft movement she caught the falling coin, twisted her hands together as if washing them, and presented them, palms up. The coin was gone. The girl laughed.

"I give up," said Doc, shaking his head. "You're getting faster than Luke Brooks at making money disappear."

"Guess where, Doc?"

"Sleeve?"

Mercy shook her head, showing the tight cuff at her wrist.

"Sash?"

"Warmer."

"Bodice?"

"Yes. You didn't see, Doc? It was just a guess?"

"That's all." Doc nodded. With a sigh he added, "I take it you mean to keep it?"

"I do," said Mercy. "That eagle nests till we leave here."

"There's more where it came from." Doc wasn't arguing. He put the other two coins away. "Last night was just first blood, Mercy. Today's the big day."

"Ever know Luke to lose twice running?"

"Luke didn't lose. He just let me skim a bit of the cream." Doc accepted a steaming mug from Mercy, sipped it, and shuddered. "I ain't never seen such a wild game, Mercy. Some of those stakes got as much as fifty dollars on the table."

Mercy whistled. She said, "Doc, be careful. That's like pitting our Duke against race horses."

A dreamy smile spread across Doc's face. "Their money was sounder than their play, my dear. Along about midnight a gentleman from Boston sat in. They are opinionated in that city. Very opinionated. But not, I am pleased to say, always correct. We left him poorer but wiser."

"And folks talk of hard times!" The girl was indignant.

Doc shrugged. "This is a Whig shindig, and they're blaming hard times on the other side. So they can't act too tightfisted. Besides, it's a celebration." He waved at the campers around him. "Moths'll fly out of some of these pocketbooks, but they'll get opened just the same."

Their breakfast was interrupted by yells and shouting. People ran past, called to each other, pointed. It was much like the scurrying toward the dance on the previous evening, only this time the crowd pressed in the direction of the road. Time after time the noise thundered out, until it blended into a single roar.

"Treason!" cried Doc. "My head! What's the cause of these ructions?"

Mercy balanced on the hub of a wheel to see better. "There's a whole new bunch marching into the clearing."

"So early?" Doc's surprise brought him to his feet. "They must have come by night. What manner of folk are these?"

A man hurrying by caught the query and answered, "It's the Cambridgeport crowd."

"Cambridgeport." Doc repeated the name.

"They have a sign, Doc," called Mercy from her perch. "Two men out in front have a big sign." She tried to read the words. "We were . . . We were . . ." Flapping her hand angrily she lost patience with herself. "Doc, come on. Read it to me."

The fat man hoisted himself up on the wagon. Doc removed his spectacles, polished the lenses with his thumbs, put them back on. He peered over the rims and read aloud. *We were once blind but now we see.*

"What's that mean, Doc?"

"I guess this bunch used to be Democrats."

Whatever the reason, the new arrivals were welcomed with an enthusiasm reminiscent of a besieged city greeting a relieving army. This first influx assured the faithful already in the clearing that the Convention was going to increase in size and excitement. The newcomers were accepted as the initial impetus to the day's activities, a pledge of the great Dan'l Webster himself. If the greeters considered themselves hosts by reason of possession, the guests were felt necessary to the success of the party.

Once started, the flood of visitors continued. The first contingent had hardly finished unhitching when the second arrived. The second was still being met when the third came up the road. The intervals between arrivals grew progressively shorter until they ceased to exist, and, from both directions, an unending stream of people, animals, and conveyances poured into the clearing like waters meeting in a pool.

This swelling of the clearing's population multiplied the scenes of the previous day. More people gaped at the log cabin; the volume of human voices rose to a tumult and stayed there. Banners proclaiming Tippecanoe's virtues seemed to increase by geometric progression. Whig standards were planted before tents, nailed to wagons, hung from lapels. The sight of fresh bands arriving sent last night's musicians scurrying for their instruments.

While new travelers flowed into the clearing from the road, one man walked out of the forest from its upper edge. He appeared at a spot not yet reached by the mass of humanity, and, except by Doc Merrifield, this lone arrival passed unnoticed. The medicine man happened to be gazing at the unbroken green hedge of the trees. So suddenly was the man visible against that background that Doc grunted in surprise.

"What is it?" asked Mercy and turned.

"For a moment," said Doc, mocking himself, "I thought Birnam Wood was on the march again." He stared at the approaching stranger. "I knew they'd come out from under rocks for this Convention, but I didn't expect Dan'l Boone or Davey Crockett."

"Doc!" Mercy squealed with delight and clapped her hands. "He has a bear cub!"

The man was of medium height and slender, but with a slenderness that suggested strength like a drawn bow. He wore a long deerskin coat over homespun shirt and trousers. A round fur cap and moccasins completed his costume. He carried a rifle in the crook of one arm, and, somersaulting beside him at the end of a thin chain, was a chubby black bear cub.

Mercy hurried to get a closer view of the little animal. Doc Merrifield followed, more interested in the man. The latter walked with an easy slouchiness that looked lazy and covered ground rapidly. Beneath the fur cap, dark hair fell to his shoulders

Not bothering with formalities, the girl greeted the cub first. She said, "Hello, feller. Hello."

The cub stopped frisking and gazed at her.

"Can I pet him, mister?"

"Jones," said the man. "Tate Jones." His voice was low but almost toneless. His gaze was as shyly interested as the tiny bear's.

Doc Merrifield introduced himself. Mercy dropped on her knees and held out a hand toward the cub. Squatting on its haunches, the bear wriggled backward.

"He's afraid," said Mercy.

Jones said, "She." He twitched the chain; it rubbed on the cub's leather collar. "You. It's all right. You be nice."

"Is that her name? Hugh?"

Tate Jones looked at the medicine man. "E-yah. Just you."

You made up her mind, reached out both front paws, and clasped Mercy's hand. In another two seconds the cub was in the girl's arms, cuddling.

In his travels Doc Merrifield had met many backwoodsmen, but he expected them farther west. He said, "Come far?"

"No."

"Live around here?"

"E-yah."

Mercy was petting the cub. They were both uttering wordless noises at each other.

"Going to be a big day," said Doc.

"E-yah. Ain't no game. All this ruckus scared it away." The hunter surveyed the milling crowd and shook his head. "Won't see hide or hair or feather for weeks."

"Wherever did you find her?" asked Mercy.

"The cub? Shot her mother."

Deep in the woods a dog barked, the sharp sound barely discernible through the babble of voices in the clearing. Tate Jones cocked his head, listened, and said, "Fool dog. He ain't never caught a squirrel yet."

Doc Merrifield stared. "You mean you know what he's chasing? From here?"

"No." Jones smiled. "But it's something small. That's one of my dogs." He strolled deeper into the clearing and cast a professional glance at the log cabin. "Lot of good wood in that building. Sort of a waste, ain't it?"

The medicine man laughed. He said, "You must be a Democrat."

"Not me." Tate Jones shrugged. "I ain't taking sides. Far as I can see it don't make much difference whether you get treed by a wolf or a catamount. This Tippecanoe, now."

"E-yah?" Doc prompted.

"He's supposed to be a sight better woodsman than the other feller. Well. Maybe." The hunter nodded his head toward the log cabin. "I ain't never seen no woodsman ever had a place as big as that. Seems to me there's a whiff of skunk somewheres."

"Then you do favor Van Buren?"

"I don't favor nobody, mister. Van Buren's the government, ain't he? Well. It's the government that comes around bothering me to work on the roads to pay taxes. I don't use the roads! And it's the government that says when I can shoot a deer and when I can't. As if I didn't know my own business. Nope. If you want the truth without molasses I ain't got a mite of use for any part of this election foolery."

"A plague," said Doc. "A plague on both their houses!"

"What's that?"

"You're neutral."

"E-yah." Tate Jones chuckled. "And talkative."

Mercy, scratching the cub's neck, said, "But, Mr. Jones, it's just a gathering."

"E-yah." The fur cap dipped in a nod. "But I never did care much for gatherings, miss."

Doc Merrifield grinned. "But you came."

"Curious. Plain long-nosed curious, Doctor. Always been my worst failing." The hunter reached out and flicked a finger against the cub's muzzle. "You! You stop that!"

"She wasn't hurting me."

"I know, miss. But there ain't a mite of sense to let her teeth on your finger that way. No point giving her the taste for it."

Although out of sight, the Chittenden farm was within earshot of the clearing. The noise of the encampment was present in the barnyard like the humming of many bees. Four yards from the front door of the farmhouse the rattling passage of the travelers was a constant, closer counterpoint, loud or soft depending on the passer. During the first hour of daylight, busy with chores and breakfast, the Chittenden family ignored both clatter and buzz. Such calm indifference was due neither to congenital deafness nor will power. It was the result of Eratus Chittenden's express command.

166

Eratus was fully determined to enjoy every minute of the Convention. He had welcomed his guests the previous evening, and he looked forward to the coming festivities with no more reservations than a child unwrapping a present. But since the Chittendens, like the Torrey family on the western slope, were within walking distance of the meeting, Eratus refused to disturb the normal course of their existence until the last possible moment. Having made this clear to the family and friends, the big man found the continuing racket in front of his home an ever-increasing irritant.

As he showed William Kidder the flock of black-faced sheep, the high-pitched scream of wheel on axle made Eratus wince. He glared balefully at the road and its offending wagon. Self-control and the remembrance of his orders held the deep voice down to an angry rumble.

"Tophet! You'd think some folks never heard of axle grease!"

"E-yah," said Will Kidder. "It's going to be the biggest gathering ever seen in these parts." The visitor was a wiry man whose middle had gone its own fleshy way. On Kidder's spare figure the smooth curve of his stomach looked like a burl on a tree. With the pride of a delegate sharing in historic events, he had made the same remark five times since rising.

The host transferred his glare from stranger to guest. Eratus said, "What's that got to do with the price of eggs? I was talking about a man taking care of his wagon!"

"Everything hinges on this election, Eratus." Kidder spoke with pompous authority. "The cost of wagons. The price of eggs. Everything." He tapped Eratus on the shoulder with a forefinger to emphasize his points. "It's Tippecanoe or tyranny, Eratus. Mark my words. Each man who climbs this mountain, delegate or plain voter"—Kidder coughed—"adds some small part to the cause."

Nothing annoyed Eratus more than being prodded by someone addressing him. The big hands opened and closed once. Eratus swallowed and stifled his desire to pitch his friend into the horse trough. "Will," he said, "do you have to go around Robin Hood's barn? That axle ain't adding a blame thing but a screech that sets folks teeth on edge!"

"What axle?"

Kidder's honest surprise stunned Eratus into silence. He lowered

167

his head like a bull about to charge and took a deep breath. Before he could speak the other went on with his discourse.

"I guess you weren't listening, Eratus." Kidder might have been explaining to a child. "This is revolution! The people are aroused against their yoke! And once more, on this mountain, Vermont shows the way! Just like we did when old Ethan took Ticonderoga while the other colonies were still talking about Lexington!"

"Thunderation!" Eratus exploded. His roar sent the sheep tumbling over each other in flight. "You ain't comparing this to that!"

Stepping back, Kidder blinked. "It invites the comparison, Eratus. This Convention too will leave an indelible imprint on history. The first blow against corruption!"

Unmindful of his own Whig principles Eratus settled into the argument. He spread his legs and dug his heels into the turf. "Will," he said. "You're letting that badge ribbon on your coat addle you. Talking ain't the same as fighting! If it was, old Van'd be a better man than Tippecanoe. Slicker talker, ain't he? And . . ."

The interruption came from the road. There was a grinding crash, a splintering of wood. A man shouted; horses whinnied, shrill with fear. Another crash was followed by the thudding, frenzied slams of an animal pitching between shafts.

With a whirling bound Eratus Chittenden started toward the noise. As he ran with long, swift strides, his shouts summoned his sons. "Boys! Peter! Charles! Amos! Henry!"

The younger Chittendens were in the barnyard with a speed that indicated they had been, against orders, watching the passing. As the rest of the family, followed by guests, poured from the front door, Mary Chittenden's admonition was loud and clear.

"Eratus! Your good clothes!"

Not even glancing at a man stretched prone on the roadside, Eratus leaped for the bridle of the struggling horse. The beast, haunches pinned in the wreckage of a two-wheeled chaise, was kicking and rearing in its efforts to rise. Fingers twined in the leather, the big man pulled the horse's head down. Charles was beside his father an instant later, and the two exchanged crisp remarks that cut across the animal's screaming.

"Get her loose!"

"Tangled!"

"Easy. Up you come."

168

"I got her, Pa."

The horse scrambled to its feet and stood trembling. Both men stayed at her head. Charles soothed her with talk and petting. Eratus made a quick survey of the scene.

The upset chaise was jammed against the rear wheel of a farm wagon. Henry Chittenden was holding one of the wagon's horses, Amos the other. The driver, his wife, three children, and two other adults who occupied the wagon were as frozen and still as a group of statuary. Fright was in every face.

It had happened so fast that Will Kidder was still hurrying to the accident. His son and Peter Chittenden were bending over the figure sprawled beside the road.

"He hurt?" asked Eratus.

"Don't know," said Peter.

"Can't tell," Will Kidder said.

The man rolled over and sat up. He began to moan in a dazed, shaken way.

Holding the horse, Charles Chittenden watched the others right the chaise. It was a light carriage and, with so many hands, there was no trouble about moving it off the road. Charles scowled at the white face of the young man who had been spilled. Milksop, thought Charles, aware that the other's brown curls and rich clothing reminded him of the Southerner who had taken Lovina home. He cursed all foreigners—blast them, coming up here in their fine feathers just to smash carriages and turn girls' heads!

With a sudden aching sense of loss that surprised him, Charles remembered the past winter days when he and Lovina had been so close. Under his breath he damned the Convention. He was certain now that, if all these people hadn't come to upset things, he could have patched up his quarrel with the girl. The problem of marriage, with Peter home and his wife expecting, was ignored as beside the point.

Passing his palm up and down the mare's nose Charles let his unhappiness turn to anger and harden into resolve. If Lovina wanted to waste her time with that Virginia peacock he'd show her it meant nothing to him. Lovina Chester wasn't the only trout in the pool. He'd gone to the parsonage last night and all the way out to the clearing to make up with her, and then she hadn't even danced with him once. All right, Charles decided savagely. All right! She was small loss, anyway. He hunted for the right word to apply and settled on "fickle." She'd certainly proved that. First with Nathan Patch, and then with this Tom Dunbar. All Lovina was interested in was money. Well, there'd be plenty of other girls at the Convention. Girls from everywhere. He wondered if he'd see Lovina in such a mob. He tried to tell himself that it was only to show her his complete indifference and failed. Charles knew he was lying. He did care. I wish, he told himself, that this damn day was over.

The rattle of the farm wagon as it started away roused Charles from his reverie. The road was clear; the chaise stood on the grass, broken wheel propped on a stone, one shaft split, its top sagging sadly.

Another carriage followed the farm wagon and another. The whole line moved again; vehicle after vehicle lurched past the Chittendens.

Peter Blodgett stayed carefully behind the trees that bordered the Somerset road. Others who went on foot walked in the ditches to avoid the close press of vehicles on the narrow roadway. The boy had a different reason. He was afraid to expose himself to a fellow pedestrian. Anyone might turn out to be a neighbor who would recognize him as the Lymans' bound boy. Every step Peter took he knew was breaking the law.

Beneath the screening shadows of the forest he trudged up the mountain. Peter was small and thin for his thirteen years, with a shock of hair as bedraggled as a hay stack. He seemed to move inside his clothes, which were cut down from some of larger size. Barefoot, boots wrapped in the jacket under his arm, the boy walked at a dogged, steady pace that looked mechanical.

He was tired. He had come six miles, and he had no idea how far it was to the place where Daniel Webster was going to talk. He had no fear of losing his way, however. From the road came the din of those with the same destination. In spite of his fatigue, he did not stop to rest. He didn't dare risk it. Somebody might come along and ask for his folks.

Peter Blodgett had no folks.

He told himself that there was no reason to fear pursuit. His pursuers were ahead. Joe Lyman, his wife, and daughter, Stella,

170

had started before dawn; they should be at the meeting by this time. Peter's face was pinched and hard when he thought about them. He could still hear Joe's cackle.

"You'll stay to home and mind the stock!"

The boy was grimly satisfied that Joe's order had produced neither argument not tears. Argument was useless; Peter had long since abandoned tears. He only cried when Joe birched him. It shortened the whipping and was deliberate.

Bas-tard! Bas-tard! Bas-tard!

Peter marched in time to the word, stamping a foot forward on each syllable. It seemed to make the walking easier. It also expressed his opinion of Joe Lyman. He had been bound to Joe for as long as he could remember. He accepted his drudgery because it was the law.

The-law! The-law! The-law!

Not understanding exactly why, Peter was afraid of the law. He had heard about it often; it was a terrible thing and responsible for his being at the Lymans' in the first place. The law meant prison. Prison was worse even than Lyman's. The whippings were worse; the food was worse; the work was harder. And, worst of all, they shut you up. Stella Lyman had explained it all.

Stel-la! Stel-la! Stel-la!

He didn't use her name for marching very long. He didn't like Stella. She was older, taller, skinny as a fence rail. When they were younger she would pinch him, get him in trouble, tell her father on him. Peter frowned. Lately Stella had taken to brushing against him when her parents weren't around. He didn't like that, either; it bothered him.

Peter tramped along, taking his beat from Mrs. Lyman.

Old-sow! Old-sow! Old-sow!

Mrs. Lyman was a fat horse, always sniffing, always smelly. She could think up lots of things for Peter to do when he came in from the fields. She whined about how much he ate. It had been her suggestion that Peter stay home.

The stock didn't need him. He was going to hear Daniel Webster. Everybody said Webster was a great man, a spellbinding talker.

Peter Blodgett felt he had to see and hear him. He had to find out how you got to be great. Great enough to make all the Lymans eat dirt. He had to know.

There was a rustle of leaves. The boy stopped; his heart skipped. He didn't think of the law or capture. He worried about bear, catamount, and wildcat. If it was one of those he was sure he'd be killed. He started to shake.

A porcupine waddled out of the underbrush. The hedgehog glanced at Peter, sniffed, toddled off.

Peter stood very still, watching. The porcupine began to climb a tree. Peter laughed. He couldn't help it. He thought the animal looked just like a little fat man in a short fur coat.

He went on, so relieved that he felt less tired. He wondered how far he still had to go. He settled back into his steady pace, silently chanting the rhythm of his steps.

Bas-tard!
Old-sow!
The-law!
Stel-la!
Web-ster!
Web-ster!

Peter Blodgett climbed higher and higher.

The kitchen of Joel Patch's house was never bright in the morning. This was due partly to its situation and partly to the fact that its owner was more crotchety before noon than after. Not that any mood affected Patch's appetite. For a man his size the sawmill owner ate a surprising breakfast. On the day of the Stratton Convention Patch consumed, in order, a bowl of porridge, three fried eggs, a rasher of bacon, two cold pork chops with hot potatoes, half a loaf of bread, and a sizeable slab of apple pie. He washed this down with numerous mugs of tea and felt out of sorts. He couldn't place the reason for his peckishness, but it was based on food. Patch resented his help stuffing themselves without working. It was bad enough on Sunday, but here it was a weekday. Whenever daylight failed to bring the creak of the mill wheel and the whine of the saw, Joel Patch was an unhappy man. All he could think about was that his mill was idle, not making a penny.

Breakfast had been later than usual, and that irritated Patch too. He'd risen at his accustomed time. He thought the others were taking advantage of his kindness at granting them the day for the Convention.

172

Patch glared around the kitchen. "Where's Clem?"

Clem's wife shrugged. Lizzie's face was ruddy from bending over the fire. She said, wearily: "I don't know."

"Don't know? Don't know?" Patch's voice rose on the repetition. "Well, if he can't get here in time for breakfast he can go without. We ain't aiming to hold meals at all hours, you know."

"He ain't come home," Lizzie said.

"He ain't? Not all night?"

"No."

"Getting a mite big for his boots, ain't he?" Patch had an inner struggle in which pleasure that Clem wouldn't eat costly victuals vied with annoyance that he wasn't on the place. "Suppose I needed him?"

"You said it was a holiday."

"E-yah," admitted Patch. "But something might come up." He found another cause for worry, and his voice sharpened. "Where'd he go? Did he go off with one of my horses? If he's kept a horse out all night—doing I don't know what—I'll have a bone to pick with Clem Galusha!"

Nathan Patch looked up from his plate. "He didn't, Pa."

"How do you know?"

"He went down road with me. I give him and Tim a ride down to the crossroad."

"That right, Tim?"

"E-yah."

"How'd you get back?"

"Walked." Timothy Frost pushed his plate away.

"Where was Clem, then?"

"Inn."

"Tippling, I suppose."

Lizzie said, "You've got no call to suppose any such thing, Joel Patch." Cook or not, she was Clem's wife and she wasn't letting anyone give him a bad name. Lizzie was sure that her husband had gotten too drunk to come home. "There's plenty of places Clem could have spent the night. He has friends."

"Friends!" The exclamation held a sneer.

"E-yah. Friends." Lizzie didn't give an inch. She was cold and definite. When Patch glared she faced him without flinching.

Since Lizzie was a good cook and cheap, Patch shrewdly de-

173

cided not to force the issue. He glanced around, seeking another target for his ill temper. "Nathan!"

"Yes, Pa?"

"I heard you get home!"

Nathan sighed. He wasn't surprised. His father never failed to wake up at any night noise. He waited.

Patch rocked in his chair, pumping his anger. "A fine hour! Regular young buck, ain't you? Got nothing else to do but waste the whole night gallivanting. Swilling in the fleshpots. Wasting time and money!"

"I wasn't."

"Don't contradict! You ain't no hoot owl, are you? No? Then, you must have idled the night away!"

"I went to a dance."

"A dance?" Sarah Patch turned to her brother. For the first time that morning the girl's sallow face showed color. "Where, Nathan?"

"The clearing. In the Tippecanoe cabin."

"Who was there? What was it like?"

Nathan expanded under his sister's interest. He noticed that even his father was waiting to hear. The hired girl, Rhoda Hapgood, held a piece of bread halfway to her mouth, listening. Lizzie and Tim Frost were both looking at him. I'm the only one was there, thought Nathan, they won't know Lovina went home with the Southerner. He glanced at his father, calculating the best way to tell about the dance so there'd be no further mention of his late homecoming.

"Tell us, Nathan!"

Nathan said, "I never seen such a crowd. I seen some folks passing yesterday but I had no idea that there was so many already camped in that clearing."

"How many?" Patch snapped the question.

"You couldn't count them, Pa. Must have been eight, nine hundred. Maybe more."

"E-yah." Tim Frost added confirmation. "Tarbox's inn was packed tighter than a cord stacks in a woodshed."

"The dance, Nathan!" Sarah wriggled with impatience. "Go on about the dance!"

"Mostly," said Nathan, "they was strangers. Our folks sort of got lost in the shuffle. But there was three fiddlers. And two fel-

174

lers took turns calling. Both good. They lit the cabin with torches mostly. Pine knots, I'd say."

Patch said, "Waste of wood!"

"Oh, no, Pa," Sarah objected. "I wish I'd been."

"You were better off to home," Patch said, "than dancing with that rag, tag, and bobtail. Nobody that is anybody is coming till today! Bad enough that Nathan put in his presence! Suppose them torches had set fire to the cabin. Ever think of that? That cabin's an important part of the Convention!"

"It didn't get hurt, Pa."

"Might have." Patch rapped on the table. "Ain't sensible to risk it, is it? The Tippecanoe cabin's the point of the whole campaign. Nobody but a blame fool takes chances with the thing he's selling."

"Yes, Pa." Nathan figured his lateness was forgotten. But his father proved him wrong with the next sentence.

"And dancing most of the night ain't helping anybody get ahead. You hear, Nathan? When you fritter away your rest we all suffer. I can't get my sleep; you can't get your sleep; the horse you take can't get its sleep! I won't have it!"

"But we ain't working today!"

"Don't bring that up again!" Patch was so irked he spluttered. "We have things to do. I'm expecting Humphrey Dunklee, and there's no telling when he'll get here."

Tim Frost said, "Not this morning."

"What? How do you know?"

"I walked down to the road," said Tim. "After I did the milking. Folks are coming up from West Jamaica in droves."

"What's that got to do with Humphrey Dunklee?"

"Coming from Bennington, ain't he?"

"E-yah."

"Has to turn off at Stratton church, don't he?"

"E-yah."

"Well, you ain't seen the crowd. Nobody's going to get far bucking against that stream. It ain't going to let up till the meeting's over. Anybody on the road this morning is going to the clearing or they ain't going anywhere."

"Like that, eh?" Patch pondered and smiled. "Good thing I figured on so many shingles. We'll meet the Dunklees at the clearing. Maybe we'd better get ready. I've a seat on the platform, you know. Sarah, get your bonnet on. Nathan, hitch up the matched Morgans." He scraped back his chair, jerked a nod, and tramped from the room.

Sarah followed her father. Nathan went out toward the barn. Tim Frost looked at the cook and the hired girl. He said, "Mighty nice of Joel to offer us the extra horse and wagon that way. Saves us walking to the clearing."

Lizzie Galusha gave a sharp laugh. Rhoda, looking scared, glanced toward the door. Lizzie said, "Tim. Was Clem bad?"

"Not so bad, Lizzie. Last I saw."

"He didn't have much money."

"Well, he won some. Playing cards."

"Oh, my." Lizzie scratched at a stain on her apron. "Clem ain't himself when he drinks too much. I wish he'd come home."

Rhoda said, "He'll be all right, Lizzie."

"No. No, Rhoda. I know. He gets sort of crazy. And all these people and excitement and talking politics—anything could happen. I—I hate to ask but I'd be real beholden if you'd help me look for him."

"Of course, Lizzie."

"E-yah." Tim nodded. "He wouldn't have wandered far. Clem ain't overfond of walking, and I know for a fact that he's aiming to take in that Convention."

"What Clem aims to do before he starts drinking and what he does after are two different things." Lizzie sighed, shaking her head. "The sooner we get hold of him the better. You go along, Rhoda. I'll take care of the dishes."

"Ain't you coming?"

"Later. Either one of you's better than me. You're his friends. I'm Clem's wife. When he's like this, he don't take kindly to any words from me. He's a good man, Clem is, sober. But somehow my trying to slow his drinking makes him do it the more. Please go."

Tim Frost rubbed his chin. "I got to shave, Lizzie."

"Then, you, Rhoda. I'll feel better if I know somebody's looking for Clem."

"All right. Don't worry, Lizzie." Rhoda touched the other woman timidly. "I'll hunt him up."

There was no delay while Rhoda Hapgood made her toilet.

176

She ran a comb through her hair and snatched a shawl from a hook. Rhoda was already wearing her best dress; her other one was even more patched. Shoes and petticoats remained the same no matter what the occasion. They were all she had. Still, the girl had added something special to her apparel in honor of the great day. She wore a much-darned pair of striped stockings discarded by Sarah Patch.

She left the house by the side door because there was less chance of Joel Patch seeing her go that way. Rhoda was afraid that her employer might yet decide not to let her attend the Convention. She hurried, jogging along with short, quick steps, holding her skirts above her high shoe tops.

The Patch mill and buildings were a good rifleshot from the main road. Patch's land ended at a rude wooden bridge that crossed the stream that fed the millrace. Rhoda didn't feel free until her heels clattered on the planking.

She stopped on the bridge, staring ahead. She could see the opening where the lane entered the West Jamaica road. The banks of the lane, covered with grass and bushes, made a green frame, filled every few seconds by a moving vehicle. Watching, Rhoda gasped. The foot of the lane was blocked and clear, blocked and clear, as the travelers passed.

"Land!" said Rhoda. She went on more slowly, a little frightened. Her footsteps sounded hollow on the bridge, were muffled in the dirt.

Sprawled on the brookside beneath the bridge, Clem Galusha never stirred. He was sunk in the heavy, drugged sleep that follows intoxication. The splashing of the stream drowned his labored breathing.

At the end of the lane Rhoda turned toward Stratton church. The heavy traffic drove her off the road. Where it was dry, the wheels raised dust; at the wet spots there was mud. Rhoda didn't want her dress splattered. She was excited by the number of passing conveyances but fearful, too. It was totally beyond her experience. Too timid to request a ride, too shy to accept one, Rhoda walked along the bank and in the ditch. She was hot and a little tired by the time she reached the Brayton farm. She sat down to rest on a stone fence.

"Rhoda! Rhoda Hapgood!"

177

The hired girl turned. She saw a hand beckoning from the front door of the Brayton house. The door was barely ajar, but Rhoda had no doubts about the hand's owner. She called, "Morning, Miz Brayton."

Zilpha Brayton didn't bother to return the greeting. She cried, "Come along, Rhoda. Come in and set a spell."

Rhoda was used to obeying orders, and she was thirsty. She climbed the slope between the fence and the house. She pushed open the door and paused.

"Come in, come in. And shut the door. I got out of the way so those folks wouldn't see me." Zilpha's chuckle came from the shadows. "That'd tie up the whole parade!"

Rhoda closed the door, blushed, and averted her glance. Zilpha Brayton was clad in her shift and not another stitch. The single garment reached her knees, but legs and feet, arms and shoulders were bare. Under the thin lawn of the tight shift the rest of Zilpha was more outlined than suggested. Rhoda was shocked; she had never seen so much white skin in her life.

Noticing the girl's confusion Zilpha laughed. "I was washing myself," she explained. "Just happened to glance out and see you. Lucky for you I did."

"Yes, ma'am." Rhoda wasn't so sure.

"Old cross Patch too skinflint to give you a ride to the meeting?"

The obvious nickname made Rhoda giggle. She thought it very clever and filed it away to tell Lizzie. She relaxed, stopped blushing, and managed to look at Zilpha. "I don't mind walking, Miz Brayton."

"Fiddlesticks! The road ain't safe today. Ever see such a herd of folks?" Zilpha was brushing her hair. It reached almost to her waist, its red vivid against the white shift. It seemed to ripple and change color as the brush swept through it. "I'll see you get a ride!"

"Thank you, ma'am." Rhoda tried not to notice how Zilpha's breasts bobbed with each brush stroke.

"Don't thank me. It ain't my carriage. We got a couple spent last night in our shed. An old couple." For the space of one sweep of the hairbrush Zilpha's face hardened, and her eyes were like green stones. Then, laughing, she went on. "They're from Dummerston Center. The old feller's real interesting. He got took fighting the British back in '13. Spent more'n a year in prison in

Canada. Like to died. He wasn't no chicken even then." Zilpha knew that the high spirits she felt were making her babble, but she didn't care. Her excitement had been mounting all morning. This day was different from all other days.

"Maybe I'll be in the way, Miz Brayton."

"Nonsense, Rhoda. They don't care. They paid Lem half a dollar just for a shakedown in our shed. There's plenty of room in their wagon."

Rhoda was grateful. She was flattered that Mrs. Brayton, whom she didn't know very well, should go to all this trouble. She said, "Could I have a drink of water?"

"Help yourself." Zilpha brandished the hairbrush in the direction of the kitchen. "There's nobody here but me. Asa slept down to the inn—he's working there. And Lem left early to sell Tippecanoe badges."

When Rhoda returned from getting the water Zilpha called her into the bedroom. The girl was pleased to find that Mrs. Brayton had donned several of her petticoats and an underwaist. With deft, swift movements Zilpha was pinning her hair into place. She grinned at Rhoda, took two hairpins from her teeth, and slipped them into position.

"Rhoda."

"Yes, Miz Brayton?"

"You walked all the way from Patch's?"

"E-yah."

"Meet anybody?"

Rhoda laughed. Zilpha's chuckle blended with the girl's laughter. "That was silly, wasn't it?" said Zilpha. "I meant anyone we know. One of the neighbors maybe. The Carpenter family? Isaac Mead?" She hoped the last name sounded casual enough.

"No, Miz Brayton."

"Nobody at all?"

"No."

"Well," Zilpha said, beaming at her image in a scrap of mirror, "I guess they'll all be at the clearing. We'll meet everyone we know there."

"I hope so."

"Eh?" Zilpha Brayton pivoted and considered Rhoda. "Aiming to meet your beau, Rhoda?"

179

"Oh, no, Miz Brayton."

"Oh, no." The woman mimicked the protest. She put her hands on the girl's arms and shook her gently. "Why not, Rhoda? Why not? This is a perfect day for such a thing. Exciting. Different. There'll never be another day like this on Stratton." She laughed, turning away from the girl. Poor little mouse, thought Zilpha. She wondered if Rhoda ever had known a man. Probably not. You had to be a woman to understand that reckless flutter inside that you meant to satisfy no matter what the cost. Thinking of Isaac Mead Zilpha felt weak in the knees. She sat down on the bed to draw on her stockings.

Rhoda was careful not to watch. She said, "I haven't any beau, Miz Brayton."

"Then who did you hope to meet?"

"Clem Galusha."

"Clem?"

"His wife asked me to. Clem—well, I guess he's been drinking. He didn't come home."

"You poor child." Zilpha meant it; she was sorry for any girl who was not meeting an interesting man today. She was suddenly certain that she and Isaac would find each other at the Convention. She was sure. Somehow this meeting would be unlike all their other meetings, as unlike as the Convention's great events were to the normal routine of the mountain. There would be no more simply gazing at each other, no more mouthing polite phrases. They would be beyond dancing in the same square. In the clearing, in a few hours, for the first time since that spring day, they would be alone, Zilpha and Isaac, alone in a multitude, secure in a crush of thousands where it would be easy to lose Lem Brayton. She had no plans beyond the actual encounter, but she knew that would be the beginning. "You poor child," repeated Zilpha. Her laughter was so quick and brittle that Rhoda stared.

"Oh, Clem oughtn't to be too hard to find, Miz Brayton," Rhoda declared. "Drunk or sober he'll be up there listening to Senator Webster. Like everybody else."

"E-yah." Zilpha picked up her dress, thrusting her arms into it. She held it over her head, hands apart, stretching the material. "Help me into this, Rhoda. I just finished fixing my hair."

The hired girl eased the dress over Zilpha's head. No one else

180

on the mountain, not even the woman who wore it, would have thought the black dress fine, but Rhoda Hapgood did. She fingered the coarse wool and smoothed out the wrinkles with tender care.

Zilpha Brayton was knotting her bootlace when they heard the singing on the road outside. She stiffened, listening. Bent over, not looking up, Zilpha said, "See who's making all that fuss, dear." The tightness of her voice might have been the result of her posture.

Already at the window, Rhoda said, "It's Mr. Mead, Miz Brayton. With a whole wagonload of young fellers."

"E-yah." Zilpha looked out over the girl's shoulder. "It is, ain't it?"

Nick, Isaac Mead's walleyed horse, was stepping along in front of the Brayton house. The wagon he pulled held half a dozen young men. It was easy to judge that Isaac had picked them up on the road and was taking them to the clearing. They were all singing. Isaac Mead, standing up to drive, was beating time with his whip.

The song roared out in full-throated chorus.

> It's step her to your weevily wheat,
> It's step her to your barley!
> It's step her to your weevily wheat,
> To bake a cake for Charley!

Showing off, Zilpha said to herself. She saw the quick turn of Isaac's head as he glanced at the house and away. Zilpha bit her lip to keep from giggling aloud.

The Mead wagon passed. It was out of sight when another fragment of the song drifted back to the two at the window.

> Oh, Charley, he's a fine young man!
> Oh, Charley, he's a dandy!

Rhoda Hapgood sighed. "They are having a time, ain't they?"

"E-yah."

"Miz Brayton. If you ain't leaving soon, I'd better get along. It won't be easy to locate Clem in that crowd."

"Wait, Rhoda." Zilpha was beside herself. At the dance Isaac had sung the words of the tunes and now again. Ain't nobody, she thought, sung anything to me in years. A phrase, with a

181

change of name, kept running through her head. 'Isaac, he's a fine young man! Isaac, he's a dandy!' She wanted to dance, to clap her hands. She wanted to do something for somebody, for Rhoda. "You set yourself on that bed, Rhoda. It's time a body took you in hand."

"Me, Miz Brayton?"

"You. A woman can't go traipsing off to a meeting big as this one without looking her best." As she talked, Zilpha rearranged Rhoda's hair. The girl sat, bewildered, her head rolling beneath the brush as if she had no neck muscles. "I ain't got a stitch to lend you, Rhoda, but I do know a trick or two."

Zilpha rummaged in a drawer and produced a string of white beads. She answered Rhoda's protest by fastening them around the girl's neck.

"You hush, now. They ain't worth hardly anything. And you can bring them back after. They look real nice on that blue dress."

"Oh, Miz Brayton."

Two pieces of red ribbon, of close but not exact match, completed the additions to Rhoda's costume. Zilpha fixed one as a jaunty bow in Rhoda's hair; the other became a sash around her waist.

"Oh, Miz Brayton."

"Wait a minute." Zilpha, enjoying herself, bustled off and came back with a dampened strip of red flannel. "Let's rub this on your cheeks. What you need is color, child!"

"Oh, I couldn't."

"Stand still. There. Now look at yourself."

"Oh. Suppose Mr. Patch sees me?"

"Tell him to . . ." Zilpha stopped and coughed. "Tell him the womenfolk on this mountain don't get many chances to have a good time. And they ought to make the most of it!"

"It—it does make me look different." Rhoda was awed by her reflection.

"'Course it does. And there ain't a soul going to know you used it unless you tell. You're a sight prettier with some color in your cheeks, Rhoda. Any woman is. I noticed that when you blushed."

"Somebody's calling you, Miz Brayton."

"I hear him. That's the old feller. They must be ready to set

182

out." Zilpha looked down at the wet flannel, smiled, and tossed it aside. She wouldn't need that today. She swept up her bonnet and put it on.

"I don't know how to thank you, Miz Brayton."

"Then don't."

"But—you went to all this trouble. . . ."

"Ain't anything at all."

"You did, too! Nobody else ever . . ."

"Rhoda Hapgood! Get a move on! They're waiting!"

"But—oh, Miz Brayton—I—you—you're so—so . . ."

"E-yah?"

"Good."

Zilpha Brayton's smile vanished, she was quiet for so long that Rhoda thought maybe she hadn't heard. At last Zilpha said, "Just you have a good time at that Convention, Rhoda. You have a good time no matter what. That's what I'm aiming to do!"

On the speaker's platform beside the tamarack tree a bugler raised his instrument. Sunlight gleamed on the horn's polished brass as he blew a long call.

The blared notes reached over the heads of the clustered crowd to the edge of the great clearing; they echoed, thinner and tinny, from the mountainside above. When the bugle stopped the clearing was amazingly quiet.

A man stepped in front of the bugler and held up his hand.

"Fellow Whigs. Fellow citizens. An announcement."

The nasal voice reached only the ranks nearest the platform. These passed the words back through the crowd. The murmur rolled through the multitude like breaking surf and was almost as visible. The announcer held up his hand again. He read from a slip of paper.

"The delegates from all townships being accounted present, the Whig party of this, the First Congressional District of the State of Vermont, in Convention assembled on Stratton Mountain, have chosen Dr. W. R. Ranney of Townshend as President of the day."

Not being able to hear, the crowd gave only scattered applause. The nasal voice continued.

"Selected as Marshal of the day—Colonel Baker of Arlington."

Folding his paper the man bowed. He had reached the steps

of the platform before the assemblage realized the announcement was over. Speech broke out in every section of the gathering, as simultaneously as guns fired on signal.

"Is that all?"

"Hey! Wait!"

"Where's Webster?"

"E-yah. When's Dan Webster get here?"

"We rode a long way!"

"Is he coming or ain't he?"

The shouters were not delegates but the masculine half of the spectators. The fact that people were still arriving showed that more than delegations had climbed the mountain. Political argument was the countryside's avocation; the Presidential election was its most popular contest, an intensely exciting game in which everyone could take part. This summer the interest of all had been centered in the Stratton Convention. They had been promised a speaker who was almost a legend. Naturally suspicious of strangers, present at a gathering where strangers outnumbered friends, the visitors voiced a quick demand for that speaker. The one thing a Vermonter cannot stand is to be tricked into doing something, even if it's something he wants to do.

There was a hurried conference on the platform. Another man cupped hands to his mouth and shouted information. "Just be patient! Senator Webster is on his way! We've had word he's left Townshend!"

This time there was a spontaneous roar of approval. The crowd dispersed; men discussed the distance between Townshend and Stratton, speculated on how fast it could be covered. They didn't mind waiting as long as they weren't being fooled.

Under the tamarack tree two men talked in low voices. One was the Man from New Hampshire. He said, "Is that true, Captain? About Webster?"

"E-yah. Feller rode in with the message."

"That's a relief. I'd hate to see this mob get out of hand."

"Me, too." The Captain grinned.

"How many people you think are here?"

"Ain't counted."

"I'd say at least ten thousand."

"Nearer fifteen's my guess."

184

"And still coming!"

"And still coming."

"God!" The Man from New Hampshire was impressed. "How in blazes are you going to keep them happy?"

"I don't know," said the Captain. "But those bands better take turns playing. There's ten or more of them. That'll help." He sighed. "It's bigger than anybody expected. It's like the biggest damn county fair ever. But nothing's really going to start till Dan Webster gets here."

The multitude found its own amusements. Some, an ever-changing gallery, watched the delegates proceed with the business of the Convention. The band music was unceasing; it came first from one part of the clearing and then from another, as each group took up where the last had left off.

With a sure sense of timing, Dr. Portus J. Merrifield hoisted Mercy onto the open back of their red wagon. "Now," said the fat medicine man, "is when we do business. They're waiting and a mite restless and willing to listen to anything."

"I can't sing against that band music," Mercy said.

"We won't try." Doc was stacking bottles of his Elixir. His voice rose suddenly in a summons like a war cry. "Good Whigs this way! Good Whigs this way!"

"That'll fetch them." The girl listened to the tune being played at the moment. She grinned and said, "And this'll keep them." Without preliminary she started to sing in a clear, sweet soprano.

> What has caused this great commotion,
> Motion, motion,
> Our country rolling through?
> It is the ball a-rolling on, on.
> For Tippecanoe and Tyler too,
> Tippecanoe and Tyler too!

"Hold!" Doc Merrifield had been calculating the size of the audience and judged it had reached its proper magnitude. His patter was swift and smooth. He smiled down on the upturned faces as if he were father to them all. His breath seemed inexhaustible.

"Tippecanoe and Tyler too! Worthy names! Victory sit upon their helms! Friends, Whigs, and countrymen, lend me your ears!

'What has caused this great commotion, motion, motion'? You know the answer to that, my friends. We come to bury Caesar! The Caesar in the White House—the fox of Kinderhook—the Dutch profligate who lolls on cushioned divans and eats from golden vessels! *That* 'has caused this great commotion, motion, motion'! Health! Our country is sick and must be healed! Healed, cured, made well! We have the remedy! Tippecanoe and Tyler too!"

Doc bowed; Mercy led the applause.

"E-yah! I thank you, my friends. There is no greater boon to mankind than a remedy for ills—a cure for those sicknesses the flesh is heir to! But do we come only to heal our country? What of ourselves? Unless you—the citizens of the country—enjoy well-being, can the country have it? Aye, there's the rub! Tippecanoe and Tyler too can help the nation but not you. Not you, madam, nor that rosy-cheeked child in your arms. He looks like you, madam. The same fair hair, the same wonderful health. But! You are a mother! You have known the slings and arrows of outrageous fortune. You have known the worries when that child was ill. Am I correct? I see by your face I am. And you, sir, I judge you to be a man of common sense. Yet I daresay you too have known moments when someone dear to you needed a remedy! Some faithful beast, perhaps, among your livestock! You, too. And you, fair maiden. And your blushing companion! We are all—all—owners of sad memories that should not be stressed on this great day."

Mercy touched a handkerchief to her eyes. Doc sighed. His next word was like a gunshot.

"But! We do not have to face the future unarmed, defenseless, turning like a weather vane before each ill wind! No! I have here a discovery of my own. A mixture of herbs and soothing liquids blended by a recipe handed down in my family. Is there a doctor among my listeners? No? Too bad. I would tell any surgeon or physician the scientific manner in which my little remedy was concocted. And he would laugh. Yes—er—E-yah! Laugh, my friends. It would be a thing of infinite jest and chuckles. Doctors are like that. You have all heard them sneer at some home remedy, some ointment perhaps that was your heritage from a dear grandmother. Why? Because they have studied? I have studied! Because they know Latin? I know Latin! *Ipso facto!* No—because they are afraid I will put them out of business!"

Mercy handed Doc a bottle of brown glass. He held it up in one hand and slapped it with the other.

"Merrifield's Epizootical Elixir! Good for man or beast! It too has caused 'a great commotion, motion, motion,' wherever I have sold it. Twenty-five cents the bottle. A quarter of a dollar. Not cheap. I will have naught to do with cheapness. A bargain, yes. But no shoddy! For your quarter you get full value. For man this Elixir will ease many things."

Doc shut his eyes and rattled a list of the things.

"Colic, croup, piles, boils, inflammation of the bowels, eruptions of the skin, ague, chills, fever—black, yellow, or tropical—spider bite, snake bite, liver complaint, and bile. Headaches, heartburn, coughs, colds, declines, rheumatism, dizziness, vapors, eye spots, female sickness, and growing pains! All for one-quarter of a dollar!"

Mercy got down, arms full of bottles, and began to pass through the audience. Doc's eyes opened at each clink of coins.

"Taken externally, rubbed or applied to the afflicted spot, Merrifield's Epizootical Elixir is equally soothing. Cuts, wounds, scrapes, slivers, hangnail, corns, sprains, wrenches, contusions and abrasions, chafing, chapping, felons, fistulas, bruises, swellings, discoloration, and proud flesh! It also has been known to remove warts! All for one-quarter of a dollar!"

Doc flipped the bottle, caught it, and held it out. A woman paid him a quarter.

"You won't regret that outlay. If you own animals, that's the best quarter you ever spent! Good for lameness, heaves, swellings of flesh or bone in horses. You've seen my horse? Had a bowed tendon! E-yah! A free bottle if you can guess which leg! What's that? Wrong! The gentleman loses. Mercy, sell him a bottle. That your dog, sonny? Fine-looking hound. A little Elixir will keep him free from mange. Thank you, sir. You must get it now! Merrifield's Epizootical Elixir! I may not pass this way again for another year. But when I return you'll thank me! E-yah! Thank you, ma'am. That bottle when empty is very handy in the kitchen. Just the right size for maple syrup! Thank you, young lady. Wait for your change! This is an honest business. Only a quarter of a dollar! One bottle to a customer!"

"Pa! Pa!" A boy charged yelling into the crowd. "They're holding an ox-pulling contest yonder!"

187

"Oxen!" cried Doc. "Wonderful beasts! The Elixir makes their hides firm and their hair sleek. Tones the muscles! Good for man or beast!"

The new attraction scattered Doc's listeners. The medicine man took a quick look at his stock and, in a whisper, lowered the price for the small amount remaining. When the last purchaser wandered away, the red wagon had no more bottles of Merrifield's Epizootical Elixir.

"Doc! We did it!" Mercy shook a heavy sack of coins.

"E-yah." The fat man mopped his face. "Sometimes I wonder where I get the wind! Have any trouble?"

"No. They couldn't buy them fast enough. I hardly used my eyes at all. One man patted me, so I palmed his half dollar."

"Mercy!" Doc's round face was stern. "I told you to holler if . . ."

"I was all right, Doc. Why make trouble?"

Tate Jones suddenly appeared around the corner of the wagon. He was carrying the bear cub. He said, "Miss Mercy. The little tyke's a mite weary. Woud you care to mind him a while?"

"I'd enjoy it."

"Here, you. Go to the lady."

"Did you hear my talk?" asked Doc Merrifield.

"E-yah." The hunter nodded. "I heard it. Beats a blue jay for chattering. What's that brew of yours got that bear grease ain't?"

"Doc," Mercy said and laughed.

The two men left her and went to watch the oxen. It was an impromptu contest. A couple of farmers, who had made the journey by ox cart and been roundly cursed for their slowness on the road, had started comparing teams. Discussion led to argument, argument to challenge, challenge to the test. For want of a proper stoneboat they had lashed saplings into a rough raft and weighted it with rocks.

Both teams were in prime condition. The Captain, delighted at the chance to provide entertainment, governed the trials. In close-packed ranks the spectators surrounded the ragged ellipse of ground that served as an arena.

The first farmer hitched his oxen to the raft. He was a tall, heavy-set man with bowlegs. Goad in hand he stepped into position and nodded to the Captain.

"Pull!" cried the Captain.

A wordless shout commanded the oxen. The two great beasts stopped being placid and stiffened. For a breath they were as immobile as stone images. Then the two wide white heads lowered slightly, the thick neck muscles tensed, the yoke quivered.

As swift as a fencer's rapier the goad darted out. The bowlegged man stabbed twice; each ox felt a prick.

The rock-piled raft jerked forward. The team settled into it, legs working, and pulled the burden slowly across the ground.

The crowd shouted. Most of the farmers watched quietly; their comments on the team's points were low, professional. Younger men, city folk, picked favorites, made bets. Some women admired the show of strength; a few knew oxen; most were frankly bored.

The rival ox team was hitched in place. Their driver was tall, too, but thin. He said little and chewed tobacco. Hands in pockets, he checked the position of the yoke and nodded.

"Pull!"

"Ho!" cried the driver. He clapped his hands.

Again the raft scraped along the ground. The driver stopped his team. He stood in front of it and put a palm on each wet muzzle. "Double the load," he said and spat.

"Double?" asked the Captain.

"Double?" echoed the bowlegged man.

"E-yah."

There was little talk from the crowd as the heavy stones were lifted into place. Farmers looked at the mound of rock and exchanged glances. Several shook their heads. Silently, as if pushed by some unseen hand, the whole circle of spectators edged closer.

"Pull!"

"Ho!"

The strain was visible. Everything that was engaged in the task became taut with effort. Muscles bulged beneath the oxen's hides; their legs trembled. The lines were straight and shivering; the yoke seemed to twitch.

"Ho! Ho! Ho!" The driver beat his palms together.

Slowly the raft moved. An inch—six inches—a foot—a yard—

As the watchers cheered the bowlegged driver slammed the point of his goad into the ground. He left it there, vibrating, walked over, and shook his rival's hand.

The removal of the rocks from the raft turned into an exhibition of feats of strength. There were no entry restrictions. Sections of the crowd would call loudly for their town favorites. The champions, big men mostly, would step forth, shed their coats, and try their hands at the weights.

It was soon apparent that two men were beating all comers. One was a giant from Londonderry; the other, equally big, represented Bellows Falls. They were evenly matched. Both heaved up the largest of the stones and managed to toss it a few feet.

"Draw!" called the Captain.

"Wrestle it out!"

The two stalwarts eyed each other; neither was willing to accept this suggestion. But each was reluctant to back down or yield to the other's supremacy.

The Captain didn't favor a wrestling match; he was too afraid of a brawl. Trying to think of an excuse, he noticed Tate Jones leaning on his rifle. "Wait a minute!" he shouted. "Now, hold on, everybody. What do you say they shoot it off?"

"A shoot!"

"A shooting match!"

"E-yah!"

Yells of approval instantly endorsed the plan. The one inalienable right of free men that both Whigs and Democrats agreed upon in the state of Vermont was the right to bear arms. Their fathers and grandfathers, fine shots, had held the state against all enemies, white or red, foreign or domestic. They had been raised in the tradition that at some time in boyhood every male sighted along the barrel of a gun and, being a Vermonter, became a good shot. Even in the cities it was accepted as a fact, as natural as growing. Most of them owned guns and used them. The better shots, the crack marksmen, were recognized as the only true aristocracy.

Nobody, however, intended to let a shooting match be confined to two opponents. Men who had brought them raced back to their wagons for their guns. Others complained bitterly to their wives because pet rifles had been left at home. A line was quickly formed; a mark selected. Dozens of pieces, of all sizes and makes, made an appearance.

Tate Jones refused to participate. He said, "I do not waste powder."

"No," said the guard by the cider.

190

Tom Dunbar rode his gelding into the clearing and watched from the saddle. He said something to Hoc, who was beside him. The Negro nodded and patted his saddlebags.

Under the tamarack tree Put Chester argued with Seth Purdy. "But, Seth! You're a good shot! You might win!"

"No gun." Seth tried to shrug, failed.

"If you ran home . . . No." Put punched his fist into his palm. "No time. They're starting."

Jabez Tute was the first to shoot. Stepping to the line the lad, with his leggings and coonskin cap, looked to the crowd like a character from the widely read novels of James Fenimore Cooper. His old fashioned, long-barreled rifle added to the picture. It was as tall as Jabez, but he had no trouble handling it. The long barrel swung up, steadied.

The gun cracked. Bark flew from the thin, white-birch sapling that had been chosen as the target.

"A hit," Jabez Tute said. He showed his teeth. "In the clout!"

Others stepped forward and fired. Shot after shot rang out, sounding like a shutter slamming in the wind. The giant lifter from Londonderry hit the sapling; the other missed. A well-dressed, stout gentleman also sent a ball into the tree. He was the banker from Bennington, Humphrey Dunklee.

Put Chester tugged at Tate Jones. "Tate! Tate! You can't let them win! It's our mountain! You can't let outsiders be the best shots. You can beat all three of them!"

The hunter smiled down at the boy. "Don't take on, Put. Anybody can hit a mark."

"Please, Tate." Seth Purdy supported Put. "It's our mountain. We ought to show these folks!"

Tate Jones looked closely at his young neighbors. He saw more of Stratton's youth than he did of its adults, and Seth's father was his closest friend. He scorned the shooting match as a wasteful frivolity, but he could see that it was important to the boys.

"Tate! Tate Jones!" Lem Brayton pushed his way through the crowd. "You ain't going to let these blame foreigners beat, are you?" Lem's voice was a shrill whine. He'd been brooding and envious ever since he'd watched the ox teams; he resented the knowledge that both teams were finer than his own.

At first glance the hunter thought that Brayton's clothes were

191

in tatters. Then he saw that Lem's jacket was adorned with many white ribbons. Never having liked Lem Brayton, the woodsman didn't bother to answer. He turned to watch the marksmanship.

A more difficult target, a white strip of birch bark, had been hung from a distant tree. Jabez Tute's shot sent it fluttering to the ground. Rehoisted, it stayed untouched as both giant and banker fired and missed.

Whooping over the general applause, the Bondville roughs pounded their leader on the back. The Captain was pointing to Jabez Tute, when Tate Jones spoke.

"Hold on a minute."

The Captain stared. "You shooting?" The company, sensing drama, became quiet and listened.

"No. But the boy is." The hunter thrust his rifle into Seth Purdy's hands. "All yours, Seth. Seems I recall you know what it's for."

Put shouted, "Go on, Seth! Show them!"

Seth was too surprised to move. He'd never known Tate Jones to lend his gun to anyone. He stared down at the flintlock, incredulous and uneasy.

Jabez Tute's laugh was mocking. He said, "Lo! A puking babe!"

"Even money he does!" Doc Merrifield bet on the hunter's judgment.

The stout banker said, "Taken for a dollar."

Scowling, Seth Purdy took his position. For an instant he wondered if his father would approve of his taking part in these Whig games. Still, maybe he could show they weren't the only ones could shoot. He planted himself firmly and raised the rifle.

"The piece is too big for the stripling!" said Jabez Tute. His followers tittered, but the spectators, interested, hissed for silence. There was no sound but the distant strains of a band.

Seth, squinting, sighted along the barrel. The target was a white daub among the green foliage. The boy took a deep breath, held it, and gently squeezed the trigger.

The shot crashed; the bark jerked, turned over, and floated lazily down.

"E-yah!" said Tate Jones.

Put Chester turned a handspring. Doc Merrifield collected his dollar. Only the Bondville roughs refrained from cheering. Women waved their handkerchiefs; men nodded and shouted approval.

"Good lad!"

"That's shooting."

"Showed him, didn't he?"

"Luck, maybe."

"Hit it clean!"

"Next shot'll tell."

Tate Jones reloaded his rifle. He measured the powder carefully into his palm, rammed home wad and ball. Examining the flint in the hammer, he replaced it with a fresh one. When the gun was ready the hunter returned it to Seth.

The Captain placed the contestants facing away from the forest. Another strip of bark was affixed to a different tree. "At the word," said the Captain. "Turn. Find target. And fire. Ready?"

Jabez Tute nodded.

"Go!"

The tail on the coonskin cap stood out straight as Jabez Tute whirled and fired. Leaves ripped from the tree where the target hung, but the bark was not hit. A gasp came from the watchers.

"Missed!"

"Foot off!"

"Close enough!"

"Maybe."

"The boy's turn."

Jabez Tute kicked the ground viciously and stepped aside. Seth Purdy waited, gripping his gun so hard his knuckles showed white.

"Ready, son?"

"E-yah."

"Go!"

The boy pivoted, sweeping the rifle up. He set himself and squeezed off the shot. The ball tore through the strip of bark, sent it spinning.

"He beat!"

Unexpected victory appealed to the crowd. They broke ranks and clustered around the victor. Seth Purdy tottered under congratulatory buffets, was shaken by a succession of enthusiastic handshakes. Tate Jones had to reach across a dozen heads to retrieve his rifle. Forced away from his friends by the press of heavier bodies, Put Chester yelled and cavorted. When his breath ran out, Put remembered his dignity and his age. He strutted, informing each bystander that Seth was a resident of Stratton and he was Seth's best friend. It was Put Chester who first noticed the strange actions of the visitors from Virginia.

As quietly as if they were alone in the clearing, Tom Dunbar and Hoc were busily preparing to put on a show. They had hitched their horses, and now the slave was solemnly stepping off twenty paces. He dropped a white handkerchief to mark the spot and returned to his master. Hoc was carrying an oblong mahogany box.

Tom Dunbar was well aware of the crowd, though he seemed to ignore its presence. Excited by the reception given the shooting match, he intended to show these Northerners that there were no finer shots than the gentleman planters of the Old Dominion. Tom also welcomed the chance to display his grandfather's dueling pistols. He was proud of them and proud of his skill with them. With evident indifference, confident that he could capture the center of attention, he took the box from Hoc and opened it. Against green velvet two pistols nestled snugly in their grooves. Four brass squares gleamed from the inner corners of the box, lids for the compartments that held powder, shot, wads, and folding scales.

Smiling, Tom Dunbar plucked a pistol from its nest. He felt his customary pleasure at the weapon's perfect balance.

"Can I?" asked a voice at Tom's shoulder.

The Southerner turned. Tate Jones held out his hand. The hunter's glance was fixed on the pistol. Tom bowed and passed it. "Certainly," he said. "But it's loaded and has a hair trigger."

Holding it as if it were breakable, Tate Jones inspected the gun. It was beautifully made, long and thin, butt and stock a single piece of dark wood. The sunlight glittered on silver trim.

"E-yah," Tate Jones said, in tribute.

Tom said, "My grandfather had them made. His own design. Executed by Grierson of London."

"For dueling?"

"Naturally." The pistol's owner frowned. He was ready to refute any objections to the code duello. It was the last vestige of chivalry; it was trial by combat, a gentleman's answer to slurs cast upon his honor. Only in the Southern states were these fine distinctions understood. Tom was aware that the cruder North had neglected the practice and had even passed a law in Washington after that duel a few years back ended fatally for a Congressman. He was ready to point out that such an attitude was cowardly and plebeian.

"Ain't no mistaking its purpose," said Tate Jones, sighing. "Kind of a shame, too."

"A shame?"

"E-yah. I ain't never seen a better bit of gunsmithing. But I ain't never seen a weapon made just for killing humans before. You used it?"

"No, sir." Tom's soft speech held true regret. He felt that the one great lack in his life was that he had never set foot upon the field of honor. It was not becoming to a Dunbar of Pulchramonte and the possessor of the finest brace of dueling pistols in the State of Virginia. He made his apology. "They've been blooded, but not by me. I have never had that privilege."

The hunter, face impassive, returned the gun.

"Hoc," said Tom. "Position." At least, he thought, I can demonstrate that I'm ready if the opportunity should ever arise.

Hoc set the box on the ground and walked to the spot he'd marked. The slave, grinning, stretched out an arm. His black fingers gripped the lower edge of a playing card.

"Ready, Mr. Tom."

Ignoring the excited buzz of voices, Tom Dunbar placed himself carefully. He had been trained in the *salon d'armes* of a Napoleonic veteran and he knew the proper procedure. Erect, standing sideways to the Negro, he held the gun correctly against his right thigh, muzzle down. He said to Tate Jones, "Would you do me the courtesy of giving the word, sir? 'Fire. One. Two.' In that exact tempo, please, if you'd be so kind."

"Fire. One. Two," repeated the hunter.

"Perfect, sir."

"That's a mighty short count," Doc Merrifield said.

Tom Dunbar glanced at the medicine man and bowed. It was the recognition of one gentleman who understood dueling for another. "For some, sir. I prefer rules that stress quickness and skill, not merely an exchange of fire. At your convenience, sir." He turned his head, gazed at his mark, and waited. He did not see Tate Jones give a puzzled shrug.

Smiling coolly, the young man knew he made a striking picture. There was no stiffness in his stance; he was poised and easy. For a brief moment in the sunlit clearing Tom Dunbar believed that he represented the South in all its gallantry. These Yankees would see how a gentleman proudly defended his sacred honor. He was as lost in his performance as the most volatile of actors.

"Fire. One. T . . ."

The pistol spat. It was a sharp, flat report like that of a riding crop slapped on a table. The playing card seemed to be pushed from Hoc's grip. Picking it up, the slave put a black finger through the hole in the card and twirled the thin rectangle. He called, "Almost in the middle, Mr. Tom. It sure enough eliminated two of them pips." Hoc was acting, too; he spoke as if his master gave such exhibitions every day.

A murmur of appreciation came from the spectators. They were too reserved to accord this stranger the acclaim that had greeted Seth Purdy's victory. They admitted, reluctantly, that it was fine shooting, but resented Tom's attitude. This Southern feller—with his slave and fancy clothes and pistol tricks—was going out of his way to put on airs.

Tom Dunbar accepted the murmur as indicative of the deep impression he'd made. He blew through the gun's touchhole and exchanged it for its mate. With a slight inflection of boredom, he said, "The coin, Hoc."

"Yes, sir, Mr. Tom." Hoc took a coin from his pocket, breathed on it, rubbed it on his sleeve. Holding the rim with thumb and forefinger, the slave extended his arm. The sun turned the silver into a gleaming disk.

"Could I trouble you again, sir?" Tom asked. Once more he took the duelist's position.

Tate Jones glanced from master to slave and shrugged. "They're his fingers," he said.

Tom's smile was superior; he waited.

"Fire. One. . . ."

Again the pistol came smoothly up and cracked. The coin went spinning. Hoc blew on his fingers, wriggled them, and grinned. He disdained to retrieve the coin, but Put Chester plucked it out of the grass. The boy's voice was uncertain with awe. "It's a regular half dollar!"

This time the crowd's murmur was louder. The bystanders were shocked by such cavalier treatment of real money. What Tom

Dunbar took for admiration was in fact repressed anger. To subject a silver coin to such indignity was regarded as immoral. The feeling was intensified as Tom called out to Put.

"You can keep that, young one."

Put closed his hand over the twisted metal. He figured the half dollar was spoiled but knew it would have value as a curiosity. He smiled his thanks and silently agreed with the disapproving comments of his fellow Vermonters.

"Never seen the beat."

"Using a half dollar for a mark!"

"Like they wasn't difficult to get!"

"E-yah. And good hard money, too!"

"Must think it grows on trees!"

"A half dollar! A half dollar!"

"Hell of a way to act!"

"Southerners!"

"He ain't never earned a red copper!"

"E-yah. Their slaves do the work."

"He'd have shot the black if he'd had the mind."

"Don't doubt it."

"A half dollar!"

Lem Brayton was speechless with fury. He wanted to punch Tom Dunbar's head.

"Supposed to be a Whig, too!" Humphrey Dunklee told his wife. The banker snorted. "Even a Loco-foco Democrat'd have better sense than to treat good money that way!"

"From Virginia," said Isaac Mead. "Like Tippecanoe and Tyler too." The comment was practically treason and startled his listeners. They hastened to dissociate young Dunbar from their candidate.

"That don't follow, Isaac."

"There's Virginians *and* Virginians!"

"E-yah."

"Harrison ain't lived there for years."

"He went West long ago."

"It ain't the same if you don't stay there."

"He wouldn't throw money away."

"Lives in a log cabin, don't he?"

"This—whippersnapper—strikes me as a bad lot."

"Probably ain't even welcome in Virginia."

197

"Left home under a cloud."

"Maybe killed somebody. Dueling."

"Shot him dead with those fancy pistols."

"Wouldn't surprise me none!"

"No sense mentioning him and Tippecanoe in the same breath."

"All I meant," protested Isaac, "was that it's surprising the same state could produce them both."

"Don't prove nothing," said old Peleg Nason. "Wasn't the Lord and Judas Iscariot both from Palestine? Washington was from Virginia. He'd know how to handle this young rascal."

"Well. I don't know. Threw that dollar across a river, didn't he?"

"Don't you tell me nothing about General Washington. You didn't fit the Revolution with him like I did."

Put Chester had to show the coin to dozens.

Seth Purdy wondered how much a pistol would cost.

The Captain again coveted the black gelding.

Doc Merrifield planned and discarded several ways of separating the young Southerner from other half dollars.

Tate Jones decided his cub had more sense than some people.

The slave, Hoc, snubbed the Yankees by ignoring them as he cleaned the pistols. Hoc thought his master had proved they were quality.

Thomas Jefferson Dunbar, well pleased with himself, was sure he'd upheld the banner of his State and section. These people weren't likely to forget soon how a Virginia gentleman acted. He began to search for another kind of target, something in a bright dress, the prettier the better. He didn't think he'd have much trouble brightening the life of some lucky Puritan girl.

For as long as it took a band to play one selection, those gathered in the clearing had a topic more engrossing than politics or the time of Webster's arrival. Even the delegates neglected their balloting to discuss the shooting exhibition. Most agreed that the Southern bloc of the Whig party was a source of constant trouble. A few expressed a distaste for Tom Dunbar's behavior at a Convention designed to show Whigs as poor, honest, common folk and Democrats as wealthy wastrels. All, though silent about it, were distressed by the presence of the Negro slave. He was a visible reminder of a question it was safer not to discuss.

The sun climbed higher. The shortened shadow of the tamarack tree was frequently disturbed by the movements of the people it fell upon. But the shadow slowly changed position, shifting around the clearing like the mark of a sundial's gnomon, as it always did when there was sun.

At each of the two front windows in the parsonage parlor a clergyman gazed out at the passing. The Reverend Matthew Butterfield was a head shorter than the Reverend Jedidah Chester, but more than twice as broad. The Reverend Butterfield would have been insulted by being likened to any Papist, even so literary and legendary a one as Friar Tuck, but his host had already made the irreverent comparison. The visiting preacher did indeed resemble the descriptions of Robin Hood's chaplain. He was fat, jolly, and bald. A fringe of hair, white and fluffy like a rabbit's cottontail, passed around the back of his head from temple to temple, as if it had slipped back from his smooth pate. The gaunt Stratton parson took a certain pleasure in his guest's baldness; it was the one physical attribute they had in common.

There were many differences. Both wore black broadcloth, the uniform of their profession, but the Reverend Chester's was shiny and had patched cuffs; the other's suit was new. The taller man seemed to become quieter as his companion talked more. The Reverend Butterfield's robust health made the country parson appear ill. An observer on the road, catching them framed in the window like twin portraits, might easily have decided that they represented Famine and Plenty.

"Jed," said the Reverend Butterfield, with a laugh. "You've got the world on your doorstep. And from the looks of the way they're jammed in that crossroad it may stay there." He found his observation an excuse for more laughter.

Jedidah Chester sighed. He'd forgotten that his fellow clergyman laughed too much and too easily. Matt had always been like that, even when they were both students at Williams College. He marveled again at the laughing man's wide reputation for giving a congregation gooseflesh with his thundering accounts of the wages of sin. The thin parson said, "Babel must have sounded like that the day work stopped on the tower."

Outside tempers shortened and voices became louder as the drivers of four vehicles blamed one another for a delay. A chaise drawn by matched Morgans had swung out of the branch road into the turnpike, locked wheels with one wagon, scared the horse of another into tangling its harness, and effectively blocked both roads.

Matthew Butterfield laughed at his colleague's remark and attempted to better it. "Or the Ark's gangplank when the animals got to fighting. Except that beasts would use less profanity. Well, there's your next Sunday's sermon, Jed." He tapped a fingernail on the windowpane and chuckled.

The Reverend Chester winced, as much at the laughter as at the strident power of one voice that rose above the others outside. Man's cursing man, he thought, may be a subject for a sermon but is scarcely one for levity. Then, ashamed of his moralizing, he said, "E-yah."

"That feller driving the Morgan team. He's to blame and he's raising the most fuss."

"Joel Patch. An impatient man."

"One of your sheep, Jed?"

"Well," said Reverend Chester, forced to grin at the thought, "one of my congregation. I wouldn't exactly call Joel a sheep. Not under any circumstances."

"Hardly. Listen to him. Think he'll really smash that feller's wheel off like he says?"

"Not Joel. It might cost money." The parson spoke without thinking, then hastily amended the remark. "Not that he doesn't contribute to the church, Matt. He's a Deacon."

"Oh." The visiting cleric thought Patch worthy of another look. "That's a fine team. A man of means, this Patch. Whig, of course?"

"Of course."

With much bumping and swearing the Patch chaise managed to untangle itself. The passage of the travelers resumed its steady, noisy flow. Matthew Butterfield lost interest and turned from the window. He glanced at the clock on the mantel, checked its accuracy with his silver, hunting-case watch, and said, "Getting late, Jed. We'd best take our departure."

"E-yah," said the parson. Then, without rancor but firmly, he added, "The clock's right."

"E-yah," the Reverend Butterfield said blandly. "I noticed. You know, Jed, I envy you today. Instead of a wearisome trip along highway and byway, you have the Convention a stone's throw away."

Jedidah Chester grinned. "Couple of miles, Matt. Real stout throw."

"I was speaking figuratively, Jed." The plump man waved a hand toward the windows. "That melee out there is bedlam! Can't even go your own pace. Just follow the leader! Oh, I envied you sitting here comfortably."

"Mmm." The murmur was polite but unimpressed. Reverend Chester had his own ideas about the comfort enjoyed while thousands rattled past one's front door.

"Not that I'd have missed it, Jed. You don't get to hear Daniel Webster every day. Finest speaker in the country. The Defender of the Constitution."

"I know."

"General Harrison himself wouldn't get all these people up here. You'd heard there was some fool talk of selecting Webster to run with Tippecanoe instead of John Tyler?"

"No. We're a little removed up here."

"Well, the position just wasn't worthy of Webster's talents!"

"I don't know, Matt. Van Buren held it. And Calhoun before that."

"E-yah. And the Red Fox got to be President. But not by sitting in that chair in the Senate. It's a waste of four years, if you ask me. That rascal Johnson had degraded the office till no first-class man wants it!"

"Tyler, too?" asked the host.

"Oh, well." Matthew Butterfield shrugged and chuckled. "He might help swing a few votes." The visitor hooked both thumbs in the pockets of his waistcoat and frowned. "This is a mighty important election, Jed. Four more years of the Democrats and this country will be worse than Sodom and Gomorrah!"

"Whig chances are getting stronger, Matt."

"E-yah. But it'll be a fight. The forces of Satan never give in without a struggle! They're an irreligious lot those Democrats—atheists, radicals—and they fear neither God nor man. But this is the year of their judgment!"

201

With the knowledge of the trade, Reverend Chester noted his friend's voice becoming louder, more pompous. Sighing, he wished Matt would save his sermons for the pulpit.

"It's our duty to guide our congregations in these matters, Jed."

Jedidah Chester's eyes narrowed behind their glasses. He said quietly, "It's our duty to preach the Lord's word."

"E-yah. Against wickedness and immorality. The Democrats stand for both."

"Maybe."

"You're too easy, Jed! Every other minister I've talked to agrees with me!"

"I know. But I can't see making stump speeches in my church."

"Does your Methodist friend follow your course?"

"Well, no. He's a fiery feller and . . ."

"Exactly! You're making a mistake, Jed. When a man shares his church with another denomination the way you do he has to give fuller measure than the other feller. Now I've half a dozen sermons I've already used all written out. There's one in particular where I likened Van Buren to anti-Christ—it went very well—you wouldn't have to change a word. . . ."

"Thanks." Reverend Chester kept the word toneless. Acceptance was easier than argument. He had no intention of using any sermon he hadn't written. "But we don't have to preach today, Matt. Webster's doing it for us. Finest speaker in the country."

Matthew Butterfield gave his host a sharp glance, but the other's smile pricked him into laughter. The plump minister could take a joke with anybody, even when he couldn't see the point. He said, with affection, "You always were a humorist, Jed. All right. Come along."

They went into the kitchen. Big as the room was, it seemed crowded with females. The two Butterfield daughters chattered with the four Chester sisters. The talk was of dresses, styles, social activity. Lovina Chester was the gayest of the group. Her comments on young men had an acid quality that kept her listeners in constant giggles.

One look at his wife's face was enough for Jedidah Chester. The parson guessed at once that Mrs. Butterfield had been enumerating in full the material blessings that the Lord had showered upon His servants, the Butterfields. Mrs. Chester wore the patient, pained expression of a woman forced to listen to unwanted advice. Since the duties of a hostess had prevented her from glaring at her guest, she greeted her husband with a glare as sudden as a broadside.

"My dear," said Reverend Chester, trying to apologize for his shortcomings with two words. "I'm afraid it's time to leave."

Mrs. Chester rose with the energetic relief of a puppy bounding out of water. "Girls! You heard your father."

There was a great rustling of skirts as the women hurried for their wraps. Little Josepha had her nose wiped by all three of her sisters until she took refuge in flight. Mrs. Chester reminded everyone that the pies were packed in the wagon and not to be sat upon. For the first time since they'd settled on the mountain, the parson, at his wife's request, made sure that all doors and windows were locked.

The families were seating themselves in their respective vehicles when, above the clatter of the passing, Lovina Chester heard a hail. She stood up and found it came from across the road. "It's Mrs. Tarbox," said Lovina. "She's waving to come over. Something must be the matter."

"At such a time!" Mrs. Chester was exasperated. "Sit still, Father. Lovina! Go across and see what she wants!"

Lovina waited until a Concord coach, horses flecked with foam, lumbered past, and then darted to the other side of the road. Mrs. Tarbox came to meet her. The innkeeper's wife was upset; her eyes were swollen with weeping. She started talking before the girl could ask a question.

"Oh, Lovina. I need your father. Or somebody. Davey's too small to drive, and I won't let Marcia, and I can't—not with the road crowded this way—and I will not walk to the clearing! Not with a horse standing in the barn! I won't! I won't! I won't!" Mrs. Tarbox drummed her heels on the ground.

"Why, Mrs. Tarbox," Lovina said, wide eyed with surprise. "Has something happened to Mr. Tarbox?"

"E-yah. I don't know just what's come over him but something has! He ain't going to the clearing!"

"Not going?"

"He's afraid he might miss the chance to make an extra dollar. As if we hadn't all been working our fingers to the bone since early yesterday! It's turned Dan's head, Lovina. Turned his head!"

Tears welled up; Mrs. Tarbox sniffed them back. "He ain't been himself since this business started!"

"I guess nobody has," said Lovina Chester, thinking of the night before.

The innkeeper's wife wasn't interested in excuses; she recaptured her anger. "He lit into me like he'd gone crazy. Just because I reminded him that my family'd be spending the night. That's the Fairbanks family from Arlington. My uncle and aunt and cousins. They wrote they was coming. I told Dan weeks ago. Now he begrudges the room they'll take up! My own father's brother's family! 'I could get money for that room,' he said. And the names he called them! My own father's brother's family that I haven't set eyes on in seven years!"

Embarrassed, Lovina looked away. She knew that married people fought; one neighboring couple was famous for its fisticuffs. But such quarrels were carefully kept at home and only leaked out through gossip. The fact that Mrs. Tarbox could make her woes public showed that the poor woman was beside herself. The girl said, "I can drive you, Mrs. Tarbox."

"Would you, Lovina? Would you? He ain't even letting Asa Brayton go! 'I'm paying you by the day,' he said. 'And a day's got twenty-four hours!' I never saw anybody so—so—mean!" Mrs. Tarbox couldn't choose between crying and talking. The result was a prodigious hiccup. She clapped a hand to her mouth. "I beg your pardon. I'm awful upset."

Lovina's sisters were calling her. She turned and shouted, "I'm going to drive the Tarbox family. Mr. Tarbox can't get away!" She saw her father and mother consult. Mrs. Chester's permission was called across the road.

"All right. Meet you at the clearing!"

After the Butterfields and Chesters had driven off, Mrs. Tarbox led the way to the barn. With transportation assured, the lady already regretted her outburst. "Lovina," she said, "Dan's always been a good husband."

As if summoned by his wife's first kind remark the innkeeper burst from the dark doorway of the barn. His face was flushed with anger. "All right!" he said. "I've hitched you up! You needn't go telling the neighbors you had to do that for yourself!" He gave Lovina a curt nod. "Some people have more important things to

204

do than fritter away time and money!" He stamped on toward the inn. Dan Tarbox felt abused and deserted. He couldn't understand how his wife and children preferred listening to a speech to making money. There'd never be another chance like this Convention. "I'm doing it for them," he said, to the empty kitchen.

He opened several bottles of rum and hurried into the common room. The party leaders of the district, two miles from the clearing, were holding a caucus to decide the business of the Convention.

It was a small group of men, but it had paid well for privacy. None of them held public office; all of them had something to say as to who did. They paid no attention to the innkeeper but went on talking in low, assured voices.

"Hiland Hall for Congressman."

"E-yah. That's settled."

"Hiland ain't big, but he's well thought of."

"Congress ain't exactly manual labor."

"Any objections to the slate the State Convention picked?"

"Nope."

"My bunch'll endorse it."

"Silas Jenison for Governor. David Clark for Lieutenant Governor. E-yah. They'll be hard to beat."

"Don't forget Silas was born in Vermont."

"E-yah. First time we've had a Governor could say that."

"Make sure it gets said."

"We'll spread it. Folks'll take to the idea."

"That's right. A real, home-grown Vermonter for Governor."

"All in the family."

"When you're whooping it up for Tippecanoe, don't forget Silas."

"You needn't worry."

"One other thing."

"E-yah?"

"Railroads."

"Railroads?"

"Uhuh. They're coming, boys. They're coming sure as doomsday. We'd be a mite forehanded to do some thinking about them."

"Now?"

"The sooner the better. There's lines running over in York State. And down to Massachusetts. And more building all the time. It won't be long before the rails come into Vermont."

205

"Money in it, ain't they?"

"E-yah. A fistful."

"Well, let's see that we have Whig railroads."

"My idea too."

"All right. Now some of you better get back to the Convention. The Marshal's gone down to meet Webster."

"Ain't you coming?"

"Nope. I've heard a lot of speeches in my time. They get votes, but they're not my idea of enjoyment. Anyway, Webster said a few words down to Brattleboro night before last. That'll do me."

"This crowd expects more than a few words."

"They'll get them. Don't worry. Ain't nothing measly about Black Dan. He'll go on till the cows come home. The old cuss likes to talk."

Listening, Dan Tarbox nodded in approval. There were more important things to do than listen to Webster. But the longer he talked, the thirstier his listeners would get. That hard cider they had up to the clearing wouldn't last forever. The innkeeper wondered if he could raise his prices. Just for the one night.

It was well past noon when Lot Purdy drove the log cabin on wheels around a familiar curve. The stage driver knew that the settlement was just ahead and, cracking his whip, he sent the six white horses forward at a gallop. He had planned it that way. Twice he had pulled out of line and idled in a roadside field, watching the passage of those more eager to reach the Convention. At one place Lot counted three hundred vehicles as they passed. He hated a clogged road and, since the turnpike was his daily route, he felt the pilgrims to be intruders.

Now the roads were less crowded, and Lot intended to thunder into the settlement at full speed. He had saved his team carefully for that purpose. He lived in Stratton, and his neighbors were going to be more impressed by the way he handled six horses than by the fact he was driving an outlandish Whig log cabin. Grinning, Lot Purdy sent his whiplash snaking out over the heads of the running team and snapped it with an expert fillip.

They raced past the outlying houses. Lot stared as he rounded his own home. There was no one about; the small house stood deserted in the afternoon sunshine. The stage driver grunted. He guessed that his wife and son had already left to attend the Convention.

Then, swaying, the log cabin rounded another curve, and he could see the crossroad ahead.

It, too, was deserted. Church, inn, and parsonage stared at him blankly. Lot thought there was some movement behind the inn's windows, but he couldn't be sure. The entire stretch of road through the settlement was vacant of life. The smithy was closed and padlocked; Peleg Nason's house had every shutter closed.

"God Almighty," Lot Purdy said. "There ain't even smoke coming out of the chimneys." He had braced himself so strongly for the entrance into his native hamlet that he could only gaze dumbly, letting the team race. He passed through and went on, and there was not a soul to see.

As the road plunged in among the trees, Lot slowed his horses. He was still bewildered by the surprise of an uninhabited Stratton. "Hell of a homecoming," he said aloud. "Like everybody was dead." He knew they had all gone to the clearing, but it was too unlike his usual arrival on the stage for the driver to accept the fact calmly. He had an uneasy feeling of dread, as if some disaster had visited the community and wiped it out in his absence.

"A deserted village," Lot Purdy announced. He knew there was a poem by some such name. He hadn't read it, but he had once heard a Democrat orator quote from it in a speech against the Bank. He tried to remember the lines, thought he had them, recited them over the drumming of hoofs and the clatter of wheels.

> Ill fares the land, to hastening ills a prey,
> Where wealth accumulates and men decay.

"'Ill fares the land'!" repeated the driver. The words had a foreboding melancholy that suited his mood. He wasn't sure that anybody was accumulating much wealth since the Panic, but he was sure that men were decaying. Turning Whig and rampsing off to hear a man talk. Like chickens with their heads cut off. No sense. No sense at all.

He saw a group of horsemen filling the road ahead of him and reined his team to a walk. The riders came on, separating to let him through. Lot noticed that they wore sashes and sabers like irregular cavalry. One of them hailed the log cabin's driver.

"See anything of Senator Webster?" The horseman motioned toward the road behind Lot.

The stage driver shook his head. The group jingled past, reformed their lines, and trotted off. Leaning far out to look back around the corner of the cabin, Lot Purdy watched them out of sight. Welcoming escort, he guessed, going to meet the guest of honor.

He heard music and shouting ahead as he approached the clearing. The road was narrowed by vehicles parked along its edge. Lot glared at them; it was like the Whigs not to care who came along later. He wanted to strike back somehow, to show that there were Democrats still left in Vermont. Since he had to take this fool log cabin right into the clearing, he ought to do it in a way folks would remember. Heedless of the congested roadway he urged his horses to greater speed.

Lot Purdy drove the cabin up the bank into the clearing at a speed that sent people scurrying out of the way. Beneath him the cabin bounced and slammed. He noticed a smaller cabin on wheels with a live raccoon leashed to its roof. The size of the crowd amazed him, but there was no pause in his singing. At the top of his lungs Lot Purdy was bawling a Jackson campaign song.

> . . . Jackson he was wide awake
> And was not scared of trifles,
> For well he knew Kentucky's boys,
> With their death-dealing rifles!
> He led them down to cypress swamp;
> The ground was low and mucky;
> There stood John Bull in martial pomp,
> And here stood Old Kentucky.

When he noticed his employer's face Lot Purdy pulled the team to a stop. He saw people staring at him and knew they had recognized the song. Flinging the reins aside, Lot's voice was loud and clear.

"Here's your goddam cabin!"

Fred Streeter's feet hurt. He couldn't decide whether his boots pinched worse than the drum straps dug into his shoulder or vice versa. The drum seemed to get bigger and heavier with each step. It bumped him as he marched. The boy was hot and very tired; perspiration streaked the dust on his face. He slogged along, not even trying to avoid the mud puddles in his path, head down, watching the heels of the man in the rank ahead.

"Close up, there! Close up!"

Fred placed the voice. The band leader. That meant they were going to play again. Wearily, he wondered why. There was no one to hear but the trees. He raised his head, stirred by a faint hope that they might be nearing the end of their march.

The musician beside the boy said, "Webster's up ahead."

"Who?"

"Webster!" The man stared at the question. "You feel all right, Freddie?"

"E-yah." The boy forced his shoulders back. He was the youngest in the militia band, and he wanted to show he was as rugged as anyone. "Just tired, that's all."

"Me too."

"Halt!"

The command came so suddenly that Fred nearly bumped the man in front. He swayed, wishing they hadn't stopped. The relief of halting wasn't enough to equal the effort of getting started again. He took off his cap and mopped his face. He said, "What are we stopping for this time?"

Voices called the reason back through the ranks. "The escort's come down for Webster. Cavalry!"

Cavalry, thought Fred Streeter. Cavalry rode horses. Mr. Webster rode in a carriage. Folks rode in carriages, chaises, wagons, carts. He'd even seen one feller driving a log cabin on wheels. The boy was filled with a dull hatred for all riders. Their feet didn't hurt. He was sure he had several blisters.

"Much farther?" he asked.

"Don't know, Freddie."

The hot sun beat down on the road, caking the mud spattered on Fred's boots and legs. He slid the straps off his shoulders and lowered the drum to the road. The taut skin of the drumhead was warm to his touch.

A canteen passed from hand to hand. The water was lukewarm, but the boy rinsed his throat gratefully. He wished he dared drink; he was very thirsty. But in the July heat he was afraid he'd swell up like a horse with the colic.

Somewhere in the band's ranks a voice cursed the delay. Others took up the complaint.

"Let's get a move on!"

"What are we waiting here for?"

"We going to that Convention, or ain't we?"

"Standing here baking!"

A horseman guided his mount along the edge of the road. "Come on, boys," he said. "The settlement's just ahead. And the clearing's only a couple of miles beyond that."

The musicians looked up at the rider. He was young, excited; he grinned down at the men on foot.

"Let's take the Senator there in style, boys. He's a Great Man. Play your best, now."

Easy for you to talk, said Fred Streeter silently. On your big gray horse, with your fancy sword and all. You ain't walking.

"Attention!"

The rider wheeled his horse and trotted away toward the head of the line.

With a groan, the drummer got into his harness. He took his sticks from under his belt.

"'Yankee Doodle!' With the left foot!"

Fred grunted and poised his drumsticks. He hoped he could play for a couple of miles. He wasn't even sure he could march it.

"Forward—march!"

The boy slammed down on his instrument. They were moving again.

Yankee Doodle went to town

E-yah, he thought. To town. He didn't set out to climb no fool mountain that didn't have a top.

Riding on a pony

Marching, Fred Streeter beat his drum grimly. Riding again. Everybody that had any sense rode places.

Stuck a feather in his hat,
And called it macaroni.

The Great Man was tired and bitter. Daniel Webster wished that the band behind his barouche would stop that infernal racket.

210

Yankee Doodle wasn't exactly soothing music. His head ached, the pain behind his eyes burned, and he kept snorting in a vain effort to clear the pressure in his nose. Catarrh again, he thought. That was all he had needed to make the trip perfect.

It was hot in the open carriage, and the Senator pushed his hat back on his head. He wished the speech were over. It was a fool idea to come all the way up a mountain just to make another speech. He should never have agreed to it. He was Webster, and those that wanted to hear him should make it more convenient. This was all Rufe's fault.

Rufe grinned from the seat facing Webster. He said, "Nearly there, Senator."

Webster snorted. He glared but kept quiet out of deference to the three local men who shared the barouche.

"Over ten thousand people, Senator."

He gave the informant a thin-lipped smile.

"Nearer twenty."

"All for Tippecanoe."

Daniel Webster's swarthy face darkened. Tippecanoe! Even after all the speeches he'd made supporting William Henry Harrison the man's nickname filled him with impotent rage. Harrison was a blundering, uncouth military-politico, who was no more fit to be President than a red Indian. Henry Clay would have been a better choice: unreliable, but at least intelligent. My worthy opponent, thought Webster, dropping naturally into the phraseology of debate. Clay was that, anyway—worthy of opposition and hate. And he and Clay, between them, were working like beavers to elect a lesser man. Because the party, more than anything else, needed to win.

The Great Man shut his eyes, and his companions preserved a respectful silence. The Vermonters nodded to each other; they were certain that the Senator was thinking of the coming speech. Rufe, knowing better, wondered if his leader would bother to put any freshness into the oration. Rufe was worried about the circles under Webster's eyes. Not that they'd matter if the old master decided to talk his best.

Jolting along, Webster admitted that he'd been wrong about the campaign. The log-cabin business seemed to have caught the public fancy. Harrison had a good chance to win, especially if they all kept hammering away that Van Buren was to blame for hard times.

211

He rubbed a finger against the ache in his forehead. There'd be a lot of speeches to make before November. The thought irked him. He'd worked hard to get where he was; the United States Senate was a far cry from a New Hampshire farm. Now he stressed the farm and ignored the office. He told people he was a simple, common man and didn't believe a word of it.

They hadn't thought he was ordinary in England. There the admiration—both of lords and ladies—had been manifest.

Cheering broke out ahead of him and came closer. Daniel Webster opened his eyes. He sat up straight, smiled. Even after so many cheers, so many applauding crowds, he still liked the sound. He noticed meadow rue along the wayside and the smell of hay-scented fern. He'd known country like this in his youth.

People lined the road, yelling and shouting. They trampled fern, grass, and flower flat.

"Almost two," said Rufe, looking at his watch.

The shouting came in volleys, like a cannonade.

Senator Daniel Webster, smiling, raised his tall hat in acknowledgement. He was pleasantly astonished by the size of the throng. It looked like a multitude. He was Webster, and it was his name that had brought these people to the mountaintop.

He smiled at them—the same smile that had been used successfully on judges, juries, statesmen, and rival card players. It masked the weariness and the pain and the bitter knowledge that, if the cheers were for Daniel Webster, the votes would be for Tippecanoe.

The tamarack tree stood majestically above the crowd and cast its shadow across the speaker's platform. Around the platform the great throng spread in ever-widening arcs, more closely packed than the trees that had once filled the clearing. The massed ranks were colorful with dresses of all hues. From the top of the tamarack the human circles must have looked like a gigantic rag rug stretching from the road to the edge of the forest and covering almost three hundred acres.

Of the people on Stratton Mountain that day, some sat in their wagons or in the windows of the log cabin; others were perched on the building's roof, on old stumps, or on boxes brought for the purpose. One elderly lady rocked in her own chair, carried from home. For the most part, the visitors were content to stand in the bright July sunshine.

No one actually counted the numbers. Some said ten thousand, some fifteen, some twenty. Everyone was impressed by the attendance and certain that any of these estimates could be accurate. Everyone was aware that there had never been such a gathering in the neighborhood. It was much just to be one unit in that stupendous sum. It was a fact that would be told and retold to those unfortunates who hadn't made the trip, to any future visitor from other parts, to children yet unborn.

After the first wild enthusiasm that greeted Daniel Webster's arrival, the multitude waited quietly. This was the climax of the meeting, the high point of the Convention, the promised reward for the journey.

Few in that gathering had ever seen the famous Senator before; those who had heard him speak were even fewer. All knew him by reputation, however; there were many who could name his more noted orations. The individual who could speak right out in meeting was admired in New England. Men were proud of this farm boy whose speechmaking crowded the galleries in Washington city. The Hayne debate of ten years before was already legend; they felt that Webster had spoken for the whole North on that occasion, and that he had outsmarted the alien, Southern aristocracy. He was from the same soil that they tried to harvest. He had been born in neighboring New Hampshire, and their state had once been called the Hampshire Grants.

Waiting now for their guest of honor to speak, the Vermonters scrutinized him carefully, filing away his appearance for future reference. This orator was the living proof that any farmer's son could attain the high places in the nation. It was typical of their instinctive wariness that they preferred other men for the Presidency. Daniel was a Great Man. Everybody knew that. But he talked too much.

They waited patiently through Hiland Hall's brief address. They had chosen Hall to represent them in Congress. They knew he was physically small and that Webster towered over him; they were nervous lest his speech be too far below the standard of the famous visitor. When Hall acquitted himself worthily, the throng's applause was sudden and relieved.

Then it came. Hiland Hall's voice rang out.

"Friends and fellow citizens. The Senator from Massachusetts.

213

The Defender of the Constitution. Our distinguished guest—Daniel Webster!"

Daniel Webster, resplendent in a blue swallow-tailed coat, the sun twinkling on his bright buttons, stepped forward. The ovation that greeted him rocked the platform, echoed from the surrounding forest, frightened the horses hitched in the clearing. Webster smoothed his buff waistcoat and waited.

As the tumultuous acclaim died down there was an interruption. A man directly in front of the speaker's platform shouted. "I've been robbed! Somebody picked my pocket!"

George Stiles, standing beside the victim, was loud with indignation. "I saw a man push you! What's missing?"

"My pocketbook! Somebody stole my pocketbook!"

The rest of the audience craned, stretching on tiptoe to view the bustle at Webster's very feet. The Senator leaned over, shook his head. He said—and the remark reached all in the clearing—"Was it a Subtreasury pocketbook?"

Shouts of laughter answered the question. Everybody knew of Van Buren's Subtreasury bill, and the connection between it and pocket picking was the cream of the jest. Husbands nudged their wives in appreciation. He was a sharp one, Dan Webster was.

Webster knew he had them. He gazed out across their many heads, noted a fluffy cloud in the clear blue sky over the distant Taconics, and found his opening. He started formally, the great voice rolling out with ease, plainly audible to the farthest listener.

"Fellow citizens, I have come to meet you among the clouds!"

As the awaited speech began, the usual residents of Stratton Mountain were scattered through the huge gathering like buttercups through a field of clover. The families tried to stay together but did not always succeed. Put Chester and Seth Purdy were squatting on the roof of the log cabin; their parents were at opposite ends of the clearing. The Chittendens clung together, an island in a sea of strangers, while Eratus stared at the speaker, impressed by the powerful voice, and Charles, head never still, looked around for Lovina Chester. That young lady, by some quirk of chance, could see many neighbors in the segment of crowd surrounding her. Nathan Patch was beside her; Lem Brayton only a yard in front of her. To her left the girl could make out the half-hidden figures of the blacksmith's family and old Peleg Nason with his spinster daughter. Far ahead, through a forest of strange head-gear, Lovina recognized the bright bonnets of her sisters. She saw nothing of either Tom Dunbar or Charles Chittenden.

Everybody could see Joel Patch. The sawmill owner was in the group on the speaker's platform, preening himself and holding Daniel Webster's hat. Patch's shrewd eyes were never still. He kept trying to find acquaintances among the listening multitude. He wanted to be sure they all knew of his exalted position. Patch smirked at the minister, winked at Lizzie Galusha, bowed to Mrs. Tarbox. He reminded himself to tell Humphrey Dunklee the cost and make of the Senator's hat.

Rhoda Hapgood, the Patch hired girl, was thankful that she was too far back in the crowd to worry about her employer's gaze. A sudden charge of people during Webster's arrival had left Rhoda stranded among strangers. She'd been unable to see and too timid to complain until a soft-spoken gentleman had noticed her. Now she shared a stump top with the gentleman, who dressed very finely and introduced himself as Luke Brooks.

None of these people and no one else saw Zilpha Brayton slip away. The orator hadn't finished his third sentence when she backed toward the edge of the clearing, turned, and darted into the shadows of the trees.

The mighty voice seemed to follow Zilpha in her flight. She hurried to escape from it, lifting her skirts and running. Her heart pounded as she twisted her way through a maze of evergreens; her feet crunched on the matted carpet of needles. Even when the sense of the words was lost, the sound still drove her on. To Zilpha there was something more than human in the power of that unseen speaker. It was like the Bible said about God calling to Adam from the heavens: the voice would search through the hidden thickets of the darkest forest, find the sinner, and punish him.

"It's only Dan Webster," whispered Zilpha, panting. She tried to control her panic but, when she found a path, she raced along it even faster. Leaning forward, stumbling in her haste, one stocking loose and fallen, Zilpha Brayton didn't stop until she could hear nothing but her own tortured breathing.

She leaned against a tree, sobbing for breath. Hot, disheveled, her first thought was for her appearance. Tugging her stocking into place, Zilpha was furious with herself for bolting.

"A fine one you are," she scolded aloud. "Running like a scared rabbit!" Her scorn stiffened her. She was Zilpha Brayton, a woman who feared nothing. Still, she was alone in the forest, and the sudden flight of a bird startled her. She said—she was not sure to whom—"I haven't done anything wrong."

She went on until the path crossed a stream, then stopped to bathe her forehead. Feeling refreshed, Zilpha took the note from her bodice and reread it. She felt again the excitement of the moment in the clearing when Isaac Mead, casually passing, had slipped it into her hand.

It was a single sheet of lined foolscap, jagged along one edge, creased with the many folds that had made it small. The writing was in ink, the crooked, tight hand of a man not used to holding a pen. Every small *s* had a tail like an *f*.

> Mrſ. Zilpha Brayton.
> Dear Mrſ.
> While Dan'l Webſter oraitſ I wood be greatful for a word with you. At your houſe if the neareſt. Go threw the foreſt croſlotſ. It iſ qiker & cutſ out fum diſtantſ.
>
> > Yr. Mſt. Obednt. Serv.
> > Iſaac Mead.

Zilpha Brayton smiled. The note somehow raised the quality of the rendezvous. Wouldn't it, she thought, have been terrible if I couldn't read. And Isaac so well written. Her husband had never sent her a letter in his life. Using the stream for a mirror, she made sure she looked her prettiest before she went on through the woods.

Even walking diagonally instead of going around by the angle of turnpike and branch road, it was no little distance from the clearing to Brayton's. Zilpha didn't dawdle; she trudged along sturdily, certain of her direction. She had no fear of the forest now, but felt very secure and hidden behind the tall, straight trunks. Climbing a slope she broke into a small, cleared space. From it she could see a patch of her own roof. The rest was simple, and Zilpha took the straightest possible path.

The farm looked sun-drenched and deserted as Zilpha cut across the barnyard. She had never known it so quiet; it made her nervous. She went into the barn, her footsteps sounding loud in its

216

emptiness. Oxen and cow were out in the pasture. She could just hear the faint tinkle of the cow's bell. She examined every outbuilding as if it might conceal a hidden enemy. Nothing. A few drowsy chickens in the hen house.

There was no sign of Isaac Mead. She went in the back door, through the house, out the front. Zilpha felt she had to keep moving; mounting excitement drove her restlessly into activity. She looked up and down the road. In both directions as far as she could see it was a brown, shining, empty strip.

"You wouldn't think it was the same road," said Zilpha, remembering the morning. The stillness forced her to whisper. Even then her remark sounded overloud.

Suddenly aware that any passer-by could see her Zilpha went back into the house. Not that there'd be any passing with everybody up to the clearing. But it was better to be careful. She paced around her parlor like a caged cat. Impatiently she yanked off her bonnet and threw it in a chair.

"Where is he?" she asked. "Where is he?"

Maybe Isaac wasn't coming, Zilpha thought. Maybe he couldn't come. Maybe Lem had somehow discovered they were meeting and stopped Isaac. At the sudden horror of this suggestion, Zilpha sank into a chair, chewing her knuckles. She was up again in an instant, pacing.

"Don't be a fool," she told herself. Lem didn't know a thing. Even if he did, Isaac could handle him. Isaac was twice the man her husband was.

Once more she read Isaac's note. She tried to rehearse the things she would say. I got your note, Mr. Mead. But he knew that; he'd given it to her. You have something to say to me, Mr. Mead? That was better. No need to rush things. She wouldn't want him to think she was easy. First they'd talk, and then she'd make some tea, and— there was plenty of time—after that, after Isaac had said nice things, after . . . Zilpha Brayton grinned and shook her head as if to clear it of her thoughts.

She stalked into the bedroom and stared at herself in the mirror. She didn't look a bit different. Then the eyes looking back at her widened as she heard the front door creak.

"Who?" Zilpha rushed into the parlor.

Isaac Mead, blinking, was standing in the doorway. His big

frame filled the opening. He twisted the hat in his hands awkwardly.

"You." Zilpha forced the word out.

Isaac nodded. His lips moved, but he didn't speak.

They stared at each other across a tension almost visible. Upbringing, marriage bonds, adultery, church meeting, Scripture, death, judgment, and hell-fire were all in the room with them. Until they faced each other, alone as they had planned, this affair had been a titillating game. Now the reality of it frightened them.

Zilpha Brayton was the stronger. Her face whitened; her lips were like a fresh wound. She laughed in sudden, reckless defiance. She said harshly, "Shut the door."

The click of the iron latch blended with their quick steps toward each other. Their meeting was more a collision than an embrace.

Straining herself against the man Zilpha could feel Isaac's hands on her back. She clutched him, her lips seeking for his. This is what I wanted, she thought. This. This. She wasn't conscious that a strained cry was coming from her throat.

"Ah. Ah. Ah."

Senator Daniel Webster, just getting into his stride, reminded the great audience that he, too, was a common man of humble origin like their candidate General Harrison. He did not mention his salary, legal fees, unpublicized retainers, or property.

On the outer fringe of the throng, only his wife's hand restrained Lot Purdy from speech. The stage driver spat.

Clem Galusha awoke with a raging thirst and a throbbing head. He didn't know where he was except that water ran beside him and there were planks over his head. His mouth seemed stuck together, but a swallow of the cold water nearly made him sick. Clem crawled painfully out from under the bridge.

He tried squinting up at the sun's position to discover the time, but the sun danced crazily and seemed to come right at him, a white-hot ball that seared his eyes. He gave up after three tries, cursed, and discovered that the moon had risen. Swaying, he gauged the height at which the moon was pasted against the blue daylight sky. Clem thought it looked like a piece of threadbare white rag.

218

"After two," he said, muttering. He had climbed to the lane before the hour penetrated into his still-drunken brain. Two! Clem said, "Oh, my God!" He knew, strangely but with certainty, that it wasn't Sunday, but he wasn't sure just what day it was. Patch would skin him alive for sleeping away a working day. Lizzie and me, Clem reasoned, may get thrown out of work in these hard times.

He began to run toward the mill. His feet seemed like lead; they tripped him up frequently. Every jolting step sent fresh pain into his aching head.

Something heavy in Clem's coat pocket kept slapping against his side. He pawed at it, fumbled it loose, stared. It was a brown bottle, half-full and corked.

Clem pried the cork loose and sniffed. He said, "Rum!"

The raw liquor burned his throat, made him cough. He drank in long, shuddering gulps. When the bottle was drained, he threw it away. After another spasm of coughing he felt better, a new man, ready to face Patch, and sure he could excuse his absence.

Thinking one explanation at a time enough, Clem skirted the house in order to avoid Lizzie. Rigidly erect, he walked straight to the sawmill. Twice he lurched as a knee buckled without warning, but each time he recovered. By the time Clem reached the mill, he was swaggering and belligerent.

"Tim!" he roared. "Tim Frost!"

The name bounced from the wall of the empty shed. There was no answer but the murmuring of the mill race.

Stumbling over the sill, Clem went inside. He stared into the shadowy corners. He said, tentatively, "Tim? Joel?" He listened, shook his head in bewilderment. His voice was dull and puzzled.

"No work. No work."

He faced about in the doorway and shouted toward the house. "Hey! Where is everybody?"

When there was no reply, Clem sank on a bench and tried to figure things out. Something, he decided, must have taken Patch and Tim and Nathan away. Even Lizzie must be gone. Everybody. He had a vague belief that somebody had told him about it, but he'd forgotten the details. It didn't matter. Gazing at the still half disk of the circular saw, Clem grinned. His eyes narrowed with a shrewd, wonderful plan that brought him to his feet.

"Show them," he mumbled. "Show them all. Be working when they get back. E-yah."

It took time and no little trouble to get the big wheel turning. Hoisting a log onto the carriage was almost too much for Clem's drunken strength; only with the help of an iron crowbar did he finally manage it. He was drenched with sweat and panting when he turned toward the saw.

"Ain't afraid of you!"

The gleaming steel arc seemed to return his glare. Clem shook his fist at it.

"Ain't afraid," he repeated.

He grabbed the starting lever, took a deep breath, moved it. With a click the big saw began to spin.

Clem hurried to the carriage, guided it forward. The shimmering edge of the whirling blade came closer. The hired man watched it as if hypnotized. Whir changed to high shriek as the saw's teeth bit into the log. Clem stood back and stared while, with sawdust spraying, the saw inched the length of the log.

When the cut plank dropped, he laughed in triumph. "Told you," Clem said to the humming saw. "Told you!"

He reached up, fumbling, to the tally board and moved a peg over one notch. As his fingers released the peg he lost his balance, tottered.

Neatly, with swift precision, the saw sliced the side out of Clem's right trouser. Feathery light as the blade's touch was, it plucked the man off his unsteady feet. That saved him; he fell away from the hooked teeth.

Shocked almost sober, Clem stared at his leg. The white skin stood out from the sheared cloth. A thin red line was suddenly drawn along Clem's thigh, as if by an invisible pencil. It was only a flesh wound but, at sight of the blood, the hired man started to scream.

Snatching up a hammer, he hurled it at the saw. It struck with a resounding clang, ricocheted.

The screaming continued as the hired man grabbed his crowbar. He rose, swinging in raging frenzy. He smashed belts from their wheels, splintered wooden supports, sent the tally board, shattered, to the floor. With quick strokes Clem beat at the mechanism until the saw stopped. Then, with a new high note in his shrieking, he belabored his enemy, pounding with the crowbar while the shed shivered before the ringing clash of metal on metal. The blows crushed the bright circle into a scarred and twisted wreck, crumpled like a discarded sheet of paper.

Clem stopped at last, exhausted, drained. It was then, for the first time, that he felt the pain along his leg. Clem fainted.

The orator scornfully described the manner in which Van Buren and his followers had brought the country to the brink of ruin, as exemplified by the recent, tragic Panic. The orator could scarcely be expected to discuss his own debts.

Reverend Jedidah Chester, listening, noted several tones of the voice, a gesture, that might improve his sermons and benefit his congregation.

Dr. Portus J. Merrifield, listening, noted the same tones and the same gesture, that might improve his speeches and sell Epizootical Elixir.

"Ain't tight-mouthed, is he?"

Jabez Tute was bored. The loss of the shooting match still rankled; he'd been beaten by a measly whelp of a stripling. Listening to Daniel Webster for an hour had not improved young Tute's temper. With a sign to his cronies, he had led the way down the road away from the clearing and voiced his question. The other four roughs were quick to agree with their leader.

"A bellows! A mewling bellows!"

"More wind than a tempest!"

"Lays on, don't he?"

The chorus made Jabez Tute grin. He said, "Noll, you set word to it. We didn't drag our butts here to harken while yon bellows bag broke wind!"

Oliver Butler guffawed at the crude jest. He slapped one thigh under his ragged knee breeches. The others, laughing, pushed and shoved each other in appreciation. Little Wat Fisher's tricorne was knocked into the road. He snatched it up, clamped it back on his head. "Jabez," he said, "you've a plan?"

"E-yah. We come to frolic, didn't we?"

"And drink!"

"And stuff our bellies!"

The two who mentioned their appetites were the Dale brothers, Cedric and Oswald. They were gangling, loutish lads with pockmarked faces older than their years.

Jabez Tute halted his band. He glanced along the line of vehicles drawn up beside the road. The coonskin cap dipped as Jabez bent his head and beckoned his listeners closer. "You're not against lining your pockets, lads? Putting a twist on one of these whey-faced psalm singers whose bony wenches think themselves too good for us?"

"How, Jabez? How?"

"We walked here. Let's ride back in high style." Jabez Tute waved toward the hitched horses. "There's plenty to choose from."

Wat Fisher chortled. "Aye! Let others walk!"

The Dale brothers exchanged a glance. "Go back to home?" Oswald asked. "Now? Without sampling that cider?"

"There'll be merriment come night, Jabez." Oliver Bulter objected. "Feasting, and maybe a wench."

"Noll's been thinking of wenching," said Wat Fisher, "since he saw my sister Patty in the hurly-burly back there. And that doxy friend of hers with her. That Dorcas White."

"That jade," said Butler, calmly.

Jabez Tute cursed them into silence. "Wait till a man's done, will you? Who spoke of leaving? There's risk enough without putting our mark to the thing. We take the swag and stow it in a safe place. Tucked away where the horses can feed and no one the wiser. Then we double back to the clearing through the woods. Before old windy guts has done, we're there a-listening like we'd never left."

"And on the morrow we go our way."

"That's it, Noll. Now scatter and find the prize. Toward the end of the line. The farther from yon clearing, the easier the plucking."

There was much argument as to the merits of horseflesh. The Dale brothers wished to take a horse for each rough and were roundly cursed for their greediness. Wat Fisher selected a huge farm wagon but the team looked tired. It was Oliver Butler who shouted he'd found their prey.

"Look at these, Jabez. As matched as two eyes in the same head."

"Softly, Noll. Softly."

"But look."

"Small, ain't they?" argued Wat Fisher.

222

Jabez Tute was scornful. "Small, aye. And sturdy. And fleet. Have you never seen Morgans afore, fool? You choose well, Noll. The chaise is neat made, too. We'll have these."

Quietly, with Cedric Dale posted as watch, the roughs unhitched the horses and led them down the road. They had taken Joel Patch's chaise and team of matched Morgans. The horses went docilely enough; the rattle of the wheels sounded loud only to the nervous robbers. Jabez Tute kept his band controlled. They were past the Chittenden farm before he allowed them to clamber into the chaise.

"Now, we pelt along," said Jabez Tute. He slapped each horse with the reins. They went toward Stratton church.

The Morgans swept down the deserted road at a spanking trot. The three younger members of the band wanted to shout over the venture's success, but Oliver Butler silenced them.

"Hush your tongues. We ain't past the houses yet!"

Jabez halted the team before the settlement came in view and sent the Dales and little Wat ahead to scout. The trio came running back all a-grin and excited.

"Not a soul about, Jabez."

"Hide nor hair!"

"We could sack the place, Jabez."

The leader scowled at Wat Fisher's ferocious suggestion. "You'll hang before your beard grows, Wat."

"But, Jabez . . ."

"No! Blast your eyes! No, I say! Highwaymen don't stoop to rifling houses!"

Butler said, "Like common thieves!"

"Go to," said Wat, but subsided.

Jabez Tute drove through the settlement at a nice, steady pace, not slow but not racing. The others watched carefully for any witnesses to their passage. There were none. No one glanced from any of the inn's windows as they turned into the branch road.

Dan Tarbox heard them pass. For the first time in his life the innkeeper felt he'd had his fill of people passing. He didn't bother to rise and look out; he barked an order at Asa Brayton.

"Get on with your sweeping. The road's no concern of yours!"

Frowning, fingers busy among coins and paper, the innkeeper

went on counting his receipts. The money piled on the table convinced Dan Tarbox that the Panic was over. Thanks to the Whigs, he reflected.

He swept a stack of eagles clinking into his hand as the noise of the chaise faded in the distance.

The Defender of the Constitution spoke at length of that document, explaining, expounding. Only the Whig interpretation of the Constitution was acceptable; Democrat Loco-focoism twisted its principles for corrupt reasons.

The girl Mercy, listening, wondered if Doc and she were going to be Whigs the next place they went.

Tom Dunbar, listening, agreed with the speaker. The Constitution was, after all, a gentlemen's agreement.

Hoc, the slave, listening, didn't understand the long words but admired the way the white man used them.

Peter Blodgett was happy. The bound boy forgot how tired he was from the long climb up the mountain and gazed steadily at Daniel Webster. Peter's knowledge of the Senator had been based on hearsay, and he found the reality different and finer than his imagination had pictured. He ain't really big, thought Peter, but he seems to get bigger when he talks. He tried to memorize every detail of the orator's dress and bearing, every movement. For the first hour of the speech the boy gave his whole attention to what his idol was saying.

He didn't understand all of it, but he didn't want to miss a single word. Somewhere in the easily flowing sentences, the moments of biting invective that brought a responsive murmur from the audience, the emotional appeals, was the key that might loose the chains that made Peter a bound boy. All the Lymans would stand in silent awe if he could talk like Mr. Webster. He realized that maybe he couldn't learn how just by listening, but he was determined to try. If you could outtalk somebody it didn't matter if you weren't so big or so strong or couldn't lick them. It meant that the day might come when you could even overwhelm the law and only work where you wanted.

Mainly the great throng stood in silence. Webster's speech was entertainment, education, history. Later the people would discuss and dissect, analyze and quote; now they listened with an atten-tiveness both flattering and polite. It was enough, while the Senator spoke, to know that they, too—farmers, townspeople, even womenfolk—were one with the noted figures of the outside world who had heard the Great Man. There was little movement. At intervals applause burst forth and swept across the clearing with the sudden, crackling passage of a forest fire.

These bursts of clapping disturbed Peter. The boy was never sure just what Mr. Webster had said to produce such a reaction. He felt he had to know. It took some time for him to tighten his courage to the point where he began to edge forward. But it was the motionless solidity of the multitude that made him timid. He had forgotten the Lymans were present, somewhere, in the crowd.

He was far back from the speaker's platform and wanted to be closer. He walked cautiously, carefully weaving between spec-tators, trying not to disturb anyone. He stopped often, listening, selecting the path of his next advance. During one of these pauses Peter had the prickling, uneasy feeling that someone was watch-ing him.

The boy looked around. All his neighbors seemed to be gazing toward the speaker. Shrugging, Peter concentrated on the words. The feeling forced his head around again. This time he saw the watcher.

It was Stella Lyman. Her eyes, narrowed and doubtful, stared at Peter from between a man's shoulder and a woman's bonnet. Even as the boy looked, angry recognition replaced the doubt in her gaze.

She was five yards away, and there were a dozen people be-tween them. Peter Blodgett saw that at once. He took one startled step and bumped into a stranger.

"Be still, son," said the man.

"Yes, sir."

Stella Lyman tried to push her way toward Peter. The result was an instant rebuke from several listeners.

Peter saw no sign of Stella's parents. He watched the girl as a deer watches an approaching human.

They began a slow, edging game of hide-and-seek. Neither wanted a scene; both, with Vermont reserve, tried not to create a disturbance. It was a private feud, and the two might have been alone. Stella tried to lessen the distance and numbers between them; Peter was determined to keep the barrier.

One step here. Two there. Peter never moved unless the girl did.

Gradually she forced him toward the edge of the assemblage. He let her, knowing that the fewer listeners gave him greater maneuverability. Stella was still hemmed in by close-packed ranks when Peter walked swiftly out of the crowd.

Then he ran. He raced between two tents, dodged around a wagon, startled hitched horses, and plunged into the woods. He looked back, but there was no sign of pursuit.

Peter Blodgett put his forehead against a tree trunk and cried. Damn them, he thought. Damn Stella! Damn the Lymans! They had beaten him after all.

He could hear the voice, but not the words.

He couldn't see Daniel Webster at all.

Godlike Daniel denounced executive tyranny as the enemy of freedom and the Union. No reference was made either to the Hartford Convention or South Carolina's Nullification Act.

Tate Jones, the hunter, thought it sounded fine and didn't believe a word of it.

Abner Reed, the blacksmith, thought it sounded fine and believed every word of it. .

Joel Patch, nodding agreement, thought such sentiments would help elect Harrison.

Peleg Nason dozed and didn't hear at all.

Idly wondering whether the shadow of the tamarack tree would completely cover Senator Webster before he finished, Lovina Chester was startled to discover that somebody had taken hold of her hand. She knew Nathan Patch was beside her; he'd been at her elbow since her arrival at the clearing. Turning, she shook her head and tried to withdraw from his grasp.

Nathan held on, unsmiling but not rough.

"Nathan!" The rebuke was whispered.

"I got to talk to you, Lovina."

"Not here."

"It's important."

"Shh. Not now."

A woman in front of Lovina turned around and glared. She flounced her shoulders and tossed her head as she returned her attention to the speaker.

Lovina made a face at the woman's back. She frowned at Nathan, put a finger to her lips, and again tugged the captured hand. Far from releasing it, Nathan reinforced his hold by clasping both his hands around the girl's.

"Nathan. Let go."

"I aim to speak my piece."

"This is no place. You're bothering folks."

"Come away, then."

The girl flushed. She began to be angry with Nathan and tried to cow him by frowning at him. The young man's superior smile increased her anger. He looks exactly like his father, she thought irritatedly, after he's made a sharp trade. She glanced toward the platform and found confirmation in Joel Patch's pleased smirk. Lovina pinched the back of Nathan's hand, nipping the flesh between her fingertips and twisting.

"Won't help any, Lovina."

She realized that her essay of force had pleased him. He considered it another advantage gained. He's tricked me into this position, the girl decided, on purpose. With Mr. Webster talking and all these folks standing around, he counts on me not giving him a piece of my mind. Now I've either got to go somewhere and listen to him or stand here holding hands like a silly goose.

"Nathan, please."

"Nope."

Lovina resented having to make the choice. But the hot, moist feel of her hand between Nathan's decided her. She nodded her surrender, and Nathan led her through the throng. By the time they reached the ranks at the back, near the turnpike, the girl was white-faced with suppressed fury. I must look a pretty sight, she reflected, with Nathan dragging me along by the hand as if I was a naughty child. The puzzled stares of strangers goaded her into a rage so blind that she never saw the Chittendens, wasn't aware of them, until she heard Nathan's pleased greeting.

"Afternoon, Charles."

The whole Chittenden family was grouped together, and Nathan led Lovina through their midst. Eratus paid no attention; the big man was watching Webster. Lovina uttered a horrified gasp as she saw Mrs. Chittenden's eyebrows rise in surprise. After that she noticed no one but Charles. Charles was looking straight at her.

Charles said, coldly, "Afternoon, Nathan." He glanced from Lovina to young Patch, then down at their entwined hands. Deliberately, Charles turned his back.

Biting her lips lest she cry out, Lovina tried to wrench free from Nathan. But the strong fingers kept their grip. Nathan clumped on and Lovina, not wishing an undignified struggle, followed.

They stumbled down the bank onto the turnpike. The road was deserted except for hitched horses and empty conveyances. Nathan stopped beside one and turned.

"Now, Lovina . . ."

There was a report like a cracked whip. The mark of the slap was red on Nathan's face.

Nathan stepped back, letting go of Lovina's hand. He said, "No need to do that."

Not saying a word, eyes blazing, Lovina swung again.

He caught her wrist. She lashed out with the other arm, and he captured that, too. "Lovina." He was frightened and pleading.

"You! You worm!" Lovina spoke from between clenched teeth. She didn't struggle.

"I was only aiming to talk to you."

"Nothing you have to say could interest me!"

"But, Lovina . . ."

"Making a show of me in front of . . ."

"Charles?"

"Everybody!"

They stood, faces close, snarling at each other. Nathan had lost all his poise; the fingermarks on his cheek were like a fresh burn.

"You didn't think of my feelings last night!"

"You have no feelings, Nathan Patch!"

"Going off with that Southern popinjay!"

"What I do is my business!"

"I was going to overlook that!"

"Indeed?"

"E-yah. I'm a moderate man. A girl can pick and choose till she decides."

"Well! Thank you!"

"I was aiming to ask for your hand, Lovina!"

"You got it! The only way you'll ever get it! Across your face!"

Nathan Patch's anger left him; he wilted. He said, "I thought —lately—Charles wasn't around. You're mad, Lovina. I was only seeking to get you alone so's I could speak out."

"Will you please let go of my wrist?" asked Lovina. Her voice was cold and cutting. "I won't strike you again."

"Aw, Lovina." Nathan knew he was beaten. He released her but tried to recapture his shattered strategy. "If you'll just listen. I'm making a bona fide offer, Lovina. I'd be a good husband. Pa thinks highly of you. There'd be no trouble there. You'd never want for a thing. I'd work my fingers to the bone." He was speaking quickly, without thought, trying to convince her with hasty sentences before she turned away.

"For the last time, Nathan. I am not interested." There was no pity in the girl; she was rigid with anger. "You can save your tricks for someone else. Someone who likes being treated as if she was livestock!" She turned and caught her breath, startled.

A man stood at the top of the road bank staring down at them.

"Mr. Brayton!"

The scowl on Lem Brayton's face stayed as if painted; there was suspicion in the forward thrust of his head, the narrowed eyes, the clenched fists dangling by his side. He raised a finger slowly to his hatbrim and said, "Miss Lovina. Nathan. Didn't mean to scare you. Heard voices. Wondered." Lem spoke reluctantly as if he blamed them for the necessity of speech. "Wondered," he repeated, and there was antagonism in the word.

Lovina sensed it and blushed. Nathan Patch spoke quickly. "We had something to discuss."

"E-yah." Lem suddenly raised an arm, pointed. "That there's Isaac Mead's horse and carryall, ain't it?"

Both Nathan and the girl glanced in the indicated direction. Everyone on Stratton knew Isaac's walleyed Nick. Lovina said, "Of course."

"E-yah. That's Nick," agreed Nathan.

Lem Brayton nodded. He hesitated, then blurted his question. "Seen my wife?" When both answered the inquiry with a head-shake, the farmer seemed forced to explain. With a smile that was more a grimace, he said, "Sort of misplaced her. The crowd, you know. Like looking for a needle in a haystack. The whole world's here listening to Webster."

"I wanted to hear him, too," said Lovina, with a glare at Nathan. "And I've no intention of missing any more." The girl climbed the bank with swift, angry strides. She didn't look back.

Nathan Patch made no move to follow. He watched Lovina out of sight, then plunged his hands into his pockets and gazed at the ground.

"What's the matter with her?" asked Lem, without interest. He was still wearing several white Tippecanoe badges, and he pulled at a loose thread of one. "Buy a badge, Nathan?"

"No."

"Ought to have a badge."

"No."

"All right. No cause to get riled. I didn't put your nose out of joint."

The young man was too crestfallen to resent the sneer. Not answering, he turned to walk away. He had only taken a few steps when Lem's hand on his arm checked him.

"You're sure you ain't seen Zilpha?"

"I told you. No." Nathan shook the other off.

"Well, you don't have to act so uppity. Civil question." Lem whined after Nathan's retreating figure. The farmer licked his lips and glared at Isaac Mead's horse. There was one other question he wanted to ask, but he didn't dare link the names. He couldn't find Zilpha anywhere in the clearing. There was no sign of Isaac Mead, either. Lem cursed the size of the attendance. You couldn't be sure of anything in that mob, he figured to himself. Inquiring after Isaac would just start talk. His neighbors would laugh behind his back. He spoke to the walleyed horse in a fierce whisper, shaking with hate.

"Goddamn you to hell anyway!"

Nick's ears went back, and he swung his head toward the speaker.

With hurried, skipping steps, Lem moved away. The ugly brute looked mean; he'd make a nasty bite. But didn't his presence prove that his owner hadn't left the clearing? Isaac Mead wouldn't go off without horse and wagon. Unless maybe, the argument formed in Lem's mind against his will, the other man wanted folks to think exactly that.

"You ain't fooling me," Lem Brayton said to a mental image of Isaac Mead. He wandered down the road, muttering every filthy term he knew. But it was aimless cursing, almost unconscious, and without satisfaction. It was the audible sign of his growing suspicion and, like that suspicion, the swearing was bitter but uncertain.

Nothing was sure, he told himself. That was it. Nothing was sure. He might have missed Zilpha in spite of all his hunting. Isaac Mead could be in a dozen places. Inside the big log cabin, though he'd searched there. Or in somebody's wagon, though he'd scanned the vehicles. Lem argued with himself, answering his doubts, questioning his answers. The only certainty was the cold vise that seemed clamped, ever tightening, around some tender vital in the depth of his stomach. He knew that was happening, he could feel it. It was fear.

Lem Brayton was afraid.

He was afraid that his wife was really with another man; he was afraid he wouldn't find out for sure. He feared Zilpha and cuckoldry and Isaac Mead. He was too frightened to face the problem of what to do if his suspicions proved correct, yet he knew he would have to do something. "I'd kill her," he said aloud. "I'd kill them both." Even to Lem's own ears it sounded like a lie.

The clearing was well out of earshot when Lem left the road and started through the woods. If they were together, he reasoned, it was a hopeless task to look for them. Yet part of him refused to accept that conclusion, and he went toward his own farm.

Under the quiet gloom of the trees Lem felt very lonely. He expected to discover nothing; he expected to discover everything. He wasn't sure which would be worse.

Twice the man stopped, listening. He held his breath and strained every nerve, not knowing what it was he tried so hard to hear. There were no sounds but the usual forest noises: the rustle of leaves, a bird on a branch, a squirrel's chatter. Each time he was sure it would be wiser to return to the clearing. Zilpha was there. Of course she was. But he plodded on, driven by the fear inside him. Once he found he was weeping—soundless, weak tears at the futility of his search.

He came out onto the Jamaica road only one curve away from his own house. Lem didn't follow the road. He crossed it and slipped from tree to tree, slowly, carefully. He crept close to the road bank, parted the bushes with his hands, and peered out.

The farm looked still and empty in the sunlight. Each of the windows in the side of the house facing Lem sparkled with reflected gold.

Smoke curled from the chimney.

A sob came from Lem Brayton when he saw the wisp of gray against the blue sky. The thin, wavering line of smoke was certain proof. Any other day it belonged there. Today it meant that Zilpha Brayton was not at the clearing but at home, and her husband knew she was not alone.

He lay there, watching the house, his fingers digging at grass, clawing it out by the roots, as if they worked independently of the man. He waited a long time. The ground near Lem seemed scratched bare by some animal before Isaac Mead came out.

Lem Brayton tensed and rose to a crouch.

Isaac glanced up and down the road. There was nothing furtive about him. He walked away from the Brayton farm with a jaunty stride that was almost a swagger. After a few steps he took out a plug of tobacco, bit off a huge chew, and grinned. It was the grin of a man well pleased with life and himself.

He passed within four feet of a figure huddled in the underbrush. Isaac Mead was humming as he strode along. He spat into the mud of the road.

Lem could see every line of the other's face. He was shaking with rage and hate. He wanted to hurl himself at Isaac's throat, but the betrayer was too big. If he beats me, thought Lem, he'll know I know. Everybody on the mountain will know. Lem Brayton has horns on his head.

The chance slipped away while Lem argued with himself. Isaac Mead went on down the road, around the curve, out of sight. Lem opened his mouth to shout after him, curse him, revile him, but no sound came. He stayed there, trembling, reasoning with himself that it wasn't cowardice, that Zilpha wasn't worth fighting over, that the shame would be less if Isaac didn't know he was aware of what had happened.

After a while Lem crawled back away from the house. He didn't want to face Zilpha just yet. Zilpha. He cursed his wife. It wasn't bad enough that she treated him like a slave, nagged at his failures, but she had to betray him. *Thou shalt not commit adultery.* Lem repeated the Commandment. A lot Zilpha cared that she'd grievously sinned. She was a devil, with her red hair and green eyes. *Thou shalt not commit adultery.* Lem felt a smug satisfaction in being, for once, the abused party. Even Scripture was on his side and against Zilpha.

"Stoned," he said, remembering. "They stoned them! It would serve her right. I'll fix her!"

He went straight down the road to the Tarbox inn. Lem hesitated a moment in the doorway, but the common room was empty. There was no sign of Isaac Mead.

Dan Tarbox hurried out when Lem rapped his coin on the bar. The innkeeper said, "Hello, Lem. Is it all over?"

"What's that?" Lem asked, thickly. Did they know already?

"The meeting. Did Webster finish speaking?"

"Oh. That. E-yah. I guess so."

"Guess so? Weren't you there?"

"'Course I was," Lem said, almost shouting. "'Course I was! I—I came away early to get out of the rush. Give me a drink. Brandy."

"Brandy?"

"E-yah. I got the money. I've been working." He gripped one of the badges, ripped it off. "Selling these."

"I know."

The flat strip of white satin was dirt-stained and smudged. But the lettering was still clear. The words stretched across Lem's palm. *Like Cincinnatus. He leaves the plough to save his country.*

Plough, thought Lem. Wasn't there an old saying about ploughing another man's pasture? He gulped his drink, thrust out the cup. "Another, Dan."

"E-yah."

The taste of the brandy was hot and sharp in his mouth. Lem Brayton stared at the slogan on the Tippecanoe badge. He had a

233

vague impression that the badge and the Convention and Dan Webster and all the rest were somehow hitched up with Zilpha and Isaac and their crime.

He leaves the plough to save his country.

"Damn fool," said Lem Brayton. "He ought to stay home." He drank, draining the cup. "Another, Dan." He was beginning to feel better.

Daniel Webster ended his speech with a stirring peroration that made the election of "Tippecanoe and Tyler too" sound like a summons to a holy war. He gestured for the last time, stilled his great voice, and relaxed. The Great Man had spoken for two hours, and he wasn't even slightly tired.

The audience roared. The immense throng burst into a sustained ovation, unorganized, spontaneous; it was a cataclysm of sound, rising from more than ten thousand throats, as unintelligible as thunder, as frenzied as an earthquake. The noise exploded from the clearing, vibrated through the forest, drowned the mountain's very echoes. Folk screamed, cheered, applauded, wept. The tamarack tree seemed to sway with the force of the tumult. Three deer, grazing a mile away, looked at each other in panic, wheeled, and fled.

Webster accepted it, bowing, with a gratified smile. The tribute kept on for minutes, uncontrolled, violent. There was nothing niggardly about the Vermonters' appreciation of the speech. Senator Webster had come a long way to address them; he had earned the payment of their acclaim. They paid in full.

The other men on the platform pressed around their guest. Compliments and congratulations came from every member of the committee. Joel Patch shook the Senator's hand and surrendered the tall hat. Hiland Hall was beaming; the Marshal had split his gloves applauding. Even Rufe, grinning, winked his approval at Webster. You never can tell, thought the campaign manager. He didn't say one damn thing different from what he's said a hundred times, but today it sounded fresh and important.

On the grass of the clearing the concerted cheering slowed, became scattered. The women subsided first; they had less interest in the political importance of the meeting and considered it a social gathering. Men were recalled to their dignity by a dryness along their larynges. They stopped shouting and began to make comments.

"Nice bit of speechmaking, hey, Annie?"

"Worth the trip, wa'n't it?"

"Well, you heard Dan Webster, son."

"Spoke right out, didn't he?"

"Clear as a bell. E-yah. No mumbling."

"Never heard the beat!"

"Don't know where he gets it. He ain't so big."

"In the chest, Ira. Chest like a barrel."

"Godlike Daniel!"

"Fits. Fits. He sounded like a voice from above."

"What was that he said about the Constitution?"

"Don't just recall."

"Tell her, Horace."

"He was for it."

"E-yah. That's right."

"Defender of the Constitution, ain't he?"

"But what did he say exactly? I want to remember."

"Heard him, didn't you? Stood right next to me!"

"Bet they heard him down to Bennington."

"Right smart orating."

"Black Dan'l."

"Ain't a Democrat can match him."

"Whig, either. 'Cept maybe Henry Clay."

"Clay ain't Webster. Southerner. Kentucky."

"E-yah. They don't talk the same."

"Worth every step we come."

"Lift the baby up, Ma. I want him to see."

"Finest speaker in the country!"

"E-yah!"

There were few dissenting voices. Here and there a Democrat, attracted to the proceedings from curiosity, complained that the speech had contained little of policy or principle. Nobody, these solitary critics carped, had made any concrete suggestion as to how Tippecanoe was going to cure hard times. But the dissenters were howled down by their neighbors and took refuge in sullen silence. Only Lot Purdy, the stage driver, refused to be overwhelmed by weight of numbers. He glared at the speaker's platform until his attitude attracted the Stratton blacksmith's attention.

"Afternoon, Lot."

"Hello, Abner."

"What're you looking at?"

"Webster."

"Oh. Hear the speech?"

"E-yah. What there was of it."

"Two hours."

"Talked a lot. Didn't say much."

Abner Reed was a mild man, and he liked Lot. He smiled. He said, "Folks took to it, Lot."

The stage driver shrugged. "They bought the horse blind, Abner. It ain't easy to admit you've been swindled."

"Ain't been swindled, if you're satisfied."

"Some folks're easy to please. Little Hall made a better speech'n Webster."

Mrs. Purdy bustled up, fearing an argument. She said, "Lot, forget politics. Folks are getting ready to eat. We don't want to miss out on the victuals." Grinning, she addressed the blacksmith as if her husband wasn't there. "He takes on like Mr. Webster did something to him personal."

"Blue-light Federalist!" said Lot Purdy, shaking his fist at the platform. He knew he was fighting a hopeless battle and allowed his wife to lead him away.

Others were hastening to prepare the outdoor supper. Throughout the clearing there was a feeling that the important events of the Convention were over; another lesser orator had trouble capturing an audience. Several of the dozen bands blared forth popular selections. The huge throng broke into segments; the younger folk strolled about or gathered in clusters, gossiping. Women stirred the campfires into life. Hard cider made its appearance. The Captain drove in the bung, drew off the first tankard. Once more the gathering had the look of a festive picnic.

There was no central, organized commissary. Every delegation had its busy group of womenfolk engaged in cooking and serving. Each church was represented by the combined efforts of its lady members. The Methodists of Stratton uncovered their Election cake; Mrs. Chester sent her daughters as couriers to gather assistants who would distribute the Congregational treasury of pies. Senator Webster and party were guided, more formally, into the big log cabin, where the Great Man's table habits would have privacy. Webster was aware of the etiquette the occasion demanded; he toasted the candidate in hard cider.

In spite of the hard times there was food enough for an army, and of better quality than the Republic's armies generally ate. Thousands of bean pots were heated to produce countless servings of baked beans, and each pot held generous slabs of salt pork. Thick slices of bread—brown, black, and white—attended the beans as the common nucleus of the meal. The variations added to these staples depended on individual tastes. There were cold meats: mutton chops, ham, fowl. Some of the guests had brought pickled vegetables. Cold boiled potatoes were in evidence, as well as others roasted and raked from the fires, their charred jackets too hot to hold. Hundreds of cakes waited to be cut. Cakes of every description—Election cakes, Independence Day cakes, egg cakes, fruitcakes, nut cakes, molasses cakes, maple-syrup cakes, cakes named for some noted local cook, cakes without names.

Naturally, everybody had at least one piece of pie.

Plates came from a pile of thin shingles. The chips held an incredible amount of food, and most of the eaters gobbled too fast for any liquid to seep through the wood. Joel Patch, chuckling, called Humphrey Dunklee's attention to the rude trenchers.

"Had them all guessing, Humphrey. My idea."

"Your lumber, too, eh?"

"E-yah." The sawmill owner jerked his head in quick nods. "Arranged it with the committee. A copper the half dozen. Never counted on so many folks, though. Wish I'd made more."

The banker gazed around, noted the number of shingles in hands, on laps, being passed, and grunted. "You did well enough, Joel. It ain't likely you used your best timber."

"Ain't saying I did."

"Thought not."

"Clem and Tim—they're my hired men—figured I'd gone stark crazy. Even my son Nathan was worried." Patch's cackle was as triumphant as a rooster's crow. "A man's got to think pert to get ahead these times, Humphrey."

"Banking's the same, Joel. Worse, maybe."

"Wait'll Van Buren's licked, Humphrey. Things'll get better."

"E-yah. If he gets licked."

"Ain't today a good weather sign?"

Dunklee lowered his voice. "Webster fetched them, Joel. He made a good speech, too. Didn't say too much; didn't say too little. But he made a whole passel of good speeches for the big Bank back in Jackson's term. It didn't save the Bank, did it?"

"No."

"A banker's got to go by facts and figures. Speechmaking and cheering ain't going to beat the Dutchman. Money's the answer. That holds for hard times, too. Money makes money."

"I've been aiming to talk to you about some such thing, Humphrey." Patch gave the banker a sideways glance and picked his words carefully. "Better times'll mean better chances. There's rumors of the steam cars coming into Vermont. That'll take a lot of lumber. Fuel, building, all sorts of things."

"It'll be at least a couple or three years, Joel."

"Pays a man to wait sometimes. And look ahead. Ain't I always stood by the bank, Humphrey? I have. I take it you won't forget that after Tippecanoe gets in and things improve some. Money makes money, like you said. I just might get a notion to spread out one of these days. At the usual rates of interest."

"All depends on election, Joel." Dunklee parried neatly. "If Van Buren wins we're really in the brine. I don't mind telling you I've contributed a good deal to the Whig cause."

"E-yah?" Patch was wary of the trend the conversation was taking. Bankers, he thought, don't put on a poor mouth for no reason.

"It's up to us men of substance—like yourself, Joel—to do our share. If we want to reap the harvest, we've got to plant the seed. You follow my meaning?"

Patch followed it only too well. Instead of making any promise about a future loan, the banker was hinting that Patch donate something to the Whig coffers. The sawmill owner's mouth tightened. He was too old a trader to make the angry retort that occurred to him. A loan was a lot different from a gift. He smiled at Humphrey Dunklee. "Ain't nobody planted more seeds than me in these parts. This mountain's for Tippecanoe and Tyler too. I ain't saying it's all my doing, but I ain't been idle."

"Never knew you to be, Joel."

Stalling, decided Patch. Well, two could play at that game. He said, "Let's get our share of the supper. We can leave talking till later. You and Mrs. Dunklee are spending the night with us, of course?"

The banker was instantly jovial. "Now, you ain't aiming to go to no trouble. . . ."

"No trouble, Humphrey. No trouble at all. Everything's set to accommodate you. Besides, I want to show you my mill. Finest circular saw in these parts. In the whole State, maybe." Have him by the hip, Patch gloated, well pleased, once he's accepted bed and board. There wouldn't be so much talk of a gift while the banker was stuffing himself at Patch's expense.

"You're certain we won't crowd you?"

"Not at all. Sarah and me will ride back in your carriage, if you don't mind. Leave the Morgans for my son. He maybe has some courting to do. The minister's daughter, you know." Patch gave the information deliberately, to impress Dunklee with his connections.

The two men paused by the cider barrel. They had to wait for their drinks. Five youths in very old-style clothes were jostling each other for precedence at the spigot. The sawmill owner identified them with a whisper.

"A rough tribe. From up Bondville way. Live back in the woods like Indians."

"That one in the leggings and coonskin cap," said Humphrey Dunklee, "can shoot. But I must say they start drinking young."

Little Wat Fisher lowered his mug and glared. "So did you, lard belly. Mother's milk!" He drank again, the tankard tilting up under the three-cornered hat so that only Wat's chin was visible.

Banker and sawmill owner swallowed their cider hastily and departed. Patch was explaining that the women of the church of which he was Deacon would be hurt if he didn't taste their supper, when he heard his name called.

"Mr. Patch! Mr. Patch!"

"Just speaking of you, Mrs. Chester," Patch answered and dragged the banker toward the lady.

Using the parsonage wagon as a booth, directing four assistants like a general, Mrs. Chester was dispensing pie. She pointed her knife and asked briskly, "What kind?"

"Apple for me. Humphrey?"

239

"E-yah. Apple."

"This one's from Mrs. Chittenden," said the parson's wife, cutting out a wedge. "She's one of our very best." She slid the wedge onto a shingle and thrust it at the banker. "Have you seen my Lovina, Mr. Patch?"

"No, ma'am. She's likely with Nathan somewheres."

Mrs. Chester smiled. "Maybe. I haven't set eyes on him, either. Not surprising. I've never seen such a crowd." She suddenly raised voice and knife, brandishing the latter. "Miss Nason! Oh, Miss Nason! Come and try our pie." Her helpers tittered, and Mrs. Chester explained in a triumphant whisper. "She's Methodist, and they had an Election cake. But it didn't last five minutes. I'm heaping coals!"

"Where's the parson?"

"Over yonder. That way. Lot of our neighbors over there. Regular church social. Reverend Chester's introducing folks to Reverend Matthew Butterfield. This is Mrs. Butterfield. Mince? Who's that asking for mince? Well, you'll have to take a thin portion, Seth. You already had three helpings, and we're running a mite short on mince."

"You, lad," said Humphrey Dunklee. "Ain't you the one took the shooting match?"

"Yes, sir." Seth Purdy took his pie and ducked away through the crowd. He was supplying Put Chester, who wished to keep away from his mother while there was work to be done. Both boys had stuffed themselves and sampled the cider. Seth joined his friend in the circle around the fire where the men of Stratton Mountain had gathered.

Reverend Chester was enjoying himself. The preacher found few opportunities to engage in the masculine talk of his community. He felt no compunctions about visiting the tavern but, being shy, had concluded that his presence put a constraint on conversation. Only on special occasions did he manage to ignore the restrictions placed on his position and cloth by the male members of his congregation.

The Convention was a very special occasion; the overwhelming majority of strangers had forced the neighbors to herd together. Tate Jones, silent and smiling, was in the group. Eratus Chittenden, broad shoulders supported by a wagon wheel, sat between two of

240

his sons, Amos and Henry. Except for the Reverend Matthew Butterfield, the others were the usual loungers of smithy and inn. The blacksmith fed the fire. Peleg Nason, wide awake now, huddled on a box. Tim Frost had, with foresight, fetched a jug of cider from the barrel, and the blue Bennington-ware pitcher passed from hand to hand.

Only nods greeted the arrival of Joel Patch and the banker. Lot Purdy was telling a story. The stage driver had buried his political opinions in the general conviviality. He was twitting the hunter, his best friend, about the latter's well-known trait of seldom laughing.

"E-yah," said Lot, grinning a welcome to the newcomers. "I was just telling Tate that his not bothering to laugh out loud shows a mean streak. It ain't that he can't laugh. I know for a fact he can!"

"How's that, Lot?" asked Eratus Chittenden.

"Well, you know, once in a while, when I can get off the stage, Tate and me goes hunting together. He lets me tag along. Ain't that it, Tate? And one night last fall we was out after coon. It was a good night for coon, and you know Tate, he can see in the dark better than most animals. You're an educated man, Reverend, maybe you can explain why that is."

Reverend Chester chuckled. "Might come from looking instead of laughing. I've noticed that folks who laugh too much miss things sometimes." The parson glanced at the Reverend Butterfield, who laughed.

"Maybe," said Lot. "Maybe. Anyways, we was out with them two hounds of Tate's. We tramp for a good spell, then sit down and wait. First you'd hear one hound bay, then the other. Tate, here, wouldn't even stir. Rabbit, he'd say. Or hedgehog. Knowing the way of their howling, you see. It's a good trick and a nice lazy way of hunting."

"Fiddlesticks! I don't believe it!"

"I'm telling how it was, Joel. All at once both dogs start making a fuss together. It sounds a long way off, but Tate gets up and says come on, they've treed something. Remember, Tate? They had, too. We found them both sitting under a tree yapping away. It was as dark as the devil's hip pocket in that tree—begging both your pardons, Reverends, but it was. Tate, I says, they've treed that coon too blame well. Well, says he, go on up and shake him out, and I'll shoot him. Wasn't that the way of it, Tate?"

The hunter smiled at his friend and nodded.

"So I propped my gun against a rock and shinnied up the tree. That coon was so high I was a mite surprised. But I finally made out the lump of him. And just as my head gets level with him— he leaps right at me, spitting and snarling! And he ain't a coon **at all, but a wildcat!**"

The stage driver paused, shaking his head. He said, "Pass that jug, will you, Abner?"

"Finish the story!"

"What happened?"

"Never mind the cider!"

The narrator ignored even Eratus Chittenden's booming protest. He took the pitcher in both hands and drank noisily. His audience waited with impatience. Lot wiped his mouth on his sleeve.

"That's better. Well. This wildcat he comes close enough to kiss me! His eyes are like live coals, and I never saw so many claws and teeth in my life! I felt his breath and spittle on my face, that's how close he was. I let out a yelp and let go of everything. Wonder I didn't fall right out of the tree and dash my brains out. But a couple of boughs, they held me.

"And that wildcat turned on himself faster than a wink and jumped. He must have lit twenty feet from that tree, and he lit running. And the dogs after him!

"Tate never did get to draw a bead, did you, Tate? And you know why? When I climbed down out of that tree, still shaking, he's sitting on the ground laughing fit to bust! E-yah. I learned something then and there."

"That Tate could laugh, Lot?"

"What he thinks is funny?"

"Not to go hunting with him?"

"Them things, e-yah. But something else, too." Lot Purdy looked around the group and nodded solemnly. "You know, I ain't never climbed a tree since."

Laughter broke out around the circle. Both ministers threw back their heads and roared. Eratus Chittenden guffawed. Old Peleg cackled and pounded his stick into the ground. Even the stolid blacksmith and Patch, who wanted to speak, laughed. Seth Purdy thumped Put's arm and gazed proudly at his father.

Tate Jones, grinning, said, "My sympathy was with the wildcat. He was there first, and you came horning in."

"E-yah," said Lot. "And if he'd bit a chunk out of me, you'd still be laughing."

"Let's have that jug, Lot."

"E-yah. Pass it along."

"For a Democrat you're right fond of Whig cider."

"I ain't choosy, Will. I'll drink with anybody."

"We've noticed."

"Just shows I'm a true Democrat."

The parson leaned back, convinced that the stage driver could take the jesting insults at his loyalties and return better than he received. It was Joel Patch who abruptly switched the talk back to politics.

"How'd you like Webster's speech, Reverend?"

Jedidah Chester frowned, but his answer was mild. "I liked it fine, Joel."

"Ought to be a subject for a sermon next Sunday, don't you think?" Patch was attempting to impress Humphrey Dunklee. His tone was a little too mandatory.

It brought a sudden silence on the group. Lot Purdy hunched forward and watched the preacher. Tate Jones became blank-faced, withdrawn. Every man in the circle waited for their parson to speak.

Reverend Matthew Butterfield laughed. "Just what I've been telling you, Jed!"

Heads turned and regarded the outsider. Even Patch scowled at the visiting clergyman. The men of Stratton saw no reason why their parson should heed advice from any off-mountain source. Peleg Nason, a Methodist, voiced the general feeling. With the blunt frankness of the very old, he said, "Nobody asked you!"

The parson refused to be forced into taking sides. He placed his fingertips together, contemplated them, and addressed himself to Patch. "A sermon, Joel? Next Sunday? That's hard to say. Sunday's a long ways off."

"What's that got to do with it?"

"I like my sermons to be important."

"What Webster said was important!"

"Maybe, Joel. I'm not claiming it wasn't. But I might choose to take my text from Scripture. I figure that what the Lord said is likely to be just as important as what the Senator said."

A murmur seemed to drift around the circle. Some of the listeners grinned openly. Patch wasn't overpopular, and the group enjoyed his obvious annoyance.

The sawmill owner blustered. "Nobody claimed it wasn't! I'm asking you right out—are you going to give a sermon about Webster's speech or ain't you?"

"Coming to meeting next Sunday, Joel?"

"Don't I always?"

"E-yah. Well. You'll hear my sermon then." The quiet voice was unruffled. "Speaking as a Whig, which you all know I am"— the parson looked at Lot Purdy—"I liked the speech while Webster was giving it. Speaking as a man, I like it less the more you talk about it. Speaking as a minister of the Gospel, our little church is not Tippecanoe's log cabin. At services you will not find this multitude, any bands, hard cider, or a speaker of Senator Webster's reputation. But you will, I think, find the word of God. Now, Eratus, may I have the jug, please?"

Eratus Chittenden rose and carried it to the minister. The big man handed the jug over and turned to Patch. "You asked him, Joel. He told you. Now let it be!"

Before Patch could speak there was the sound of cheering. It grew louder. Tim Frost stood up and stared. "It's over by the big log cabin."

"Wonder what it's for?"

"Don't know."

"Some more speeches, likely."

"Aim to go see, Tim?"

"Not me. Walk? With all I ate?"

"Me, neither. I'm too cozy here."

"E-yah. Would you pass the cider this way, Pars—I mean, Reverend?"

Isaac Mead joined the group and explained. "Webster just announced he'd sleep in the clearing tonight. I heard him. Said he wanted to camp with the Green Mountain boys on the summit of their famous hills. Folks were pleased."

Every man in the group knew that he'd sleep that night in his usual bed. They felt detached from the delegates and campers.

They grinned at each other with pleasure. They had stayed at home, and even the great Webster had climbed their mountain to sleep out in the open.

Tate Jones glanced toward the setting sun. "They're going to have a fine night."

"E-yah."

"Isaac." Reverend Chester beckoned the man closer.

"Yes, Reverend?"

"I've been looking for you. Where've you been keeping yourself?"

Isaac Mead swallowed hard. It would be, he thought with sudden panic, the minister who asked. For a breath the age-old awe of priestcraft frightened Isaac. He wondered if the parson could, in some strange way, know all that had happened in Zilpha Brayton's bedroom. He lied, quickly, half expecting an accusation. "Right here in the clearing. Yonder."

"I wanted to talk about something."

"E-yah?" Fighting a desire to flee, Isaac felt cold sweat break out on his forehead. He was afraid to look at the preacher. Don't let him say it, he prayed, here in front of everybody.

"E-yah. I'm going to need help with my haying. If you'll lend a hand with mine, I'll do the same for you."

"Is that all?" Relief made Isaac's knees shake. Of course he doesn't know, he told himself. Nobody knows. He said, "Glad to help you out, Reverend."

"Thank you. I figured I could count on a good church member."

Isaac Mead laughed, hoping it sounded better to others than it did to himself. Everything the parson said seemed to mock the farmer's hidden guilt. "Let's have a turn at that jug," said Isaac, stumbling away from the minister. When he captured it, he drank long and thirstily.

"Hey, Isaac."

"Don't be a hog!"

"Leave some for others!"

"You empty that, you'll have to go fill it!"

"Don't dribble."

"E-yah. He's dipped his nose before today."

"No wonder the Reverend couldn't find him!"

Grinning at them, Isaac noted Lem Brayton's absence. He

245

shook the jug, listening to the gurgle. "Plenty left. Wasn't my fault nobody found me in this mob. Nobody looked in the right place."

"Where was that?"

"I found me a spot," said Isaac. He didn't think anybody'd seen him come out of the woods, but he had his explanation all prepared. "Up near the edge of the trees. I could watch the whole clearing and Webster, too. Never expect to see the beat. Close to twenty thousand folks standing quiet, listening. Prettiest sight anybody ever laid eyes on."

"Not me," Peleg Nason said. The old veteran waved his cane. "Not me, Isaac Mead. Don't you go including me in that."

"I mean for looking at a crowd."

"So do I. So do I."

"You've seen prettier, Peleg?"

"E-yah, Parson. Once." The ancient's thin voice quickened as it always did when he referred to his Revolutionary service. "Once. Years ago, over to the highlands just before the Revolution ended."

Reverend Chester settled back, smiling. He prompted, "Tell us." But the words weren't necessary; Peleg had only paused for breath.

"We—the Continental Army, that is—or, leastways, Washington's part of it—was sitting watching Clinton in New York. Sir Henry Clinton, you recall. We watched him the way a cat watches a mousehole. Only in a sort of backwards way like we was the mouse and the British was the cat. E-yah. We'd been sitting there till we'd worn out the seats of our britches and put corns on our souls. There ain't much about that campaign in your history book, Parson. Ain't much about it anywheres!"

The parson nodded. "Washington was keeping Clinton bottled up in the city."

"Bottled up! That's one way of putting it. Bottled up! Well, I was part of the cork, and it was no picnic. Months on end, day in, day out, rain or shine, it was the same thing over and over. Sit in quarters, move to the outposts, back to quarters, man a fort, back to quarters. Go here, go there, do nothing! And drill! We drilled so blame much my stomach'd turn at the sight of a musket!

246

Spit and polish! Spit and polish! Till we wore our clothes to rags and dried up our spittle. E-yah. An army fighting is bad enough, but an army sitting is worse. I'll never forget that terrible waiting.

"I was a young feller in those days, and impatient. I'd been to Bennington battle, and I'd been to Saratoga when Burgoyne quit, and I'd burnt some powder at Monmouth, down Jersey way, where we'd have won again only for that bastard Charles Lee. I ain't aiming to soften the word. Washington called him a whole lot worse, and rightly. E-yah. I was farther from Washington than I was from Dan Webster today, but I heard him a sight plainer. When the General took to cussing it sort of carried.

"Well, I was used to winning not setting, and I was young, like I said. I wanted to go home. It'd been more'n a year since I'd set foot in Vermont. I ain't never figured why I didn't just up and set out like some others, but I didn't. Each day seemed like a year. Every morning I'd be wishing the British'd come out and hoping they wouldn't. Them Redcoats had a nasty habit of killing soldiers, win or lose.

"The captain sent me out foraging one day. The country round our camp was picked cleaner than hen bones in a fox's den, and I had to wander a mite farther than you'd expect. Not that I minded. Even walking along by myself seemed a nice change from the usual!

"All at once I heard soldiers marching. You get so's you can tell soldiers just by sound. There's a sort of tramp and jingle and scuffing all in time. And regulars sound different from militia. This was regulars. A lot of regulars. So many I figured they must be British, though the sound was from the wrong direction, and I didn't see how the Redcoats could have gotten way around behind our lines that way. Not even the British Army can fly!

"I was on a little hill, and I reconnoitered. I crawled up to the top on my belly, keeping down, and peered out from behind some brambles. Below me was a valley, and coming down it, winding like a stream, as neat and glittering as you please, was an army.

"They was in marching column and doing quickstep, and they was regulars all right. E-yah. Ranks tight, and gaiters flashing together, and gun barrels as even as the pickets in a fence. They had their colors muffled, but every man jack of them was in uniform, and there wasn't a red coat in sight. A lot of white and some blue and a splash or two of green. E-yah. And enough gold braid to trim a barn dance. That told me. They was Frenchies.

"Rochambeau's bunch. Washington hadn't thought to tell me they was coming, and he never did get around to telling Clinton. Six thousand or so of them coming from Newport. Not much of a crowd compared to this here Convention maybe, but real soldiers, regulars, all spruced up and slick as a whistle.

"I was raised in Vermont, and I ain't got much use for Frenchies. Heard too much about them sic-ing the Indians or leading them down from Canada. E-yah. But I came near to busting out crying at that army. It meant the end of the waiting! Things were going to happen!

"It was the prettiest sight I ever laid eyes on. Bar none!"

"I can understand that," said the preacher. "They helped us take Yorktown."

"Yorktown, my foot!" Peleg Nason snorted. "Who the hell was thinking about Yorktown! I figured with all those fresh troops I'd get a furlough and come home!" The old man giggled. "E-yah! I was madder than Clinton and Cornwallis and King George lumped together when Washington dragged me all the way down to Virginia!"

"Hello," said Peter Blodgett.

The lad bathing his feet in the brook reached for his drum before he looked up. Fred Streeter saw that the speaker was younger than himself and scowled. He said, "Hello."

"You're in one of the bands, ain't you?"

"E-yah." The drummer's tone was truculent. "Look, if they sent you to fetch me, you didn't find me! I've done all the marching and drumming I'm going to for a while!"

Peter blinked in surprise. "Nobody sent me."

"Then what are you doing off here in the woods?"

"Nothing." Peter looked away. He couldn't explain that he was afraid to go back to the clearing. Stella Lyman had found him once, and next time she'd be looking for him. He said, "Did he leave?"

"Who?"

"Daniel Webster."

"No. He's spending the night. Last I saw he was still eating."

"Oh." Peter was very hungry. The smell of cooking had driven him away from the edge of the clearing. He couldn't bear it, and he didn't dare leave hiding to eat. By this time the Lymans probably had the law after him.

Fred Streeter took his feet from the cold water and sighed. He examined a stone bruise and, having an audience, complained. "We marched all the way!"

"So did I."

"Well, you didn't have to carry no drum! And play it! And then have everybody watching you and ordering you around just because you're youngest! Try to have some fun, and they say they'll tell your folks!"

"Have you got folks?"

"Sure." Fred stared. "Ain't you?"

Peter shook his head. He said, with admiration, "Folks! And a drum!"

There was a cracking of brush across the stream. Peter stiffened, looked toward the noise. He saw two figures through the foliage and heard a giggle. "I'd better get along." Peter took a quick step.

"It's only a couple of girls."

"E-yah. I know." The bound boy moved away. It might be Stella, he thought. Taking no chances, he darted between two trees and ran.

Fred Streeter gazed after Peter, shrugged, and dried his feet, using his socks as towels. He felt very superior to anyone who was afraid of girls. Still, he remembered, they did have a strange way of laughing at a fellow, and he hurried to don his boots. He wasn't fast enough; one foot was still sockless when two girls suddenly emerged from the brush on the opposite bank.

One was fair, plump, and blowzy. The other, slim and dark, had an uptilted nose and a pointed chin. Both gaped at the young drummer. The plump girl gave a cry of dismay; the dark one spoke.

"Ho! What have we here?"

Fred Streeter looked at them. He guessed they were about his age. That and their clothes put him at ease. He hadn't seen anybody dressed like that outside of an old picture his mother owned.

Patched, short-sleeved blouses, none too white, and homespun skirts above their ankles. Neither girl had bonnet or boots. He was openly staring.

The dark girl stuck out her tongue at him.

"I beg your pardon," Fred stammered, reddening.

"Come away, Patty," said the plump one.

Patty ignored her, pointing. "Your drum?"

"E-yah."

"I'm Patty Fisher. She's Dorcas White."

Dorcas stamped her foot. "Patty! I'm in haste!"

"Go then. I'm not."

Dorcas exploded into shrill cursing that brought Fred bolt upright. With a swish the plump girl flounced off through the brush.

Unruffled, Patty Fisher giggled. "Dorcas fears she'll wet herself. Would serve her right." Ignoring Fred's blush, she hoisted her skirt knee-high and thrust a foot into the water. "Devil's stones! 'Tis cold!" She waded across with quick, sure steps and leaped out beside Fred.

"Have you a name, lad?"

"Fred. Fred Streeter."

The girl plopped herself on the bank. She laughed and said, "They have a cask in the clearing. My brother Wat is drunk as a lord. Are you?"

"Me? No!"

"No. Not you." Patty reached out and tapped two fingers on the drumhead. "Boots and a drum! Your purse is fat, Fred. But your face is long."

"Well, I came here to enjoy myself, and . . ."

Patty laughed, interrupting, and said, "I know. I thought the oafs'd never stop talking, too, but there's time. The day's not gone nor the night started. There's time, Fred."

Fred shook his head, puzzled. He had never encountered anyone like her. Maybe, he thought, it would be worth the journey after all. Now that his feet had stopped hurting.

Too disturbed to eat, Lovina Chester wandered to the edge of the clearing. In spite of the noisy presence of so many people the girl felt lonely. She cherished the feeling by staying carefully away from all her friends and neighbors. For her, Lovina reflected, the

250

day was over. She supposed it had been a great success; the way folks were carrying on indicated as much. Strolling couples increased her melancholy. She found the shouting of children, the chatter of adults, the music of bands an annoying bedlam. Probably, she thought, her very own family was enjoying itself, little knowing she was so miserable, alone, and unhappy. Well, they would never know. She would carry her burden secretly to the grave.

Lovina mentally brought the grave from the far-off future to some not-too-distant date. Thoughtfully, she selected every detail of her mysterious decline, her last fatal illness, her deathbed in the midst of a weeping family. Charles Chittenden would not be there. He would ask to see her, but she would refuse the request. When Charles heard it was over he would weep and tear his garments like they did in the Bible. Nathan Patch, also brokenhearted, would confess the trick he had played the day Daniel Webster spoke in the clearing. Charles, wild with regret, would kill Nathan. No, Lovina changed her mind, Charles would not kill him because her dying wish, repeated by her father, would be that the two should be friends and forget. They would shake hands and become as brothers, but neither would every marry. Lovina sighed. It was very sad.

She gazed up at the tall tamarack tree and decided she would like to be buried in the clearing. It was fitting, she considered. Here Charles had shattered her dreams of marriage. Here she had met Tom Dunbar and started her lapse into sin. Here, too, Nathan Patch had destroyed her last hopes of healing the rupture between herself and Charles. Yes, the girl agreed with another sigh, it was fitting. Let them dig her grave beneath the tamarack tree that had been a silent witness to all the important events of her life. There she would lie, alone, with a simple stone at her head.

> Reader pause, as you pass by,
> As you are now so once was I.
> As I am now, you too shall be.
> Prepare for death, and follow me.

The noises of the great crowd intruded on Lovina's silent but dramatic recitation of the familiar epitaph. She turned away, seeking a quieter sanctuary under the trees. The long shadows, the sunshine dappling the ground, the columns of trunks suited her mood better.

She walked for a while aimlessly, contemplating the tragic future. Lovina found a melancholy pleasure in accepting it as a just punishment for her wayward behavior with the young Southerner. The wages of sin were death. She had enjoyed those kisses and caresses. There was no doubt in her mind about that. Blushing, she remembered every touch. She wasn't worthy of Charles; she deserved her untimely demise.

Lovina stopped, startled. For a heartbeat she thought the Southern voice another figment of her imagination.

"Annis Rockcliff," Tom Dunbar said, gently stressing each syllable. "That's very lovely. My compliments to your parents, Miss Annis. They sure found the proper name."

A lattice of foliage screened the speaker from Lovina Chester. Well, came her first indignant thought, that's almost exactly what he said to me. She heard the girl's answer, primly accepting the compliment.

"Thank you, Mr. Dunbar."

Lovina stretched, trying to catch a glimpse of the couple. It was difficult to do without making any noise. They were quite close; Tom's soft suggestion was clear.

"Tom."

A polite laugh rebuked him. "We've barely met, Mr. Dunbar."

"We were properly introduced in the cabin, Miss Annis."

"I was formally presented to Senator Webster, too. Would you expect me to address him as Daniel?"

"Not at his age, Miss Annis."

With a disapproving frown Lovina recognized Tom's impudent, laughing tone. A gap in the leaves gave her a good look at the girl called Annis. Against the white circle of a small parasol the girl's face, framed by a white bonnet, was heart-shaped, with even features. She's lovely, Lovina admitted with some irritation, and no bigger than a minute. Chestnut ringlets moved as Annis tossed her head. Lovina judged that her dress was white, too.

Tom Dunbar said, "Meaning no disrespect for the great Webster. I am his eternal debtor. I went into that cabin to pay tribute to an orator-statesman and found a vision of loveliness."

"So far from Virginia, too, Mr. Dunbar."

252

Frankly eavesdropping, Lovina listened.

"I admit that Vermont's beauty has astonished me."

"Have you seen our lake?"

"Lake?"

"Champlain. I live at Burlington, you know. We made the passage to Whitehall on one of Father's steamboats."

"Your father owns steamboats?"

Tom sounded impressed; Lovina shared his feeling.

"E-yah. Several. Steamboats are entwined with the history of my family, Mr. Dunbar. Father and mother met in a rather romantic fashion. They were aboard the first *Phoenix* the night it burned. That is romantic, don't you think?"

"It sounds so, Miss Annis. But I thought phoenixes were indestructible."

"The *Phoenix* was a steamboat, Mr. Dunbar." Annis Rockcliff was cool and reproving. "It caught fire in September, 1819. The fifth of September. Six persons lost their lives. The flames could be seen shining across the water for miles. My father and mother were on the boat. It was a famous tragedy."

"I'm sure it was, ma'am."

"I, myself, Mr. Dunbar, though a mere child at the time, recall the night word came to my father that the second *Phoenix* had collided with the *Congress* off Port Kent. We were at dinner. My father turned as pale as the tablecloth. My mother fainted. I, myself, Mr. Dunbar, shed tears. That was in 1826. I shall never forget it. One person was killed."

The eavesdropper nodded in admiration. Miss Annis Rockcliff, she thought, had certainly led an interesting life. Steamboats!

Surprisingly, Tom chuckled. He said, "You have convinced me, Miss Annis. I shall take care never to embark on a steamboat named *Phoenix*."

"Mr. Dunbar!"

"Miss Annis?"

"Your jest is unseemly."

"Your pardon, ma'am." Tom Dunbar changed the subject with gracious ease. "My interest is more personal than nautical. How far is Burlington from here?"

"Very far. We would not have made the journey at all except that I, myself, begged Father. I found the State Convention at

Burlington last month most exciting. And I desired to hear Senator Webster."

"Strange."

"My desire to hear the foremost orator of the day?"

"No. That from such great distances—Burlington and Virginia —you and I should come to hear Webster and meet . . ."

"Yes, Mr. Dunbar?"

"Each other."

Lovina Chester tiptoed away. She had heard enough. The glib Southerner was beguiling another girl with fine manners and flowery talk. Certainly, Mr. Dunbar had no scruples about what had happened behind the Chester barn. Somehow this fact made Lovina furious. More angry at Tom, she was less scrupulous with herself. She refused to be upset over a few kisses that meant nothing to the other party involved. The worthless rascal, she thought.

She walked briskly back to the clearing, wondering if it was too late to get something to eat.

At the spot where she reentered the clearing Lovina was forced to pick her way more carefully. Hundreds of horses, hitched or hobbled, grazed in a common pasturage. They were of all colors, and they munched docilely or twitched at the noise of so many humans. Lovina was not afraid of horses; she thought the beasts seemed puzzled at their unaccustomed inactivity. One mare nickered at the girl, and she paused to stroke its nose, then went on.

Suddenly, straight ahead of her beside a vivid red wagon, she saw Charles Chittenden. He was talking to a fat man and a girl. Lovina remembered that Mrs. Tarbox had pointed out the fat man as Dr. Somebody, who sold medicine. The girl was the same one Charles had rescued the night before. Not being able to see Mercy plainly, Lovina recalled her as much prettier than she was.

At that moment Charles laughed. The watching girl couldn't hear him, but she knew the characteristic movement of his head. Lovina bit her lip. Men, she judged scornfully, were all alike. There was Charles, enjoying himself, laughing, while she ate her heart out.

Digging her heel into the turf, Lovina changed direction and strode off on a tangent that took her well away from the red wagon. She noticed that the crowd seemed a little more boisterous, gayer, but no one bothered her as she pushed through an audience listening to one of the bands. She did not want to meet anyone she knew; it would mean stopping to talk. Naturally, the first person she bumped into was her mother.

Mrs. Chester greeted her daughter without preliminaries. "Lovina! Where have you been?"

"Nowhere."

"What have you been doing all this time?"

"Nothing."

The parson's wife sharpened her tone and tried to slice through Lovina's attitude. "Lovina Chester! I'll thank you not to answer back like that! I wasn't even sure you'd gotten here till Mrs. Tarbox came looking for you! The poor woman naturally expected that you'd drive her home, but you had to go gadding off. . . ."

"I'll be glad to drive Mrs. Tarbox home," Lovina said and walked away.

"Lovina! You come back here this minute! Lovina!"

Ignoring her mother's angry summons, the girl kept walking. She was well aware that she had committed unpardonable rebellion by refusing to listen. She didn't care. All right, Lovina thought, let her be angry, let her punish me. With the whole world uniting to spoil Lovina Chester's life, one more wouldn't make any difference. It wasn't that I meant to be rude, Lovina told herself, fighting back tears, but there are times when I just can't stand Mother's voice.

By the time she reached the place where she'd left the Tarbox wagon, Lovina had recovered her poise. She found Mrs. Tarbox anxiously peering at every passing female.

"Lovina! Oh, I'm so glad to see you! Davey! Marcia! Lovina's here!"

"Yes, Ma."

"I see her, Ma."

"I was getting a mite worried, Lovina. I know it's early, but I promised Mr. Tarbox I'd come back right after the supper." The innkeeper's wife shooed her children into the wagon and climbed up beside the driver. "It's good of you, Lovina."

"I don't mind."

"No. It is. And I won't forget it! I do hope I haven't spoiled your good time."

"You haven't," said Lovina shortly, not stressing the pronoun in her voice. "I was aiming to leave, anyway."

David Tarbox stood up in the wagon bed and shouted with all a small boy's lung power. "Hoc! Hey, Hoc! Hoc! Over here! It's me! Davey!"

"Davey!" said his sister.

"You hush that shouting!" Mrs. Tarbox said, threatening.

"But it's Mr. Dunbar's Hoc!"

"Well, you don't have to take on like it's the end of the world."

The slave rode his horse alongside the wagon in time to hear the remark. He said, "Mind your mammy, Master Davey." Hoc raised his shiny hat and bowed respectfully to the ladies. He was leading the black gelding. "Mr. Tom told me to take Ebony home, ma'am."

Lovina Chester remembered Ebony only too well. She gazed straight ahead.

David said, "Hoc. You promised me. Remember?"

A grin flashed from the black man's face. "Yes, sir, Master Davey. I'll be waiting to oblige your friends any time you say. You'll find me moseying around the stable."

Jockeying the horse carefully out of line, Lovina turned it toward the settlement. There was little traffic; few of the great throng were leaving the clearing so early. The Tarbox wagon jolted past the long rank of parked vehicles. Hoc, a self-appointed outrider, rode behind the tailboard.

The girl concentrated on her driving. The noise and tumult of the Convention had faded behind them by the time they passed the Chittenden farm. On the wagon seat Mrs. Tarbox's chatter was incessant and excited.

"I'm aiming to tell Dan every last detail. It ought to make him a mite sick that he missed it. Serve him right, too! Ain't Mr. Webster a fine-looking man? In a plain sort of way, that is. E-yah. I guess us folks haven't heard speechmaking like that since Ethan Allen's day. Not that I ever heard him talk, but I've heard about it! Maybe Mr. W's a mite more polished, but he didn't spare the rod any. Called a spade a spade, didn't he? And all them bands. It was even better than the orating in a way, wasn't it? I ain't never heard so much music all at once. And I always was fond of a good tune. E-yah. Many's the good time Dan and I had in the old days singing right out together at church meeting. Supper was tasty, too. 'Course the baked beans I got was soupy. And I always add a dollop of maple syrup to my own beans. I didn't see any signs of the hard cider, did you? Guess there was some all right, but I wasn't much interested. I see enough of that around the inn. E-yah. You know—in a way—Mr. Webster reminds me of my own Dan. The name being the same. And stout in the shoulders. And, of course, both being very outspoken. Especially for Tippecanoe and Tyler too."

Not listening, Lovina watched the ears of the horse bobbing ahead. She didn't blame Mrs. Tarbox; everybody else had apparently had a fine time. I've heard enough about Tippecanoe and Tyler too, the girl thought savagely, to last a lifetime. Doesn't anybody ever mention those men separately? She managed to keep the horse at a decent pace; it was anxious to get home, too.

The shadows of the settlement's houses were dark, and the road was no longer quite deserted. Several carriages were drawn up in the inn's stableyard. Lovina pulled up, smiled politely at Mrs. Tarbox's effusive thanks, made her good-bys. She walked slowly across to the parsonage.

Toby, the cat, was miaowing at the door. Lovina found the key and let them both in. The tomcat streaked into the hall, disappeared.

She wandered through the empty house. She couldn't remember another time when she'd been there alone. Forlornly she mounted the stairs to the bedroom, took off her bonnet, let it drop to the floor. She flung herself across her bed and stared moodily at the window. There were no tears; the girl felt too drained to cry.

It's all over, she thought. The Convention, the speeches, everything. Lovina listed the events one by one. Nathan Patch had widened the breach between herself and Charles. She'd refused Nathan in a manner that left no chance for future peace. Tom Dunbar had revealed himself as a flirt and a scoundrel. Even Charles was fickle. And, just to complete her defeats, she'd aroused her Mother's anger and could expect repercussions.

Lovina Chester sighed. Her voice was clear in the quiet of the room.

"What a horrid day!"

The sun, rose-colored and tinting near-by clouds, was low in the west when Lizzie Galusha turned into the lane that led to the Patch house. The cook's broad face was puckered with worry. She had left the clearing reluctantly, and her anxiety had mounted as she walked the six odd miles back to the sawmill. She knew she hadn't skimped in hunting for her husband. She'd gone through that crowd like a comb through hair. There had been no sign of Clem.

Lizzie shook her head. She'd asked several neighbors. Rhoda Hapgood had reported nothing but, Lizzie judged, Rhoda seemed much more interested in a well-dressed stranger than in the search for Clem. The parson hadn't seen Clem either, nor had Isaac Mead nor young Seth Purdy. She couldn't understand it.

Drunk, of course, Lizzie told herself. But her faith in that theory had been shaken when she'd stopped at the inn. Dan Tarbox had admitted Clem's tippling the night before but hadn't seen him all day. With all that free hard cider up to the clearing, Lizzie was puzzled by her husband's disappearance.

Then she saw Clem.

He was stumbling toward her up the slope from the mill. Clem looked like a scarecrow, hair wild, arms flapping. One pant leg hung raggedly, a strip of cloth that gyrated as Clem staggered. Even as she hurried forward Lizzie could hear her husband's hoarse whimpering. She thought he must have the horrors.

Clem fell into his wife's arms. She smelled the liquor as she held him up.

"The saw!" wheezed Clem.

"Clem. Brace yourself."

"The saw, Lizzie!"

"E-yah. All right. The saw."

"The Goddam saw!"

Lizzie was having trouble with his shifting weight. She yanked Clem around to get a firmer grip. That was when she noticed his leg. "Clem! My God, what happened?"

"The saw. Killed me."

He went limp so suddenly that she tottered and almost pitched to the ground. She left him lying there while she ran for water. She ran like a woman unused to swift movement, her head and shoulders thrust forward, throwing her feet awkwardly at the ground.

Lizzie breathed with relief when she bathed the wound. It wasn't half so bad as it looked once she'd removed the layer of clotted blood. Clem's leg had a long, nasty-looking scratch, but that was all.

"Clothes saved him."

Clem gripped her wrist; his eyes opened. "Killed me, Lizzie."

Her voice was sharp with angry reaction. "Killed, nothing! You're drunk! That's no worse than a bad nick."

"Won't kill anybody else! Fixed it!"

"Fixed it?"

"The saw! Fixed it good!"

Lizzie stared. She had an arm around Clem's shoulders, and she started up so abruptly that his head bumped on the ground. Once more she ran, plunging down the slope toward the mill at a headlong pace. She only managed to stop herself by grabbing the jamb of the shed door.

Dusk was gathering in the corners of the mill, but there was light enough to see. The place was a shambles.

Lizzie said, "Oh, my God!" She thanked Providence that she hadn't asked Joel Patch if he'd seen Clem. There would be no holding Patch when he discovered the wreckage of his mill, his circular saw. He'd send Clem to prison for this.

Her face was grim and stubborn when she returned to Clem. She tugged him from the ground, silently helped him to their quarters. Clem objected at first, but Lizzie was strong and unyielding. Since his wife wouldn't let him lie down and die, Clem obeyed her. He fell on their bed groaning. Lizzie left him there.

She returned in a minute with a bowl.

"Drink this, Clem."

"My leg."

"Your leg's all right. Drink!"

Clem drank. With a scream, he leaped from the bed and bolted for the outdoors.

Still holding the bowl, Lizzie watched her husband's heaving shoulders. She said, "You ain't poisoned. It's mustard, vinegar, and water. You're going to be sober when Joel Patch gets home, or I'll know the reason why!"

Clem rolled over and stared at his wife. The hired man's mouth kept opening and closing; tears were streaming down his cheeks. His voice was a begging croak. "Water! Water, Lizzie!"

"No."

"You burned my insides out."

"Aimed to. You've got to get rid of that liquor."

259

"Water!"

"Drink more of this."

"No, Lizzie! No!"

"Drink! You ain't lost enough yet!"

"Lizzie!"

"Listen to me, Clem Galusha. You're a worthless fool! But you're my husband, and you ain't going to prison while I can stop it!"

"Prison?"

"E-yah! You wrecked that sawmill! But as far as Joel Patch'll ever know you were with me the whole day! Hearing Senator Webster! I mean to have you sober when it comes time to tell them lies! Now drink!"

Sunset, the subject of so much speculation the previous evening, was a minor attraction to the great throng that now filled the clearing. Farmers glanced at the crimson glow out of habit. Wives who dreaded a wet homeward journey smiled at the pink promise of the clouds. The light grew a little dimmer; the shadows of the surrounding forest thickened. Slowly, imperceptibly, the bright green of the tamarack tree began to darken. The multitude was much more interested in enjoying the last hours of the day than in watching how they changed to night.

Fires flared brightly as people burned the thin wooden shingles that had served them as trenchers. With flames leaping from this tinder and the green wood hissing, the campfires suddenly became bonfires. The talk switched from friendly conversation to hilarious shouting. One by one the bands stopped playing, laid down instruments, and sought the cider barrel. The organizers felt that their important work was finished; the visitors tried to ignore a feeling of finality by whipping up excitement. The Captain made sure that Senator Webster was in responsible hands, sighed with relief, and rode away from the clearing. He seemed to take all semblance of order with him.

There were many who yielded to weariness and withdrew from the celebration. They retired to tent, wagon, or shelter and hoped that the riotous noise would stop before it was time to sleep. Children, overfed, were fretful. Mothers, overtaxed, were exhausted. It had been a long journey and a long day. Now it was over. They had come to the giant Convention on Stratton Mountain; already

260

they thought of it in the past tense. They had heard Daniel Webster. They had shouted themselves hoarse for Tippecanoe and his running mate. Now it was over. Tomorrow they would go home. They were the respectable, the fatigued, the outstanding citizens. They were only a part of the gathering in the clearing.

Doc Merrifield was more interested in the other parts. The fat medicine man frowned at the silhouettes leaping before the fires. He had seen too many fairs and race meetings end in trouble when the rougher elements got out of hand. He glanced up at a sky which had faded to gray and said, "Mercy."

"Yes, Doc."

"Maybe it ain't such a good idea. Staying here."

"It'll be dark soon, Doc."

"I know. But if this crowd gets ill-tempered . . ." Doc shrugged. "Well, we're on a mountain, and there's no sense trying to get off. The roads are jam packed with vehicles. And that ain't much of a moon. No bigger than a shaving."

"They're just enjoying themselves, Doc."

"Now. But you're forgetting our friends of the road. George Stiles. Crimpy. Let one of them filch the wrong purse, and there might be an ugly mess."

Mercy sighed. She wasn't afraid, and she was eager for another chance to talk to Charles Chittenden. He might return to the clearing tomorrow. She said, "What about your game?"

"I dunno. I don't like leaving you alone. We made a pile today, and somebody may have noticed."

"Not with all these folks around. And you're not taking it to the inn. Luke Brooks would get it sure. It's a lot safer hid in the wagon."

"Maybe." Doc's voice dropped but remained calm. "Don't turn around, Mercy."

The girl was motionless. She knew the tone; it was a signal of danger. She said, very softly, "Sheriff?"

"Don't act like one. Never knew a sheriff to come creeping along the ground. My daughter or my ducats, more likely. We'll let whoever it is get a little closer."

Mercy, not turning, said, "Nobody we know'd bother our wagon."

"Nobody we know. But there's over ten thousand folks here, and we don't know them all." The medicine man took out a cheroot, dropped it, bent to retrieve it. "A rat, a rat, Mercy. The shadow

261

is careful not to be seen. And the back of our wagon is the prize all right. I'm going to amble around, careless-like, and welcome our visitor."

"Be careful, Doc."

"It is not a big shadow, my dear. And conscience—or something —doth make cowards of all sneak thieves." Cheroot clamped firmly between his teeth, hands in pockets, Doc sauntered away.

Mercy remained where she was. She glanced casually around, as if distracted by an outburst from some near-by merrymaker. The girl saw the quick movement by the wagon's rear wheel and ignored it. She judged that the thief had sneaked down from the edge of the trees, past the horses. I'm decoy again, thought Mercy, and while he's watching me, Doc will pounce. She waited, neither nervous nor still but moving naturally. She crouched, raked at the fire, straightened, hummed a snatch of tune.

There was a yell of fright. The wagon shook as a body slammed against it.

Mercy raced toward the sound. Doc Merrifield's voice was raised in anger, almost drowning out a boy's pleas.

"You thieving brat!"

"Don't hit me, mister. I wasn't going to do nothing."

"I'll teach you to steal!"

Doc had a firm grip on the struggling boy. When the youngster saw Mercy he stopped trying to free himself and burst into tears. His face was white and frightened.

"Doc. You're hurting him!"

"I ought to thrash him." Doc didn't loosen his hold. "I caught him fumbling in our wagon, Mercy."

Sobbing, the boy appealed to Mercy. "Please, Miss. I didn't mean no harm. I was hungry, that's all."

"Hungry?"

"You lying little whelp!"

"I ain't lying, mister. Honest, I ain't."

A fresh outburst of weeping brought a frown to the medicine man's pudgy countenance. The girl hid a smile; she knew how Doc hated tears. Hiding his uneasiness with a gruff tone, Doc said, "How could you be hungry? With all the food at the supper! Enough to stuff an army!"

"I didn't get none. I was scared to till it started to get dark."

Mercy and Doc stared at each other. Both looked quickly around. The girl's question was a whisper. "Scared? Scared of what?"

"If they see me they'll set the law on me."

"The law!" Doc Merrifield cursed. With a sudden movement he swept the boy off his feet and pitched him into the wagon. Mercy followed swiftly, using Doc's clasped hands as a step. The boy, bewildered, started to protest, but the girl's command hushed him.

"Shh. Be quiet."

While Mercy lit a candle, Doc climbed in and lowered a curtain across the back of the wagon. In the boxlike body of the vehicle the candlelight was thin and yellow. The three exchanged glances. Though his cheeks glistened with tears, the boy had stopped crying. He even risked a wan smile, like a homeless kitten's first overture toward kindness.

"You're really hungry?" asked Mercy.

"E-yah. I ain't et since breakfast."

The girl found bread and cheese, a pitcher of milk. The boy's fingers tore a chunk from the loaf, thrust it into his mouth. Doc Merrifield relaxed with a sigh. "You're hungry, all right. What's your name?"

"Peter. Peter Blodgett."

"The law's after you?"

Peter stopped eating. Mouth full, he nodded. His eyes, wide and pleading, shifted as he glanced from man to girl.

Mercy said, gently, "Eat. You're safe with us."

"Is this a dagger that we see before us," said Doc. He was worried and scratched his head. "We can't afford to shelter nobody, Mercy. Sheriffs ain't too fond of us as it is. You, Peter! What is it you've done?"

"Run off."

"You mean from home?" asked Mercy.

"From them."

"Them?"

There was guilt in Peter's nod. He hid his face in the pitcher, gulped milk. He took a deep breath and spoke.

"The Lymans. I'm their bound boy. If I don't do what they tell me they'll sic the law on me. That's what he's always saying. Joe Lyman. And Stella, too. They told me to stay to home, but I did want to hear Mr. Webster. I run off."

263

"And they know it?"

"E-yah. Stella saw me. She chased me. That's why I hid in the woods till sunset. I—I was aiming to go back tonight. Honest! I just wanted to see Mr. Webster. But I don't dast go back now that Stella knows. They'll sic the law on me. Joe'll beat me." The last sentence was an afterthought and much more calmly expressed than the rest of the story.

"Can they set the law on him, Doc?"

"I don't know."

"I do," said Peter, miserably. "They can."

"You're bound by articles? Papers?"

"E-yah. I've seen them, mister. Till I'm twenty-one. 'Course I couldn't read them, but it's so, all right. Joe Lyman took me from the poor farm. I shouldn't have run off, but . . ." Peter raised his head; his thin face was proud and defiant in spite of the milky moustache that lined his upper lip. "I ain't sorry! I ain't a mite sorry!"

"Just scared?" asked Mercy.

"Yes, Miss."

Doc Merrifield laughed. "You've come to the right place, Peter. There ain't much I don't know about running off. And you'd better start learning right now. You've got to keep running."

Peter looked at the man, puzzled. He said, "How's that?"

Mercy grinned. She seemed much older than Peter and spoke as if he were a younger brother. "You can't go back there to be beaten, Peter. You said so."

"It ain't the whipping. I've been whipped before. It's the law."

"All right," said Doc. "Take to the road. Run by night. Hide by day."

"How does he eat, Doc?"

"E-yah," Peter said and finished the milk. He smiled again. "I ain't spry at snatching food. I just found out." The boy's forehead puckered in a frown. "Besides, I ain't got no place to go."

"You came here."

"E-yah. But I wanted to hear Mr. Webster."

Mercy glanced at Doc; he looked back at her over his glasses. "No, Mercy. 'Tis pity, but 'tis true. We'd be crying havoc down on us and letting slip the dogs of the law. And you know blame well we can't manage an extra mouth to feed."

264

"For a while, Doc?"

"No. He can sleep here in the wagon tonight. That's safe enough. As long as you stay out of sight, Peter. When the crowd thins out tomorrow you skedaddle on your way."

"E-yah. Thank you, sir." Peter sounded sincere. "Where do you figure I should go?"

The medicine man gave an exasperated snort. Mercy said, "You see, Doc? He's a lamb. He wouldn't last two days."

"It ain't our business, Mercy."

Mild as the discussion was Peter Blodgett realized that he was its cause. He blushed. "I ain't aiming to be no trouble, Mr. Doc. I was just asking."

"Look at him, Doc," said Mercy, laughing. "He's peaked enough. A fine specimen for the Elixir. And we could use a boy to start the buying. One more to feed won't ruin us."

Peter didn't understand what they were talking about, but there was sudden hope in his voice. "I don't eat a great deal, Mr. Doc."

"It ain't the victuals," said Doc. "You know it ain't the victuals, Mercy. But he's likely to have every sheriff in the county looking for him."

"There's other counties. Other States."

"We ain't in them. If that Lyman kicks up a fuss they'll be hunting for him. Must be twenty, thirty constables and sheriffs in this crowd. I noticed a couple of them when George Stiles was helping that bumpkin complain about his pocketbook. No. I'll try to think of some way to help you, Peter, but we can't risk having you found with us."

"Don't worry, Peter," Mercy said. "We'll think of something. There's milk on your lip." The girl cocked her head, listening to the sounds of revelry through the thin sides of the wagon. "Before we decide anything, Doc, hadn't you better find out if folks are looking for Peter? Then we'll know what's in store."

Doc Merrifield gave her a long look. "Nymph," he said. "In thy orisons you'd better ask forgiveness. You wouldn't wheedle an old man, would you?" He reached up to the wagon's ceiling, unlaced a canvas strip, and took down an ancient, short-barreled blunderbuss. "All right. If anybody bothers you, Mercy, stow Peter under your trundle and have this in their faces. I ain't never fired it, as you know, but it's still the wickedest-looking firearm I ever saw."

He left the weapon on a chest, bowed, poked the curtain aside, and dropped to the ground.

Night had settled over the clearing. The sky was dark above the trees, but the glow from the many fires seemed to dull the stars directly overhead. Black figures cut the leaping orange flames into strange shapes. The medicine man was too old a campaigner to go blundering off without a destination. He paused by the wagon for a moment and gazed at the entire scene.

Campfires—there must have been a thousand—were scattered around the half-moon shape of the clearing. Some were small, difficult to see, in front of silent wagons, dark tents. Others sent flames and sparks shooting high, and in their glow were many ruddy faces. Around one blaze men and women leaped and cavorted in a noisy, impromptu war dance. The long log cabin, lit by torches within and without, was the rallying point for the loudest, most riotous of the throng. But it was the panorama that impressed Doc Merrifield. It was a fine show, and he felt himself to be something of an authority on fine shows.

"On such a sight," said Doc, softly. "That silly Troilus atop his wall was sighing his soul out. Uh-uh." The medicine man nodded. "The Grecian camp must have looked just like this clearing. As if somebody'd built a giant fire and then kicked it and scattered the brands all over the place." He was pleased at the picture and embroidered it. "Some one-eyed Cyclops kicked the fire and made a lot of little fires."

Doc considered the crowd around the cabin and rejected it. There was too much light there. The people he sought had no great fondness for light. He walked toward the upper edge of the clearing, skirting the larger fires, glancing at the faces around the smaller ones. His path was a devious one; he kept out of the brightness and watched from the shadows. When he saw a lantern make a bright square in a patch of darkness, Doc grunted. He measured the distance from the lantern to the nearest campfire and chuckled.

"Like a good deed in a naughty world," Doc said. "I don't think! Vice versa would be nearer the truth." He went toward the lantern as if it were a beacon. He admired the illumination selected. A lantern threw light but not too much light; it was mobile and easily doused.

The medicine man heard giggling from beneath a wagon as he passed and smiled an indulgent smile. Of course, he thought, in such a place, on such a night. Troilus, methinks, was a fathead not to have realized that.

He went close enough to see that the lantern was suspended above a group of men. Doc Merrifield stopped and lit his cheroot. He made no effort to hide the match flame but held it before his face until the cigar's end was a cherry circle. With a gust of smoke, Doc blew out the match and waited.

"Doc?" The voice was close and quiet.

"Had I three ears I'd know you, George." Doc sounded surprised. "I was looking for you, but I didn't expect you'd be Crimpy's sentinel."

George Stiles chuckled. "It's a pleasure, Doc. Anybody bets against Crimpy shows where he keeps his purse. If Crimpy don't empty it, I do."

"Don't wear out your welcome, George."

"Oh, I'm getting real choosy, Doc. It's been a big day."

"There's a sheriff nosing around."

"For me?"

"I don't know. But he don't sound right. Says he's hunting for some boy that's run off."

"Oh, the bound boy." The pickpocket was relieved. "I know about him, Doc."

The tip of the medicine man's cigar brightened and dulled as he puffed. "You mean it's true, George?"

"Looks that way. There's a feller claims he's the one the boy run off from. Mean-looking cuss, too."

"Another sheriff, maybe. Don't take chances."

"He ain't no sheriff, Doc. A big farmer. I asked around. His name's Lyman, and he won't bother us any. He just wants to get his hands on that runaway."

"Lyman, eh? I'll take pains to stay out of his way. An angry man's a dangerous man, George. We wouldn't want him in Luke's game down to the inn."

"No fear." Stiles laughed. "He couldn't cover Luke's lowest bet. Anyway, he's set himself down by that Tippecanoe cabin. Thinks Webster will draw the boy like honey draws a fly."

"That so?" Doc seemed tired of the conversation. "Is Webster still there?"

267

"I dunno. But he was there. This Lyman says the boy—the runaway—is touched about Webster." Stiles grunted. "But Lyman ain't shy about tapping that free cider while he waits."

Doc Merrifield yawned. "It ain't our business. Well, I just wanted to pass the word. Might have known you'd know more about it than I did myself."

"Thanks anyway, Doc."

"Good night, George." The medicine man saluted by raising his cigar and walked away. He didn't make straight for the cabin but took a roundabout course. When he reached it, Doc paused outside the wavering semicircle of torchlight and watched.

This segment of the encampment was a large one, mostly masculine and raucous. One noisy group was rolling a fresh barrel of cider into place; three men wielding axes were smashing the empty keg to pieces with joyous destruction. A barrel hoop fell off. A drunken farmer snatched the hoop and, lurching, began to roll it. Others tried to wrest it from him, but the farmer, with quick strokes of his hand, whipped the hoop in and out through the jostlers, dodging, doubling, keeping possession of his toy until it split. Another had a cowbell hung around his neck, like some heathen, bronze amulet, and the clang of the bell's tongue was never still. Human tongues, too, raised a constant clamor.

"Set it here! Here!"

"Who has the tool?"

"Tool?"

"The bung starter! Give me that!"

"I can tap a barrel!"

"Don't crowd! There's plenty for everybody!"

"That's all you know!"

"Hurry up. I aim to wet my whistle!"

"Goshen! You fellers aging that cider? Or broaching it?"

"Think you can do better?"

"E-yah. Might."

"Now, wait. Wait! We got to have rules!"

"Who in blazes are you?"

"Rules! In a sow's ear!"

"We got to! The cider's getting low!"

"Got enough rules, now."

"E-yah! First come, first served."

268

"Get out of my way!"

"Pushing sort, ain't he?"

Doc Merrifield recognized a face here and there. One of those fussing around the keg was the lad in the coonskin cap, Jabez Tute. Another was his companion who wore knee breeches. They were both flushed and swaying. The two ox drivers of the morning's contest were present; they seemed to be inseparable comrades. The Londonderry giant pushed help aside and wrestled the barrel up onto a box. On the fringe of the lighted space the medicine man saw Tom Dunbar with a pretty girl. The Southerner stood in a rank of well-dressed spectators, most of whom watched the antics of the drinkers with disapproval. Doc wondered which of the strangers was Joe Lyman.

One way to find out, he thought, and stepped forward into the light. A howl went up from the group around the barrel and, for a second, the medicine man had the startled feeling he had caused it.

"E-yah! That's it!"

"New rules!"

"Anybody drinks has to swear!"

"Swear they'll vote for Tippecanoe!"

"Whig cider for Whig voters!"

"Whigs only!"

"Nothing for Loco-focos!"

"Anybody drinks has to vote for General Harrison."

Smiling, Doc approached the cider barrel. He was instantly surrounded. The cowbell man shook his music in Doc's face. Hands grabbed his arms.

"Want to drink?"

"Got to vote for Tippecanoe!"

"Swear!"

The medicine man's voice rolled out, sonorous and powerful. "Friends, Whigs, and countrymen. You know me. Dr. Portus J. Merrifield, at your service. A Whig since I could vote, gentlemen, and always willing to abide by Whig rules."

A big-shouldered man with a narrow mouth thrust his chin in front of Doc. "You promise to vote for Harrison?" His fingers dug into Doc's shoulder.

Doc Merrifield plucked the hand away as if he were removing

269

an insect. He said, "I was not aware that anyone else worth mentioning was running."

A roar greeted the sally, and willing shoves hurried the medicine man to the barrel. He raised a brimming tankard and removed his hat. The crowd quieted and listened.

"I give you General Harrison, Daniel Webster, and the most faithful of all Whig patriots—the Green Mountain boys!" Doc drank and bowed his acknowledgment to the cheers. As others came forward, promised, and drank, he mingled with the crowd. He noticed that several times the big-shouldered man was addressed as Joe. Nudging the cowbell wearer Doc asked casually, "Ain't that Joe Lyman?"

"E-yah. The big feller. Hopping mad, too. Seems his hired boy's missing. Joe Lyman, of Somerset."

"Thought I recognized him," said Doc Merrifield and wandered away. He was still a yard from the shadows when Lyman's shout rang out.

"There he is! You won't get away, Peter Blodgett!"

The medicine man swung around. He saw Lyman plunge into the darkness beyond the torchlight and drag back a boy. One glance told Doc that the boy wasn't Peter. But before Lyman realized his mistake there was a blur of movement, the spat of a blow, and the farmer was flat on his back.

"Keep your hands off my son," said Lot Purdy.

With a bellow of rage, Lyman scrambled up, crouched, and charged. Men scattered, clearing a place for the combatants. Lyman was bigger than the stage driver, but Lot moved in to meet him. One smashing punch rocked the farmer before they closed and crashed to the ground.

They rolled over, kicking, pommeling. It was frontier-style fighting, primitive, without rules. The farmer managed to get a grip on Lot's throat and darted a hooked thumb at the driver's eye. The gouge missed. Lot slammed an elbow against the other's windpipe, snapped both knees into his stomach. Twisting, the driver broke free, gained his feet.

Lyman made the mistake of trying to clutch his opponent without rising. Lot kicked him in the face. Blood spattered as the farmer went over backward, legs doubled under him.

Snarling, Lot Purdy took a step, ready to fling himself on his fallen adversary. His son grabbed his arm, hung on. Seth's shriek was hysterical. "No, Pa! No! Let him be!"

With a gasp the horrified crowd broke into movement. Men pressed between the fighters. Some pushed the driver back; others ministered to the senseless Lyman whose face seemed as featureless as a crimson handkerchief. For once the voices of the cider drinkers were hushed, stunned by the sudden violence.

"Great Godfrey!"

"Happened so fast!"

"All over in two shakes!"

"Might have killed each other."

"God's blood! That was a fight!"

"You see the big one's face?"

"Ain't dead, is he?"

"Nope. Bleeding like a slaughtered pig, though."

"Well, he tried to gouge the other."

"That's right. Seen it."

"Regular dogfight, wasn't it?"

"You mean wolf."

"E-yah."

Doc Merrifield was in the group that led Lot Purdy away. The stage driver was docile, trembling with reaction. He seemed ashamed of his ruthless ferocity. His apology was to his son. "Seth. Seth, it's all right. I—I don't know what come over me. I guess maybe I took out a lot of bile on that feller."

"Name's Lyman," explained the medicine man. "He mistook your son for somebody else."

"E-yah. I'm sorry. I didn't stop to think." Lot sighed. He kept shaking one hand like a cat with a wet paw. The buckskin gloves were splashed and discolored. "Feels like I broke some knuckles, too."

Doc cut the glove off with a knife. He peeled back the leather. Lot's hand was swollen and purple. The medicine man's pudgy fingers gently prodded the swelling. Color drained from Lot's face; the long scratches on his cheek stood out like welts. Doc said, "It ain't too bad. Be all right in a week or two."

Lot Purdy said, "God Almighty! I don't know what come over me!"

"Don't feel too bad," said Doc. "I've got a feeling this Lyman had a thrashing coming to him." He advised soaking and a tight bandage for the injury, mentioned regretfully that he had no Elixir at present, and left the group. He felt very grateful to the stage driver. As far as Doc could judge Peter Blodgett was not going to be bothered that night. Not by Lyman, anyway.

The young Southerner was standing nearby, and Doc, raising his hat to the girl, asked after Lyman.

Tom Dunbar shrugged. The soft voice was cool and disapproving. "He's being cared for, sir. Your Northern manner of settling disputes seems more fitting for gamecocks than human beings."

"It was horrid," said the girl. "I fear I feel faint." She swayed; Tom's arm was around her shoulders instantly.

"Miss Annis!" The Virginian was solicitous but unflustered. He glanced at Doc Merrifield. "Some water, please. If you'd be so kind, sir."

Doc said, "Better than that. Be back in two shakes." He plunged off toward the rear of the log cabin.

"Miss Annis. May I express my most abject apologies. Your father did me the honor of entrusting you to my care. I feel that I've been wanting as an escort."

"It's not your fault, Mr. Dunbar."

"Your kindness does not excuse my neglect."

The medicine man returned with a cup. "Drink this, Miss. It won't hurt you none. Just a dram of spirits."

Annis Rockcliff drank. She choked, coughed, and sighed. "Thank you," she said. A faint flush tinted her face like firelight shining through thin china. "I'll be all right now."

"Your obedient servant, sir." Tom Dunbar bowed. "May I ask your indulgence in leaving my compliments till some future time? I intend to remove Miss Rockcliff from the scene of her distress at once. My arm, Miss Annis."

The girl curtsied, took the proffered arm, and they walked away from the cabin. Once beyond the circle of torchlight Tom Dunbar's feeling of protectiveness increased. With the disdainful anger befitting a Southern gentleman, Tom was furious that a young lady should witness such a bestial exhibition while in his company. Naturally she was revolted, he thought, and near to fainting. Miss Annis was a well-bred, cultured young lady; he was a good judge of manners and quality. The Virginian scowled. He'd enjoyed every minute of the girl's company, and he hoped his anticipations weren't going to be spoiled because of a brawl.

"Tom."

"Yes, Miss Annis?" It was the first time she'd used his Christian name; he was pleased and alert.

"I'm not given to vapors."

"Miss Annis! You're not apologizing for a weakness induced by that disgusting . . ."

Annis chuckled. "Don't take on, Tom. You couldn't help my seeing the fight. Nobody knew it would happen."

"I should have foreseen it."

"Nonsense. It's a fine night. Let's not spoil it."

They stolled on through the clearing, avoiding the dark clusters of people, the ruddy glow of fires. They didn't speak; somehow the promenade made speech unnecessary. They were one couple walking in the midst of thousands, unseen, silent. Voices babbled around them, whispering, shouting, guffawing. A couple argued; a group of women squealed at a jest. Somewhere in the darkness a fiddler scraped out a tune. Tom and Annis heard all the noises of the great encampment and were aloof from them. They drew closer to each other and walked in step. Dark shapes hurried past; boots thudded. Once a man with a torch staggered drunkenly across in front of them. They met no one they knew.

They had reached the western edge of the clearing when the girl looked back. She said, "Let's not take the turnpike."

"It's the only road, Miss Annis."

"No. We're staying on the west side near the Torrey place. And one of the Torrey children showed me a path through the trees. A short-cut. It's much more pleasant."

Much more romantic, too, thought Tom. He said, "But can you find it? Now? In the dark?"

"I can find it." Annis Rockcliff laughed. "You just take a bearing on that tamarack tree yonder. I'm not a steamboat owner's daughter for nothing, you know."

They passed between packed ranks of wagons and tents, dark and silent except for snores. Annis kept glancing over her shoulder at the black top of the tree. She led Tom around the stampings and ghostly shapes of the horses and plunged into the forest. They were on a narrow path.

Tom Dunbar laughed admiringly. "My compliments, Miss Annis. You find your way like an Indian. And a stranger here like myself."

"It's all in knowing where you wish to go."

It was quieter under the trees, and the darkness was thicker, impenetrable, no longer dotted with campfires. They followed the path away from the clearing, single file, the girl in the lead. It was easy walking. Overhead the stars were clear and cold, like ice chips strewn on deep, winter water. Annis took off her bonnet and swung it by the ribbons.

The Southerner watched the girl's figure as it swayed in front of him. Starlight had dulled the white of her dress, and the shadows of the foliage fell across it like a design of black leaves. As Annis walked the leaves moved across her dress, dropped off, were replaced in an ever-changing pattern. She's very shapely, Tom thought. Very shapely. It was apparent that even Puritan young ladies could walk in exciting fashion.

Annis looked over her shoulder. Her face was a pale heart framed by dark ringlets. "It's not far now, Tom."

"More's the pity, Miss Annis."

Not far, he repeated to himself. He smiled fondly at the undulating skirt ahead. Annis Rockcliff was smaller than most girls. Delicate, too, Tom thought, remembering her reaction to the brawl. Yet she strolled through the woods unchaperoned, at night, with a young man. The Virginian felt very wicked. This would be the final test in his investigation of Vermont femininity. He was already proud of his chosen experiments. Tavern girl, minister's daughter, wealthy young lady of fashion. Tom Dunbar grinned. *Q.E.D.*—Puritan girls were not much different from Virginia belles. Of course it depended on the gentleman in question, he decided, with a mental bow to himself. But he highly recommended the study. It was considerably more amusing than mathematics or Latin.

Annis will be frightened, he thought. Probably nobody had ever kissed her goodnight. She wasn't a country girl like the others. He vowed he'd be gentle, tender, but irresistible.

They came out into an open meadow that sloped gently down to where lights shone in the dark bulk of a house. Annis stopped; Tom stepped beside her.

"The Torrey cabin," said Annis Rockcliff.

"Journey's end," said Tom Dunbar. I warrant, he thought, that little Annis will remember our fond farewell.

One of the innumerable stone fences barred their path. Annis sat down on it. Tom took off his hat and sat beside her.

"You leave tomorrow?" asked Annis.

"Yes, Miss Annis. And you?"

"E-yah."

Tom sighed; he put his arm around the girl. She turned her face toward him. Too easy, he thought, and bent his head.

It was as if he'd fired his dueling pistol aimlessly and a mountain had exploded in his face.

They kissed. Somewhere in the middle of Tom's triumph he realized he was being kissed. Annis was kissing him. The girl slid her arms around him, pressed her body against his. She held him tightly, kissing. They swayed on the stone wall.

"Wait," said Annis. "Come." She drew back.

Tom Dunbar gasped. That was a kiss, he thought. Jove! A little longer, and he'd have forgotten that he was a gentleman and Annis a Puritan lady. As it was . . .

"Come, Tom!"

He stared. For a pulse beat he thought she'd fainted.

Annis was lying beside the wall; she had his hand, was drawing him down. Yielding, Tom was aghast. Annis Rockcliff couldn't know what she was doing.

She seemed to know. She put his hand on her breast, nibbled along his cheek, kissed him so hard his teeth hurt. Well, I declare, thought Tom, bewildered. He felt the girl's hands moving on his back, drawing him over her. Annis arched herself beneath him, went limp. Tom was panting, excited but amazed. All his notions about Puritan girls disappeared in another silent exclamation. Well, I declare.

Annis fumbled with his waistcoat, slid her palm inside his shirt. Her touch drove all thought from Tom's mind. Quivering with desire he managed one gasped word. "Annis!"

"Don't talk," she said fiercely. "Don't talk!"

* * * * * *

If ever before our friends abroad have doubted the Green Mountain Boys would do their part, could they have witnessed this pageant, we know they would have said, "Let the Green Mountain Boys alone, they'll do their duty." All classes were assembled, the laborer, the mechanic, merchant, farmer, all left their accustomed duties, many of them at a great sacrifice and expense, with a determination fixed and immovable that if anything could be affected by them to bring about a change it should be done. Here you might see young and old, rich and poor, mingled together and discussing freely on the political state of things in that country. Oh, that Buchanan, Benton, Wright, and even Van Buren himself could have been present to have seen this mighty gathering of people. They would no longer claim Vermont as a Van Buren state but in the height of their anguish would exclaim, "She's gone, hook, line and sinker."

The Man from Boston handed the sheet of foolscap back to the Captain and nodded. Stroking his chin, he said, "Neatly put, Captain. Not precisely expressed in the highest literary style but, on the whole, neatly put."

"Sounded all right to me," said the Man from New Hampshire.

"Fixed *and* immovable," the Bostonian said. "Still, I daresay it makes its point."

"You daresay!" The New Yorker snorted. "Where was it you said it'd be printed, Captain?"

Folding the manuscript, the Captain put it away. "The *Vermont Phoenix,* gentlemen. Next issue. Feller from the paper wrote it all out. I got him to make me a copy. There's more to it, of course." He tapped his coat pocket. "This is only a sample."

"It went off real slick, Captain."

"You ought to feel a mite proud tonight."

"Senator Webster was in fine voice, wasn't he?"

"E-yah." The Captain's head tilted back as he drained his glass. He gazed around the noisy, full common room of the Tarbox inn and blinked wearily at the fog of tobacco smoke. "Damme, I'm tired."

"All right to talk here, Captain?"

"Why not?"

"A trifle public, don't you think?"

"Where do you talk business in Boston? The churches?"

The Bostonian gave his New York colleague a pained look and waited. The Man from New Hampshire, leaning close, said, "Shucks, I figure everybody's too busy drinking and saying their own say to listen to us! Ain't that the right of it, Captain?"

"E-yah."

"We'll take the good news home, of course. But how about a few pointers?"

"For our own rallies."

"We'll have log cabins, naturally."

"The trick," said the Captain, lowering his voice, "is to have enough hard cider and not too much. Here we got twice as many folks as we expected, but it worked out all right because lots didn't bother to drink."

"Can't count on that in my State," the New Yorker said.

"Or mine!"

"In Boston the cider barrel is more a symbol than a source of refreshment."

"All right!" said the Man from New Hampshire. "All right! You can get Dan Webster to give a speech on every street corner in Boston! We know that! He lives there! But if you ain't got Webster you've got to have cider!"

"Damn right!"

"Gentlemen." The Captain's rebuke was annoyed. "You've seen what can be done. You'll have to adapt your methods to your own people. That's all. You know the essentials. Some sort of log cabin. Cider."

"Bands."

"The best speaker you can get."

"Banners and badges."

"E-yah. We've got the money and money talks. It says, 'Van is a used up man'! It says 'Tippecanoe and Tyler too'! Keep driving those nails home. Folks can't seem to get enough of them. God alone knows why."

Charles Chittenden turned away from the parsonage door and walked moodily across the road toward the tavern. He had just delivered young Put Chester to his home after practically dragging the protesting boy all the way from the clearing. Charles scowled and kicked at a pebble. He wished now he'd let Put run wild; he was guiltily aware that he'd spoiled the lad's merrymaking in order to see Lovina. It had all been for nothing. Mrs. Chester had answered the door, clamped stern fingers on Put's ear, and thanked Charles coldly. An inquiry about Lovina had brought the clipped

277

reply that she had retired. Charles didn't believe it. The parsonage was bright with lights, and he had heard the girls laughing. It's plain enough, thought Charles. Lovina had told her mother not to admit him.

Every window of the inn was like a checked patch of yellow cloth. Even in the upstairs bedrooms beams of light streamed through the many small panes. Charles was not surprised. It was late; the moon was near to setting. But no one would try to sleep with the din that was rocking the tavern. Charles thought it sounded even worse than the noise in the clearing. He realized that the neighboring church, so white and chaste and silent, emphasized the racket of Dan Tarbox's hostelry.

Wanting company, Charles had almost reached the inn's front door when it was pulled open from within. A shaft of light shot out, caught Charles directly in its path. There was a knot of struggling figures in the doorway, a shifting, many-legged mass that suddenly ejected a single man.

The man came hurtling toward Charles as if flung from a catapult. Only the force of his headlong thrust carried him across the intervening distance. Charles caught him just before he crashed to the ground.

"And don't come back!" Dan Tarbox's voice shouted.

With a slam the inn door cut off the shaft of light. Charles smelled liquor fumes. He had no time to speak before the drunkard tore himself loose, swayed, and swung a wild punch at his benefactor's head.

He missed and pitched, sprawling, on his face. He made no effort to rise but lay there, cursing in a thick, dull voice.

Charles recognized Lem Brayton. He bent over to offer assistance.

"Slut!" shouted Lem.

"Mr. Brayton."

"Slut! Goddam slut! Whore!"

With an apprehensive glance toward the parsonage, Charles pulled Lem to his feet. Trying to quiet the shouting he said, "It's all right, Mr. Brayton. You don't have to holler. I hear you."

"Who're you?"

"Charles Chittenden."

Lem glared in disbelief, then slumped, hanging on to Charles.

278

"Charles, eh? Let me tell you, Charles. Listen to me, Charles. They're all sluts! Every one of them. Women are sluts!" The last three words were roared.

"Shh, Mr. Brayton."

"Don't you shh me."

"Then hush up!"

"Who's going to make me? Who, eh? Who?"

"Me."

Nodding drunkenly, Lem seemed to ponder. A whining note came into his speech. "Threw me out. E-yah. Dan Tarbox threw me out. Get even with him. Own son didn't stick up for me. My own son. Asa. No good. Like mother, like son. Fix him."

Charles sighed. "Let's go around to the horse trough, Mr. Brayton. Make you feel better."

"Saw her," said Lem, paying no attention to the suggestion. "Saw her with my own eyes. Came in with that gambling feller. Upstairs now. If he can, why can't I? Good enough for her, ain't I?"

"Stop that talk." Charles was annoyed.

"Saw her. Rhoda. Patch hired girl. Rhoda. Upstairs now." Lem twisted around and spat toward the inn. "Brothel!"

I would get saddled with him, Charles thought. He wanted to throw Lem into the nearest ditch but decided it was his duty to take care of a neighbor. He said, "Even if it's true, it's none of your business. Come on, I'll take you home."

"Home!" Lem Brayton sprang back, staring at Charles. "Don't want to go home. She's there! Brothel!" Suddenly whirling, he started to run up the road. Lem couldn't keep a straight course, but he ran with startling speed.

After one step, Charles gave up the pursuit. Shrugging, he turned toward the inn. He figured Lem's flight saved everybody bother. The man couldn't go far in the state he was in, and when he stopped he might sleep himself sober. All I need, reflected Charles, to complete this day, is to take a drunken husband home to his wife.

The common room was crowded when he entered. Charles pushed through toward the bar. He had never seen the inn so packed; the heat was as stifling as that of a brush fire and the smoke almost as thick. The noise was even more impressive inside. Charles wondered how anybody could hear himself think.

Dan Tarbox and Asa Brayton were trying vainly to keep everyone supplied. The innkeeper's broad face was red and glistening. Asa was shaking with fatigue; whenever he carried a tray its contents rattled. Dan's daughter, Marcia, was behind the counter filling glasses, tankards, cups, the family's entire supply of drinking vessels. No matter how fast the three worked there were always cries for more drinks and impatient pounding on tables. When Charles tried to greet the host, Dan brushed past with a curt nod.

Feeling shy and awkward, Charles looked around. Every chair was occupied; men stood in the spaces between the tables. None of the usual residents of Stratton seemed to be present. Charles recognized only one group listening to the man they called the Captain.

"Charles! Charles Chittenden!"

The hail came from a far corner, and Charles shoved toward it eagerly. He wasn't sure who had called; any neighbor was preferable to standing out like a sore thumb. He saw the blacksmith's muscular shoulders and waved.

"Evening, Abner!"

The smith beckoned. Charles had almost reached the table before he noticed that Abner's companion was Nathan Patch. The two young men eyed each other like rival roosters.

"Hello, Nathan."

"Lo, Charles."

Abner Reed ignored the suspicion in the two voices. He kicked a milking stool out from under the small table. "Have a seat, Charles," said the smith. "Fetched that with me. E-yah. Been saving it for someone I knew."

Nathan Patch, remembering the encounter during the oration, was worried. If Lovina had told Charles of his trickery there was likely to be trouble. Nathan pursed his lips and kept them closed.

Remembering the same meeting, Charles Chittenden was worried. He clamped his clenched fists between his knees. If Nathan mentions Lovina, he thought, I'll throw this milking stool at him. He was not going to be crowed over in defeat. Charles admitted the defeat, set his lips, and said nothing.

Abner Reed, impassive, said, "Walk down from the clearing, Charles?"

"E-yah."

"Sensible. Too many vehicles sitting in the road."

"E-yah," agreed Nathan. "I was more than a mite pleased Pa took the team off without me."

Charles nodded. He waited while Asa Brayton set a drink in front of him, then lowered his voice as the boy hurried away. "Ran into Lem Brayton. Outside."

The blacksmith frowned. Nathan said, "Lem's tongue is hinged in the middle sometimes. Pa wouldn't like that kind of talk. Pa's a stickler."

"He needn't know."

"E-yah, Charles. I sort of figured that."

The two young men exchanged a grin and felt better. Each believed the other was the more successful rival; both were determined to hide their disappointment. They were careful to behave exactly alike. Nathan drank sparingly; Charles made each drink last a long time. Conversation became a matter of a few guarded sentences and a great deal of silence.

"Your pa got guests, Nathan?"

"E-yah."

"Mine, too."

If Abner Reed was amused, he gave no sign. He seemed content to watch the inn's thriving trade. Whenever his companions spoke, the smith cocked his head and listened. He seldom offered a remark.

"Charles."

"E-yah?"

"Your Pa aiming to raise that young bull?"

"E-yah. Guess so, Nathan."

"Just wondered."

Even when the throng in the room began to thin as weariness and late hours drove men to their beds, the young neighbors sat on. Each was reluctant to make the first move toward departure. He ain't going to outset me, Nathan Patch told himself. All right, thought Charles, I can wait as long as anybody.

"Getting late, boys."

"E-yah."

"You got the right of it, Abner."

It became a contest. The room held more empty tables than crowded ones when Luke Brooks made his appearance. Casually, the gambler, fingering his white neckpiece, surveyed the attendance. He walked to a deserted table and sat down. Several men joined him as if by a summons.

"Owns the earth, don't he?"

"That's the gambler feller. Name of Brooks."

"E-yah," said the smith. "Luke Brooks."

Charles recalled Lem Brayton's remark and wondered what had become of Rhoda Hapgood. He didn't ask. Nathan's ready information about the gambler rankled. Figures he bested me that time, thought Charles. A few minutes later when Doc Merrifield entered, Charles saw his opportunity for revenge.

"Evening, Doc!"

"How now, Charles!" Doc called, waving. "Well met. Tippecanoe hath murdered sleep." The medicine man hurried to the card game and took a place.

Over the rim of his tankard Charles watched Nathan and waited. He counted on the sawmill heir's curiosity. Finally young Patch licked his lips and yielded.

"Friend of yours, Charles?"

"E-yah. Dr. Portus J. Merrifield."

"Talks a mite peculiar, don't he?"

"It's his trade." Charles smiled patiently. "Doc sells patent medicine. Told me about it today."

Except for the card game and the Stratton trio the room was soon deserted. Marcia Tarbox disappeared. Asa Brayton, exhausted, sprawled across a table and slept. The innkeeper, yawning but dogged, slumped into a chair with his neighbors.

"Sold out," Dan said, hoarsely. "Every blame drop! Scraped the bottom of the barrels. Could have sold more."

Abner Reed pointed to the card players. "They're still drinking."

"E-yah. Couple of bottles set aside. Mr. Brooks paid extra for the service." In the midst of a jawbreaking yawn the innkeeper heard his front door open and swung around as if he hadn't seen a customer in months. He jumped up. "Mr. Dunbar!"

Thomas Jefferson Dunbar slammed the door behind him. The Southerner looked disheveled. Grass stains streaked the light trousers. Tom's white hat was on the back of his head, and his cravat was askew. There was a wide, foolish grin on the handsome face. The young man swaggered to the center of the room.

"Drunk," muttered Nathan Patch.

The Virginian swept off his hat and swung it in a wide arc as he bowed to the assemblage. "My compliments, gentlemen." He straightened and laughed delightedly. "My compliments." The slurred speech was slower; each word came separately. "I'm afraid I bring sad tidings. A drought is on the land. There just is no more nectar up at Tippecanoe's plantation."

"Nectar, Mr. Dunbar?"

"Nectar, sir. Ambrosia. Hard cider. Whatever the libation is called, mine host, there is no more. No more, sir. Gone."

At the card table the Captain shrugged and picked up the deck. He said, "It lasted longer than I expected."

Tom Dunbar laughed again. "Not long enough, sir. My thirst and the last barrel ran neck and neck. But the barrel quit in the stretch, sir. I'd sure be pleased if you gentlemen would oblige me by quaffing the flowing bowl with me."

The innkeeper wrung his hands.

Charles Chittenden shook his head.

"Folks that ain't used to hard cider," said Abner Reed, "shouldn't fool with it."

Luke Brooks looked at Doc Merrifield. The medicine man sneaked out a tiny foot and hooked a chair toward the card table.

"Care to sit in on the game, Mr. Dunbar?" asked the gambler. "Innkeeper. A glass for Mr. Dunbar." Brooks waited till the glass came, then poured it full. "We've no more cider, sir. But that's middling-fair whiskey."

Swaying, Tom Dunbar raised the glass. "A toast, gentlemen. A toast. I give you the hard cider and soft ladies of Vermont. Both somewhat deceiving. Mild as milk, sirs, and containing hidden fire!" He drank, gulping the brown liquid with a speed that made every man present stare.

Charles glanced at Nathan Patch. This Southern dandy is talking about Lovina, he thought. He saw the agreement in Nathan's face. Silently, with a look, the two rivals joined forces. It was Nathan who addressed the alien.

"Sir," said the sawmill owner's son, "this ain't the place to discuss ladies."

Laughter rocked the slender figure. "Begging your pardon, sir," said Tom, still chuckling. "I was addressing these gentlemen." He turned his back and sat down at the card table. "Deal me in, sir. But I give fair warning. Tonight I can't lose at anything. Puritans!"

The bottle clinked on the glass as he poured another drink. "A toast to the Goddess of Fortune—a Puritan lady who pretends indifference but is most generous with her favors."

Doc Merrifield glanced over his shoulder at the two glaring young men. He said, "Deal, Captain. Shall we play cards, Mr. Dunbar?"

Eyes glazed, Tom Dunbar stared into space. The merriment faded from his features. He shook his head, puzzled. "Jove," he said, as if speaking to himself. He seemed to be unaware of any listeners. "Jove. I can't get over it. A well-bred girl like that. And she practically raped me."

There was an instant of stunned silence. For all the easy, tavern talk, the loose jocularity about passion and potency, Tom's remark violated a New England ethic. He'd been bald and specific. For several seconds the men in the room couldn't believe their ears.

Nathan Patch's voice ripped out, shocked beyond control. "He's a liar!"

Lovina. The name flashed into Charles Chittenden's mind and touched off his fury as a spark will powder. Everybody knew this Dunbar had taken Lovina home, and Charles wasn't going to leave her defense to Nathan.

He was moving across the space between the two tables in a white blur of rage. Charles scarcely saw Doc Merrifield's attempt to intercept him. He shoved the medicine man away with one stiff thrust of his arm.

Tom Dunbar blinked at the innkeeper's warning shout. He had time neither to rise nor turn before Charles was upon him.

As if handling a down pillow Charles plucked the Southerner from his chair, whirled him around, and hit him.

It was a short, upward blow, and it thudded viciously against Tom's jaw. The Virginian's body curved backward. He crashed across the table, upset it. Wood splintered; coins rang as they bounced on the floor. Tom's white beaver rolled until it hit the far wall.

The card players were all on their feet. Luke Brooks had leaped nimbly away from the table. He held an ugly, short-barreled derringer in one fist. It was cocked, and no one had seen him draw it. The gambler said, quietly, "I wouldn't have done that. The man was drunk."

"E-yah." The Captain agreed.

Another card player, a stranger, nodded.

It was suddenly the mountain against the valley. The blacksmith and Nathan Patch stepped to each side of Charles. Dan Tarbox, innkeeper as well as neighbor, was speechless with indecision. But Asa Brayton, roused by the noise, shuffled forward and ranged himself beside the smith.

"He deserved it," said Nathan.

Doc Merrifield's voice was unruffled, neutral. "Gentlemen. Gentlemen. Much ado about little. The fault is equal. I say let's have apologies all around, and let all be well that ends well."

Charles, not listening, was tense, ready to renew the battle. All his unhappiness—the quarrel with Lovina, the bitter deadlock of circumstance—was centered in the tall figure stretched on the floor. I'll smash him again, thought Charles, and go on smashing until he swears he lied.

Thomas Jefferson Dunbar rose slowly. He drew himself erect, chalk white, eyes narrowed to slits. A trickle of blood ran down from the corner of Tom's mouth and was ignored. With a strange, cold dignity the Southerner's glance traveled from man to man, fixed on Charles.

"A coward's blow, sir." Tom sounded remote, detached. There was no emotion in the lazy voice, yet it was somehow deadly. He was cold sober now.

Staring, Charles was bewildered. The other's calm reaction was beyond his experience. Bewilderment held him motionless but lashed his anger. Charles said, "Worth your mettle."

"You'd fight, sir?"

"E-yah!"

"You have the advantage. I have small knowledge of your Northern style of fighting." Dunbar of Pulchramonte permitted himself a contemptuous smile.

Charles flared out at the Virginian's iciness. "I'll fight you any style! Any place! Any way you want! If you're man enough!"

Tom Dunbar bowed. "You all heard the gentleman? I believe that constitutes a challenge."

Doc Merrifield sighed. Luke Brooks pocketed his pistol. Nathan Patch said, "A challenge? You—you mean a duel?"

The Southern voice might have been discussing the weather.

285

"Will you do me the honor of acting for me, Mr. Brooks? And you, please, Captain. The choice of weapons is mine. Pistols. I suggest tomorrow at dawn if the gentleman's friends will agree. I will have to leave Stratton afterwards."

"Now, hold on," said the blacksmith.

"We don't stomach dueling in these parts," Nathan objected. "It ain't a mite better than murder!"

Tom Dunbar's look made Charles flush. He said, "Hush up, Nathan. I'll fight him."

As if he had no further interest in the matter Tom Dunbar held out a hand. "My hat, if you please, innkeeper." He accepted it from Tarbox, settled it firmly on his head. "Thank you." Tom had complete control of the situation, and he knew it. Each word and action was scrupulously correct. "Good night, gentlemen." He bowed only to the card players. He walked past the men of Stratton as if they did not exist.

They all heard his footsteps mount the stairs; a door closed.

"Land of Goshen!"

"He means it, don't he?"

"E-yah."

"Dueling!"

"Charles, you ain't aiming to go through with this tomfoolery?"

"I ain't scared of him!"

"Charles!"

"Don't be a fool, boy. What is honor? A word."

"Stay out of this, Doc. We'll need you as master of ceremonies."

"Luke, you've got to stop this. We'll have the authorities down on us!"

The gambler shrugged. "Young Dunbar wants satisfaction. He's capable of demanding it of me if this gentleman won't oblige. Things have gone too far, Doc. I doubt if that fire-eater would accept an apology now."

"He ain't likely to get one," said Charles. "Nathan. Abner. Make the arrangements."

Doc Merrifield stared. "Are you weary of this great world, Charles? I've seen that Southerner shoot. You're a sight bigger target than a silver coin. And Dunbar punctured one at twenty yards."

"Maybe," said Charles stubbornly. "But the coin wasn't shooting back."

"You ever handle a pistol?" asked the blacksmith.

"E-yah. Couple or three times."

"Couple or three times!" The medicine man mopped his forehead. "I give up. You'd better spend the rest of this night with me out at the clearing. I'll tell you all I know about dueling. And . . ." Doc Merrifield sighed. "You might want to get your affairs settled —while there's time."

Dear Lovina.

I write this under strange conditions, by candlelight in a wagon in the clearing which we have so often visited. It is very different now. It is after three o'clock and everything is quiet and dark. You never saw so many wagons, and tents—all black now. You wouldn't know it was the same clearing in which Sen. Danl. Webster made his speech this afternoon. The only noise now is over by the Tippycanoe Log Cabin where somebody keeps ringing a cowbell.

I am not much at writing letters. I have a lot to say and I go on about the clearing. It is hard to remember that you won't read this unless the worst happens. The girl who brings you this letter will tell you what the worst is. Her name is Mercy.

I hope for once I can tell you all I want to. I've never been able to, but this may be my last chance. First—don't think I believed that Southner for a minute. I hit him because I wanted to, and I'm duelling him because I won't give him the credit of going down to where he lives and saying Vermonters are cowards. You are the finest girl I ever knew. I loved you, Lovina. I figured we would get married some day. I only put off asking you because there was no room at home with Peter there and Jenny expecting. I thought we had lots of time, but there has never been anyone else. Now, there isn't any more time.

Doctor Portus J. Merrifield has directions about my things. Please accept the gold chain. I was saving it for a watch, but I want you to have it. You could hang a locket or something from it. It is real gold.

I'm sorry we quarreled. Very sorry.

Goodbye, my dearest Lovina. You have my best, sincerest wishes for all future happiness.

Yr. loving frnd.
Charles Chittenden.

Miss Lovina Chester.
By hand.
8 July, 1840. Another day.

THE THIRD DAY
July 8, 1840

SLOWLY, AS the sky above and behind it paled, the ridge of Stratton Mountain's summit detached itself from its background. The curved spine that resembled a crouching cat grew clearer against the blue of a false dawn. One by one the stars were surrounded by a spreading flood of light, struggled briefly, and were drowned. The fresh, first breeze of morning whisked the mountaintop free of clouds and mist. In the huge clearing on the mountainside, fog and shadow were draped around the countless angles of the vast encampment. The base of the tamarack tree was hidden by folds of smoky vapor.

From road to trees, across the acres of the half-moon shape that held wagons and tents, cabin, shelters, and booths, the great field was still under a hush that muffled the natural noises of sleeping thousands. No lights showed; no more than a dozen red smudges marked the ground where yesterday's fires had died. The beasts that were bringing men to the spot were as quiet as the beasts that waited for them to leave. All four of the riders passing along the turnpike sensed that they were intruders.

They walked their horses, clopping in single file past the long black rank of parked vehicles that hedged the roadway. The Captain knew the way and led. Tom Dunbar's black gelding followed, stepping delicately through pools of mist. Hoc kept his mount a neck behind the gelding, and Luke Brooks, on a sturdy cob, came last. They had ridden up from the tavern in that order; while the road stretched beside the clearing none of the four spoke.

Tom Dunbar strained his ears for any outcry at their passage. The Southerner wished to avoid questions about their destination at that hour; he knew that dueling was not a popular practice in New England. It was his first duel, and he didn't want it stopped or spoiled. Walking, it seemed to take hours to pass the encampment and, even then, the line of conveyances stretched endlessly ahead.

The Captain held up an arm, waved it. He turned his roan into a branch leading off to the south. The branch was narrower and rougher than the turnpike, but the Captain spurred his horse to a canter.

With a grunt of relief Tom sent the gelding forward. He drew alongside the leader and called, "Is it far now, sir?"

The Captain shook his head. "Just ahead."

Hoofs drumming, they rode on. Tom was forced to hold in the gelding; the big black horse wanted to go first, but the other was the guide. Boot to boot the two riders thundered down the road. Once the Southerner glanced back. Hoc, bent low, was several lengths behind. Beyond the slave Tom could make out the dim figures of the gambler and his horse.

"There it is!" shouted the Captain and reined in the roan.

Tom caught a glimmer of gray through the tree trunks. For a moment, as he slowed his gelding, he thought it was a mist-covered field. Then the Virginian saw that the wide, flat surface was water.

They dismounted in the rank grass at the bank of the pond. The darkness was thinning, and the ripples on the water were like the quick scribbles of an inked pen.

Hoc's horse skidded to a stop. The slave said, "This here place, Mr. Tom?"

"Yes, Hoc. Tie up Ebony. And you'd better get a fire started. I want my hands warm." Tom walked to the pond's edge and stared across it. His reflection was a shadow at his feet. Aware that the Captain had followed, the young man asked, "What do they call this place, sir?"

"Holman's Pond. South Pond. It's got a couple of names."

"I can't make out if the ground's level."

"E-yah. It is. Level enough."

Luke Brooks joined them. The gambler's face was suddenly clear as he lit a cheroot. "Can I offer you gentlemen tobacco? Captain? Mr. Dunbar?"

"Not now." Tom shook his head. "Later, perhaps."

292

"E-yah. Me, too."

"Nervous, Mr. Dunbar?"

"No." The reply was short. Tom glanced at the gambler with irritation. Damn it, he thought, how did the fellow guess? Of course he was nervous. Not scared, or anything like that, but a man wanted everything to go perfectly on the field of honor. Especially the first time. He said, "I'd like to get it over, Mr. Brooks. It's sure enough an uncomfortable hour to be out in."

"Sun'll be up any minute."

"E-yah."

"You're sure they'll come, sir?"

"They'll come."

"I figured we'd be first. They'll walk over from the clearing." The Captain paced a few steps worriedly. "I wish we had a surgeon."

"So do I," said Tom. "It's proper. And there'll be need for one." He was proud of his casual, quiet tone.

The gambler shrugged. "Doc Merrifield will have to do. He isn't a bad substitute. Doc's seen shooting wounds before. He knows how to treat them."

"Ah!" said the Captain. The other two turned and followed his glance. Above them, over the trees and far up its slope, the summit of the mountain was limned in golden outline. The sun was rising.

Tom Dunbar walked back to the fire the Negro had kindled, stripped off his gloves, and extended his hands. The slave, squatting to feed the flames, looked up at his master. "Mr. Tom."

"Yes, Hoc?"

"You going to kill this man dead?"

"He struck me, Hoc."

"Yes, sir, Mr. Tom. You done told me."

"Well? Isn't that answer enough?"

"Sure, Mr. Tom. Sure. But . . ."

"But what, Hoc?"

"Nothing, Mr. Tom. Nothing, sir."

"A duel's a duel," said Tom, annoyed at himself for attempting to explain. "He'll have to take his chances the same as I am. I've been insulted beyond amenities, Hoc. I intend to get satisfaction in blood." Increased annoyance shortened the Southerner's temper. His voice became crisper. "You take care of the pistols! I'll take care of the shooting."

"Yes, sir, Mr. Tom. You don't have to tell me!"

With a snort Tom ended the conversation. He didn't expect Hoc to understand that there was no room for sentiment in the code duello. I'm going to teach that Chittenden a lesson, thought Tom, with a ball through his body. He was irked that the slave had introduced the subject of death. If a man died as a result of a duel it was an unfortunate but honorable finish. He remembered his tutor's edict. He could hear the French accent and see the cavalry moustaches of the man now. "The true duelist, mon petit, has only the one rule. Kill or be killed. Mais, oui! Leave nicenesses for the funeral, or it may be it is your funeral."

Massaging his right hand, Tom stood and watched the morning brighten beautifully. It was going to be a lovely day. Dew glistened on the grass; the trees along the edge of the pond began to assume shape and color. The duelist could see that the place of combat was entirely suitable. A strip of flat ground paralleled the bank of the pond. The principals would have water on one side and a fringe of trees on the other. Neither would have to face the sun. Only each other.

Impatiently, Tom frowned at his seconds. From their murmuring he didn't think they seemed very concerned that the other party had not yet appeared. Punctuality was important in dueling. It was unforgivably rude to keep your opponent waiting. He was sure that the others were late.

"Mr. Tom."

The Southerner looked down. Hoc jerked his head to point. Tom stared in the direction indicated. He could see figures approaching; voices murmured. He wondered if they were discovered and was surprised that the possibility didn't upset him. Then he recognized the round contours of the medicine man.

"Brooks. Captain."

The two turned, hurried to meet the newcomers. Tom Dunbar put his right hand inside his coat and spoke to Hoc. "My compliments to Mr. Chittenden's seconds, and their man may use the fire if he wishes."

"Yes, sir, Mr. Tom."

He walked away from the blaze and strode to the pond bank. He stood there, his back to the company, gazing out over the water, well aware of the picture he made. He'd changed to a complete black outfit, buttoned high, with only a touch of white linen at the throat. Tom regretted that he'd only brought one hat. The tall, white beaver was jauntily cocked, but it was scarcely the correct garb for the occasion.

A hermit thrush awoke in the woods and sang. The bird's melody startled Tom Dunbar. He listened, surprised at his own emotion. A lump rose in his throat, and a soft weakness flowed into the pit of his stomach. It had been years since he'd heard a bird greet the sun, and he remembered Virginia. Pulchramonte was suddenly far away from this cruder Northern land. Tidewater, at once greener and bluer, would lap more gently at his feet than did this mountain pond. This, he thought, with an aching rush of homesickness, would be a hell of a place to die.

"Mr. Dunbar." The gambler was at his side.

With an effort Tom managed to turn calmly. "Yes, Mr. Brooks?"

"Ready, sir."

He took the place indicated, and saw that Charles Chittenden was in position. The Vermonter stood with his legs spread. He hadn't changed his clothes, but his jacket was snugly fastened at the neck, and his hat was pulled down over his eyes.

"They wouldn't change the stance, Mr. Brooks?"

"No, sir." The gambler smiled. "That young Patch is no one to argue with. A sharp trader. You're to front each other, facing."

"A wider target."

"You can thank Doc Merrifield for that. I'll wager it was his idea. Gives young Chittenden a better mark and less chance of a vital wound."

Luke Brooks stepped aside to allow Hoc to present the mahogany box. One of the velvet grooves was already empty. Tom Dunbar took the other pistol. "Thank you, Hoc."

"Yes, sir, Mr. Tom." The Negro rolled his eyes. "Now you be careful, sir."

The note of fear in the slave's voice brought panic to the master. What's Hoc afraid of, he thought. Hoc knows I'm a good shot. But Chittenden had a pistol, too. The mate to the one in his own hand. One of Grandfather's wonderfully made pistols. What was it the hunter said? Made for killing. A lucky shot could kill as surely as an aimed one.

"Good luck, Mr. Dunbar."

Tom Dunbar smiled, but there was no blood in his lips. Hoc and the second walked away. The Southerner felt very much alone—alone and vulnerable. There was something more to dueling than the fine, formal speeches, the ceremonious combat; something more than chivalry or honor. He had cherished every rule of the code duello, but he had never realized that death could come to either duelist. Death was the something more. Death faced him in the stolid figure of Charles Chittenden, twenty paces away. Death gleamed from the pistol barrel by the other's thigh. Tom Dunbar's palm was wet on the smooth butt of his weapon; a tendon behind one knee began to vibrate like a plucked fiddlestring. He was afraid to die.

The medicine man was speaking. Tom had to concentrate in order to hear the words. "If either gentleman would accept an apology, there would be no reflection on anyone's honor."

Charles Chittenden said, "No."

He can't answer for both of us, thought Tom. Maybe I'm the one should apologize. He couldn't remember what he'd said before Chittenden's blow. Something about girls. But he hadn't mentioned any names, and he'd been in liquor. A man wasn't to blame for what he said while drinking. He was bitter at his opponent's refusal to apologize; the stubborn bumpkin would get them both killed.

Thomas Jefferson Dunbar looked like the perfect duelist. He seemed cool and poised. No one could see that the tendon twitched or that he gripped his pistol too tightly.

Doc Merrifield took the Virginian's silence for disdain. "All right," the medicine man said. "The word is 'Fire. One. Two.' No shots are to be fired before or after the signal." Doc hitched his wicked-looking blunderbuss forward.

He won't hit me, thought Tom. He can't possibly hit me. But there was fearful doubt in his belief. With a coldness that prickled along his spine Tom Dunbar decided that he didn't like dueling. He'd been badly misled.

"Ready, Mr. Chittenden?"

"E-yah."

"Ready, Mr. Dunbar?"

The Southerner took one last, wild look at his surroundings.

The sunshine was driving the mist from the pond, and beneath the rising wisps there were glints of blue and gold. The trees were green, now, and lovely. It was a lovely morning. He felt like weeping. He could no longer hear the thrush.

Tom Dunbar focused on his opponent, took a deep breath, and nodded.

"Fire. One. Two."

The reports blended together. Their echoes came flatly back across the lake like two quick handclaps.

An unseen force stabbed Tom's left shoulder. It shoved him off balance, sent him staggering back with jerky, uncertain steps. Pain, warm and flowing, boiled over into his arm. He dropped his pistol, clutched at the wound. Blood seeped through cloth, wet his fingers. His blood.

I'm killed, he thought. I'm killed.

He never noticed that Charles Chittenden had spun half around, slipped to his knees, and pitched forward on his face.

Thomas Jefferson Dunbar, of Pulchramonte, in Virginia, sat down on the ground and began to cry.

Senator Daniel Webster gazed at his image in the mirror. The white lather beard that covered the lower half of his face softened its contours, masked the thin line of the mouth. The man that stared back from the glass was a tired man. Under the smooth, noble dome of the forehead the eyes were ringed by dark circles. He was used to early rising, but he had retired late. Besides, his catarrh was bothering him again.

The Senator opened his straight razor and tested its edge. It was a fine piece of steel. He liked the things that money and position brought—good clothes, expensive shotguns, blooded stock.

He started to shave with long, even strokes. The swarthy skin bared by the razor might have been polished wood.

Webster's mouth was a soap-rimmed zero as he shaved his upper lip. He heard Rufe's hail from outside.

"Senator?"

He waited until he saw Rufe behind him, reflected in the mirror. Webster said, "Morning, Rufe." He went back to his shaving.

Rufe sighed. Like that again, he thought. By this time he knew all his charge's moods. With a hasty glance around he asked, "Comfortable night, Senator?"

The Great Man drew his finger along the razor and flicked soap into the basin. He grunted and ignored the question.

Hands in pockets, Rufe contemplated the broad, slightly hunched shoulders in front of the glass. Webster's linen shirt was tautly stretched; his legs were solidly planted. There's no doubt about it, thought Rufe, sighing, he's a fine figure of a man. No wonder he impresses the Supreme Court when he argues those cases. In Rufe's opinion Daniel Webster had every quality for a successful Presidential candidate except one—in the final test he wasn't popular enough to get the nomination. Well, that was water under the bridge now.

The politician waited until Webster had splashed his face and was busy toweling it. He said, "We have to make a fairly early start, Senator. We're making for Bellows Falls."

"Speeches?"

"A few words, maybe, to local lights. Nothing big."

The Senator rubbed at his chin and tossed the towel aside. He pondered a moment before speaking. "Rufe."

"Yes?"

"He's going to win."

"Tippecanoe?"

"Harrison. Yes! I wasn't sure in the beginning, but I am now. This crowd—there must have been close to twenty thousand listening yesterday—they took care of the last doubts I had. We're going to lick Van Buren, Rufe."

"That's the idea, isn't it?"

"William Henry Harrison, President of the United States." Senator Webster closed his razor with a snap.

Rufe shrugged. "There's many a slip, Senator. Election's in November. This crowd—well, they came to hear you more than anything else."

"They'll go for Harrison."

"It looks like they might."

"Rufe." The Great Man's voice lowered, but his gaze was steady. "You're sure they know what I want?"

"They know."

"There's Henry Clay."

"Clay's been Secretary of State. He has other plans. Don't worry, Senator."

298

"Secretary of State." There was no emotion in the pliable voice. "You might see if breakfast is ready, Rufe."

"Sure, Senator." Rufe recognized dismissal. "Right away."

Left alone, Webster finished his dressing. He shrugged into his coat and stepped before the mirror. The big, farmer's hands smoothed the hair over his ears.

Daniel Webster stared at Daniel Webster. He thought of the tremendous gathering in Stratton's clearing. He still didn't understand this new force of the people, but he recognized its power. It had elected Andrew Jackson; it would elect William Harrison. Webster didn't like it much. He preferred the earlier days when men of property—patriotic, of course—had controlled the nation's votes. Now it was bread and circuses. The first death rattle of Republics.

The thin lips in the glass moved. The words were low and bitter.

"Tippecanoe and Tyler too," said Daniel Webster. "The damn fools. The damn, blind fools!"

The clearing was alive with activity when Luke Brooks thundered back down the road toward Stratton church. Several men dodged into the line of vehicles to avoid his galloping cob. Brooks ignored their shouts, but he took a good look at the encampment as he passed. Smoke curled up from hundreds of breakfast fires; people were milling about busily. The gambler thought of his stealthy passage a half hour before. It was difficult to recognize this wide, sunlit field with its bustling noises and hum of voices as the same place. He swerved to avoid a chaise turning onto the turnpike from the clearing and rode on. Some early riser was starting his homeward journey. Luke Brooks smiled with approval. He and the unknown chaise driver seemed to share the same opinion. Beat it, thought Brooks, while your shoes are good. Before the roads become clogged. Before there's trouble.

He felt sure there was going to be trouble. He'd expected it since the challenge in the tavern and had laid his plans accordingly. Two nights of gaming had been profitable, and Luke Brooks was determined to be far away when the authorities started to talk about murder.

Churning the roadbed beneath its hoofs the cob carried him past the Chittenden farm. The gambler's quick survey noted the smoke from the chimney, the man carrying milk pails from the barn. Young Chittenden's father, he judged and, without thinking, spurred his horse.

Years of gambling had taught Luke Brooks to spend little time bewailing the events of yesterday. Now, however, he had a moment's regret at the duel's outcome. He remembered his surprise when Chittenden had hit the Southerner. Then Doc's girl, Mercy, had come running from the woods and bent over the fallen Vermonter. One glance at her face, and the gambler had known Chittenden's wound was serious. Brooks had fought several duels and witnessed more. He had no faith in recovery from stomach wounds. He hadn't examined Charles Chittenden; that was the medicine man's job.

Dunbar was more scared than hurt. Luke Brooks grinned at the memory of the Virginian's tears. The pistol ball had ripped a groove across the top of Dunbar's shoulder. It would soon respond to the slave's tender care.

Hammering through the settlement, the gambler drew rein behind the inn. He dismounted and hurried inside. Dan Tarbox met him at the door. Brooks answered the question in the innkeeper's face. "It's over. They were both hit."

"Both?" Dan's eyes widened. "Bad?"

"Young Dunbar's all right. A deep scratch. Left shoulder. Might curb his spirit a little." The gambler pushed past and went toward the stairway.

"Mr. Brooks."

"Yes?"

"What about—the other—Charles?"

Luke Brooks frowned. He said, "I can't say for certain. He—well, he looks like a stout lad. Maybe it'll be all right." He left the innkeeper gaping behind him and mounted the stairs. He had a front room, and it was only a step from the stairhead.

The girl was still in his room. That surprised him.

Rhoda Hapgood turned from the window where she'd been looking out. Rhoda was fully dressed. She smiled timidly, uncertain.

Luke Brooks shut the door. He said, "My dear. I thought you'd be gone by now." The gambler's rebuke was gentle.

Blushing, Rhoda gazed at the floor. "I—I wanted to see you again," she said. "I wanted to say thank you."

300

"Thank you? To me?"

"E-yah." The bowed head moved in a nod.

Brooks glanced at the table. The two eagles lay side by side like golden spectacles. The girl hadn't touched the coins.

"I—I don't want the money, Mr. Brooks. And I thought if I just left it you might figure I was sorry or angry or . . ." The girl's fingers moved futilely. She glanced up; her voice faltered. "So I waited."

The gambler walked over to her. Rhoda cringed slightly as if expecting a blow. The movement brought a pained expression to the man's eyes. Two eagles, Brooks thought, must be a fortune in her life, and yet she's refused them. He wondered if Rhoda were playing for higher stakes. He put a finger under her chin, tilted her face up. "Rhoda."

"E-yah?"

"What will you do now? You were going to be gone before the inn was awake."

"I know." Rhoda shrugged. "I don't care." She was suddenly looking straight at him, her hands linked together. "I ain't aiming to be trouble, Mr. Brooks. I did want to thank you. Nobody ever was nice to me—that way—before. You—you treated me like a lady. You were kind."

"Rhoda, Rhoda."

"I ain't a mite ashamed. I'm glad. I guess I ain't a very good girl."

Luke Brooks chuckled. He picked up the coins, looked at Rhoda, and tucked them in his waistcoat pocket. He took the heavy saddlebags from the back of a chair. "I have to be off now, Rhoda."

"I know." Rhoda's eyes were wet, but she smiled. She reached for the saddlebags. "Let me carry those downstairs for you."

"No."

"I want to."

"A gentleman never lets a lady carry burdens."

Rhoda flushed with pleasure. She bowed and placed her hand on his arm. "All right, Mr. Brooks."

They went down the stairs together. The inn's entire staff was grouped in the hallway, but Rhoda's step never hesitated. She held her head proudly, smiling.

Luke Brooks saw Mrs. Tarbox's mouth pop open with shock at

301

seeing Rhoda. The innkeeper's wife gasped and said, "Rhoda Hapgood! You—you were upstairs?"

"E-yah, Mrs. Tarbox. Guess I was."

Dan Tarbox coughed uneasily. Asa Brayton and Marcia stared. "Well!" said Lydia Tarbox. "I never heard the like! I thought you were a nice girl, Rhoda!"

"Mrs. Tarbox," said the gambler, coldly. "Your thoughts are no concern of ours. Please, step aside."

"Dan! Are you going to let him talk like that to me?"

"Hush up, Lyd," said Dan Tarbox.

I can't leave her to all this, the gambler decided. Old Patch will be even worse from what she's said. She'll be a drag, yes. Slow my getting away. But it won't be the first time I've played against heavy odds. Grinning, Brooks said, "Miss Hapgood has done me the honor of agreeing to accompany me on my journey."

Rhoda's head turned. She stared, amazed, unbelieving.

"Miss Hapgood, indeed!"

The girl didn't seem to hear Mrs. Tarbox. Her lips trembled; her face was radiant. She said, "Mr. Brooks!"

"We have to get along, Rhoda."

"E-yah!" Rhoda fumbled at her neck, took off a string of white beads. "Asa. Will you give these back to your mother? Tell her thank you for me. Tell her thank you very much."

Asa Brayton stared at the necklace. "E-yah, Rhoda," he said. "E-yah. I'll tell her."

Mrs. Tarbox finished. "You'll regret this, Rhoda Hapgood! He's a common gambler! He'll desert you somewhere!"

"No, Rhoda," said Luke Brooks, "I always back my chances."

"Chances!" Rhoda Hapgood laughed. "E-yah. And at least there's chances, Mr. Brooks. There ain't never been none for me here. Never!"

Gambler and hired girl went out together. Mrs. Tarbox whirled on her husband. "Dan! You knew that—that hussy was up there! In my house! My house!"

"It's an inn! He paid for everything!"

"Paid? Ain't there nothing you won't do for money? My family wasn't good enough to stay here. Oh, no! I had to beg and plead to get them a night's shelter. But you could turn a respectable, decent inn into a—a—a . . ." Mrs. Tarbox couldn't find the proper

302

word, but her meaning was plain. She saw Asa and her daughter listening and stamped her foot. "Asa! Marcia! Get along out of here! I ain't talking to either of you!"

The boy and girl went into the inn's big kitchen. Through the closed door they could hear Mrs. Tarbox stridently berating her husband. Marcia said, "I ain't never heard Ma take on so. She's really hopping mad."

Asa nodded. "I know."

"Asa! Did you know Rhoda was up there? Did you?"

"Well. E-yah."

"Asa Brayton!"

"Don't you start," said Asa. "I wasn't sure. But last night my Pa . . ." He hesitated; he wasn't used to discussing his pa. He knew that Marcia had seen Lem so drunk he could hardly stand. Lem's son flushed and turned away.

"Everybody drinks," said Marcia, quickly. "It ain't nothing, Asa. Shucks! There's lots worse than your Pa!"

Asa doubted that but smiled.

"Tell me how you knew? About Rhoda?"

"Pa said something."

"Then—then she was up there all night?"

"E-yah."

"In a man's room!"

Asa looked at Marcia. He thought of returning home that evening. No matter how much money he brought home Lem was likely to beat him for not having more. The boy hadn't minded the hard work in the tavern. For two nights he'd slept without fear of his father. Somehow it was different working for pay. Dan Tarbox had run Asa's legs off but never lifted a hand to him. With sudden understanding he knew why Rhoda Hapgood had left with the gambler. Asa was sure that Joel Patch was no easy taskmaster. He said, "Marcia. It ain't for us to judge."

The remark was surprisingly adult. Marcia blinked and gazed at Asa with new interest. "I guess maybe it ain't," she admitted. "I guess maybe them things happen."

"E-yah."

Little David Tarbox came in from outside, slamming the door. "Hey," he said. "What's Rhoda Hapgood doing riding off with that Mr. Brooks?"

"Hush up, Davey," Marcia said.

"Huh? Who're you telling to hush up? I just asked . . ."

Asa scowled. "Do like your sister said, Davey!"

David stared. The two were smiling at each other. David had seen his parents smile like that when they'd refused to answer his questions. But the small boy had other things on his mind than Rhoda Hapgood and he changed the subject abruptly. "Where's Hoc? He ain't in the stable!"

"He left early," explained Asa.

"Left? For good? He ain't gone?"

"He'll be back."

"Oh." David blew his breath out in relief. "I didn't get much chance to show him yesterday. Only Josie Chester came. And there's Put and Seth Purdy. They ought to pay a copper to hear Hoc sing, don't you think, Asa?"

"I dunno."

"He sings good. Hymns and things. He sang 'Old Hundred' for Josie. And something else I never heard before." David noticed that the others weren't listening.

"Asa," Marcia asked. "Why did Mr. Brooks leave in such a hurry? E-yah. And why are Mr. Dunbar and Hoc off somewhere? What's behind it all?"

"Your Pa'd skin me if I told."

"I wouldn't tell. Cross my heart."

"Davey?"

"E-yah. I swear! I won't say a word!"

Asa lowered his voice to a whisper. "There was a fight last night. Charles Chittenden hit Mr. Dunbar." The tall boy showed his teeth in a grin. "Knocked him out from under his hat!"

"Do tell!"

"Yow!" David punched at an imaginary opponent.

"But that ain't all. This morning they went off somewhere to finish it with pistols. Dueling, they calls it."

"You—you mean shooting at each other?"

"E-yah." Asa Brayton frowned. "And your pa says it sounds like Charles was hurt some. The way Mr. Brooks acted. I mean bad hurt—shot."

"Dead?" asked David. "Dead, Asa?"

"Davey!"

304

"I don't know the whole of it, Marcia." Asa addressed the girl. "But everybody was scared for Charles. It seems like this Mr. Dunbar is a crack shot."

The door burst open, and all three started guiltily. Dan Tarbox filled the doorway. From behind the innkeeper came the sound of his wife's weeping. Dan was red-faced and angry. The trio recoiled from his glare.

"Well," said the innkeeper. "Are you aiming to stand here talking away the morning? There's work to be done! That common room's got to be cleaned! Folk'll be wanting victuals! You hear, Asa?"

"E-yah. All right, Mr. Tarbox."

"Marcia!"

"Yes, Pa. Right away."

"Davey! Fetch water for your sister!"

David nodded, then jumped as his father slammed the door. He gulped, staring at the panel where Dan had been. David said, "Marcia. What's the matter with Ma?"

"Just don't ask questions, Davey! That's all!"

David watched his sister follow Asa Brayton from the room. The small boy, puzzled, moved closer to the hall door and placed his ear against the wood. He could hear his mother's wailing and the deeper, angry rumble of his father's arguments. Suddenly he stiffened, wrinkling his nose. From the fireplace came the smell of cooking, and David realized he was alone in the kitchen.

He charged at the table, peering under the cloths that covered the plates. David piled cheese on bread, scooped pickle slices from a dish to top the cheese. He crammed the combination into his mouth with one hand, while the other darted out and captured a piece of pie.

Mouth filled, munching, David Tarbox was completely happy.

"Gently," Doc Merrifield said. "Gently, now. Don't jostle him."

Sweat ran down Nathan Patch's nose and formed a drop at its tip. He tensed his muscles, shaking in the effort to lift smoothly. Nathan spoke as if his collar were choking him. "Got him, Abner?"

"E-yah." The blacksmith nodded. "Just a mite higher, now."

They were lifting Charles Chittenden into a wagon. Charles, wrapped in a blanket, had his eyes open watching the operation.

The wounded youth's face was as colorless as canvas, but he was the calmest of the group. Smiling, he said weakly, "I ain't likely to break in two. Stop playing pat-a-cake and put your backs into it."

Mercy was folding blankets into a pillow. She glared at Charles. "You be quiet!"

"I'm all right, Mercy."

"Be quiet!"

It was an open wagon, and they eased Charles onto its bed. He gazed up at the bright blue of the sky, sighed, and closed his eyes. There wasn't much pain except at moments; mostly he felt uncomfortable from the tightness of Doc's bandaging. But he had no desire to move. They're all making too much of it, he thought. Instead of calling me all sorts of a fool for getting into a duel in the first place, they take on like I was going to die. Well, the duel was over, and he was still alive, and he had no intention of dying. He wasn't even mad at Tom Dunbar. He wasn't mad at anybody. Remembering, he spoke without opening his eyes.

"Mercy?"

"I'm here."

"Got that letter?"

"You mean the one for Miss . . ."

"E-yah."

"I've got it."

"Tear it up."

"Now?"

"E-yah. Now."

"I will if you'll promise not to talk any more!"

Charles smiled in the direction of the girl's voice. "I promise, Mercy."

The wagon driver had been summoned by Hoc and paid by Tom Dunbar. He was from Dorset, and he found the whole affair puzzling. He tugged at Doc Merrifield's sleeve and nodded toward the wagon. "What's the matter with him?"

The medicine man scowled over his spectacles. "Fever!"

"Fever?" The driver glanced at Doc's hands. "With all that blood?"

"Fever!" repeated Doc fiercely. "And I bled him for it! Now stop baying the moon and climb up and get your nag moving. And walk him, mister! Walk him! I don't want that boy bouncing over any more ruts than you can help!"

The Dorset man grunted. "Whole blame turnpike is ruts after yesterday!"

Abner Reed said, "You ain't deef, are you? The man said walk your horse." The blacksmith strode to the horse's head and grabbed the halter. "Come along, now."

The wagon started. Doc waved Nathan Patch after it. "Go on," he said. "I'll catch up in a minute." The medicine man trotted back to the pond and washed his hands. He was drying them by waving them in the air as he hurried along when the Captain hailed him.

The politician leaned down from the roan's saddle. "Young Dunbar's gone back to the inn. How's Chittenden?"

"God knows," Doc said. "He's got a hole in his side you could stick your finger through. It looks clean, and the ball went clear through. Far as I can tell it didn't hit nothing important."

"That's good."

"There ain't nothing good about getting drilled with a pistol ball. This one ain't as deep as a well, nor as wide as a church door, but it may serve. I poured brandy in to clean it, and I patched him front and back, but that boy ain't out of the woods yet."

The Captain nodded. "E-yah. Complications?"

"No telling. The more I see of bullet holes the less I know. Some men can carry a half pound of lead in their innards and never turn a hair. And I've known others to go around bragging how they won a duel and just got nicked a little, and three days later they topple over dead."

"Well," said the Captain. "As long as he hangs on till nightfall everything'll be all right."

"Nightfall?"

"E-yah. The Convention'll be over, and we'll all have left by then. Including me and Dunbar."

"Dunbar!" Doc waved both arms. "God made him, I guess, therefore we'll let him pass for a man! But there wouldn't have been no trouble if that blame Virginia planter had stayed to home. He comes up here with his Southern horses and his Southern manners with the ladies and that brace of dueling pistols, and nothing will suit but that he has to show off all three!"

"E-yah. I know. Them Southern Whigs is always trouble. But they've got votes same as Northern folks."

Doc grunted. "Votes? I forgot that. When it comes to electing

307

Tippecanoe let no dog bark! I'd better get back to Chittenden."

The Captain walked his horse beside the trotting medicine man. He said, "You taking him home, Doc?"

"Yes!"

"You ain't aiming to mention any names?"

Doc Merrifield's answer was angry. "I'm aiming to tell his folks that the Whig party held him while Dan Webster used him for target practice. Try not to be a damn fool, Captain." He broke into a shambling run and left the horseman staring after him.

He caught the slow-moving wagon before it reached the clearing. Doc climbed up over the tailboard. Mercy wriggled her fingers at him and held one to her lips.

Doc looked at Charles. The young man's head was on Mercy's lap; his eyes were closed, his breathing regular. The medicine man used the same side-of-the-mouth whisper that he employed before audiences. "Asleep, Mercy?"

The girl nodded. "He didn't get much last night."

"Sleep will help. Knitting up the raveled sleeve, and so on. His color's a mite better. It's too early to say, but he just may pull through."

"He's got to!"

Doc Merrifield gazed at his ward. "Mean that much to you, Mercy?"

"Not the way you mean, Doc." Mercy smiled. She smoothed a fold in the blanket. "But he was friendly and nice. Last night he talked some about his family and the farm. It's a big place. And he has brothers and sisters. It sounded—well, he's just got to be all right."

Slowly they passed along the edge of the huge clearing. The medicine man stood up, swaying with the movement of the wagon, and scanned the encampment. There was a different bustle in the multitude this morning; it was a purposeful scurrying that prepared for departure. Men were busily packing vehicles; women collected belongings and children. A long file of horses was winding from the night's pasturage to the wagons; dozens of beasts were already between shafts. Even while Doc Merrifield watched one of the banners near the tamarack tree fluttered to the ground. The Convention was striking its colors.

There were other indications that the great throng intended to

308

dissolve. Most of the men had discarded their coats and hurried about with rolled-up shirtsleeves. Gowns and lapels were bare of party ribbons and badges, so universal on the previous day. Though the morning sunshine glinted on the brass of band instruments, there was no music. Only the log cabin showed that the Convention was still sitting. Delegates hurried into it; messengers hastened out. But, even here, in the temple erected for the occasion, there were signs of an impatient briskness.

Doc Merrifield chuckled. Nobody, he thought, is as anxious to get home as the man who's had a fine time. The travelers had come to hear Webster and cheer Tippecanoe. Having done both they saw no need for wasting any more time. Politics was an engaging sport, a fierce contest, an important choice—but only on definite occasions, apart from the daily routine. There were homes to return to, farms to tend, stock to be cared for, business to be conducted. The medicine man understood the feeling as well as most; he knew he'd have to find a stream and concoct a new supply of Epizootical Elixir.

By the time the wagon reached the Chittenden farm three other vehicles were sluggishly trailing behind it. A trio of drivers cursed the leader's pace; Doc Merrifield ignored them. Charles awoke when the wagon wheeled into his father's dooryard. He started to stretch and winced.

"Lie still," said Mercy.

"Do as you're told," Doc said. He jumped down and started for the house. A big voice, booming from the barn's dark doorway, checked him.

"Tophet! What is it this time?"

Eratus Chittenden came out of the barn scowling. The big man glared at the strange wagon. Then he saw his neighbors, Nathan Patch and Abner Reed, and shouted a greeting.

"Morning, Nathan! Abner!"

The two looked at each other, turned to Doc Merrifield. Eratus noticed their hesitation and came forward with swift, long strides. "Something the matter?"

The blacksmith nodded. "E-yah, Eratus."

"It's Charles," said Nathan.

"Charles!" Eratus stopped, glanced toward the house, and lowered his voice. "What's happened? He didn't come home! Wasn't here for chores! Why? Speak out!"

Doc Merrifield said, "He's been shot, Mr. Chittenden."

Color slowly drained from the big man's face, then as slowly darkened it. "Shot!" The word was violent. "What sort of nonsense is this? Who're you? Where's my son?"

"He's here in the wagon, Mr. Chittenden."

Eratus charged past them, swung around the tail of the wagon. "Charles," he said. "Charles." He took the tailboard in his strong hands and shook it.

"Hello, Pa," said Charles.

"You blundering idiot!" Eratus, relieved, took refuge in bellowing. His glance missed nothing in the wagon. He noted his son's pallor, the arrangement of the blanket, the girl Mercy. "Ain't I told you never to go hunting with strangers? Too many folks lose all common sense when they pick up a fowling piece! How'd it happen?"

Mercy answered. "He wasn't hunting. It was a duel."

"A duel?" Eratus stepped back as if he'd been struck. He wet his lips, frowning. With a sudden movement he whirled, shot out an arm, and grabbed Doc Merrifield's coat lapels. "Who did it? You?"

"What's done's, done," said Doc. He was pulled up on his toes by the big man's grasp, but he made no attempt to struggle. "It was not my doing. And the boy needs attention, not talk!"

"E-yah!" Eratus thrust the medicine man away. The shouted summons thundered across the barnyard. "Peter! Amos! Henry!" The big man swung back to his stricken son. "Don't worry none, Charles. We'll get you fixed. I'll send Peter to fetch a doctor."

Charles said, "I'm all right, Pa. Doc bandaged me right snug."

"Doc? Doc who? Who's Doc?"

"That's me," admitted the medicine man. "Dr. Portus J. Merrifield. I ain't a regular practicing doctor, but I know a mite about bullet wounds."

A sniff from Eratus displayed suspicion. He beckoned his other three sons to him with a wave of his arm. His face changed as he saw his wife in the doorway of the house. He called, "Mary. Get a bed ready. Downstairs. Charles is hurt."

"Charles?" Mary Chittenden put a hand to her throat.

"E-yah." Eratus sounded curiously gentle. "Now it ain't nothing to fret about. He'll need some tending, that's all. Go on, Mary."

He waited till his wife disappeared, then asked the blacksmith. "Did I lie to her, Abner?"

"I don't know, Eratus."

"Nor I," said Doc. "But I hope not. The wound's clean. The ball went through. It's just a question of healing."

The younger Chittendens ranged themselves behind their father and stared at their brother. None of them spoke, though Henry's eyes were frightened. Charles winked at his youngest brother and said, "It ain't nothing, boys. I hit the other feller, too. It came out even."

"Kill him?" asked Eratus.

"No, Pa."

"Then it ain't even yet. You boys get up in that wagon and hand Charles down to me. Hurry!"

The trio scrambled into the wagon. With Mercy directing, they lifted Charles. Eratus braced himself, held out his arms. He took his son's tall frame against his chest, handling the young man like a baby. "Put your arm around my neck, son. Steady. E-yah." With no apparent effort, Eratus carried Charles toward the house. He called over his shoulder, "Keep out from under foot. Get the details from Nathan and Abner." He didn't notice that Doc and Mercy had accompanied him until the girl pushed open the door. Eratus thanked her with a nod.

Nancy was helping her mother make up a trundle bed in the front room. Eratus eased his son onto the cot. Charles said, "Thanks, Pa. Sorry to make such a fuss. Hello, Ma."

Mary put her palm on her son's forehead. "Well, Charles," she said. "You ain't feverish, anyway." Her voice shook very slightly.

"Blankets," Doc Merrifield ordered. "And a fire in that fireplace. Keep him hot in case of a chill. Get his clothes off. I'll make him a warm drink that'll help him sleep." He touched Eratus on the elbow. "I think we'd better leave him to the women."

"E-yah." The big man nodded. "See you in a couple of minutes, Charles." He followed the medicine man into the kitchen, shutting the door. Eratus stopped in the middle of the room and glared down at the smaller Doc. "Now, mister. I aim to hear the whole story, and I'd like to hear it plain."

Doc Merrifield shrugged. He described the words, the blow, the challenge, and the duel. He spared no one and named names.

311

Throughout the recital Eratus Chittenden's only show of emotion was his heavy breathing.

"That's all, Mr. Chittenden."

"Thank you." Eratus glanced toward the long-barreled squirrel rifle over the kitchen mantel. "If my boy dies, I'll find Dunbar if I have to go all the way to Virginia."

"That won't mend anything."

"Maybe not. I'm beholden to you, Doctor, for taking care of Charles. But there's no denying I think part of the blame's yours for not stopping that duel. You're an older man. You ought to have more sense than either of those young fools!"

"I admit the impeachment," Doc said. "I did try. Charles wouldn't apologize!"

"Naturally!" Eratus roared. "Why should he! The other was at fault! Charles ain't no whining coward!"

The medicine man smiled. He said, softly, "You see?"

Eratus Chittenden glowered, then thawed. He nodded. "E-yah. Guess it was like untying bobcats with their tails lashed together. Blaming you was a mite hasty. I take it back." He paced the room, his boots thumping on the wide planks of the floor. Behind his back one hand clasped his wrist; the other was a tight fist. At each turn he rumbled into speech, but the words were not addressed to the medicine man. Eratus was talking to himself. "Dueling. My son. Outlandish custom. Comes of having strangers here. Southern blackleg! Took advantage! Crack shot, ain't he? Charles should have thrashed him. Slaveholder! Charles is strong. Good blood. Blood?" Eratus stopped and pointed a finger. "Doctor, did he lose much blood?"

Doc was stirring a mixture in a cup. "Enough. But that ain't what I'm afraid of. If he's all right inside, and it don't fester or get poisoned, the bleeding won't matter."

The door opened and both Mercy and Nancy entered. Eratus spoke instantly. "He ain't worse, is he?"

"No, Pa. Ma sent me out."

Mercy said, "Doc. That drink." She took the cup he offered and sniffed it. "Laudanum."

"And hot rum. Make him take it all."

The girl nodded and went back into the sickroom. She put her

312

arm around the wounded man's shoulders. "Here, Charles. Drink this."

"I'm all right, Mercy."

"Do as she says, Charles."

"E-yah. All right, Ma."

Mary and the girl smiled at each other. They were already friends, drawn together by their common task of ministering to Charles. The mother appreciated Mercy's efficient help. Her first suspicions about the girl's presence were gone; Charles spoke to her like a cousin. Now, gazing at Mercy across the bed, Mary realized that she was much younger than she seemed. Her grave, mature manner was deceiving only until one looked close.

After he drank, Charles wanted to talk. But neither of his two nurses would permit it. He didn't bother to argue; he was warm and comfortable. After a while he drifted off to sleep.

Mary Chittenden relaxed and put her head in her hands.

"He'll get well, Mrs. Chittenden," said Mercy. "I'm sure he will."

"I'm sorry." Mary raised her face; her eyes were brimming. "Of course he will. But—well, I wouldn't dare cry in front of Charles or my husband." She smiled. "It would scare Eratus half to death."

"I know. Doc's the same way about me."

"Your father?"

"No." Mercy's voice was low. She glanced down; her fingers plucked at her breast buttons. "Doc ain't my father. He—he found me. I never had any parents. But Doc's just like a real father!" Her defense of the medicine man was vehement.

"I'm sure he is, Mercy."

Charles stirred in his sleep, and both the watchers stiffened alertly. Mary waited till her son was peaceful. Smiling, she whispered a question, "How old are you, Mercy?"

"I think fourteen, about. I don't know for sure."

Fourteen, Mary thought. Only a few years older than my Miley, two less than Nancy. She had married Eratus when she was sixteen, yet this waif seemed much older than her daughter, older than she remembered herself as a bride.

Tossing his head on the pillow, Charles muttered. Then he said clearly, "Lovina."

Mercy started; Mary explained, "It's a girl he knows, Mercy. I think he's fond of her."

"Yes'm. I know." Mercy felt the folds of the letter in the bodice of her dress. She stood up. "I'll be back, ma'am. He ought to sleep a while now. I'll be back." She left the room.

Eratus Chittenden jerked out of his chair and took a step toward Mercy. The girl shook her head at the fear in the big man's eyes.

"He's sleeping, Mr. Chittenden."

"That good, Doctor?"

"Fine, Mr. Chittenden. Just fine."

Mercy went out into the yard. The wagon that had carried Charles to the farm was gone. There was no one in sight but Nathan Patch. The young man was sitting on a stone watching the turnpike, he swung around at the sound of Mercy's step.

"Charles?"

"Asleep," the girl said.

"Better, then." Nathan was genuinely glad. He'd been wondering what his chances would be with Lovina Chester if Charles succumbed. He felt guilty about such speculation. It had bothered him all morning. Even standing beside the pond watching the two stiff figures face each other in the duel, Nathan had been troubled by the sudden thought that Charles and the Southerner might kill each other. He had shaken the thought away; he'd never wished such a thing. But he knew it had come to him as to a man who was considering every possibility in a trade. That was why he so hurriedly took the more optimistic view of Mercy's announcement.

"E-yah. He'll be better after he sleeps."

"Where is everyone?" asked Mercy.

"Mr. Chittenden sent the boys back to work. The wagon driver hurried off soon as he got it straightened out there'd been a duel. And Abner went along to the smithy." Nathan sighed. "I guess I'll mosey along myself. To home." He didn't relish the prospect.

"Do you know where Lovina Chester lives?"

"Lovina? E-yah. The parsonage."

"I know that. And I know it's at a crossroad and across from an inn. But I've never seen it. Are you going that way?"

"E-yah."

"Would you show me the house?"

"E-yah."

Mercy smiled her thanks. She had no idea that Nathan had any interest in Lovina Chester. All she knew was that Charles had

314

quarreled with this Lovina and was upset about it. Mercy was a great believer in desire as a basis for cures. She'd seen too many folks pay for Epizootical Elixir because they wanted it to help them, and she'd even heard that, sometimes, it did. That was why she hadn't torn up the letter from Charles.

They walked out onto the turnpike and went toward Stratton church. There was traffic moving down the road; every thirty yards or so the two drew aside to let a vehicle pass. People were leaving the clearing; it was the early trickle that warned of the flood to come.

Nathan said, "Another hour or so and this pike will be worse than yesterday."

Mercy needed most of her breath to keep up with his long strides. She merely nodded.

Nathan Patch plodded along gloomily. He thought he knew why the girl had inquired about the Chester house. Charles had sent for Lovina.

"Mr. Patch?"

"E-yah?"

"Can you read writing?"

Surprised at the question, Nathan stopped and stared. The girl took a folded sheet of paper from the top of her dress. She said, "You're his friend. You were his second. And I want to be sure I'm doing what's right."

"How's that?"

Mercy unfolded the letter and gazed at it. "I can't read it. Hardly any of it. I can only read big print, and this is writing. It's a letter from Charles to Miss Lovina Chester."

"We ain't got no right to read it!"

"But I have to know. I think it would do Charles a heap of good if she'd come to see him. Make him want to get better. But maybe this letter won't fetch her." She thrust it at Nathan. "Read it to me."

Nathan put a hand out, took it back, reached again and held the letter gingerly. He said, "We ain't got no right to read it." His eyes shifted from left to right—again, again, and again—as he scanned the writing.

"Read it to me," said Mercy, surprised. "I want to know if it'll fetch her."

With a sigh Nathan refolded the page and handed it back. It was a gesture of renunciation. "I know Lovina," he said. "You needn't fret. It'll fetch her."

"You're sure?"

"E-yah. Sure."

"That's fine, isn't it?"

"E-yah." Nathan Patch strode on down the road. Mercy had to skip to stay beside him. If it hadn't been for the frequent pauses necessitated by the carriages that overtook them, she would have been winded long before the settlement came into view.

As they passed between the houses that faced the road Nathan Patch's pace slowed; when they reached the blacksmith shop he came to a full stop. He pointed out the parsonage for Mercy. "You can't miss it. Right there. That's the inn t'other side of the road. I want to tell Abner the latest about Charles." He did not want the Chesters to see him conduct Mercy to their house.

Mercy thanked him and went on. She looked at the parsonage with great interest. Mercy thought it was nice but not grand. Still, it was a lot grander than a red wagon, and for a moment she envied Miss Lovina Chester. Not that she didn't prefer Doc Merrifield for a father to a parson. Mercy didn't like clergymen; several had kicked up a fuss about the Elixir.

She straightened herself, wished she was wearing a bonnet, and walked straight to the front door. Mercy knocked.

The door was opened by a formidable-looking woman. The woman gazed down her nose at Mercy and sniffed.

One of those, thought Mercy, and sniffed right back.

"E-yah?" asked Mrs. Chester.

Mercy was polite. "Miss Lovina Chester lives here?"

"E-yah."

"Can I see her, please? It's important."

Mrs. Chester hesitated. She tried to learn a little more about the reason for this visitor's appearance. "I'm Lovina's mother." Mercy bobbed in a curtsy and offered no information. "I'm not sure my daughter is receiving." Mercy smiled, blinked her eyes, and waited. "If you'd just give me your name . . ." Mrs. Chester stared. She'd been outmaneuvered. She didn't know just how it had been done but the girl was over the threshold.

"Thank you," said Mercy. "But your daughter doesn't know

316

me." She folded her hands together and attempted to look as meek as possible.

Annoyed, Mrs. Chester wasted no more time. "Lovina! Come here! Someone to see you!"

Lovina Chester came into the narrow hallway, saw Mercy, and stopped. She glanced from her mother to the visitor. Lovina said, "Yes?"

The older girl's recognition puzzled Mercy. "Miss Lovina Chester?" she asked. When the other nodded Mercy said, "Mercy Merrifield." She smiled at Mrs. Chester. "Thank you, ma'am."

It was a polite dismissal, and it almost worked. Mrs. Chester took two steps toward the kitchen, then, flushing, swung around. The parson's wife folded her arms and glared at Mercy. She made no further move to leave.

Mercy shrugged and surrendered. She took out the letter and offered it. "This is for you, Miss Chester." Then she watched carefully while Lovina opened the folded paper and read.

"What is it, Lovina?"

The paper started to shake. "Oh, no," said Lovina. "Oh, no." When she looked up from the letter she was frightened, mutely appealing.

"Lovina!" Mrs. Chester reached out for the letter, but her daughter brushed her arm aside. Lovina ignored her mother's exasperated snort.

Mercy relaxed. It's all right, she thought, this girl does love Charles. She answered the unspoken question. "He ain't dead, Miss Chester. But he's bad hurt."

"Who?" Mrs. Chester exploded. "Lovina Chester, if you don't tell me what's going on this instant . . ."

"It's Charles," said Lovina. "Tell me, Mercy."

"Him and that Southern fellow fit a duel. Charles was hurt in the side. Serious. He don't know I brought you the letter. I can't read writing, but I figured out the kind of letter it was, and I thought maybe you'd like to know."

"Dueling is wicked!" Mrs. Chester announced. "Let me see that letter, Lovina."

"No." Lovina folded the sheet. She said, very simply, "Thank you, Mercy. You can tell me the rest as we go."

"Go? Go where?"

317

"Wherever Charles is."

"We took him home."

Mercy was opening the door when Mrs. Chester barred her daughter's way. "Lovina! You can't go dashing off this way! It isn't right! What will the Chittendens think? It isn't as if you could do anything!"

"She can," said Mercy.

"I think so. Please step aside, Mother."

There was nothing forceful about Lovina's speech. Her voice was strained and trembling. But Mrs. Chester stepped back, staring at her daughter as if she'd never seen her before.

The door closed behind the two girls. The parson's wife admitted defeat. It was Charles Chittenden with Lovina; the look on her daughter's face had made that plain. She was concerned with her daughter's happiness and felt momentary anger at Charles. She'd always said he wasn't a good match for Lovina, and now he'd proved her right. Getting mixed up in a duel, Mrs. Chester thought, and being shot. It wasn't at all respectable. Lovina would have her hands full with that man when they were married. She can't say I didn't try to warn her, the mother told herself.

Remembering that Charles might be dying, Mrs. Chester stood for a moment and bowed in silent prayer. She had no intention of allowing God to make Lovina unhappy by punishing young Chittenden. She informed the Almighty that she wished a complete and rapid recovery; Lovina was not to be saddled with an invalid for a husband. When she had given these directions, Mrs. Chester went about her business.

The elderly couple who had spent the night in the Brayton barn hitched up right after a scanty breakfast. They were pleased with yesterday's events and felt that the convenience of having a head start toward home was well worth the expense. When the first wagon rattled past Brayton's the old gentleman cackled at his smartness. His wife agreed with the tolerant patience that comes from a long marriage. But she prodded her husband with bitter comments when he lingered too long in saying farewell to Zilpha Brayton.

Zilpha watched them drive off with hidden amusement. She knew perfectly well what had irked the elder woman. Not that

318

she'd bother about a dry old stick like that, but he had been help-
ful with the morning milking and feeding the stock. Zilpha pressed
her lips together. It was like Lem, she thought angrily, to leave
the farm to run itself while he caroused all night. She wondered
where her husband was, shrugged, and went into the house.

She threw two logs on the kitchen fire and poked them into
place. Somehow she'd expected that this morning would be different, but it wasn't. There were the same dull farm chores; the same
household tasks. It was almost as if yesterday and Isaac Mead
had never happened.

But it did, Zilpha said silently. It happened, and it's going to
happen again. She was surprised and a little proud that she felt
no guilt. She intended to light into Lem for staying away. It was
good policy. He'd be so busy making excuses he'd never suspect
a thing.

Basking in the warmth from the fire Zilpha relived every minute of her meeting with Isaac. She had no faith in the man's
promises, but she intended to see that they were kept. She made
the inevitable comparison between lover and husband, and scornfully decided she was stronger than both. But Isaac had the advantages of being new and sinful; she was tired of Lem. E-yah,
thought Zilpha, I can make them both dance to my tune.

Smiling at the flames, she relished her remembered excitement
and considered how to choose the presents Isaac had offered her.
They would have to be things that Lem wouldn't notice or that
she could explain away.

Zilpha didn't know her husband was in the room until he spoke.
"Morning, Zilpha."

"Lem!" Startled, she turned so abruptly that she caught her heel
in the hem of her skirt and nearly lost her balance. Tugging the
cloth loose, she said, "Do you have to sneak up on a body like that!
Ain't it bad enough I've been worried about you all night without
you trying to scare me half to death."

"What are you scared about?"

Zilpha Brayton looked at her husband. Lem's clothes and boots
were muddy; his best coat was torn. Unshaven, his eyes blood-
shot, he was a model for a picture on the evils of drink. But Lem's
pink-rimmed eyes were fixed and unblinking as he repeated the
question.

"What are you scared about, Zilpha?"

He knows, Zilpha Brayton thought. A shock of fear like the twitching of a nerve passed through her and was gone. She met glare with glare. "You're sight enough to scare an Indian! Did you sleep in somebody's pigsty?"

"You slut."

The whisper seemed to repeat itself until it filled the room. Zilpha saw the purpose come into Lem's face, saw it in the clenching of his fist, the crouch of his shoulders. Stooping, she snatched up the poker and stood at bay.

For a moment neither moved, then Lem lunged.

The poker missed his chin by inches. He felt its wind on his face and jumped back.

Zilpha Brayton took a step and swung the iron again. This time her husband ducked to avoid the blow. Relentlessly, not saying a word, Zilpha pursued, swinging the poker, driving the man before her. She knew what she was doing. She was going to crack Lem's spirit or his skull.

"Zilpha!"

Lem stumbled against the table, dodged around it.

"Stop! Put that down!"

The poker whistled through the air, slammed a corner of the table.

"Zilpha!"

The man turned to run. Zilpha Brayton laughed.

It was mirthless and mocking. Lem Brayton bowed under the gale of laughter and shivered. When it ended, he spoke in a defeated tone.

"You slut."

"What do you aim to do about it?"

"You admit it, then?"

"I ain't admitting nothing. You're doing the name calling. What is it I'm supposed to admit?"

"You know!"

"Maybe. And maybe not. Speak out!"

Still gripping her weapon Zilpha Brayton dared him to make the accusation. She knew Lem was sure of her adultery. He wouldn't have tried to strike her on mere suspicion. The coward, she thought, watching the way he eyed the poker. Once he declared his knowledge there would be warfare between them. The house wouldn't be big enough to hold them both. She had no fear that Lem wanted a public scandal.

"Speak out!"

Lem Brayton was beaten. He refused his wife's challenge. He said, "I couldn't find you at the clearing."

"I couldn't find you! All them folks!"

"I hunted!"

"E-yah. So did I."

Both knew she lied. Both accepted the lie as a necessary concession to morality.

Zilpha Brayton tossed the poker aside with a clatter. "I got tired of speechmaking, Lem. And bands! And Tippecanoe!" A new note came into her voice. "I was looking for you, Lem. Know why?" She taunted him. "Know why?"

Lem Brayton stared. Gulping, he swallowed twice.

She saw the lust swell his face and laughed.

She knew how to handle Lem.

Nothing is a more common characteristic of the American public than the unchanging manner in which it goes home. A few hardy, individual souls make the first move. Others follow in increasing numbers. The bulk of the crowd wavers indecisively and tries to recall the excitement by talk. Then, almost as if by signal, there is a general bustle of preparation and a sudden flood of departure.

All morning the Whig Convention in the clearing on Stratton Mountain had followed this usual pattern. There was neither order nor plan to the dispersal; vehicles plunged out of the field onto the turnpike; horses were wheeled right or left for the descent that started the homeward journey. Some of the earliest to arrive were among the earliest to leave. Villages, townships, clubs, and organizations that had come as units and been greeted with cheers lost their unity and departed as individuals. The Convention's Great Man, Senator Daniel Webster himself, left without fanfare. Except for a few officials no one sped the traveler on his way.

The news that Webster had left spread across the clearing like a rumor of disaster and produced the same effect. It was the awaited signal for striking camp and withdrawing. Tents came down, the canvas collapsing limply; bedding was folded and

packed. Horses and oxen were shoved into their proper shafts.
Parents herded their children together. The delegates hastily wound
up the Convention's business, while a few slipped away before the
final tap of the gavel. The press of vehicles along the turnpike edge
of the clearing thickened until wheel hub rubbed against wheel
hub. The retreat became a rout, with a rout's confusion and violence. Men and beasts so choked the narrow turnpike that the
major portion of the multitude was prevented from leaving the
clearing at all.

Leaning comfortably against the trunk of the tamarack tree,
young Putnam Chester watched the shifting crowd. Seth Purdy
squatted at Put's feet. Both boys were indifferent spectators. Secure
in the knowledge that they didn't have to get anywhere, they were
no longer impressed by the size of the throng. After all, they'd
seen these thousands for two days now, and the novelty was gone.

"Anxious to get to home, ain't they, Put?"

"E-yah." Put nodded. "But they ain't going about it right."

"Packed themselves in tighter than sheep in a shearing pen."

"Tighter than bees in a swarm."

"Or frozen maple syrup." Seth grinned at his friend.

Put returned the grin. They liked the game of trying to outdo
each other describing the crowd's actions. It made them feel very
superior to the noisy, struggling mass. Put said, "They ain't going to
get far that way, Seth."

"E-yah." Seth tugged up a wisp of grass, chewed it. "Be quiet
around here from now on, Put."

"Good riddance."

"You sound like my Pa."

"I ain't turned Democrat," said Put, chuckling. "It was a fine
meeting. A right cracking time. But it ain't nothing I'd want to
happen up here every day."

"Me, neither."

"'Course you got to admit, Seth, that it proves Tippecanoe is
going to win."

"Well," Seth said, frowning. "I ain't saying it proves it. But he's
sure got a whole passel of folks that's for him."

"E-yah. I just wanted to show you. That's why I invited them all
up here."

322

"That was you, eh?"

"You never guessed?" Put widened his eyes in mock surprise.

"Can't say I did, Put. That feller Dan'l Webster fooled me. I figured he had something to do with it." Seth had trouble keeping his voice serious. He always enjoyed Put's foolery.

Put shrugged. "He asked to come. Wanted to see the finest mountain anywhere in the whole world."

"Stratton?"

"Stratton."

"Well, you could hardly refuse if he put it that way."

"E-yah. But the party's over now. They can all go home. You and me got things to do this summer before school starts." Put waved him arms at the multitude in imitation of a woman driving chickens. He turned toward every corner of the wide clearing. "Shoo! Go along, now! Shoo!"

Seth Purdy laughed. He jumped up and made the same motions. "Shoo! Go on home, now! Shoo!"

Put's dog, Cap, came out in three quick bounds from under the speaker's platform where he'd been sleeping. He looked up at his master, then barked at the crowd. Both boys thought the dog's behavior was very funny.

"That's the way, Cap. Drive them home."

"Keep them moving, Cap."

The dog tired of the game first and wandered away. Put and Seth stayed in the tamarack's shade. They were idly speculating on the future of the Tippecanoe log cabin when a somewhat older boy came through the crowd. He was looking around anxiously and, when he saw the two beneath the tamarack, he hurried toward them. He was hatless and barefoot.

"Say," called the stranger.

"E-yah?" asked Put.

The older boy hesitated, then, realizing he was taller and more aged, said, "You two from Bondville? Or anywheres near?"

"No!"

"Fire and brimstone, no!"

"I just wondered," Fred Streeter said. "Because you were both barefoot."

"So're you."

"E-yah." Fred scowled. "That's just it. I did have—I mean . . ."

He blushed and changed the subject abruptly. "Look. You ain't seen a girl with a drum around, have you?"

"A girl?"

"With a drum?"

"My drum!" The drum's owner was indignant. "She stole it. Her name's Patty Fisher, and she's from up around Bondville way. And I've asked practically everybody in the clearing. And I can't find her."

"You won't," said Seth Purdy. "They'll steal anything. That crowd."

Put nodded. "E-yah," he agreed gravely. "That's why me and Seth are guarding this old tamarack." He patted the tree. "We're making sure them roughs don't walk off with it."

Seth snickered. Fred Streeter said, "It ain't a joke."

"Didn't say it was. But how'd you come to leave a drum lying around that way? I'd say a drum was a mite hard to lose, much less get stolen."

"I was asleep." Fred's face turned crimson.

"Then how do you know this girl stole it?"

"I know." Fred couldn't very well explain that the girl had shared his blanket during the night. He'd lost cap and boots as well as his drum. And they weren't all he'd lost, either. Stammering, he said, "Look. If you see this girl hang on to her, will you? Call a sheriff or somebody. My name's Fred Streeter. From Brattleboro. And that's my drum." He strode away, the soles of his feet flashing pink at each step.

"A mite upset, ain't he?"

"Serves him right, Seth. If I owned a drum I wouldn't let no girl within ten feet of it. Feller that shiftless don't deserve to own a drum."

"E-yah. You've got the right of it, Put."

"Let's look around. A drum ain't easy to hide."

They strolled away from the tree and pushed their way through the mass of people. They didn't really search but kept their eyes open. They dodged in front of horses, walked between wagons, weaved through talking groups. They watched a family fold up its tent. Twice they saw drums, but the men who carried them were other musicians and obviously owned the instruments.

Seth grabbed Put's arm. "Put, wait." He pointed to two men a short distance away. One was big-shouldered, with a battered, swollen nose crisscrossed with strips of black plaster. "That's the man I told you about. Name of Lyman."

"The one your Pa licked?" Put stared and whistled. "He looks it all right." The boy grunted as a movement by the second man revealed a gleam of metal at the waistcoat. "Seth, that's a sheriff. You don't figure this Lyman is aiming to sic the sheriff on your Pa?"

"Why, Put? He got beat fair."

"E-yah. But he looks mean enough for anything. And why else would he be talking to a sheriff?"

"He's looking for a runaway bound boy. I told you. That's how the trouble started last night."

"Even so." Put was reluctant to give up his interesting conclusion. "We'd better keep out of Lyman's way. Seeing you might remind him."

They turned and doubled on their tracks, putting several carriages between themselves and Joe Lyman. A loud argument between two drivers brought the boys on the run. They listened while the men shouted insults at each other, wandered away when the difference ended in muttered insults.

"I was hoping there might be a fight," Put complained.

Seth Purdy thought of his father's struggle with Lyman and bit his lip. He spoke slowly. "I guess I've had my fill of fighting, Put."

"You mean us? Day before yesterday?"

"Huh?" Seth grinned and put a finger to a bruise left on his cheek. "No, I wasn't thinking about us."

"Last night, then. Your Pa."

"E-yah."

"Fire and brimstone!" Put said. He kicked at a shard of bean pot discarded by some camper. "All right for you to say you've had your fill! You've seen a fight! I haven't!"

They examined a now deserted camp site, testing the beds of boughs critically. They didn't hunt for souvenirs. There were too many people still around and they considered such scavenging beneath both their dignity and years. Besides, as Put pointed out, the clearing was theirs; they could search it at their leisure any time they wanted.

They strolled up toward the higher edge of the clearing and gazed down across the slight slope at the packed thousands. The throng was alive with movement, but neither boy could see that any progress had been made toward emptying the field.

"Mite different from yesterday, ain't it, Put?"

"E-yah. No music."

"How many bands was there? A dozen?"

"Likely. I counted ten."

"Which one did you like best, Put?"

Three days before they had never heard a band. Now they were critics, and Put weighed his answer carefully. He said, "I don't know. I think maybe the one that camped over on the east side of the clearing. The biggest one."

"E-yah. They were loudest, anyway."

"Which did you?"

Seth considered. "The first one," he said loyally. He whistled a few bars of a march. He broke off abruptly and stared. "Put."

His companion knew the tone; it was the same one Seth used when he saw game out hunting. Automatically Put glanced at Seth's eyes, followed their direction.

"The red wagon, Put. The medicine man's wagon."

A boy's head, blond hair gold-flecked by the sunlight, was visible at the rear of Doc Merrifield's wagon. Poked between the side of the wagon and the blanket that curtained its back, the head seemed bodiless. It turned as the boy gazed around and Put Chester, watching, was reminded of a wary turtle. Like a turtle, too, was the way in which the head suddenly disappeared.

Put looked at Seth. More than anyone else the two boys had made it their business to know every interesting detail of the Convention. Either could have told the number of buttons on Webster's coat or how many pieces the Methodist Election cake had made. Put said, "That medicine feller had a girl with him, didn't he?"

"E-yah."

"That wasn't no girl."

"No."

"Didn't see no boy with them, did we?"

"Nope."

With one impulse they walked toward the red wagon. They looked around carefully. There was no one within earshot. Put leaned against the wagon's tailboard. He kept his voice low.

"You in there!"

326

There was no sound from within. The blanket hung motionless. Seth reached out and twitched a corner of it.

"You hiding?" asked Put. "Come on, talk up. We ain't going to hurt you. We just want to know."

They listened, could hear nothing. Put Chester snapped his fingers. "I know, Seth. I'll bet it's the runaway boy. E-yah! I'll bet!"

Seth addressed the curtain. "Are you?"

After a long pause a voice, muffled and desperate, said, "Go away. Leave me alone."

Without exchanging a word the two boys drew aside the blanket, climbed into the wagon, and let the curtain drop back into place. There was no light in the wagon's interior, and they stood still. Put spoke into the darkness. "Where are you? It's all right. We don't like that Lyman, either."

There was a rustle of movement. "Joe Lyman? You know him?"

"My father," said Seth Purdy, "thrashed him."

"E-yah. You got a candle or something, boy? I can't see a thing."

A match flared to show a boy's face. The tiny flame moved, stopped over a candle, made another flame. The blond-haired boy said, "You ain't aiming to tell on me?"

"What do you think we are?" said Seth, with scorn.

"Not us. You are the runaway, ain't you?"

"E-yah. My name's Peter Blodgett."

Put introduced himself and Seth. Solemnly, the three shook hands. "He's looking for me, ain't he?" asked Peter.

The other two nodded. "E-yah," said Put. "I guess he is. But what are you doing here all alone?"

Peter shrugged. "Mercy told me to stay hid. She followed Doc. They went off early. To the duel."

"Duel?"

"What duel? Was there a duel?"

"E-yah. With pistols."

"Pistols?" Seth nudged Put. "That Southern feller."

"E-yah."

Put Chester gazed at Peter admiringly. Well, thought Put, maybe it ain't all over in spite of folks going home. Duels and runaways! He shook his head with pleased wonder. There seemed no end to the entertainments a Convention could bring with it. Settling back on a cot, Put said, "Tell us about it, Peter."

327

Few men of voting age, in the election year 1840, had any bashfulness about talking politics. Even those citizens who could not vote—and their number grew less each year—were ready with opinion and argument to support the candidates they would vote for if they could. Nowhere in the Union was the topic more popular than in the state of Vermont; nowhere in that state had there been more conjecture, more acrimonious debate, more concentration on the single subject of politics, than on Stratton Mountain.

The leader in this one-track marathon of polemics was, avowedly, the sawmill owner, Joel Patch. Even the most ardent Whigs in the neighborhood were tired of Patch's wordy discourses. The July Convention in the big clearing might serve as a political catharsis for many of those who attended, but no one who knew Patch expected it to do so for him. His neighbors, from parson to spinster, would have testified it was impossible for Joel Patch to refrain from commenting on the election, barring lockjaw, for a single hour. But, although he had risen from bed the morning after Daniel Webster's speech fully determined to crow about its irrefutable success, Joel Patch fooled everybody.

Of course he talked—as a matter of record, Patch hardly stopped talking after he first guided his banker-guest down to the mill to view his circular saw. He wept, swore, blasphemed, and cried out for vengeance. He never mentioned Tippecanoe or Tyler or even Van Buren. Not even Joel Patch believed that the President had wrecked his sawmill.

Humphrey Dunklee, the banker, made sympathetic noises.

Tim Frost and Lizzie Galusha were silently aghast. The cook seemed the more surprised of the two by the wreckage.

Clem Galusha swore as loudly and almost as often as his employer. To hear Clem tell it, he had loved that circular saw as if it were his child. Only his wife's stern glance prevented Clem from elaborating this theme too greatly.

From dawn till past noon Patch stormed and screamed and ranted. When Nathan Patch finally came home, trudging up the lane, his father had finished his inspection of the damage, but he was just getting his second wind denouncing the outrage. Nathan, pricked by the words his father had chosen, ran toward the sound of his voice.

"Pa!" he called. "Pa! What's happened?"

It was the wrong question. Patch choked and stopped cursing. The sudden silence was startling. The sawmill owner, glaring, strutted up to his taller son like a bantam attacking a large rooster. "You!" said Patch, poking out an accusing finger. "Where in thunder have you been?" Without waiting for an answer, he went on, rage lashing each sentence louder than the preceding one. "Out all night! Gallivanting! Rampsing around! Couldn't be home protecting the property, could you? Had to be off idling and drinking! You worthless, spineless, addlepated son of the devil's spawn!"

"Pa!" Nathan was stunned.

"Don't Pa me, you whelp! Who wrecked the mill?"

"The mill? The sawmill?"

"E-yah, e-yah, e-yah!" Patch rattled the words like a stick along a picket fence. "How many mills have we got? Wrecked! Smashed! The circular saw hammered to a pulp! Don't you understand English?"

Nathan stared at the others. Mr. Dunklee nodded. Clem Galusha said, "Some dirty vandal did it, Nathan. Ain't hardly a part untouched. Take days to fix."

"Fix!" Patch shook both fists at the heavens. "It'll take money to buy a new saw! Somebody's going to pay for this! I'll find the culprit if it takes till doomsday!"

Lizzie Galusha said nothing. Her husband spat and said, "Democrat, likely."

"E-yah." The banker agreed. "It's possible."

Patch's face was so red and white by turns that it looked mottled. He had no patience with politics when it came to catching a malefactor. "Democrat or Whig! Whoever it is! I'm out hard money, and he's going to pay! I'll find him! I'm going back to that clearing and fetch the sheriff! What kind of law have we got in this country when a man's property ain't safe? Nathan!"

"Pa?"

"Turn the Morgans around. We're going back to the Convention and . . ." He stopped, staring at the bewilderment on his son's face and visibly struggling with a thought. "Nathan. I didn't hear the chaise. Where's the team?"

"Team? Why—what team, Pa?"

"The team! The team! My Morgans!"

"Ain't they here?"

Patch jumped straight up in the air and landed kicking. He ripped out with an oath that made the banker gulp and glance up at the sky. "Have you gone daft entirely, Nathan? You took the chaise and team from the clearing."

"No, Pa. You did!"

"Don't tell me what I did! I come home with Mr. Dunklee! The chaise was gone from its place on the turnpike! It wasn't where we left it!"

"I know that," said Nathan. "I thought you'd taken it. I walked home."

"You lost my Morgans! And the best chaise in the county!" Patch was beside himself; with hands curved like claws he reached for his son.

Nathan stepped back and pushed the hands away. "I lost nothing, Pa! I ain't taking the blame for that!"

"They were in your care!"

"No more than in yours! You drove them!"

"Don't contradict your elders!"

"Don't call me a thief!"

Startled by such mutiny, Patch for once lost his voice. He sputtered. Father and son glared at each other; their likeness was never more apparent. The rougher-hewn, taller Nathan had his jaw thrust forward in exactly the same manner as his parent. Joel Patch might have been storming at his own portrait, drawn much larger than life-size. Even the shrewd speed with which the son took advantage of his father's speechlessness was a trait worthy of the elder man.

"I ain't standing the blame for what I didn't do, Pa! If the Morgans are gone, it's no doing of mine! You could do a lot better than waste time swearing and calling names!" Surprised at his own temerity, Nathan plunged on. I've lost Lovina, he thought recklessly, and I ain't taking no more from anybody. "You'd better get after them that did the taking and the wrecking!"

"Don't you tell me what to do!"

"Somebody ought! You ain't showing good sense!"

Shaking with rage Patch again tried to clutch Nathan, and again the son brushed away his father's fingers. Nathan said, "Keep your hands to yourself, Pa. Your days of whipping me are over! E-yah! And of telling me what to do! And nagging and prodding at me the whole day!"

330

"You're my son! By thunder, while you're under my roof . . ."

"I'm getting out, Pa."

"You? You ain't got the gumption!"

"Wait and see," said Nathan. He turned on his heel and strode toward the house. He didn't slow his step or turn his head when his father bellowed.

"Nathan Patch! You come back here!"

The young man went on; a screen of bushes hid his figure.

"Nathan! You hear me?"

The only reply was a slamming door.

Patch rocked back and forth, heel and toe, for a moment. He spat in the direction of the house, turned to the others. His features might have been carved from ice; his eyes were hard. He spoke, rasping but no longer shouting.

"My apologies, Mr. Dunklee. It seems the Convention was an excuse to rob me right and left!"

The onlookers, held motionless by the fury of the family fight, quailed before the man's cold vindictiveness. Lizzie moved closer to her husband. Tim Frost looked everywhere but at his employer. Humphrey Dunklee took off his hat and mopped his brow.

"You can't blame the Convention," said the banker. "Because some scoundrels took advantage of it." Even as he spoke Dunklee realized that the Whigs would get no further contribution from Joel Patch.

The sawmill owner grunted. "You'll excuse me. I aim to make sure the law does something about this! Tim! Saddle the bay!"

"E-yah!"

"Clem!"

"What is it, Joel?"

"Fetch the horse pistol. And both rifles."

"Both?"

"You're going with me."

"Oh. E-yah, Joel. Sure."

Lizzie followed her husband up the slope that led to the house. The woman kept her voice low. "Be careful, Clem. No drinking, now. Mind! You're likely to blab the whole thing if you drink."

"Not a drop." Clem glanced over his shoulder. "God, he's wild. Joel'd rather lose his right arm than that Morgan team."

"E-yah. But it blew good our way. Makes it look like somebody

331

was out after Joel good and proper. Wrecked the mill *and* stole the horses. I hope you never catch the thief."

"But—why?"

"You fool! Don't you think the feller that took the team knows he didn't touch the saw?"

Clem stopped. "Liz. Liz, I'm scared."

His wife took his arm and shook it. "Stay scared. Stay good and scared. You don't know nothing about that mill! Nothing! Just don't let on you do!"

"I wish we could leave like Nathan."

"Later. Next fall, maybe. Not before. Now come on. Don't get him thinking things about us."

They went into the house. Lizzie watched Clem collect the guns and leave. The cook went into the hall and started up the stairs. Mrs. Dunklee popped out of the parlor, smiled timidly, and popped back in again. The banker's wife knew something had happened, but she'd been trained not to ask questions.

Lizzie found Nathan in his room. His sister Sarah was wringing her hands as the young man piled his clothes into a bundle. Lizzie said, "You really aiming to leave, Nathan?"

"E-yah."

"Oh, Nathan," Sarah said, sniffling.

"There ain't nothing for me here, Sarah. It's his house and his mill and his trading! Don't worry about me. I'll make out."

"But where'll you go?"

"I ain't decided. Bennington, maybe. Or Brattleboro. Or farther. York State, maybe. Over to the Erie Canal. There's money being made over there. I think I'll try to hitch up with one of them railroads. Steam cars are the coming thing."

"Got it all figured, ain't you?" asked Lizzie.

Nathan grinned. "Pays a man to figure things."

"You got any money?"

The young man stopped lashing his bundle and glanced eagerly at his sister. "You got some, Sarah?" His face fell with disappointment when the girl shook her head. Nathan turned toward the cook.

Lizzie laughed. "You know better, Nathan."

The big shoulders shrugged. "It don't matter. I'll make out."

"Nathan. What about Lovina Chester?"

"That's one of the reasons I'm going." Nathan gazed at his sister;

332

his hands fumbled as if searching for words. There was no great affection between them, but each felt the necessity of speaking.

A tear trickled down the girl's cheek.

The brother cleared his throat. He said, "I'll write." He turned away as if finished, swung back. "Don't let Pa marry you to a wood lot or a forge. Pick your own man, Sarah. That's another reason I'm going. He liked Lovina, but he's likely to use me for trade now." It was a longer speech than he'd intended, and he stopped as suddenly as he'd begun. No sense, he thought, in listing all my reasons. Charles Chittenden had beaten him. The neighbors would laugh. He'd half wanted to leave even before his father's attack had fused the wish into a definite intention.

Lizzie said, "Good-by."

"E-yah." Nathan chuckled. "At least this is one day I'm sure of a lift down the mountain. I can pick and choose."

From outside the house came Joel Patch's high-pitched hail.

"Nathan! Nathan Patch! I want you!"

Nathan jumped, betrayed by habit. Angry at his reaction he said, "And that's the best reason of all!" He snatched his bundle from the bed and went out, clattering down the stairs.

Joel Patch, mounted, was waiting in front of the house. He looked even smaller atop the big-boned work horse. The sawmill owner scowled down at his son, shifted his glance to the bundle, darted it back to Nathan's face. He spoke like a man driving a hard bargain.

"There'll be no coming back."

"There'll be no coming back."

Clem Galusha, standing at Patch's stirrup, could hardly tell the two voices apart.

Lips tight, Joel Patch swung the horse's head and kicked it into action. He went off at a shambling trot with Clem holding the stirrup leather and running alongside.

They found the Jamaica road crowded with folk returning from the Convention. The exodus was at its height. Downhill the pace of the long line was a little faster than uphill, but the road was no wider. Patch rode his horse along the edge like a man bucking a river's current by keeping against the bank. The heavy horse was off the muddy track as often as he was on it. Patch gave every team and vehicle a sharp glance. He knew his chances of seeing his property were small, but he was not the man to miss a trick.

333

Clem was winded before they'd gone half a mile. The hired man's exertions of the previous day had weakened him; his leg began to hurt. He limped along for a few yards and let go of the strap. Patch whirled in the saddle, angry, but Clem waved him on. "I'll cut cross-lots. Quicker!" he shouted.

Using his reins as a whip Patch kept the big horse at its best speed, a slow, heavy-footed gallop that lifted great clods from the roadbed. The sight of the lone rider pounding along in the direction opposite from theirs brought comments from many of the travelers.

"Headed wrong, ain't you?"

"Meeting's over, mister."

"Hey, there! You're late, ain't you?"

"E-yah. Must have misread your calendar!"

"Been coming for days, mister?"

"Trade that horse, friend. He didn't make it!"

"Got a message from Van Buren!"

"E-yah! Wants to stop the Convention!"

"Step along, Democrat! We're bound t'other way!"

"Go-o-oin' on a wolf hunt?"

Joel Patch gave no indication that he heard a single word. He bounced in the saddle, arms flapping, but each jolt along his spine stiffened his resolution. When he came to the crossroad where the stream of vehicles eddied and split, Patch cast one agonized look after the conveyances retreating down the turnpike and turned his steed toward the clearing. His neighbors stared as he thundered through the settlement, but Patch ignored them. Between Stratton church and the clearing Patch met a hundred teams; none was his. Several pedestrians leaped from before his horse and shouted curses after him.

He had to rein in at the press of traffic surging from the clearing. The tired horse was blowing, but Patch walked him straight into the crowd. In an instant he was surrounded by protesting humanity. Men swore at him; a woman screamed. One indignant farmer grasped his bridle. Patch's glare was so baleful that the farmer let go and stepped back, gulping. The driver of a barouche swung his whip at the rider, but the lash was too short to reach.

Patch rose in his stirrups and yelled. "Captain! You there! Captain!"

The Captain, harried and weary, turned. Recognition grew as

Patch came closer. "Mr. Patch, isn't it? Just the man I wanted to see."

The greeting surprised Patch into forgetting his purpose. "See? What for?"

"That bill for those shingles." The Captain laughed. "The whole committee was tickled at your idea of using them for plates. But they were wondering if—being a leading Whig and strong for the party's choice—you wouldn't like to call the price of them shingles a contribut . . ."

"No!" Patch interrupted; he pounded his fist on his thigh. "No, no, no! I want my money for them like we agreed! I aim to get payment in full!"

"E-yah." The Captain sighed. "Well, your bill will be met in due time."

"It better be! Where's the sheriff?"

The Captain's mouth popped open. "The sheriff? Now, hold on, Mr. Patch. All the bills have to wait until . . ."

"I want the sheriff! I've been robbed! Horse thieves! Vandals! I want to see the sheriff at once!"

"He's around somewhere," said the Captain. "He ain't left yet." With a cool nod, he turned and walked away.

Joel Patch stared after the politician and cursed him. The robber, he thought. Tried to skin me on that shingle deal. Whigs! Thieves! Bad as Democrats! Steal a man's horses and make a shambles out of his mill!

He glared around the clearing, trying to find the sheriff in the noisy multitude. He cursed the sheriff. He cursed the crowd, cursed it by villages, by townships, by delegations, by bands. There were too many people to curse individually so Patch lumped them all together in one resounding string that mentioned their habits, ancestry, and deceit. The silent, heartfelt, mass damnation ended with political references. Beneath his breath he blasted the souls of Daniel Webster, Tippecanoe, and Tyler too.

"I wish," said Joel Patch, muttering between his teeth, "I'd never heard of the Whigs or their Goddam, thieving convention!"

> I got a toothache,
> An earache,
> A bellyache.
> A pain in my left side;
> A pimple on my nose!

The chorused singing ended with shouts and laughter. Spinning along behind the neat trot of the matched Morgans, the chaise was far out on the Bondville road and rapidly increasing the distance between itself and the Stratton clearing. Jabez Tute was driving. Beside him Patty Fisher beat raggedly on a drum. The girl wore a militia cap on the back of her head, and her slim legs ended in boots that looked much too big.

"God's blood," said Oliver Butler. "It was a frolic after all! And you're riding home like a queen, Dorcas!" He tickled the blowzy girl. Dorcas White squirmed, giggling.

The Dale brothers watched interestedly. Little Wat Fisher stood up on the rear seat of the chaise and doffed his tricorne. He bowed, right and left. He said, "Ho! Look at me. I'm Dan'l Webster coming to make a speech! Make way there, varlets!" He puffed out his cheeks and thumped his chest. "Fellow citizens! I greet you from on top a bloody cloud!"

A rock in the road jolted the chaise and tumbled Wat on top of Dorcas. The girl squealed, and young Butler pushed the boy away. "Set!" he said. "You're as big a bag of wind as yon Webster!"

Nudged by his brother, Cedric Dale spoke. "Why can't we keep the chaise, Jabez?"

Jabez Tute swore impatiently. "I told you, didn't I? Folks got eyes, ain't they? This ain't no shillingsworth, twopenny cart! We'll diddle them all by ditching the chaise when we're nigh home."

"We could sell it," suggested Wat.

"Get half price and be clapped in irons before it's spent? No! We'll sell the horses, maybe. Anyway, we can hide them a while. Cuff the next one that asks, Noll."

"Aye, aye, Jabez."

Patty Fisher said, "It's a handsome team. Who owns it?"

"Some fool with more gold than brains." Jabez shrugged and grinned. "I'll wager he's fit for bedlam this minute."

"Them Whigs are all miser rich," said Butler.

"Who you for, Jabez?"

"For?" Jabez glanced at Patty in surprise.

"E-yah. Like them back there was all for Tippecanoe and against Van Buren."

"That Dutchman!"

"York State bastid!"

336

"We ain't for him, are we, Jabez?"

Jabez frowned, thinking. "Guess not. But it ain't no skin off our noses either way. We ain't got no say."

"Why not?"

"It's our country, ain't it?"

"Why ain't we?"

The leader pushed back his coonskin cap and scratched his head. "I don't know. But we ain't. Maybe we live too far up in the hills. Or maybe we don't suit. They got rules, you know, same as joining a church."

"Church! God's blood! Ever been to church, Dorcas?"

"You stop, Noll Butler. 'Course I been."

"They learn you this?"

"Now, stop!"

"Patty," said Wat. "Let me beat the drum some, huh? Let me?"

"You'll break it."

"I won't, either. Come on. I'll tell Ma how you got it."

"Ma won't care. But be careful with it." The girl passed the drum to her brother.

Wat patted her shoulder and said proudly, "A drum and boots! You're sharp at filching, Patty."

"I didn't steal nothing." The girl's laugh was throaty and suggestive. "He got full measure. He was a nice lad." Again she laughed.

Wat Fisher began to pound the drum. He sang, and the others joined in. The stolen chaise rattled on.

> Home came our goodman at e'en,
> And home came he,
> And there he saw a man
> Where a man shuldna be.
> "How's this now, Kimmer?
> "How's this?" quo he,
> "How came this carle here
> Without the leave o' me?"

The banging passage of the many vehicles jolting down the mountain shook the windows of the Chittenden farmhouse and penetrated Charles Chittenden's slumber. He stirred and began to dream. It was a wild dream and very vivid. Charles saw himself and Lovina Chester atop a careening log cabin on wheels. Whitefoot was in the shafts, galloping at a headlong pace that sent the landscape whirling past. Faster and faster they went. He and Lovina were fleeing. A lone horseman pursued, a giant on a giant steed. The giant's face was sometimes Tom Dunbar's and sometimes Nathan Patch's and sometimes he had two heads and looked like both. The pursuer kept firing an inexhaustible supply of pistols at Lovina and Charles. They dashed on and on and suddenly swept into a familiar clearing. Safety was just ahead, and Lovina smiled. But Charles saw the tall tamarack tree sway and topple. He tried to cry out, to warn Lovina. The black trunk loomed over them, blotting out the sun, falling. It crashed down on them, and he felt the pain in his side.

Charles woke in a cold sweat. Lovina was bending over him, and he believed he was still dreaming. He tried to rub the sleep from his eyes.

"It's all right, Charles," said Lovina.

"Lovina!" He put out an arm, wanting to touch her to be sure. His fingers gripped a warm, real hand that pressed back. He said again, with mixed relief and wonder, "Lovina!"

"E-yah." Lovina grinned and winked at him.

"I—I was dreaming."

"I know. I was fearful you'd hurt yourself the way you tossed." Suddenly shy, the girl put his arm back under the covers and straightened his pillows. "I'll call your mother."

"Wait." Charles looked around, saw they were alone. "Lovina, who told you? How'd you know?"

"Mercy brought the letter."

"The devil! I told her . . ."

Lovina put her hand over his mouth. "I know. But I'm glad she didn't. It's the nicest letter ever." Her cheeks felt warm, but she looked him in the face. "I—if you meant what you wrote, I'll wait. I—there's never been anyone else, Charles. I—I love you, too." She blurted the last sentence and turned scarlet. "There! I said it."

"There'll be no waiting."

Her fingers muffled the words, but she heard him. Charles captured her hand, kissed it, and held it. He said, "You had the right of it, Vina. No more waiting. Out there this morning I found out. Planning and waiting ain't always sense. I never planned to fight no duel, but I might have got killed all the same."

338

"Charles!"

"E-yah. We're going to be married. Soon as we can." Charles grinned. "I mightn't be so lucky next time."

"There'll be no next time, Mr. Chittenden. And you're not well yet."

"Well enough. Sit on the bed. I'll show you."

"No." Lovina glanced toward the door.

"We're going to be married."

"We'd better be." Lovina chuckled. "With me alone in a man's bedroom."

"Sit down."

"Your wound."

"It's fine. I don't even feel it unless I move."

"Then don't move. Don't move at all. Let me." She sat on the edge of the bed, held his face in her hands. They kissed. Lovina sighed happily and thought it the best kiss she'd ever had. Bracing herself carefully, she laid her cheek to his. After a while she uttered a sound that was half snort, half chuckle.

"What?" asked Charles, not moving.

"Just thinking."

"What?"

She sat back and grinned boldly. "Oh, my! Just think when you're all healed!" Lovina smoothed her hair. "I'm a brazen baggage, Charles."

"E-yah," agreed Charles. He sounded very pleased.

"Don't go telling it around," Lovina said. She went toward the door, opened it. "Mrs. Chittenden. Everybody. He's awake now."

A moment later the room was crowded. Mary Chittenden went straight to her son's bed. Her husband beckoned Doc Merrifield forward. Mercy stayed by the door.

The medicine man looked at Charles, felt his head, and smiled. Doc said, "How're you feeling, Charles?"

"Hungry."

"Thank God!" Eratus Chittenden's prayer was heartfelt and loud. As far as the big man was concerned a desire for food was a sure sign of health. "He'll be all right now."

"Easy," said Doc Merrifield. "Easy. He's going to have to stay quiet for some days yet. And I wouldn't go stuffing him too much. I think Charles is on the mend, but it's a mite early to be sure. He ain't feverish, and his color's good. If the wound heals proper . . ."

Charles said, "It will. Shucks, Doc. I cut my foot worse with an axe when I was nine."

"E-yah. That's right. I remember."

"So do I, Eratus," Mary Chittenden said.

"Just to be on the safe side," said Doc. "I'm going to take a look. But maybe you folk'd rather have a more regular doctor."

Eratus looked at his wife. Mercy said, quickly, "Doc's cared for dozens of shooting wounds. You know as much as any sawbones, Doc."

"You've managed so far," said Charles. "No sense changing horses when there's no need. Doc patched me up, Lovina." He smiled at the girl. "And Mercy."

"I've thanked Mercy." Lovina smiled. "Thank you, too, Doc."

Mary Chittenden glanced from Lovina to her son. She saw how matters stood. Well, she thought, I've always liked Lovina. But I do wish they'd managed to settle things before Charles risked his neck. She said, "We all thank you. Since it had to happen I'm glad that Dr. Merrifield was at hand. And, of course, Mercy." She turned to smile at the latter and stared instead. Except for Charles, whose bed faced the other way, the others followed Mary's stare.

Mercy was gazing out the door into the kitchen. From the other room came a voice, polite and Southern. "Mr. Dunbar's compliments, miss. And we'd be obliged to learn about the condition of the young gentleman."

"It's the slave!"

"Hoc!"

"The nigger!"

"The devil!" Eratus roared and reached the door in two strides. There was no mistaking the big man's purpose. Wife and son called out together.

"Eratus!"

"Pa! Wait!"

"Wait? I'm going to boot him off my land!"

"No, Pa. Please." Charles spoke to his father, but he was looking at Lovina. "If Mr. Dunbar is with his man, I'd like to have a few words with him."

Eratus said, "I intend to!"

340

"Pa. It was a fair fight. And it's mine."

Eratus struggled to control his temper. "Thunderation!" he said, storming. "Ain't that slaveholder caused enough trouble!" He glared at Hoc. The Negro stood, silent, respectful, outside the kitchen door. "Where's your master?"

"Mr. Tom's right outside, sir."

"Fetch him!"

"Yes, sir." Hoc bowed and disappeared.

The group in the sickroom changed position without conscious thought. Lovina stepped closer to the bed. Eratus ranged himself beside his wife. Doc Merrifield and Mercy drew aside, less hostile. When Tom Dunbar entered the room he paused, aware of enmity.

The Virginian's left sleeve was empty and neatly pinned across the bulging breast of his jacket. Tom carried his hat in his right hand. He bowed, graceful but uneasy.

"Could you all inform me if Mr. Chittenden is badly hurt?"

"Mr. Dunbar."

Tom located the speaker and moved around the bed. He faced Charles and showed his relief. "You're looking well, sir."

Charles reached out and took Lovina's hand. "Mr. Dunbar. I don't know how you do these things in your part of the country. We ain't used to duels much up here. But Miss Chester has done me the honor of deciding to be my wife."

Eratus Chittenden opened his mouth, closed it. His wife's sigh was audible.

Looking at Tom Dunbar, Lovina blushed but raised her head. Land, she thought. I hope he isn't remembering how he kissed me. As she saw expression follow expression across Tom's face the girl's confusion changed to surprise.

Something cracked the Southerner's smooth façade. First, puzzled but polite, he started a flowery compliment. "Miss Lovina, may I wish you every . . ." He stopped and paled. Awkwardly, Tom said, "Mr. Chittenden, sir. You—you recall our argument? The—the difference that led us to the—field of honor?"

"E-yah."

Tom Dunbar fumbled for words. He realized that a ghastly mistake had been made. Jove, he thought, I might have gotten myself killed in error. The prospect appalled him. He said, "A—an argument on the merits of certain horses? Sir. My apologies. I—I declare. Believe me, sir, to use one of your own expressions, I—I was discussing a horse of an entirely different color."

"What in thunder is he talking about?"

Charles ignored his father's muttered question. He gazed at the Virginian for a long time, then laughed. He said, "I believe you, sir. I figure we've both played the fool."

"My fault, sir. There's no possible excuse. A gentleman should hold his liquor and his tongue, sir." Tom was sincere; he still remembered the duel and his fear.

"Hard cider ain't a punch, Mr. Dunbar." Charles grinned. He released Lovina and held out his hand. "Quits, sir?"

"I am honored, sir." Tom shook the offered hand. "And my congratulations concerning Miss Lovina." He had recovered his poise, and the words came smoothly. He bent in a courtly bow. "I wish you every happiness, Miss Lovina. And I thank God that our unfortunate duel didn't end in tragedy." This time his bow included the entire company. "Farewell to you all."

The white hat flashed as he turned and went out. Eratus Chittenden followed him into the kitchen and shut the door. The big man said, "You. Dunbar."

"Sir?"

"I'm Charles's father."

"Sir. It was all a dreadful mistake and . . ."

"E-yah." Eratus interrupted. "Never mind the pretty speeches. Been a mite too much speechmaking around here lately. You leaving?"

"Yes, sir."

Tom Dunbar spoke like a truant schoolboy. The role of the perfect Southern gentleman was shaken by the other's stern hostility. Behind his master Hoc worriedly watched Eratus.

"Good." Eratus, for once, was not shouting. "I ain't asking anything about the cause of that duel, Dunbar. That's between you and Charles. I'm hoping it's over and done."

"It is, sir."

"Maybe. But it ain't over if my son collapses later. It sometimes happens. If Charles dies, young man . . ." Eratus paused and spaced each word evenly. "I'll find you and kill you."

Hoc's gulp was loud. Tom Dunbar tried to stare Eratus down, swallowed, and looked away.

342

The powerful voice went on, low and filled with cold promise. "There won't be no dueling nonsense. I don't hold with that tom-foolery. You're dangerous. Like a mad dog. And I will shoot you down like one. That's all. Get out."

Slave and master left without a word. They were on their horses and in the stream of carriages before Hoc spoke. The Negro said, "He meant it, Mr. Tom."

"He did." Tom Dunbar couldn't control an involuntary shiver.

"That ain't no way for a gentleman to talk."

The master rode on in silence. He was thinking. Girls and death and dueling pistols were all mixed together in his mind. I don't understand these people, Tom told himself. I came here to witness their politics and fool with their girls. They take both a little too seriously for my taste. The fact that he might have been killed in mistake horrified him. He wasn't sure just what he had said about Miss Annis Rockcliff, but he knew he hadn't said anything about Miss Lovina Chester. With deep self-reproach he listed the events of his visit to Stratton Mountain. There was Annis; he'd failed to hold his liquor; he'd provoked a tavern brawl; he'd disgraced his grandfather's dueling pistols. He didn't try to excuse his conduct during the duel. He'd escaped more lightly than his opponent because he was the better shot, but he'd been afraid.

I've learned my lesson, Tom Dunbar decided. I'm going to change. No more wildness and less drinking. In a sudden contrite resolve he determined to be more circumspect in his conduct with the fairer sex. He knew he'd never fight another duel.

"Mr. Tom?"

"Yes, Hoc?"

"Where we going now, Mr. Tom, sir?"

"Home, Hoc."

"Home? Virginia?"

"That's right." Thomas Jefferson Dunbar slowly grinned. The Chittendens and Lovina Chester faded before the memory of Annis. Wouldn't hurt anything to pay his respects. He said, "After we've visited a place called Burlington."

"Burlington? Where's that at?"

"Oh, we'll find it, Hoc. We'll find it." He touched the black gelding. Ebony broke into a canter. Keeping to the side of the road, they began to pass the crowded vehicles.

Hoc rode behind his master. The slave looked back over his shoulder at the mountain they were descending. Folks that live in that Stratton place, Hoc thought, are just plain crazy. He wished that Mr. Tom would forget sightseeing and go straight home, but he knew it wouldn't be that way. Hoc sighed. He said to his horse's ears, "Wonder what sort of scrape he'll find to get into this time!"

When the late afternoon sun threw the shadow of the tamarack tree across the deserted speaker's platform, the throng still left in the clearing numbered hundreds instead of thousands. These, the rearguard of the giant Convention, were the laggard travelers. Some had only short distances to cover before reaching home; others had waited deliberately for the roads to clear. The delegates were gone; the officials and functionaries were gone. The political gentlemen from the several neighboring states were on their way toward those states, moving sluggishly down the narrow mountain roads. Those who had come on foot left on foot, walking in the ditches or on the banks, part of the retreating army that wound west of the clearing to Somerset or East Arlington, or descended the eastern slope through Stratton church to Jamaica or the Wardsboros. The last band to leave had marched a mile past the settlement, with its leader, lanky Luthur, herding it along. Fred Streeter, drumless and without boots, was dejectedly jolting along in a friend's wagon. The Captain, packed, was settling his bill at the Tarbox inn. The pickpocket, George Stiles, had already lifted a purse in East Arlington.

Of all those still in the clearing the noisiest was Joel Patch, who had found no trace of his lost property. Joe Lyman, constantly nagged by wife and daughter, still hunted listlessly for Peter Blodgett. Twice he passed close to the medicine man's red wagon, and each time two boys, loafing around the wagon, whistled an off-key version of "Yankee Doodle." The big-shouldered farmer watched Lot Purdy hitch six white horses to a log cabin on wheels. The stage driver, busy, using his right hand sparingly, gave all his attention to the harness.

Doc Merrifield, returning from Chittenden's with Mercy, noticed Lyman and nudged the girl. Mercy nodded. They walked on in silence. As they drew near the red wagon Put Chester and Seth Purdy hurried to meet them.

"Hello," said Put. The loudness of the greeting annoyed him, and he lowered his voice. "It's all right. We've been guarding him."

"E-yah," agreed Seth.

The medicine man stared. Mercy said, quickly, "Guarding? Guarding who?"

"Peter."

"E-yah. Peter Blodgett."

Doc sent a hasty glance in Lyman's direction. Put Chester grinned. "He ain't bothered us a mite. How'd the duel come out? Who won?"

Seth was interested, too. "Did Charles kill the Southerner?"

Doc Merrifield took off his glasses. He spoke in an awed whisper. "O' Conspiracy, where wilt thou find a cavern dark enough! How did you two find out about the duel? Or about Peter for that matter? These things were supposed to be secret."

"We know. We ain't told a soul, have we, Seth?"

"Nope."

The fat man looked at Mercy and shrugged. "They act like the first and second murderer. This Peter is a blabber. Such boys are dangerous."

"He'll learn," said Mercy, smiling.

Put Chester was puzzled by the medicine man's speech. He said, "You needn't blame Peter. We discovered him. We're his friends. I'm Put Chester, and this is Seth Purdy. We live here on Stratton."

Doc Merrifield leaned closer and asked fiercely, "Can you hold your tongues? There's work to do."

Both heads bobbed in nods. Both boys answered as one. "E-yah."

"Wait here," commanded Doc. He led Mercy to the wagon. "That'll keep them quiet, Mercy. They can carry your bundle back to Chittenden's."

Mercy clutched his arm. "Doc. I'm scared."

"They're fine people, Mercy."

"It ain't that. But Mr. Chittenden just feels beholden because you helped Charles. Maybe they don't even like me."

345

"They couldn't help it. Question is—do you like them?"

"Well, yes. But Doc. All this about me staying with the Chittendens is so sudden and everything."

The medicine man put both hands on Mercy's shoulders and looked down at her. He wasn't acting now. He said, "Mercy, it's best. You know it. They're good people. You ain't going to be charity or anything like that. We made enough at this Convention to pay for your keep for a good while. That's why I asked them straight out. Next week I might have lost it all."

Mercy didn't cry, but she looked as if she wanted to. "Oh, Doc. Who'll take care of you?"

"Peter and me will make out. I'll write, Mercy. You'll have to learn to read writing."

"I will, Doc. I promise I will."

"And if you don't like it, let me know."

"Yes, Doc."

He held her against him for a moment, then released her. Fumbling for his handkerchief, Doc blew his nose. "I'll be back, Mercy. Don't worry none. I'll be back this way again."

Mercy knew it was what he wanted. She knew, too, that it was the realization of her own dream. To stay in one place, have friends, go to school. Here on Stratton she was sure she could make friends. Charles Chittenden and his Lovina were already friendly; Mrs. Chittenden was a kindly, easy-to-know woman, and her big husband's bluster was like Doc's Shakespeare talk, a mask to hide real feeling. Mercy gazed at the medicine man and choked with unaccustomed tenderness. He didn't even plan it, she thought, but just grabbed the chance when it came—the way he sells Elixir. That was Doc. When it came to talking folks into doing things, there was nobody to hold a candle to him.

"Let's get your things together," said Doc Merrifield. He too was thinking, remembering her as smaller, recalling moments of comradeship. He cleared his throat and turned toward the wagon. "Parting is not such sweet sorrow!"

As they climbed into the vehicle Peter peered from beneath a bed like a frightened puppy. The medicine man completed the picture by snapping his fingers to summon the boy. Doc said, "Come on, Peter. We're leaving. You're going with me."

"In my place, Peter."

346

Peter's eyes widened. "They—Seth and Put—they said Joe Lyman ain't gone yet. He's looking into every wagon as it drives off."

"We've thought of that," said Mercy. She selected a dress and sunbonnet. "Put these on and keep your head down. Everybody saw me come with Doc. Everybody'll figure you're me."

It didn't take long for Mercy to gather her belongings. The clothing was piled in a wooden chest; a small basket held hairpins, ribbons, mirror, all the trivia of feminine adornment. "I guess that's all, Doc"

Doc Merrifield dropped a large volume on top of the clothing. The tan-leather binding was stained and faded, but the girl knew the book. It was the copy of Shakespeare.

"Doc!"

"I want it this way, Mercy."

Peter glanced from one to the other. He thought Mercy was crying, but he wasn't sure in the dim light inside the wagon.

"You'll get another, Doc?"

"First chance."

"And you'll stay out of trouble?"

"Always do, don't I?"

"But—you're all out of Elixir."

"Peter and me'll brew a mess tomorrow. First stream we come to. I saved out cash enough for bottles."

Mercy looked around, but there was nothing more to say. "Well," she said.

"Well," said Doc. "I'd better fetch Duke."

"You won't trade him to anybody mean?"

"No, Mercy." He pushed aside the blanket and dropped to the ground. Doc Merrifield stood a moment, holding the blanket open, gazing up into the wagon. The fat man's shoulders straightened; his head was cocked. Winking, Doc touched the brim of his hat. "I go, Mercy. I go!"

"Swifter than arrow from the Tartar's bow!" Mercy's reply was clear and gay. When the blanket dropped into place, the girl sighed and brushed a hand over her face. "Be good to him, Peter. Take care of him for me."

"I will, Miss Mercy."

"Stay out of sight till I'm gone, I'll take care Lyman doesn't see me leave." She called Seth and Put. The two boys willingly took chest and basket when Mercy explained the plan.

Put said, "Don't worry. We know a way to go through the trees." He nodded toward the upper edge of the clearing. "Circle around and come out on the pike near Chittenden's. Will you tell us about the duel as we go?" Put Chester was enjoying the drama of the escape. "Seth."

"E-yah?"

"You watch for Lyman. Once we're out of the clearing pass the word to Peter and come after us."

"All right," said Seth. "But don't tell about the dueling till I catch up."

Alone in the wagon Peter Blodgett waited for the signal. He felt more foolish than scared. I must look a sight, he thought, in a girl's dress and bonnet. He was sure that Joe Lyman wouldn't be fooled. Stella would know him in a minute. Peter sighed and decided he'd just have to trust Doc to get them away.

The boy jumped as knuckles rapped the wagon's side. He heard Seth's voice.

"Clear away! Good luck, Peter!"

Bracing himself, Peter pulled the bonnet tight. He unlaced the tarpaulin at the front of the wagon and climbed out onto the driver's seat. He sat there, hands locked in his lap and head bent, unable to see anything but the narrow strip of ground between the wagon's shafts. The noises of the crowd weren't close, but Peter felt very exposed. Sure that all the Lymans were staring at him, he strained to catch the sound of an approach.

The boy tightened at the first thud of a horse's hoof. It was close and coming closer. He risked a glance and let his breath out in relief. It was Doc Merrifield leading the dun-colored horse.

Doc backed Duke between the shafts. Without looking up at Peter, the medicine man said, "She gone?"

"E-yah. Put and Seth took her."

Doc Merrifield nodded and fumbled with a buckle on the harness.

"I know how to hitch up, Mr. Doc."

"No. Not today, Peter. You sit there. You're a girl."

"Yes, sir."

The pudgy fingers skillfully adjusted harness and reins. Doc

348

climbed to the seat beside Peter. The fat man settled his tall hat, slapped the reins on Duke's back, and chirruped. Duke pawed the ground tentatively, shook himself, and started.

They moved slowly toward the western edge of the clearing, Doc watching for a gap in the packed wall of vehicles lined up along the turnpike. Suddenly, from one corner of his mouth, the medicine man addressed the boy. "Lyman. Keep your head down." The sonorous quality he used in selling came into Doc's voice. He shouted. "Ho! You there?"

Joe Lyman turned. "Me?"

"E-yah." Doc's affirmative rang true. "Which way to East Arlington?"

The big-shouldered farmer pointed with his whip. Lyman showed no further interest in the red wagon but strode away.

Doc Merrifield chuckled. He said, "Just tell me where is fancy bred? There's more than one way to skin a cat. Sit tight, Peter." He pulled up to let a log cabin on wheels pass in front of him. The six white horses pulling the strange vehicle were prancing and frisky. Doc recognized the driver as the man who'd fought with Joe Lyman. The medicine man waved and yelled.

"How are you?"

Lot Purdy held up his broken hand. "Middling, thanks. I'm favoring it a mite." With a farewell nod the stage driver concentrated on his team. The six beauties, thought Lot, are a mite fractious. He guessed they weren't used to spending a night in the open with so many other horses. Lot Purdy wasn't worried but, with a swollen right hand, he was being careful. He had waited to be one of the last to leave the clearing, and he drove completely around its semicircle to reach the turnpike on the eastern side. He had the team settled and working together when he started to jockey for position on the roadbank.

Keeping always on the flank of the waiting line of vehicles, Lot wheeled and turned the team. He was still trying to take the edge off their temper. The tracks of the log cabin's wheels formed a huge figure eight on the trampled ground of the clearing.

It was pretty driving, and it drew attention. People forgot their impatience to be off and turned to watch. Men nodded in appreciation; women murmured admiration of the snowy team.

Lot Purdy saw his opening and a clear stretch of road. He

349

straightened the team, loosened his grip on the reins. The clumsy log cabin wagon was halfway down the bank, and the two leaders were turned into the turnpike, when the stage driver heard the whistle of the whip.

The right lead horse reared, squealing. Lot Purdy caught one quick glimpse of Joe Lyman as he lashed another horse. Then the team plunged forward in panic, and whip and man were gone. The log cabin, swaying, nearly capsized on the turn. All six horses were racing. The stage driver swore, tried to draw in his reins, felt the pain in his broken knuckles. He knew it was a runaway.

With one hand, Lot thought. He wasn't excited. He cursed the farmer's vengefulness without emotion and worried about team and wagon. The brake was useless; locked wheels would mean an upset, and a smashing one. Nothing would please the driver more than to see the silly Whig cabin-wagon shattered, but it was his charge, and professional pride came before politics. The team hadn't completed its first headlong rush before Lot decided he would have to let them run.

He gathered the reins into his good hand and applied pressure by locking wrist against wrist and using the strength of both arms. If the pike's clear, he thought, we'll manage. He was driving with all the skill he had, tightening the reins, slackening them, tightening, slackening. He wanted to remind the team that they still had a driver, were still hitched. He liked the white horses and feared a fall, a tangled horror of flailing hoofs that would end with fatal injuries. Lot Purdy knew his job. It was to keep the team in the road, running as a team, and work for the moment when the panic passed.

They thundered down the turnpike, the wagon skidding and bouncing. The trees that lined both banks of the road swept by like a solid hedge. Lot's glance kept shifting from the horses to the road ahead. He tensed for each curve of the narrow track, guiding his leaders around it, foot poised on the brake pedal. A vehicle ahead meant a certain smashup. The driver was glad he'd waited till the traffic had thinned.

The team swept into another curve, and Lot Purdy grinned. He thought he could manage them now; they were racing together and seemed calmer. The road straightened and dipped.

That would be Chittenden's ahead, Lot thought. He knew every foot of the turnpike. Another quarter mile and the danger was over. Four of the six horses were responding to his handling.

Then he saw the three figures in the road and yelled.

The two boys darted for the banks, but the girl stood as if frozen. Lot Purdy shouted. One boy dashed back, grabbed the girl's arm, whirled her away from the charging team.

The stage driver saw the boy slip in the churned mud of the roadbed. He saw the dark body that seemed to rush at the right lead horse, saw the wide eyes and the open mouth. There was no swerving the team. Lot Purdy tried his best, but the boy was gone beneath the racing horses. He felt the cabin shudder as it hit something.

"God Almighty," said Lot Purdy. "God Almighty! That was Put Chester!"

There was no sound in the parsonage parlor but the insistent ticking of the Terry clock on the mantel. Eratus Chittenden sat, filling a chair, and stared at the clock's hands. They indicated that he had been watching them a long time, but they seemed to move with a slowness only emphasized by the flash of the brass pendulum and the steady click-clack. Eratus was not used to waiting. He thought the timepiece must be broken; all that bustle and noise should move the hands faster. The big man listened but could hear no movement in the house. Eratus sighed and stirred. He remembered his pacing of the morning when he was worried about Charles. But this was not his home, and Putnam Chester was another man's son. Eratus settled back in his chair and watched the clock and cursed it under his breath.

A carriage rattled past on the turnpike outside. Eratus, glaring at the front windows, placed the vehicle's direction. One of the visitors bound for home. He realized suddenly that since he noticed the noise it must be less frequent. Most of them are gone, Eratus thought, and good riddance. He was glad his own guests had left before Charles was brought home.

The Reverend Chester came into the room and shut the door. The parson looked more gaunt than ever. Weariness deepened the furrows in his long face.

351

Eratus rose. "Well, Reverend?"

Jedidah Chester raised a hand, dropped it. He liked the big man. They were not close, but each had a healthy respect for the other. The parson sighed and rubbed his forehead. His voice was mildly accusing as if he blamed himself. "I'm not a doctor, Eratus."

"Nearest thing to it on this mountain."

"A miss is as good as a mile, Eratus. And he's my own son."

The big man's shrug was impatient. "Lot Purdy'll fetch a doctor back soon as he can. I'm sorry the Merrifield feller got away before it happened. How bad is the boy?"

"Putnam," said Reverend Chester, shutting his eyes as he spoke the name, "has broken several bones. Left leg. Right wrist. That much I know."

"E-yah."

"He's badly bruised and in pain. The leg . . ." The quiet voice faltered and went on. "The leg is bad, Eratus."

"I saw it."

"I judge that a horse broke the leg first." The parson's face was taut. "And then a wheel passed over it. Putnam may not walk for —a long time."

"What about his backbone? His innards?"

"I don't know." The words were a whispered mixture of prayer and fear. "I don't know."

The whisper made the big man look away. Gazing unseeingly at the clock, Eratus said, "Your son and mine. Why, Reverend? Why them?"

"Accidents happen, Eratus."

"Accidents!" Eratus snorted. "That duel wasn't no accident. Neither was the runaway! And I ain't aiming to blame it on God, either! The Almighty's got better things to do than go making trouble for folks. It's that blasted Convention!"

"We enjoyed it."

"E-yah. Far as it went. The speechmaking and the supper and all that. But it ain't healthy, Reverend, to have all those strangers around." Anger and suspicion sharpened the big man's tone. "It just ain't healthy!"

The parson managed a thin smile. "My friend, Reverend Butterfield, would find meat in the fact that Lot Purdy's a Democrat. And Lot's our neighbor."

352

"E-yah." Eratus dismissed the notion. "Lot wouldn't have harmed Put on purpose. He come running all the way back after he got the team stopped. And he's half out of his head about it."

"I know." Jedidah Chester nodded. "Young Seth is still waiting out back with Put's dog. One looks as lost as the other. I figure there's not a mite of use in blaming anything, Eratus. Things just happen."

"Around strangers," insisted Eratus, doggedly.

Sighing, the parson realized that he must plead a cause he didn't feel. He said, "It could be worse, Eratus. They might both have been killed."

"They might both have been unscathed, too!"

I am not going to argue, thought Reverend Chester. Not today, with Putnam lying back there injured. Not with this man whose son is marrying my daughter. We were all pleased to hear the Convention was coming to this mountain. My own qualms disappeared as I thoroughly enjoyed the great speech and the merry-making. He said merely, "What's done's done. It's over now, Eratus."

Eratus Chittenden stared, then, twinkling, allowed a grin to slide onto his face. "E-yah, Reverend. Put that in your sermon next Sunday. Joel Patch will find it a great comfort." He saw by the minister's blank look that the remark meant nothing. "I hear Joel's aiming to vote Democrat."

"Joel Patch?"

The evident disbelief brought a chuckle from the big man. "E-yah. Seems the whole meeting was held for the single purpose of robbing Joel. At least he's taking on that way. My son Peter heard about it. Joel lost that Morgan team, and somebody wrecked his sawmill."

"Oh, my!" said Reverend Chester.

"Kind of a high price to pay for the pleasure of holding Dan Webster's hat, ain't it?"

Well, thought the parson, there goes any chance of getting a new stove for the church. Reverend Chester rebuked himself. That was no way to be thinking of another man's loss. He said, "In such a great crowd there were bound to be some rascals." He could not resist a momentary quirk of the lips. "Poor Joel. The most fiery Whig of them all."

Both men suddenly sobered, annoyed at their lapse into unimportant matters. Eratus reached for his hat. "I'll get back up home. Charles will be wanting to know about Put."

The parson held out his hand. "I am very pleased about Charles and Lovina."

They shook hands. The parson promised to send word as soon as the stage driver brought a doctor. The big man departed.

Left alone, Jedidah Chester slumped down at his desk and put his face in his hands. He had a moment of weakness when his faith in his son's recovery was shaken. With cold dread he faced the possibility that Putnam, the fleet of foot, the never-still, might spend the rest of his life hobbling, crippled. My son, thought Jedidah Chester, with despair. God! The unuttered cry was a prayer, and its plea gave him strength. The parson straightened. He took off his glasses and cleaned them. It kept his hands busy for a minute and left his mind free for thinking.

Resolutely, he forced his mind away from Put. He remembered Eratus Chittenden's outspoken disapproval of the Convention and tried to smile. It was easy to disapprove after an event. Certainly the gathering had been a great success, in numbers and entertainment. Daniel Webster had spoken. General Harrison's strength in the countryside had been demonstrated. If all other log-cabin Conventions were as successful Van Buren's defeat was certain.

The parson knew that his son's accident had dwarfed Convention, election, and Presidency. Of course he would vote; every man who could vote did. Naturally he would vote Whig; his convictions lay that way. But that was doing his duty, and he didn't really care about the result. Maybe Eratus is right, he thought. Maybe the Convention made more trouble than it was worth. During its tenure, life on Stratton had been changed. In Putnam's case and Lovina's, the change was not for a few days but, perhaps, a lifetime.

Jedidah Chester recalled his position and wondered what other changes might have taken place among his flock. A material loss like the sawmill owner's was a trifle compared to sickness or marriage. Maybe there had been others.

"Speculation," said the parson aloud, "is ridiculous. Blame, also. It was a political meeting. Nothing more."

Reverend Chester put his glasses back on and rose. There was

354

no visible bracing or change of countenance. Walking quietly, he went back to where his wife sat beside their stricken son.

Sinking far to the west, the sun seemed to pull the shadows down from Stratton's summit to the clearing that scarred the mountain's side. There was no one left in the clearing now. But there was still enough sunshine to show that the wide expanse had changed. It was no longer green but churned and trampled and rutted into a muddy waste. Across its surface the many campfires had left dark smudges, like the careless fingermarks of some giant child. All around the semicircle of the forest wall were fresh white scars where men had found their fuel. The sunlight caught on a green oblong; a parked wagon had saved the grass. The great clearing looked as if it had been cleared yesterday.

There were debris scattered everywhere. A broken spoon, a discarded strap, a forgotten ribbon. The rubbish and litter that even a thrifty people leaves behind. The ground pine and cut boughs that had served them for beds marked where hundreds had slept. A scrap of bunting clinging to a nail trimmed the oration platform. The long Tippecanoe log cabin, its door ajar and windows dark, looked desolate in spite of its newness, like an abandoned toy.

Alone, in the center of the clearing, stood the tamarack tree. Tall and majestic, the tracery of its foliage clear in the sun's last rays, the tamarack towered above the deserted field. For the first time in days a bird darted into its branches, perched a moment, skimmed away. The flutter of its passage scarcely disturbed the sunset hush of the mountainside.

Still unscarred, full of years and dignity, the tamarack tree rose from its root, straight and strong, as if challenging the clearing and the axes and men.

EPILOGUE

April, 1841

ALL THAT morning it rained. Even when it stopped, around noon, there was no sun visible in the sullen, yellow-gray sky. The mountain's summit was hidden by a swollen, thick mist that clung to the trees. On the slope the forest was soaked to a dark, shapeless mass; the clearings and mowings were swamps; the roads were narrow streams of slick, brown mud. It was cold. It was a miserable April day.

Still, there were no surprises in the weather. Everyone who lived on Stratton Mountain had known worse seasons. The humans accepted the damp and chill as the natural order of a Vermont April; the birds and beasts huddled under the evergreens did not complain. Afterwards, on the days that followed, men spoke of portents, omens, and feelings. These were lies. All that the people on Stratton knew, at noon, was that the rain had stopped and would probably start again. They were not even expecting the stage.

Hub-deep in mud, its four horses floundering and slipping, the Concord coach was making slow progress up the eastern side of the mountain. Only the skill and whip of Lot Purdy himself kept the team at work. A dozen times the stage driver and his single passenger had shoved, pushed, and pried the heavy vehicle from the mire; once a horse had fallen. Men and beasts were plastered with mud. Lot Purdy resembled an unfinished clay figure. His own father would have had trouble recognizing the passenger as Charles Chittenden.

After conquering one slippery rise they rested. The two men leaned against the coach, their breath forming vapor in the chill air. Lot Purdy tried to scrape the muck from his gloves. He glanced at his horses, turned to his passenger.

"How's your side, Charles?"

Charles grinned. "I'm all right."

"Maybe."

"Honest, Lot. It never bothers me. Healed fine."

"Don't pay to strain yourself. Even to get home. You quit if anything starts hurting. I don't want Lovina around my neck for letting you overdo."

"How is she, Lot?"

The stage driver laughed and held up four fingers. "That's the fourth time, Charles. She ain't changed a mite since I told you three miles back. Your wife's real pert considering she's six months along."

They were alone on the turnpike with none to hear but the horses, yet Charles lowered his voice. Where the mud streaks allowed it the older man saw the flush. "Lot. How—how is she? How does she look?"

"She ain't too big."

The calm answer startled the young husband. He said quickly, "It's just that her last letter was a mite peckish."

"E-yah. They get that way."

"It isn't bad?"

"Nope. Don't mean a thing. Anyway, it's natural if she's upset over you being away all these months. She'll perk right up when she sees you."

"She ain't expecting me. You don't figure the shock . . ."

"I don't." Lot dismissed the subject by beating his hands together to warm them. "Come on. We'd better get along before the coach sinks clear out of sight in this mud."

They climbed up on the box. The stage driver uncurled his whip, cracked it, and shouted. The four horses lunged, pawed at the slippery roadbed, started. The coach lurched forward.

"Yah!" yelled Lot. "Yah!" His whip was never still as he tried to keep the team moving. They plowed along, spewing mud and water behind the wheels. With the driver screaming and lashing like a madman, the coach made the next rise without getting stuck. Lot reined in and rested the horses.

"You ride them newfangled steam cars, Charles?"

"E-yah. Some. Over to York State."

"You like them?"

360

"Well. Middling. They get there."

"Could they climb this mountain?"

Charles tried not to smile. He realized that the railroads irked the stage driver. He said, "Don't know, Lot. Ain't never noticed them going over any mountains much."

"Thought not." Lot Purdy spat. "They'll never tinker up nothing to replace the horse. How're the roads out West?"

"What roads?" said Charles. "I'm homesteading. This here turnpike's better than anything in the whole Illinois country."

Pleased, the stage driver proceeded to justify the young man's words. By unsparing use of lungs and arm, he stirred the horses to a splashing trot and kept them at it for over a mile. At the next level stretch they rested again.

"What's the news to home?" asked Charles.

Lot Purdy grunted. "God Almighty! The big news we're fetching drove it right out of my head that you might want to hear. I guess Lovina wrote about Put?"

"E-yah. That's good."

"E-yah! Never know he was hurt. Him and Seth was out hunting last week. Them bones knitted fine. Thank God." The stage driver said the words simply and went on. "Put's getting better's the big news. Ain't much else been happening. Old Peleg Nason didn't winter."

"I didn't know that."

"Recent. Took a chill the last week in February. Went fast. Three days. And he never said a word the whole time. Not even about fighting the Revolution."

"Well, Peleg was getting on."

"E-yah. There's a new couple working for Joel Patch. Clem and Lizzie Galusha quit. Clem told it around he come into some money, but I hear he's working for a farmer down to Brattleboro."

"Is there still talk about Isaac Mead and Mrs. Brayton?"

"There's talk. But nobody knows a thing." Lot shrugged and picked up his whip. "Folks find little to talk about. There's some made a mountain out of the way Zilpha Brayton looked at Isaac at your wedding, and the same ones gobbled about how he looked at her during old Peleg's funeral."

"You think there's nothing to it?"

"Maybe. Maybe not. It ain't my business. But Lem Brayton don't act no different. Not a mite. Hup, there! Hup! Yah!"

They jerked their way up the mountain. The journey was slow and spasmodic, but the driver never let up on his horses. Charles forgot that he was cold and damp as they drew near the settlement. Stratton had been white with snow when he'd left his bride. I've missed her, he thought, but it was safer here with a baby coming and not knowing what we'd find in strange country. He was glad Lovina hadn't faced the bleak prairie winter in her condition. Not that he was taking her back to much, for all the months of work. A shack and a lot of land. Charles smiled. It was good land, and they'd make it better. His son would grow with the house they'd build. Charles hadn't the slightest doubt that the baby would be a son.

Lot Purdy had his own ideas. He was on an unscheduled run at his personal insistence. God Almighty, he thought. I've never had news like this before. He knew, and Charles Chittenden knew, but no one else on Stratton had an inkling of what had happened. And it was in the big clearing on Stratton that the Whigs had held their Convention last summer! The stage driver was stunned by the magnitude of his message. It had never happened before; it was almost unbelievable. For a moment, knowing his neighbors, Lot wondered if it would be better to let another—Charles—make the initial announcement. It might sound better coming from a Whig than a Democrat. He decided against it. He couldn't throw away his greatest opportunity as a courier. Democrat or no Democrat, thought Lot Purdy, they all know I ain't the kind would whoop at a man's death.

The horses clambered on, hauling the big stage around curves, between dripping trees. They seemed to realize that the destination was close. The rests on the level stretches grew briefer; the coach managed to avoid getting stuck. They made the last, climbing half mile without a stop. Houses appeared on both sides of the turnpike. The grade became less steep, flattened, and there ahead of them was the white wall and squat tower of Stratton church.

Both men on the stage shouted. The horses, ears forward, broke into a run. Lot Purdy was proud that they were coming in with a flourish.

Charles Chittenden watched the parsonage. He didn't really ex-

362

pect his wife to be at her mother's, but he hoped she would be. Charles was scarcely aware that the driver was slowing the team. He saw the Reverend Chester come around the corner of the house and stare; he saw Mrs. Chester at a window. The parsonage door opened; the doorway was filled with excited girls. Charles recognized Sally Chester, Mattie, the girl Mercy. He leaned forward. If Mercy were at the Chester's, perhaps Lovina would be. The girls separated and let another through the door. With a sudden pang Charles saw his wife's swollen figure. Yelling, he leaped to the ground as the stage slid to a stop.

"Lovina! Lovina!"

Lovina Chester Chittenden swayed. Stumbling and awkward she ran toward her husband. He covered the distance with long, quick strides and caught her in his arms.

Hammering with the butt of his whip, Lot Purdy kept up a wordless, ululating cry. The unprecedented noise was accepted as a summons. Men came out of the inn; the blacksmith hurried down the road. The stage driver's wife and son knew his voice and ran from the house, frightened. The stage was not expected; the behavior of its driver was even more abnormal. Women snatched shawls and followed the men.

They gathered around the coach, standing in the ankle-deep mud of the turnpike. Faces stared up at Lot Purdy. He waited until the group was full, and no more were coming.

Reverend Chester called, "What is it, Lot?"

"Land of Goshen!" said the innkeeper. "What's got into you?"

Lot Purdy raised a hand. He gazed down at the citizens of Stratton. They were his neighbors, and he knew them all. He saw his wife's pinched fright, the minister's bewilderment, the smith's impassive watchfulness. Everyone within hearing was present. Asa Brayton stood with Marcia Tarbox. The Pierce boy grinned with his usual foolishness.

"News!" cried Lot Purdy. He paused a moment, not for effect, but to record the scene in his memory. Grouped around the stagecoach, under a bleak, threatening sky, the people of Stratton waited. The stage driver removed his hat. His voice was clear, too loud, excited.

"The President is dead!"

It did not register. The faces turned toward Lot Purdy remained blank, expectant. There was no disbelief; there was nothing. Such an announcement had never been made before in the country's short history, and the listeners couldn't grasp its import. The innkeeper's wife tugged at her husband's sleeve and asked, "Who?" The question sounded puzzled.

"The President is dead," the driver repeated. "The President. William Henry Harrison. He's dead!"

Shock and disbelief came then. Wives looked at their husbands. One man shook his head. Jedidah Chester held out a hand as if reaching for the truth. The innkeeper swore in a tight, dazed whisper. Lovina Chittenden, already tearful, burst into fresh tears and clung to Charles. Mrs. Purdy gave a relieved sigh and then covered her mouth, aghast. The group erupted into speech, pelting the stage driver with quick questions.

"Harrison?"

"Tippecanoe?"

"General Harrison?"

"Dead?"

"The President?"

"It ain't true, is it, Lot?"

"Dead?"

They knew it was true and voiced doubts. Death was accepted and natural, but not the death of a President. They felt that the highest office in the land should be inviolate, should vest its holder in an armor different from that of other mortals. It had never happened before. Here was the stunning fact. Old Andy Jackson still lived. John Quincy Adams was still active. They had shouted for Harrison, toasted his victory, rejoiced when he had taken the oath of office only the previous month. It must be a trick, a joke, a mistake. It couldn't be true, and yet they knew it was. No man called Lot Purdy a liar, but every eye held a mute appeal that he recall his words. The Reverend Jedidah Chester, a pious man, felt his own sense of loss, gazed at his neighbors, and thought that it was as if God had ceased to exist.

"Tell us, Lot. Tell us."

"E-yah."

"Is it certain?"

The stage driver nodded. "True enough. Ask Charles Chittenden there."

Every head turned toward Charles. He nodded. "E-yah. President Harrison's dead."

"But he just got in office!"

"Dan's right."

"Mighty sudden, if you ask me."

"Wasn't killed, was he?"

Lot Purdy shouted at them, trying to prevent useless speculation. "He wasn't killed! But he is dead! He took a chill and died."

Dan Tarbox said, "E-yah. Mighty sudden."

"Tippecanoe."

"Dead."

"I never heard the beat."

"Ain't sense!"

"Lot!" There was startled panic in Will Carpenter's voice. "You mean we ain't got no President?"

The stage driver sighed. He'd expected the question. He answered it. "John Tyler's President."

"Tyler?"

"You mean Tyler too?"

"E-yah."

"*He's* President?"

"Who says so?"

"E-yah. Who says so?"

"I voted for Tippecanoe!"

"Tippecanoe is dead!" Lot Purdy told them again. "And John Tyler is President. That's the way it works. It's in the books that way. He took the oath and everything."

"Couldn't wait till the man was cold!"

"Ain't decent, if you ask me."

"Ain't even fair!"

"Can Tyler do that, Reverend?"

The parson smiled. "I believe so, Abner. It's legal."

"Well," said Dan Tarbox. "He's a Whig, anyway." The innkeeper's tone carried no conviction. None of them knew much about Tyler. They had all been stirred to wild enthusiasm for Tippecanoe. They began adjusting to the President, but they were laconic and bewildered.

"John Tyler."

"*President* Tyler."

365

"Virginian, ain't he?"

"E-yah."

"You know he is."

"Whig, though."

"That's right. He's a Whig."

"Tyler."

The gathering lost its unity and broke into smaller groups. No one left. They stood in the open, cheeks reddening from the chill air, and talked. Again and again Lot Purdy told his message. They were very impressed that they had gone around for days thinking they lived under President Harrison while Tippecanoe lay dead down to Washington. Yet they agreed with the blacksmith that the news had traveled fast.

"Bad news always does."

"E-yah."

Reverend Chester wondered aloud how the nation was receiving the tragedy. This caused fresh talk. The Stratton folk figured their own reaction was something special. Hadn't they been hosts, so to speak, at the big Convention for Tippecanoe and Tyler too.

"You know. I had a feeling."

"What's that, Will?"

"That log cabin. Up to the clearing."

"E-yah?"

"Recollect how Joel Patch busted it up?"

"E-yah. Took back his lumber."

"Well, I had a feeling then."

"A feeling?"

"Knew something was wrong. Said so."

"That was way back last fall."

"E-yah. But it goes to show."

Charles Chittenden, suddenly solicitous, urged Lovina out of the cold. The rest of the Chester family followed, though Mercy stayed to watch the crowd. Folks started to depart, lingered for a last opinion. Lot Purdy was satisfied. There had never been such news brought to Stratton. He remembered his horses and was inspecting them when Asa Brayton spoke.

"Mr. Purdy."

"E-yah? What is it, Asa?"

"Didn't Pa come back with you?"

"Your pa?" Lot stared at the boy, puzzled. "Lem?"

"E-yah."

"Back from where?"

Dan Tarbox heard the question and turned to listen. The blacksmith moved closer. Asa's surprise seemed to reflect that on the stage driver's face. "Why," said Asa. "Why, back from Wardsboro. He took the stage down. Took it."

"Saw him get on," said the innkeeper.

Abner Reed nodded. Lot Purdy stared from face to face. He said, "You mean to tell me Lem Brayton ain't here?"

"He took the stage, Mr. Purdy. Pa was aiming to do some buying off the mountain."

"I know that. He started with me two days back. But he didn't go far. Said he'd forgot something. I let him off a couple or three miles down the pike." Lot looked at Asa. "Didn't your pa come home, Asa?"

The boy paled as if suddenly washed of color. He stepped back, wet his lips. "No," he said. "No." Asa turned abruptly. He walked past Marcia Tarbox without seeing her. After five steps he broke into a run. He raced down the branch road toward his home.

Dan Tarbox stared after him and shrugged. The innkeeper was wondering how he could get some custom into his tavern. A President didn't die every day. Dan said, "There's a fire inside, Lot. We'll all want to hear . . ."

The stage driver interrupted. "You ain't seen Lem Brayton?" Lot was serious, frowning. When the innkeeper shook his head, the driver said, "We'd better find out what's bothering Asa. Abner!"

"E-yah!" The smith was already moving. They ran past the inn and into the branch. Both men felt the necessity for speed. It was in the diminishing figure of the boy ahead of them. Something was wrong. Very wrong.

They were men, and neither was used to running any distance. Lot Purdy sprinted ahead of the smith, but the latter plodded through the mud steadily. Once the driver shouted Asa's name; the boy gave no sign of having heard. On the last half of the stretch Abner Reed caught up with Lot and passed him. They did not overtake Asa.

It was Asa who arrived first. He charged into the house, panting, calling from winded lungs.

"Ma! Ma! Ma!"

There was no answer. Asa Brayton reeled against the wall. He knew there was reason behind his father's pretense of taking the stage. Asa was frightened, shaking at a horror he could not name. There was a fire crackling in the room, but the heat seemed to have a different feel, a different smell.

Asa said, tentatively, "Pa?"

He was standing motionless when the men arrived. It was Abner Reed who looked into the bedroom. That was where he found them.

Isaac Mead had been shot in the face. Zilpha Brayton was huddled in a corner. Beside her was the smeared axe that had smashed through the red hair, not once but many times.

"Keep the boy out of here, Lot."

"God Almighty!"

"The boy. Don't let him see!"

"E-yah."

"And you'd best fetch the parson."

The blacksmith was sweating when he shut the bedroom door. He nodded to the stage driver. "Both of them." It was true, then, he thought, about Isaac and Zilpha Brayton. They had been carrying on. From the looks of things Lem had shot the man first, and the wife had tried to run. You couldn't run far in a small room. He must have had the axe and gun hid out when he pretended to take the stage, Abner decided. Now they would have to catch Lem Brayton. Murder was murder, whatever the reason. Lem Brayton! By all appearances, the last man to do a thing like this. . . .

Asa moaned. Lot Purdy, hugging the boy close, said, "God Almighty."

Abner Reed wished that the driver would stop using the same words. They weren't fitting in the Brayton house. The smith talked only to himself for Asa's sake. She was a fine-looking woman, that Zilpha. He wondered just when she'd kicked over the traces.

They heard the rumble of distant thunder. It sounded as if it came from beyond the summit of the mountain.

They assembled in the Brayton barnyard, quiet men, armed, talking in low voices. There was an expressed distaste for their task, yet underneath it was the excitement of the chase. All had hunted, but never for game like this.

Few blamed Lem Brayton for what he had done. They were bred to the stern Mosaic law that punished adultery. When Eratus Chittenden deplored the manner of punishment, however, he was met by grim nods. This was too coldly planned. The victims had obviously had no chance. They might not, in jury, convict Lem Brayton, but there was no question of letting him escape. The law was the law. *Thou shalt not kill* was as potent and binding as *Thou shalt not commit adultery.*

Steps had already been taken. There were no boys in the group. Seth Purdy was riding down one side of the mountain; Putnam Chester, too excited to be cautious, was racing down another. Young Henry Chittenden, cantering Whitefoot, had splashed past on his way to carry the news to the Jamaicas. The towns off the mountain would know; the roads would be blocked; the forces of authority would be warned and waiting. But no one believed that Lem Brayton had fled by the road. Any road. He was a Stratton man and therefore not a fool. His crime was committed on the mountain. It was up to them to catch him.

When Tate Jones arrived with his hounds they learned that Lem was on foot. His slow oxen were in their stalls, and the hunter had found Isaac Mead's walleyed horse dead in its shafts, a ball through its throat.

"It was off the road back a piece," Tate Jones told them. "I figure he killed the horse first. There's a trail to here."

Lot Purdy swore and checked his priming. "Lem always hated Isaac's Nick." Joel Patch estimated Nick's value.

The killing of the horse shocked and angered the men. It was senseless, the wanton act of a man filled with blood lust. Their animals were their prop and pride. They all felt that Nick had done nothing to merit slaughter. A deeper, stronger determination became part of the hunt. Fingers tightened around rifle barrels; there was less talk. The quarry was dangerous and might kill again.

They watched Tate Jones examine the ground. The thin tracker's reputation was almost legend. No one protested when he took the hounds into the house. When they came out Jones spoke to the dogs, sent them trotting into the brush.

"He went up the mountain," the hunter said.

"How long, Tate?"

"He's got an hour's start. Or more." The hunter shrugged. "All I know is he set out after the rain stopped." Glancing to where Asa Brayton stood trembling with the parson, Jones lowered his voice. "He must have blood on him. I'm trusting to the dogs."

"Over the summit," said Eratus Chittenden. "And down the other side."

"E-yah."

"Makes sense."

"He might get away at that."

"E-yah."

They waited. Eratus glanced at young Brayton and thought of his own stalwart sons. Amos and Peter were with him. He had found time to welcome Charles before the posse was formed. I'm a grandfather, the big man remembered. He loved Peter's little girl, but hoped Lovina would bear a son. He felt very sorry for Asa. What a heritage to leave a child.

In the woods one of the dogs barked. The sound tightened each man's muscles. They looked at Tate Jones.

"Well," said the hunter. He lifted his rifle to the crook of his arm and started.

The men spread out behind him. Abner Reed averted his eyes as he passed the minister and young Brayton. No one expected Asa to join them. They would have been profoundly shocked at the thought of a son hunting his father.

They went into the forest like a line of skirmishers. Tate Jones squatted, stared at the ground.

"E-yah."

"Go ahead," said Eratus. He started the word down the line. "Pass it on, Amos. Keep close enough for hearing and gather at a shot."

"E-yah."

A shadowed half-light filtered through the trees. The inhabitants of Stratton became dark, eerie figures covering the ground with quiet purpose. There was little talk. Each man was a solitary stalker, aware of his neighbors by noise and movement. One splashed through a puddle and swore; another coughed. There was always the rustle of brush, the snapping of a stepped-on twig. Ahead a hound bayed and then a second. No one thought of what was ahead of the hounds.

A hail came from a flanker.

"Still on it, Tate?"

"E-yah. It's plain track."

"So far."

"So far, Lot."

"If it rains . . ."

The hunter, walking at a steady pace that was surprisingly fast, called back his answer. "If it rains, it rains. I ain't no hawk."

Thunder grumbled a threat. Rain would wash out all traces of Lem Brayton's flight.

"The dogs?"

"Are good dogs. But they ain't used to this kind of work."

"Who is?" asked Dan Tarbox. "Who is?" The innkeeper was finding his legs out of practice for outdoor walking. He wished he'd stayed at the tavern. Not that there was any point with all his customers away on this hunt. Dan sniffed at their numbers. Since the lucrative days of the great Convention the innkeeper had been dissatisfied. Over his wife's objections and without the knowledge of his neighbors, Tarbox had put the inn up for sale. Who could make money on top of a mountain?

A cough answered the silent query. Joel Patch was the cougher. The sawmill owner was marching forward with relentless strides. Patch hated all evildoers. He was sure in his mind that Lem Brayton was making for the Bondville country, and that convicted Lem. The new circular saw had cost a small fortune, and the Morgans, recovered after months of searching, were ruined as a team. Patch thought of the man he pursued as a shiftless farmer. That, too, condemned him. He should be caught, wiped out. What kind of a lawless country were they living in? He wouldn't be surprised if there was something crooked about this business of Tippecanoe dying. Patch coughed again, spat impatiently, and kept on.

"Still on it, Tate?"

"E-yah."

Steadily the hunters climbed toward the mountain's summit. The hounds clamored angrily and were found racing back and forth beside a mountain stream. Tate Jones splashed across, pointed to a heel mark, held up a pinkish rag.

371

"Stopped to wash."

"E-yah."

"Needed it," said Eratus, grimly.

"Likely."

"How far ahead, Tate?"

"Can't say." The tracker whistled to his dogs, touched their noses with the rag, sent the two coursing ahead.

The men spread out again; a few sighed wearily.

"Get along."

"E-yah."

They climbed toward the source of the stream. It seemed to twist itself deliberately into their path. The trail finally left it, and the men were grateful.

They were making more noise now, but they moved faster. Every time one of the hounds gave voice the sound sent a quiver along the line and increased the pace. It grew colder, darker, and the thunder became more frequent.

The hunt had hold of them all, and they swore at the elements fighting against them. When the thunder drowned the dogs even Tate Jones stamped impatiently.

Around them, always, was the dripping of the trees.

No man heard the report of Lem Brayton's musket.

Once past Stratton's summit the murderer felt safe. He was panting from the long climb, but he gave a triumphant shout. He didn't pause until he had plunged a few yards down the other side of the mountain. Then he sat down and gloated. He had beaten them; he had beaten them all. They would never catch him now. He was over the crest, out of the trap of the valley, and the rest was downhill. Lem Brayton laughed through a clap of thunder and went on laughing until tears flowed down his cheeks. That frightened him, and he stopped. There was no reason to be frightened; they would never catch him now.

Twice during the ascent Lem Brayton had heard the thin wail of a hound. It was far behind—so faint he wasn't even sure it was a hound—but it had been enough to send him plunging on in panic. He had tried to beat down the panic by telling himself that it couldn't be pursuit. No one would find the bodies before Asa returned at nightfall. The father's teeth showed in a grin as he thought of what awaited the son. There was bound to be confusion. Everybody in Stratton knew he'd gone down the mountain on the stage. They'd seen him go. Lem admired his plan. He had figured on everything, even to the fact that there was nothing in the world that would make Lot Purdy break his stage schedule. Regular as clockwork, that was Lot. He started to laugh again, but checked it.

His hands were shaking with fatigue, and he was wet through, but he scarcely noticed. He had lain hidden through cold and rain and night, munching his store of food, fondling his weapons. But once he'd sent a ball into that walleyed devil of a horse, Lem Brayton had been master, drunk with power.

Hugging himself, he relived each second he'd spent in the bedroom. Isaac Mead had started up, but he'd uttered no sound before the charge smashed him sprawling back across the bed. Lem Brayton stroked the smooth butt of the musket.

Zilpha had screamed. He'd caught her with the first swing of the axe.

Lem Brayton admitted he'd been scared after it was over. Still, it was smart to take to his heels right away. They'd never catch him now, no matter what. He had beaten them all. He had won.

"E-yah," he said aloud. "Beaten you hollow!"

A sudden, lurid flash of lightning brought him to his feet, fumbling for the musket. Lem Brayton insisted he wasn't afraid. He wasn't afraid of anything. His teeth chattered, but that was cold. He decided he'd move along. It was getting darker. E-yah. And there was more thunder. He didn't want to get caught in a tempest. Caught. The word made him shudder.

Lem started down the mountain. He wove between trees, the slope pulling him into a stumbling half trot. He crossed a ledge of rock and broke into a small clearing. It reminded him of the huge clearing where Webster'd spoke while Zilpha had made him a cuckold. Well, he'd paid them back for that. That and all the other times she'd sneaked off to Isaac.

Something moved across the clearing, and Lem's heart gave a leap that stopped him frozen.

He stared, starkly afraid. He was caught.

"Oh, God," said Lem.

There was enough light to see the big black figure. It moved again, and Lem saw it was a bear.

With a frightened whimper, Lem threw up his gun and fired. The bear's bulk jerked and dropped behind a fallen tree. Lem Brayton cackled into laughter that was sharp with hysteria. He spoke to himself, once more triumphant.

"A bear! Killed a bear, too! Zilpha! Isaac! A horse! And now a bear! Killed them all! E-yah, Lem. You're a one! You ain't scared of anything! Man or beast! All the same to Lem Brayton! Go on— thunder! Go on! I ain't scared of you, either!"

Swaggering, Lem Brayton went to view his trophy. He was halfway across the clearing when the bear rose from behind the log.

Lem couldn't believe his eyes. He saw the open mouth, the fangs, the angry eyes. The bear gathered himself for a charge. Screaming, the man whirled and fled.

It was a wild, terrified flight, but it did not last long. He was still carrying the empty musket when the bear caught him.

The storm came back with redoubled fury, as if it had been pent up since noon. Clocks pointed to the milking hour, but there was no sun, and Stratton knew neither darkness nor light, night nor day. Wind lashed the rain against the mountain's summit, tossing swirls of spray like surf beating against rocks. Thunder slammed, and lightning, visibly jagged, ripped the gray curtain overhead and illuminated the slope for quivering seconds of too-vivid brightness. Beneath the trees of the forest, where wind and rain beat an unholy tattoo and darkness made all shapes strange, the men of Stratton lost touch with each other. They scattered, making their way back down from the summit by twos and threes. They brought nothing with them.

Tate Jones had led them to Lem Brayton before the storm broke, and the story of his end was tracked across the small clearing for all to read. They didn't bring Lem back. There was little to bring, and they had nothing to carry it in. They buried Lem Brayton where they found him, and it was something they would remember, with the storm threatening, and two men standing guard in case the bear returned. The hunter had picked up the broken musket. It was in two pieces, but it was recognizable.

Bent by the pounding of the rain, they straggled into the settlement. Dirty, wet, and weary, they stumbled to the Tarbox inn and slumped in chairs. Eratus Chittenden and his two sons arrived first. The blacksmith and Joel Patch came in together, followed by Dan Tarbox. Others entered; Lot Purdy and Tate Jones were the last to arrive.

Eratus gulped hot rum gratefully, but his voice still vied with the thunder. It was the big man who roared the answer to Mrs. Tarbox's question.

"A bear got Lem!"

The innkeeper's wife blanched. She said, "Please. Asa's upstairs with Marcia and Davey." Mrs. Tarbox hesitated, then gave her news quickly. "The parson's been waiting for you to get back. He's aiming to hold a service."

The men stirred. Joel Patch's voice was sharp. "Service? For adulterers?"

"No." Lydia Tarbox shook her head. "It's a special service for the President."

"Oh."

"For the President."

"For Harrison."

"For Tippecanoe."

The squat tower of Stratton church held no bell, but the men in the inn could see that light streamed from the building's windows. They went across in a body, huddled together against the rain. They left their guns at the inn.

The Reverend Jedidah Chester was standing inside the church, halfway between the two entrance doors. The parson, the skin of his bald head taut and showing the skull bones, looked very worn.

As the others passed to their places Eratus Chittenden lingered beside the minister. In a few swift words the big man told how they had found Lem Brayton. The parson bowed his head.

"Thank you, Eratus."

Jedidah Chester stayed in the rear of the little church and watched his neighbors filing to their places. Everyone on Stratton, except the boys who had ridden to inform the authorities and the two hired men guarding the bodies at Brayton's, was in this congregation. The parson passed a hand wearily over his eyes. Even the Methodists were present. He noticed Miss Nason sitting in the front row, still in mourning for her father. For once, thought the parson with a wry smile, the peripatetic Methodist preacher is being penalized for not living in the settlement.

He was very tired. He had changed to his best black broadcloth, and he still felt rumpled. It had been a miserable and backbreaking day. He had delivered Asa Brayton to the gentle mercies of the Stratton women and had stayed with the boy until he seemed calmer. Then, alone, the parson had trudged back to the farmhouse that held so much slaughter and had made the bodies presentable. Reverend Chester had no illusions as to why he had done that. He knew that Zilpha and Isaac had died in the very flowering of their sin, without chance of repentance or redemption—he refused to admit this last, though he understood that it was popular morality. . . . He had done what he could for their corporal remains, because he felt he had failed with their souls.

It was a terrifying failure, but he accepted it. I, the parson thought, Jedidah Chester, minister of the Gospel, rector of the First Congregational Church of Stratton, have failed to keep two of my flock from the paths of sin and the wages thereof. Their fall and destruction was my fault. The long, bony fingers locked behind the preacher's back and twisted against each other till the knuckles cracked. Silently he cried out, If I had known. It was the worst day he had spent since his ordination. If he had preached stronger. If he had consulted the three concerned. If he had been more perceptive and less scholarly. The conditional sentences ranged themselves in his mind and reminded him of a page in his Latin grammar. For that, too, he blamed himself.

Reverend Chester remembered the rest of the afternoon. He had persuaded the two Patch hired men, Tim Frost and the stranger, to stand watch at Brayton's. Then he had gone, on foot, to every farmhouse to summon the women to the special service. He knew what he wanted to do with this service. He had something to say. In speaking of Tippecanoe's death he was going to try to give his neighbors a message about those closer, violent deaths that it was not proper to mention. He wished he had Daniel Webster's eloquence, remembering the speech at the great Convention in the clearing. For a moment Jedidah Chester wondered what the new Secretary of State, Mr. Webster, had felt when he heard that Harrison had died.

376

The congregation was waiting, whispering but not restless. Wives told their husbands that chores were done; husbands told of the posse's finish, tersely, ignoring gasps. The group was complete when Mrs. Tarbox herded David and Marcia and Asa Brayton through the door. Reverend Chester gripped Asa's hand, shut both doors, and walked down the aisle between the rude benches.

By the time the parson reached the front benches there was no sound but the crack of his heels on the floor planks and the drumming of the rain on the roof. He mounted the platform and turned.

The people of Stratton faced him. Jedidah Chester took hold of his coat lapels with both hands. He saw his wife leaning forward, anxious, and recognized her frown as worry about his coming speech. His daughter Lovina was holding her husband's hand, and the preacher thanked God that all was well with her. He would miss her when she left for the Illinois country, but Charles was a good man and a good husband. He saw the Chittendens clustered together with the girl, Mercy, in their midst. Joel Patch was in his usual place, thin-lipped and severe. There was the blacksmith—the innkeeper—the farmers. Toward the back the parson noticed Tate Jones and realized that it was the first time the hunter had ever entered the church.

Lot Purdy sat with his wife. Lot Purdy, Democrat. Tonight it made no difference. Lot's presence reminded him that Seth Purdy was Putnam's best friend. Reverend Chester had a momentary thought about his son. It was a hard ride to East Arlington, but the boy was whole again. Putnam had been fortunate. Again, sincerely and simply, the parson thanked his God.

Jedidah Chester spoke to the townspeople.

"Neighbors. We are gathered here to pay our respects to our dead President. Not long ago we gathered on this mountain, our home, to cheer the mention of his name. We heard a famous orator speak of William Henry Harrison. But death strikes in strange ways and in unexpected places. We know not the day nor the hour. It is not for us to judge these things. A dead President; a dead neighbor. God's will be done.

"At the same time it is true that, in His merciful Providence, God has given us the future. The deeds done on this mountain, the great Convention, are history. President Harrison's life is over.

377

But our Republic has a new President; our own mountain has to-morrow! Let the past be past. Let us mourn the news we learned today. Let us forget it and go about our duties."

The mild voice stopped. For the first time in his ministry the Reverend Jedidah Chester had spoken without a planned and written sermon. He reached under the folds of his coat and took out a prayer book.

Jedidah Chester said, "We will now read a short funeral service for President William Henry Harrison—and all others who have died this day."

The rain had stopped. There was enough moon to drive by, and the stars were crystal clear overhead. The sheriff's light two-wheel chaise had less trouble with the turnpike's mud than other, heavier vehicles, and, sitting beside him, young Putnam Chester was impatient of the officer's careful driving. By the time we get to Stratton, Put thought, they'll all have gone to bed. His leg ached severely, and he rubbed it. He wondered if the posse had caught Lem Brayton.

They had stopped climbing and were going downgrade when Put noticed the break in the deep shadows of the tree-lined road. The boy leaned out and stared. He recognized the flat expanse of the great clearing where they had held the Whig Convention. Put remembered that partridge used to nest in the field. He'd have to ask Seth Purdy if they'd come back. By bending almost double and looking up, Put was sure he could see the tip of the tall tamarack tree.

"Careful, son," said the sheriff. "You'll fall out. What in thunder are you looking at, anyway?"

"Just a tree."

The chaise went on down the turnpike.